Blade of Thieves

by

Lee Roland

Guardians of the Blades
Book 2

Blade of Thieves, Book II

Cover Art by *Debbie Taylor*

The Wild Rose Press, Inc.
PO Box 708
Adams Basin, NY 14410-0708
Visit us at www.thewildrosepress.com

Publishing History
First Edition, 2023
Trade Paperback ISBN 978-1-5092-4768-4
Digital ISBN 978-1-5092-4769-1

Guardians of the Blades, Book II
Published in the United States of America

Dedication

For Woody, as always

West Oregon Mountains

Limbo is halfway to Hell. His mind kept repeating the words the previous delivery driver offered when he handed over the keys. He'd left Helle Township early. Next delivery, the town of Limbough. Then the weary drive home to hold the love of his life and watch waves of sorrow wash her soul away like tide eroding a beach.

He hated this road. The narrow, treacherous pavement cut sharp curves through the deep green Oregon forest. The steering wheel pulled hard right. He fought and slowed for a sharp bend. He almost missed seeing the fresh black skid marks and a car's roof barely visible from the road. He stopped, parked, jumped out of the truck, and rushed down the short incline.

The mangled car sat crushed against a massive tree. It hadn't been there long. Still cooling, it slowly hissed steam from the mangled radiator. The driver's door stood open. He cringed at sight of the woman slumped on the passenger side. No need to touch the blood-soaked, broken body to know she'd gone. So young and obviously pregnant, why had she not been wearing a seatbelt?

A shrill cry came from the backseat. He jerked the undamaged back door open. And there was the miracle. His hopeless dreams and fantasies suddenly came alive. Temptation—and purest evil. He was certainly not a good man, but he'd never committed such a dreadful crime.

A sudden, firm voice declared, *"Yes! Do it! This is for you."* It sounded so loud and clear he whirled to see who'd spoken. He stood alone. Doubt and guilt disappeared. He obeyed the command and lifted the child out of her seat. Up the short incline to the truck, he dragged an empty cardboard box from the back and tucked her in. He set the box on the floor, and he was away.

He glanced once in the rearview mirror. What was that? He jerked his eyes back to the dangerous road. He could have sworn he saw a mini tornado swirling furiously across the dirt where he'd parked the truck, magically erasing all tire tracks that could allow an investigation to lead to him. No, that wasn't possible. He drove on. Fate or chance—God or the devil—what was one more sin? Limbo is halfway to Hell.

Chapter One

Seattle, Washington

I hurried past the museum's star exhibition. An artist had tortured sheets of junkyard metal into the form of a giant horse. A little sign proclaimed, *Mea Equus Fabia.* My horse Fabia. I could commiserate with poor Fabia. My parents named me Katrine. *Katrine Latrine,* that's what the kids in school called me until I taught them better. School girls can kick ass too.

Poor tarnished Fabia didn't appeal to me. My exquisite prizes financially and artistically surpassed rust devoured scrap metal. I'd pilfered two artifacts. A two-thousand-year-old crystal wrapped in gold wire, looted from a war-torn Middle East, and an icon of unknown origin. The crystal had a hum that spoke to supernatural properties. Certain artifacts made powerful impressions. They would tell me stories of ancient people and places. The icon, a five-inch square tile of dead white stone, held no such mysticism.

My tiny watch said 2:00 a.m. I'd entered the building through the massive HVAC ductwork system. Plenty of entry and exit points. It let me move undetected around the building. I had time, plenty of time. A minimum wage museum employee had given me the system passwords. I had generously and anonymously compensated him in return.

A swift, rhythmic elbow slide on my stomach powered me through one of the ducts. I'm slender. Or malnourished and scrawny as the people who tried to feed me believed. But at five-eleven, I wasn't a feather weight. I also worked for and prided myself on athleticism.

I had my prizes in a backpack. A few tools of my trade filled another. Both were small and light enough not to impede movement.

The alarms shrieked. I jerked and banged my head on the top of the duct. Damn. I'd cut them off an hour ago. Encased as I was in a metal box, the clamor pounded my eardrums in rhythmic braying whoops. The uproar tore away the surety of an easy job and clean escape. I forced myself on. Faster, since the faint hiss of my thin, black catsuit across metal certainly wouldn't be a problem any longer. Completely covered except for my eyes, I'd leave no DNA in passing. The mask also guaranteed no identifying images if I passed a camera. Unfortunately, the password that allowed me entrance wouldn't cut the camera security off. *No deterrent though, I knew the game. It was not my first escape.*

Another fifteen feet and I emerged into one of many handy service closets. The alarm still sang its dreadful song. I stood to take a deep breath. Open a door and on to the *walk of death.*

I stared straight ahead. Tight balance and sure quick steps carried me over the thirty-foot, two-inch-wide beam that crossed a two-story display room below. Easier than my childhood tight-rope walking lessons. Unlike the rope, the beam didn't move under my feet. No net and a twenty-foot plunge down to a concrete floor. Look straight ahead, confident, count your steps…made it. I did look down then. A great black dog stared up at me. A dog? In the museum? Why would… No! No time. I had to go on.

Next came a tight squeeze through the vertical shaft that housed the main HVAC system and electrical conduits. Down the tiny steel ladder embedded in the concrete wall and into the basement. My hands and feet fit the rungs easily, but I pitied a large man who had to negotiate the drop.

At the bottom of the shaft, I removed yet another panel for exit into a basement hallway. The museum's interior labyrinth provided multiple points of easy access for repairs—and a highway for slick professional thieves. A deeply flawed system, but I appreciated the architects and engineer's highly specialized work.

My immediate goal, a basement utility room…there. I ducked inside, carefully closing the door behind me. At least someone had silenced the annoying alarm.

Now to finish the escape. The newly constructed storm sewers in this part of town were wonderful for thieves like me. You could drive a small car through the formidable underground pipes. So dangerous though. Millions of gallons of water rushed through them at times.

I quickly pried open the small passage door designed for city service lines. Farther down a steep set of stairs was another door that would let me access the sewer. I tossed the bag with the prizes through the door. With no immediate pursuit, I stood to stretch for a few minutes and allowed the adrenalin high to seep from my body. I removed my mask, too.

Powerful arms clamped around me. They snatched me off my feet. The man who'd captured me was taller than my five-eleven with rock-hard muscles that pinned my arms to my sides. I couldn't see him, but with my back against his chest, the thin cat suit let me feel his muscles flexing. He'd entered the room with absolutely no sound.

My grunts and hisses sounded garish as I twisted and strained to break away. At least I made him dance to keep his balance. With a single flip, he had me on the floor on my stomach. Not unnecessarily rough, he didn't injure me, but he maneuvered me as easily as he would a two-year-old. I stopped struggling to save my strength. My backpack with my tools was only on one arm, and he snatched it off first. Zippers opened, Velcro hissed, and he rummaged through the bag. When he found nothing but my tools, he shoved the pack aside. Now, he searched me too. His hands moved with impersonal swiftness.

As quickly as he captured me, he set me free.

I rolled, jumped to my feet, and crouched, ready to fight again. I wouldn't win. He stood between me and my escape hole.

And he was naked. Why was he…?

I had to stare. To call him handsome was an understatement. Breathtaking? Stunning? What's that clichéd saying? *A woman should never love a man who's more beautiful than she is.* Love? Not in my nature. Sex? Absolutely. Under different circumstances, of course.

He stood at least six-five. He had a lean muscled body and flawless bronze skin to complement his perfect face. Hair, thick and black as the deepest cavern, had artfully skimmed touches of silver at the temples. Intense gold eyes focused all his attention on me. His expression? Not angry. Maybe perplexed. And yes, interested.

He chuckled, his voice husky and full of confidence.

"And who are you, my lady thief? That was spectacular balance crossing that room. And the climb down? What was it? Fifty feet? Sixty?"

"Seventy-five. I measured." I hadn't seen him. Only a black dog had watched me.

I straightened from my laughable fighting stance. *Say something Katrine. Something clever but reasonable. Try not to antagonize him.*

"Listen, I'll split the take." I kept my voice low and hoped I sounded alluring. Seduction was not high on my list of skill sets. "I think we could be good friends. I'll even buy you some clothes." I held out my empty hands. "I hid the shit upstairs in the duct work. I…we…can come back when things settle down.

He stepped closer. I couldn't do anything to stop him. No move I could make would be fast enough. Too close. Oh, my. Damn those eyes. They had the burnished shine of vintage gold coins I'd stolen long ago. Gentle hands on my shoulders, he drew me closer, held me against that magnificent chest. *What the hell?* Was he going to throw me down and rape me there in the basement? He laid that perfect face against my neck. His tongue licked my throat in a long, slow path up to my ear. He drew a deep, slow breath. Tasting me? Smelling me?

I'd had superior ability to detect and identify certain types of odors all my life. It had served me well in my chosen profession. This man so close, so vibrant, smelled like the forest, cedar and pine, and the earth, deep and loamy after a rain. Intense, masculine, I'd know him by odor alone if I met him again, which I didn't plan to do— ever. And I had to escape first.

He released me and stepped back. Okay, I had to keep staring. I'd never met a man with such primal maleness. He radiated potency and calm determination. In another time, another place… No! Never!

How absurd. This was not the kind of man who would be attracted to a plain, ordinary looking woman like me. Years of false smiles and pretty lies, followed by bitter disappointment, had taught me well.

An honest examination in the mirror told me I'm not beautiful. I'm not repulsive, but I lacked the symmetry and perfection of facial features that beauty entailed. My hair, ashy blonde, my eyes, light blue, nothing special, nothing out of the realm of mundane. My breasts, those objects so cherished by men, are…adequate.

His grin, teasing, taunting, told me I was a silly gawking girl who had amused him. He'd moved and no longer stood between me and freedom. A few seconds. Just a few seconds and I could make it through my escape portal. Why didn't I move?

He chuckled softly. "You should run now."

Disbelief hit me like a punch in the gut. "You're letting me go?"

"Of course. If they put you in jail, I won't be able to see you again. Do you have a name?"

How stupid did he think I was? *That I was going to say my name was Katrine Dolinski. And oh, I'm single, twenty-seven years old. Should I give him my address? My phone number, too?* I guess my incredulous expression said it all. He laughed again, then turned and walked out of the room. He closed the door behind him.

What an absurd and appalling situation. I'd allowed a stranger to dangerously mesmerize me. A beautiful stranger who caught a thief—and set her free. I'd never counted on lady luck, but she was a kind gracious patroness this night. She allowed me to toss my bag of prizes out of sight first before he grabbed me.

Move, Katrine, get your ass out of there.

I forced my body through the escape door, retrieved my ill-gotten goods, and hurried down steps to the tunnel that ran parallel to the streets. I'd have to search for a separate way up and out, too. The original was too close to the museum. At least it was June, above freezing, and not raining. My flashlight lighted the way as I trudged through the foul-smelling dark. Twice I had to wade. I'd had clothes hidden above ground to cover my cat suit, but since I'd forsaken my original exit, I couldn't get to them. No loss. I'd bought them well-worn at a garage sale so they wouldn't carry any of my DNA if anyone found them.

I exited in a service building at a park. Once out in fresh air, I stalked cautiously through the shadows in my suspicious thieves clothing. I had another thrift store outfit in the car. I also had a long careful drive from Seattle to northern California. I still had to figure out what went wrong. What I did *wrong!* Albeit under bizarre circumstances, a dangerous stranger had mesmerized a skillful cat burglar. Who was he? Why had he let me go? More important—why did he believe he could find me again?

****

Four hours of sleep after a seven-hour drive from Seattle left me conscious, but barely functioning. The air in Uncle Rado's gloomy, third-floor office clogged my sinuses and gave me a throbbing headache. I could almost hear the mold spoors growing, multiplying by the billions in the walls. Thick green curtains padded the windows, and a bizarre multi-color rug, obviously woven by a deranged artist, covered the floor. Stepping on the rug could give visitors nightmares—or at least distract them from business. The looming shelves secured to the walls sagged under the weight of old leather-bound books. Some of those books whispered to me. I was the only one who could hear them. I refused to listen. I preferred paperback suspense novels. They didn't talk.

I recited my escape story while Rado listened, solemn and grim faced. I'd spoken of the shorted alarm, and how I escaped, but couldn't make myself talk about the naked man who grabbed me in the basement or my baffling and dangerous reaction to him.

Rado's thick black brows knitted together in a single line, and his mouth turned down at the edges. He'd lost most of his hair in the last few years, so he decided to do the shaved head thing. It was not a good look for him with his full fleshy face.

Though technically a success, elements of the Seattle job had gone amiss. Rado wasn't happy with the slightest deviation. Any deviation was threatening to a job planning perfectionist. He leaned back and locked his hands over his prominent belly.

"Darling Katrine, I'm sure you observed all the proper precautions." His rolling voice offered a note of assurance. "Your work is always meticulous. I'll try to find out what happened. You say a dog?"

"A dog. I have scent neutralizers, but I didn't carry them. You don't find many dogs in a museum." You did, however, find them on private estates.

Tulmic Radoslaw, my dear Uncle Rado, had

procured and fenced stolen goods since before I was born. An organizer with a keen sense of detail, he exploited my inborn skills to create an exceptional thief. He had a superb reputation for reliability and confidentiality in all endeavors.

I needed to know what went wrong in Seattle, too. I knew I should tell Rado about the man in the basement, of course, but it had been such an intimate encounter. I'd played it over in my mind so many times since I'd returned home. The man and his remarkable appearance still stunned me. Not that I ever wanted to see him again. *He was far too dangerous—like bracelets and a jail cell dangerous.*

Rado grunted. His mouth formed a huge O as he belched. He needed to lose weight. "I transferred your fee to your account, my dear. My clients will be most pleased with your acquisitions."

Acquisitions? The small crystal that hummed of secret magic and a five-inch square icon, carved of an unusual milky white stone. I knew the icon was valuable even if it did look like a bathroom tile. The crystal was unique and valuable to the person who desired such ornaments. I doubted he or she could discern its true internal power. I'd never met another person who could feel that magical pulse. If the orb were mine, I might explore, but it wasn't so I didn't bother. The other piece, the icon, was unique, too. Like the crystal, it wasn't mine to keep.

My official profession—my day job—by education and experience, is Antiquities Authenticator. I examine, date, and verify relics from the Neolithic and pre-Neolithic eras in the Middle East. I used to go to archeological digs, but that became too dangerous the past few years. War kept the business of artifacts looted from museums and sold to purchase weapons booming.

"Please be careful, Rado. That icon is late Neolithic, probably Sumerian. Your client has offered three times what it's worth on the market." The desire for an object often determined its value. Offering too much money signaled desperation—or the intention not to pay for the goods.

"Oh, yes, my darling Katrine. I assure you I've taken, and will continue to take, extra precautions on this one. Did you drop the car off?"

"Yes. It's there."

I'd left the car, an older ubiquitous white sedan, at a self-storage unit, then walked home. It was, of course, registered to a fictious person. In a tight situation, I could always leave it behind. With a single phone call, Rado would have it picked up soon and disposed of God knows where. In a week or so, another equally ubiquitous ride would take its place.

My share for the evening was a quarter million that Rado had transferred to a bank in the islands. I wouldn't leave it there, of course. I'd move it to other accounts to be safe—as safe as anything like that could be. Eventually I would launder it through my legitimate antiquity authentication business.

My immediate goal? Permanent financial security in a transitory world. My mother had an extensive bout with cancer seven years ago and getting her the best of care was paramount. It was far more than Medicare and insurance would touch. By the time they pronounced her cured, I was well over a million dollars in debt.

Rado lowered the square white icon to his desk. "I have another job for you in about two weeks, if you're interested."

"Where?"

"New Orleans. A mansion, not commercial. There's a necklace and, I'm told, inadequate security."

"Get me the details. I'll look it over."

"What about the other piece, my dear? The third one." Rado's voice turned serious. "It's not like you. Not that I mind, but holding items is dangerous. You know that."

"Other piece?" I frowned, my mind racing. "What other piece? Rado, you know I only take what I'm assigned. No deviations. Ever."

"I've heard from a contact in Seattle early this morning that three items were missing." He held up the white icon. "This, the crystal, and a knife."

"No, no knife." I was adamant on that one. "Staff? Insider?"

Not uncommon after a major theft. Items would go missing, usually into an employee's pocket so the thief would take the blame.

He held up his phone with a photo.

It was indeed a knife, a spectacular knife at that. Old, Middle Eastern in style, but I couldn't immediately position it in time or place. The hilt? Ivory, with a significant red jewel attached at the end. I'd never seen the pattern of runes incised down the blade. That type of marking was common since many ancient peoples believed it gave them mystical protection.

"It's beautiful, but no, not my target, Rado."

"I'm sorry, darling. I didn't mean to imply that I don't trust you."

"I know you trust me, Rado."

A deep frown masked his face as he evaluated the

information. He believed me, but any little glitch could throw a whole project off. That made two anomalies for this job. A prematurely tripped alarm and a missing knife. Two for him and three for me. Rado dealt with details in the entire operation, and naturally, all such disparities disturbed him. My conscience nudged me. I should tell him about the man. No. I needed to think about it more, try to find a more impersonal balance.

I went out to make the short walk to my own office across the street. The warm sun and green leafy street trees made a perfect early summer day in Northern California. The oppressive heat that occasionally blanketed the area would hopefully find another home this year.

I've always carried a cross-body messenger bag to leave my hands free. It held essentials, including a carefully designed and disguised side pocket for a 9mm Smith and Wesson pistol.

Rado and I worked in a dangerous world. We maintained a low profile, but he had enemies. And I had a man who caught me in a basement! Who was he? I had to find out. I started to go back, to talk to Rado about him. That was stupid, though. I had work in my office, and we could talk tomorrow.

Chapter Two

Rado owned two buildings in Senica, California. Close to downtown, they were sturdy, convenient, and low-key. Three-stories each, neither were spectacular bits of urban architecture. His third-floor office was in one, and mine in the building across the street. I only required a sparsely furnished single room, since most of the time I traveled to my clients for authenticating.

Senica, CA, sits west of 101, close to the Eel River, and close to the Pacific Ocean. Twenty to thirty thousand permanent souls, and God knew how many tourists during the season. *"Not far from. Close to."* Ah, the Chamber of Commerce brochures. Not a destination itself, but *close to* whitewater rafting, whale watching, fishing, and of course mountain hiking.

I loved Senica and missed it when I started college at sixteen. Massachusetts was not my kind of place. I had a master's by twenty, and kept telling myself I should get a Ph.D. I had multiple scholarships, so I'd graduated with only a small burden in loans. But by then, Mom was battling cancer. I had to make money—lots of money.

And now?

I'm an adrenalin junkie. The sheer risk of high dollar crime is my drug of choice. Last night had given me a power boost. A total high, even with, or because of, the problems. I was born with a profound degree of athleticism, and special extrasensory skills. Some would call those skills magical, but regardless, they supported me professionally and fueled my addiction.

Touch is the most pronounced of my unique skills. It's one reason I never handle artifacts without gloves. The other reasons being DNA and fingerprints. I can hold an artifact or other object in my bare hands and accurately identify its age within a hundred years. I can often tell the area of origin. Occasionally, a rare piece will give me a brief image of another time and place.

How? Why? I don't know. The mystical workings of the universe, the cosmos, the whatever. For me, the ability to receive knowledge through touching objects is a blessing and a curse.

I can also read people by touch, but I absolutely refuse to do so. Reading a person once left me mentally stranded and terrified, lost in their personality. It took years and conscious effort to control the *touch and know* thing. Until then I was the weird kid in school who wore gloves all the time. I finally found a mental off switch early in puberty. It no longer automatically overwhelmed me when I handled an object or shook hands with a person. I avoid reading weapons of any kind. Images from those are horrific. My 9mm is brand new, so it offers me nothing but cold steel.

Then comes the Push. Push with a capital P. I can, if I concentrate, thrust objects away from me. I don't usually consider it because that feat requires determined effort. I have destroyed property when I failed.

I managed a few hours paperwork before I gave up and headed home.

Mom, Dad, and I live in an expansive and recently remodeled craftsman type house originally built in the 1930s. We moved there when I was six. I met my BFF,

Danny Studstill, who lived next door. A geeky boy with thick glasses and a slight stutter, Danny accepted my weirdness.

My dad, Telek Dolinski, is a tall, lean, whitehaired man of Polish descent. I think I got my height and slenderness from him. Mom, Alina, is of Polish ancestry, too. Or at least they say they are. I have no idea about grandparents, aunts, uncles, and cousins or if they even exist. Mom and Dad did not discuss or allude to them in any way. As a curious and odd child, I once asked Dad if he had no family because aliens had dropped him on earth. He said, "Your Uncle Rado is an alien, no doubt. Your mother?" He lifted and tilted his hand back and forth. He lowered his voice and winked at me. "Don't tell her you know. She lives in perpetual denial, so we must indulge her."

They were in their late thirties when I was born. They occasionally referred to me as their miracle, their greatest gift. I think I had the happiest childhood in the world. When I heard other kids' woes, druggie, alcoholic, violent abusive parents, it confirmed my luck. The important thing? They included me in their lives. They withheld almost nothing in daily life. Today I provide financial support, but I have no chores. Some sweet person, a.k.a. my dad, makes my bed every day, my laundry is done, my meals deliciously cooked, and I come and go as I please. What more would a person want?

Well, yes, a person could want things like the love of an appropriate man and dear children. That normality had never, and would never, be mine. When you live with certain mysteries as I do, you tend not to trust anyone. A loving close companion required confidence and honesty

I wasn't now, or ever had been, prepared to offer.

****

While I sat at the dinner table with Mom and Dad that evening, stuffing myself with sausage, cabbage, and potatoes, I struggled to stay awake. Mom is short and round like Uncle Rado, but much prettier with her now gray hair and blue eyes. Partially disabled by her battle with cancer, she merrily rolls along in her new, and exorbitantly expensive, power-chair.

She tipped her head lower and her mouth formed the expectant smile that usually heralded an unusual request. "Trine, darling, will you go with me to this next week? I want your opinion." She handed me a paper. "I found it at the library."

The paper advertised a seminar on extrasensory capabilities.

Supernatural phenomena? Hoax or science?

Professor so and so, and doctor so and so, would be at the library speaking on phenomena that was *"unexplained by means known to current science."*

I winced as I read the words promising to enlighten the ignorant and uneducated. I had lived with certain forms of supernatural phenomena most of my life. Experience had taught me to always keep my abilities hidden. I waved the paper at her. "Mom. No. I can't do this." Mom sighed and pouted. That usually made me feel guilty. Oh, I was talented as a child. Certain supernatural type phenomena would erupt and spew out of me like lava from a volcano. I had lost—or suppressed—all but three skills, touch, odor, and push as I matured. Regrettably, Mom wanted me to pull specific talents out of a hat and manipulate them like a surgeon cutting into a heart.

Dad gazed out the window, longing in his eyes. There, in the separate garage, sat the divine vehicle of the glory days, our years on the road—the concession trailer we pulled behind a motorhome every summer. From carnival, to circus, to festival, it was, by now, totally inoperable. He remembered. He dreamed.

Life on the road absolutely thrilled me. No summer boredom for me when school let out. A different place every few days, I saw much of the country before I was twelve. All summer dad cooked and peddled kiełbasa sausage, makowiec, the poppy seed rolls, and anything else he could find a recipe for and pass off as Polish in origin.

Unfortunately, the only thing verifiably Polish about my Dad, Mom, and Uncle Rado, is their names. Dad couldn't speak Polish, but he could fake an accent beautifully. He only ran into trouble when he met the rare soul who could speak the language. He could fake laryngitis, too.

As usual with Mom's requests, I took the easy path.

"Okay. I'll go with you. But I'm not *Katrinka, the Child Prognosticator*, anymore. I won't ever do that again." Hunger sated, I pushed my plate away, ready for dessert, strawberry shortcake, that Dad handed over.

The smile never left Mom's face. "Yes, darling, of course I understand."

Sure, she did.

Katrinka, the Child Prognosticator, was her brilliant idea. Prognosticator meant a seer or forecaster, a fortune teller predicting the future. *I absolutely cannot see the future and never could.* I was seven years old when Mom discovered my budding talent for knowing things by touch. Unfortunately, she quickly realized my ability extended to people, too, not just objects. I could hold a person's hand and read them. I could feel their emotions, and often see adult scenes in their minds. I matured quickly during that time. Over Dad's objections, she bought a tent, decked me out in a Romani costume, and sat me in a chair where I could barely see over the table. She then proceeded to prostitu…promote me to carnival and fair goers. She coached and encouraged me to spout my forbidden knowledge of deep and desperate secret lives.

Most people didn't hang around long once my little girl voice started vocalizing their secrets. They just tossed money at me and ran. If they ran without tossing money, Mom chased them, demanding compensation. My petite mother was fearless back then. Dad made her stop when one of the customers attacked me over my spewing facts of a crime he'd committed.

I went to bed early after dinner—and dreamed of a man with a body made of lean hard muscle and a warm lush voice that stroked my senses. I dreamed of golden eyes, his breath on my face and his tongue gliding across my throat. I received nothing from that touch because it would have taken conscious effort to read him. At the time, I could barely manage rational thought. I woke twice in the night smelling the scent of the forest and the earth and filled with intense sexual desire. I climbed out of bed still tired—and still aroused.

Chapter Three

Such a beautiful morning. The breeze through the car window ruffled my hair like a soft fingered massage. I'd donned my *medium brown girl* persona. Natural blonde hair enhanced with a darker rinse and brown contacts worked. Standard beige jacket, white shirt, and navy pants created a blend-in and forgettable appearance. I can slip into the appropriate costume, then put on the face. Medium brown girl with dark downcast eyes, smoking-hot girl in a red dress, executive woman in a pinstripe power suit, and yes, cat burglar girl in black. I could be anyone I wanted—except myself. My true self was far closer to medium brown than smoking-hot or executive.

Rado and I both knew our time as premier thieves was rapidly running out. Technological advances in DNA, facial recognition, and other science continued to outpace us every day. Soon, my legitimate authentication business would be my only source of income.

I had my mind focused on upcoming travel when I headed out. I came to earth and slammed on the brakes as I turned a corner to my building. Panic seized me. Police cars blocked off the street between my office and Rado's. A crowd of uniforms gathered at the entrance to his building.

The man in the basement! Why hadn't I told him about the man? Wait. Stop. I forced my racing thoughts to slow down. I didn't know what had happened. Maybe a fire. There were other tenants. *Don't panic.* Restraint didn't work. My heart raced, the sound throbbing in my ears. A knot formed in my guts, thick and bloated like a deadly cancer tumor.

I parked, threw my messenger bag over my shoulder, and ran. Straight into a crowd of Senica's finest uniforms, who promptly grabbed me and forced me back. They weren't rough. I knew many of them personally because Danny, my BFF was one of them. *Wait, Katrine. Wait they said, please wait.* They weren't going to let me in, and they wouldn't tell me anything.

Despite my mother calling me a prognosticator, I couldn't see the future. If you have knowledge, however, you can predict potential outcomes. The museum, the man in the basement, the missing object that I didn't take, the above value offer for the icon…but Rado was the expert, years in the business. Never careless, he knew the risks.

Screw the cops!

I knew this place. I backed away. I raced around the crowd to the back of the building, thankful for my flat-heeled oxford shoes. I knew every viable way in and out. The fire escape, fifteen feet above the ground level, would only release from the last platform above. This was to keep a thief from doing exactly what I wanted to do—go up.

My ever-present messenger bag went out of sight under a thick bush. No way I wanted to get a strap caught on anything during an aerial escapade. A short run, leap, and up onto the thick eight-foot concrete block wall circling the property. No challenge compared to the two-inch beam in the museum, and wide enough I didn't have to shed my shoes.

I balanced for a few seconds, drew a couple of deep breaths, then powered forward. Run, run, push off, leap. I caught the metal ladder with both hands. I hung there, fingers aching. It creaked and groaned but held. I threw my leg up, caught a rail, and climbed on. Up the steps, don't run, I didn't want to alert the people inside.

Yes! A window into a second-floor real estate office. I knew how to open it from the outside sill. I would have shattered the glass if I couldn't have. Surprised the hell out of a meeting in progress when I dropped in, apologized profusely, and raced out into the hall.

Uncle Rado redesigned and remodeled the building interior a few years ago. Behind hidden doors on each floor is a narrow, reinforced staircase, separate from the regular public stairwell beside the elevators. It ran from the basement to the roof and had unconventional access points and escape routes along the way. I located the second-floor entry to the secret stairs and climbed to the third.

Stop, stop, slow down. Stop.

I leaned against a wall, closed my eyes. I could go into the third-floor hallway and step out, or I could climb between walls and open a lightly tacked panel into Rado's office. I chose the office. I squeezed my way through tight walls. Hearing nothing, I cautiously pushed the panel back. Empty. Multiple voices grumbled outside in the third-floor hall. I hurried to the door. Still locked as it should be. I turned the deadbolts and carefully opened the door an inch to peek out.

My beautiful, wonderful Uncle Rado lay in the hallway. On his back, arms flung wide, blood, too much blood, pooled like a vile poison around him on the floor. A lethal wound, a black-red hole in the center of his chest, said it all. He hadn't died immediately. His heart pumped enough for him to bleed out.

I'd seen violence before. Fist fights, even a couple of knife battles, a few of the carnivals and circuses I'd grown up in tended to attract volatile people. I'd walked in bars and dirty streets at times for information.

Rado had prepared and trained me for violence, gave me a gun, but it had never happened. Sneak in, sneak out had worked every time.

How long had he been there while I showered, dressed, and painted on my face? A black human-sized plastic bag spread out beside him, ready to accept his body. A bloody nightmare of shoe prints tracked the floor like a diagram for a weird dance.

Choked into silence, memories flooded me. Rado, always there, always loving, always teaching. Rado who spoiled me outrageously. His face, now a pale death mask, eyes wide in surprise...*his gun in his hand*. He'd been ready, always ready. He knew the risks of his profession. Gun in hand also meant he was expecting something—or someone. Who could have surprised him like that? It had to be someone he knew. A client?

Sorrow, longing, bitter regrets weighed on me. My body vibrated in fine quivers. It would soon shatter into a pile of bloody brittle sticks. All I could do was stand, hold on tight, and stare.

Someone noticed me in the doorway. Men's voices shouted, one sharp voice cursing above the others. Firm hands grabbed me. I didn't struggle. I couldn't. Then a familiar person arrived. Even blind with tears, I knew the masculine arms drawing me away.

Danny, my dearest friend, held me close. He supported and led me to the bench by a window at the end of the hall, away from the carnage. He sat beside me, cradling me in his arms, stroking my hair like soothing a child.

"Trine, I'm so sorry." Black sadness filled his voice.

I'd met Danny when we first moved into our home. We had both climbed the same tree on the property line to check out the new neighbors. Danny had outgrown his awkwardness and matured into a tall and handsome young man. He had also grown up with a passion for upholding the law. He'd always wanted to be a cop. He knew much about my early life, too much to be comfortable. He knew about my problems with extrasensory powers, along with the normal adolescent angst of a tall, awkward girl. As we grew older and my skill at thievery grew, I had to keep things from him. That left me with a friend I dearly loved—but couldn't allow to know the truth.

I stared into his dark eyes, his boyish face. He hugged me tighter. "I don't know what happened, honey. I'll find out. I'm so sorry. I loved him, too."

I could tell he wanted to cry, but of course, didn't dare give in to sorrow in front of his peers. Yes, Danny had loved Rado, too. Through our inseparable childhoods, Rado taught us peculiar things that we'd take to school and use to appall our teachers. Danny may have heard whispers about Rado or me in the places he walked now, but for the sake of love and friendship, he asked few questions. For the sake of love and friendship, I would take nothing in this town, in his jurisdiction. Our common ground was our years together, not our professions.

"How the hell did she get in here?" A booming voice thundered through the hall. I knew that one, too. Barnhouse, one of the five detectives in the Senica Police Department. A brash, florid man, he thought things would happen faster if he could shove and demand in loud brutal tones.

Danny started to speak. Barnhouse stopped him. "Shut the fuck up, Studstill." He yelled in Danny's face. "This isn't your case."

My friend stood, but he pressed so close to me I could have laid my head on his hip. He'd long since passed the stage where anyone intimidated him.

Barnhouse glared down at me. "Damn it, how did you get in? I told them to keep you out."

I shrugged. "Climbed a wall out back. Came up the fire escape." That's all the information he'd get. Danny sat beside me again. I could hear him muttering under his breath. He knew my athletic skill. It saved his life once when foolish kids went exploring in a building scheduled for demolition and the floor dropped out. In our wild demented youth, Danny and I explored places brave people feared to walk. Barnhouse whirled and strutted away.

"If it's not your case, what are you doing here?" I had to ask him.

His face went tight, his mouth set, an expression I knew meant something deeply disturbed him, aside from the obvious murder. "You remember when I went to that conference in Vegas last year? While I was there, I ran into an old friend from my army days. We'd kept in touch occasionally over the years. He lives up in Oregon. He's searching for certain antiquities. I recommended Rado. He came here to talk to him, found his body, and since he knew I lived here, he called me. A mistake. He should have called 911. The captain wouldn't let me…Barnhouse was assigned." Danny nodded down the hall. "His name is Garrett Dain."

I raised my eyes. *Oh, holy hell! My stomach cramped. I suddenly couldn't swallow. Impossible, Incredible…no!* The man from the museum basement, the one who'd held me and let me go a little over 24 hours ago, stood not far away, talking to one of the uniforms. An expensive gray suit now covered that magnificent golden body. Neatly groomed, he had the charming shock of black hair combed away from his face. The fascinating bit of silver marked his temples stood out as if painted with a fine brush.

I'd left no trace of myself in the museum, no sign of my identity. He was the one who found Rado's body? Had he come for what I'd stolen and killed Rado? He couldn't have located me so soon. Could he? But he called Danny.

My museum captor's gaze passed me over like a stranger. My *medium-brown girl* façade held. Danny knew about my personas but considered them a game I played. *Medium-brown girl* was for professional credibility. Could I get away quickly? Not without Barnhouse seeing me.

Garrett? Not a common name. He quietly spoke to one of the officers who was taking notes. Graceful and so incredibly dangerous. The suit amplified that danger, made it smoother, but not less deadly. I'd seen men like him a few times. I couldn't walk in my world and not come across them. Swift, strong, and lethal, but this one had an angel's face. A smile would soothe a victim before he struck.

Oh, my sweet wonderful Rado? I needed him. I wanted him here.

The stink of blood had masked odors, but then the AC kicked on. A cool stream of air brushed across my face. The stranger's eyes widened. Barely noticeable, but I was watching. His nostrils flared. Confusion crossed his face. Oh, hell, could he smell me from that distance? My sense of smell was exceptional, but not *that* exceptional. His head turned, and that golden-eyed gaze locked on me.

I wasn't completely in control, but I could function. I stared at him, mouth set, eyes narrowed, willing him to silence. Ordering him to stay away. The threat, coming from *brown-girl,* wasn't credible. A few quick steps brought him closer.

"Trine, this is Garrett Dain." Danny nodded at my basement man. To him he said, "This is Katrine Dolinski. Radoslaw was her uncle."

Garrett Dain nodded his head to acknowledge me, his expression intense but still cautious. "I'm sorry for your loss, Ms. Dolinski. And sorry you had to see him like that." Calm, in control, that deep voice I remembered did indeed carry a note of concern.

Danny stood. He laid a hand on my shoulder. "Garrett, would you stay with Katrine a minute. I'll see if I can find out what's happening now."

Garrett took Danny's place beside me. Too close. That overwhelming masculine power, his sheer presence amplified everything around me. I am strong. I have the steady nerves of a master thief. I am not a coward. If cornered, if I had to fight, I would. He didn't speak, but after a moment he grasped my hand and gently held it in his. His other hand closed over it too, fingers stroking. I fought the urge to jerk away.

Temptation to read a person by touch assailed me for the first time in years. I instantly crushed the compulsion with logic. I didn't dare risk the personal trauma.

"Is there anything I can do for you?" He spoke quietly, barely above a whisper. No threat, his voice slid through me carrying nothing but concern.

"Did you kill him?" The question I asked sounded so logical. I don't know what I expected.

"No. Please believe me. But you have no reason to trust me. I understand."

"Mr. Dain—"

"Garrett. Please." His grip tightened gently. He wasn't going to let me go. "Katrine. That's a beautiful name." He lowered his voice. "I'm glad I found you so soon. I thought about you often since I saw…" He stopped. He would know the danger of such a conversation.

I'd spent much of my life taking chances, learning, and failing to learn, control. When I am afraid, I dwell on it, then let it pass so I can act. But this deep black sorrow? This horrible ache in my chest. I wanted my Rado back. My body quivered in fine vibration. Garrett slipped an arm around me. I sat silent, trying to push the pain away. I wanted to push him away too but didn't want to make a scene.

Danny approached. His face flashed surprise. *What did he see?* He knelt in front of me.

"Trine? I talked to your dad, honey. Hated to do that on the phone, but I didn't want him to hear from a stranger. He promised to wait at home for more information." He turned to stare down the hall, then back to me. "You came out of Rado's office. It was locked, and we hadn't gone in. Would you come and see if anything's missing?"

"He wouldn't keep anything valuable there."

"I know. We have to look, though. And Barnhouse is going to want to know how you got there." He stood and stepped away.

My phone rang. "That's probably Dad." I pulled it out of my pocket.

Barnhouse—who stood glaring at Rado's body as if he could magically make him rise and name his own killer—suddenly launched himself toward me like I had a grenade in my hand. A clumsy man, he tripped. Garrett's arms circled me instantly. He snatched me to my feet. I was out of the way so fast I'd have fallen if he hadn't held me tight.

Barnhouse went down and smacked his head on the corner of the bench hard enough to vibrate the wall. He struggled to get to his feet. Head wounds bleed freely and of course, he shook his head and flung blood everywhere. A slap-stick black comedy exhibition was all I needed.

Garrett still had both arms around me, holding my back against his chest, much as he had when he first captured me in the museum. He twisted, and stray drops flung our way hit the back of his expensive suit.

I was laughing and crying at the same time. I stared back at Rado's body. "Hey, Uncle, can you see the show? It's the carnival again. Oh, you'd love it." Then I laid my head back on the shoulder of this beautiful stranger who might be his killer and gave into the pain. I sobbed heavy and deep. I wanted my Rado back!

Since I had little control, Garrett and Danny

managed to get me out of the hallway and into a neighboring office. The office lease holder, an accountant, offered me a chair. Older and wiser than many, she'd heard the shot and had not rushed to see what happened. She hid in a closet, forgetting her cell phone, and didn't come out until the police arrived.

Garrett remained at my side though by then I barely noticed him. I sat there and waited while an unfathomable ache throbbed inside. My sweet Rado who sat with me on nights when I was ill, and Mom and Dad had to work. Rado who told me wild impossible stories. My sweet scheming Rado who taught me how to open any lock and pick carnival goers' pockets.

Danny came in the office. Barnhouse followed him. He had a sloppy, lopsided bandage on his head, a blooming black eye, and an attitude from hell.

I held out my phone. "You only had to ask."

Barnhouse sneered and snatched it away. His primary attention was, however, focused on Garrett, the stranger who discovered the body. I don't blame him. If I could function, I would focus there too.

I held steady through my part of the usual investigative questions. Where was I when it happened, etc. Barnhouse kept probing, demanding, and yes, passive aggressively accusing. Murder wasn't that common in Seneca. Murder had his undivided attention. Barnhouse wanted me to go downtown so he could record and harass me further. Danny said he'd take me. Surprisingly, Barnhouse agreed.

Of course, they wanted Garrett, too. He'd found the body. Fortunately, Barnhouse didn't notice when he climbed in the car with Danny and me. I know he would have never allowed such an unauthorized action under normal circumstances. The whack on the head must have had him confused.

Garrett sat in the front seat. He lowered his phone and turned to Danny. "I've called in lawyers from the corporation for Katrine. A little over an hour by helicopter. I can represent myself."

Danny glanced at him, then back at the road. "You're a lawyer?" He sounded surprised. *I thought they were friends?*

"I'm a corporate lawyer, Dan. She needs a lawyer with criminal experience."

I leaned forward. Barnhouse was an ass, but surely, he didn't believe I'd killed Rado.

"Do I need a lawyer?"

Danny snorted. "Yes, honey, I think you do. At least for the moment. The pope would need a lawyer when Barnhouse is on a rampage. Oh, he knows you didn't kill Rado. He knows you. But he'll make demands, harass you, make you suffer. You and Rado did business together. A lawyer can stop that useless nonsense. That night at the club—"

"He touched me, Danny." I smacked my fist on the center console. Detective Barnhouse had slipped a hand up my skirt.

"I know, but you set him on his ass in public." He chuckled. "It was a righteous rejection."

I leaned back and struggled to clear my mind. I had to shove pain and sorrow aside to deal with—to survive—chaos. First thing? Suspicion. The stranger who found the body. The stranger who'd caught me in the act of a major crime in Seattle and was now buying me a lawyer. Who was he and what did he want?

"I don't like debts, Mr. Dain. I'm sure there's a

criminal lawyer here in town. I'm still not sure I need one." I strived to keep events in my life low key.

Danny chuckled. "Yeah, buddy, I was thinking the same. I mean, she should have a lawyer to cut the crap, but she doesn't need one to come from another state. What about a license to practice?"

"This lawyer can work in several states." Garrett's firm deep voice reassured him. "You remember what I owe you, Dan. In Afghanistan. You saved my ass. Katrine's important to you, isn't she?"

"Yeah, she's important." In his voice I heard the love and friendship that had always warmed and comforted me.

"Then let me help." Such a firm voice, but full of unspoken words. *I will be involved regardless of your wishes or concerns.*

I leaned back and wrapped my arms around myself, willing them to impossibly morph to thick armor. Garret's scent still plagued me in intriguing ways. It remained steeped in the forest and the earth, deep and silent—and saturated in mystery. Now, with the element of surprise fading, I could examine the fierce power that resonated from deep inside him. The conventions of civilization held that ferocity in check. Had he killed Rado? Certainly, he was capable. He turned and gave me a smile much like he had in the basement of the museum before he had let me go.

Chapter Four

The nightmare continued. Garrett steadfastly refused to answer questions about his discovery of the body until his lawyer arrived for me. Poor Danny couldn't interfere, and he had to deal with unconcealed hostility from Barnhouse. I can stand on my own, but I hurt all inside and decided it might be good to have an advocate. The ache of enduring loss kept coursing through me, debilitating my sense of self-preservation. That and I kept thinking about Mom and Dad. I needed to be with them, not here screwing with Barnhouse and answering multitudes of repetitive questions. Nasty business and waiting on a lawyer made me look guilty as hell.

The Senica PD Station wasn't a large building, seriously crowded and far from new. Things went crazy there not long after we arrived. They'd brought in Rado's computer and one of the experts down the hall immediately turned it on, searching for evidence. The expert tripped the failsafe I'd installed to prevent undesired access. The whole box, enhanced with carefully disguised and installed combustible material, burst into flame. We had to clear the building for an hour. Barnhouse refused to allow me to go home.

Once back inside, I heard angry words about Rado's office basement. I figured they'd found his vault, attempted to open it, and triggered the mechanism there, too. By the time the fire department arrived, and it cooled down, all that remained inside was a pile of ash. Rado kept few records, but they were paper. The blaze would bring great relief to his clients. I know it relieved me. No record of anything he bought and sold remained. Only the money in the bank. Valuable if they had account numbers. It was not in my best interest to offer aid. I asked Danny to call Rado's lawyer, inform him of events. I'm sure Rado had left detailed instructions. Truly, so far everything had worked according to the emergency plans Rado and I had made and constantly updated. The Radoslaw and Dolinski families, miniscule as they were, knew how to cover their asses.

All my authentication business clients were legitimate, but I objected when they wanted to search my office. I, too, had worked to maintain a reputation for client confidentiality. Then the high-dollar lawyer Garrett had summoned arrived. With exquisite, knife edge precision, she informed Barnhouse to get a warrant. She also informed him of reasons he should refrain from that action.

Damn, that lawyer was a pistol. Marisa Trent. Few women are as tall as me, but she was six feet of solid female. Six three with her superb designer shoes. Dressed in a tailored black suit, she was intelligent, articulate, and impressive as hell. Kick ass and beautiful, too. She quietly accepted instructions from Garrett. However, each time he turned away from her, I caught a glimpse of raw emotion on her face and in her dark eyes. I didn't have to touch her to read her.

I could sense the palpable rage and resentment that drove her. Obsessive burning desire for Garrett filled Trent like water behind a dam. A single crack would send fury bursting out to destroy anything in its path. She would die for Garrett—and yes, she would kill for him.

The questions went on. I answered most things truthfully. One thing Danny managed to tell me. The woman who hid in her office closet knew the exact time of the shots. Cameras outside on the street moved Garrett down on the suspect list. Finally, they released me.

Barnhouse snarled as I went out, Danny looked worried, tried to follow, but someone called him back. The moment we were outside on the sidewalk, Garrett grabbed me by the arm. Before I could think, he gently, but firmly, guided me a few short steps to an imposing limo that waited, door open wide. Surprised and exhausted, I didn't immediately resist. I climbed in. Trent was already there, and Garrett followed behind me. He closed the door. The instant it slammed shut panic hit me with blinding ferocity. Too many people, too little space—the ultimate step over the traumatic day's emotional cliff.

Terror punched me like a fist in the gut and spread throughout my whole body. At that moment, sitting in that limo, I topped out my limit of stress for the day. All rational thought raced away in a desperate rush to escape. My mind rebelled. It lashed out with fury.

"Let me out." I fought, clawing across Garrett to get to the door. He grabbed my wrists.

"Ms. Dolinski, we're only going to talk." Trent, the bitter lawyer snapped words.

Garrett, slid his arms around me, struggled to soothe me. "Katrine? Please, we'll take you home."

No way. Locked in a big black limo with strangers. *No way*.

So, cat burglar, super thief, cool, calm—not this

time.

"Let me out." I screamed the words. I fought Garrett's hands. Then I choked and set a firestorm of frenzied emotion free. Fear, sorrow, colossal rage. How many years had I held that secret power safely in check. My hands slapped on the limo door. *Body and mind, I pushed.* The enormous capital P push. It surged out of me with each breath. Metal moaned. *The door bent. Hinge and lock broke under my will.* The door exploded off the vehicle frame. It crashed onto the sidewalk and skidded away. The shriek of metal across concrete followed. Thankfully, no one was in its path.

I leaped forward and once on my feet, I whirled and raced back toward the office building, an easy two miles with my practical shoes. I sprinted first, then settled into the track team distance-runner I was in school. *Breathe, Katrine, pace yourself, think of nothing. No pain, no loss, only a steady heartbeat.* Watch the potholes, the curb...watch that car...damn. I'd allowed myself to create a disaster with the Push. I'd controlled it for years. Devastating consequences added to an already desperate situation.

I'd reached my goal. I raced around Rado's building to retrieve the messenger bag hidden under the bush. I threw it over my shoulder. Now to my car. I whirled, and Garrett stood there. He'd followed me—and kept up with me. He'd ditched his jacket and we were both covered with sweat. The foot race had one benefit for me. It dispersed the panic.

"Katrine?" He held out a hand. "I only want to help."

"I don't want your help. Or your fancy lawyer." Emotionally and physically exhausted, I couldn't bear anything else.

Wait? Didn't he want to ask about the limo door? "You need to leave me alone, Garrett. Go to the police with your Seattle basement story or go to hell. *Just leave me alone*."

He reached for me. I backed away.

"But you'll need help, Katrine. You don't understand." Desperation filled his face as if he endeavored to talk a suicidal woman from off a ledge. "Something you took from the museum has a bloody history." His deep voice turned sharp as flint rock. "Someone wants it enough to kill. You're a target. You're in danger."

"Which piece?" *Shut up, Katrine. He knows nothing for sure.*

"The white stone icon. I'll explain more later, but please, let me help you. Protect you."

"What? You think I have the stone?"

Garrett stood, feet apart, ready to act. To attack? He visibly forced himself to relax. Yeah, I admired that. Finally, a bit of clarity arrived. I had my messenger bag over my shoulder. I loosened the tab on the concealed-carry side pocket that held the 9mm.

He cocked his head as if again curious. "Katrine, you tore out a luxury car door like it was cardboard."

"Shitty workmanship. Go get your money back." How I hated the sound of a desperate lie coming from my mouth.

"The door...what else can you do?" He was mocking now. "Don't you want to know? I can tell you so much."

Touch him, Katrine, touch him, read him and you'll know.

No, no. I would not do that. And yet he offered to answer a question that had plagued me all my life. Had he experienced events like mine before? If Rado was murdered for the white icon, this man might have information I needed. *I had Danny's word Garrett didn't murder Rado. Was that enough?* I was not going to let my uncle's murder go unpunished. It was not in my nature or the nature of my family to allow lawful justice to fumble around and screw things up. I gave in.

"Let's go over to my office. We can talk there."

I couldn't run away from the situation. It owned me. Garrett kept staring at me as if I were a puzzle he had to assemble. His attitude? Different now. Different from the museum basement, different from the murder scene.

I didn't want to go into my office alone with him, but I kept my hand near the gun. I also kept my distance and wouldn't hesitate to draw. Pulling the trigger might be problematic. I practiced regularly but shooting at targets didn't mean I could kill someone. That line I hoped I'd never cross.

My computer was missing from my wrecked office. I called Danny. Told him what happened, and to check out local small fires. Someone would need an extinguisher. I had a failsafe on my computer, too.

"Are there any cameras?" Garrett asked as I stared at the mess. "We need a time. If they came here after killing Radoslaw, they probably didn't get what they were looking for from him."

"No. No cameras inside either building. So many people come and go it's impossible to tell what office they entered." Not exactly true. Cameras inside recorded everything and neither I nor Rado wanted them around. No one had trashed and searched Rado's office. Did that mean that something scared his killer away? Why shoot first before they got into the office? Rado kept nothing I had acquired for him in his office. If he'd hidden the icon in a special place, it might remain lost forever. I knew one thing.

"Garrett, you're making unsound assumptions about Rado's murder. Hell, Rado's profession alone came with enormous risk. He bought and sold millions in antiquities. Remember, he was in the hallway with a pistol in his hand when he died."

Garrett watched me and said nothing.

I didn't want to wait for the police. Garrett insisted on driving my car home. Fine. The headache building right behind my eyes threatened to blind me.

"Look, I realize you're trying to help, Garrett." I realized no such thing. "But why are you doing this?" I still wouldn't speak of Seattle.

"I recognized…" He stopped, then went on. "It involves other things we can and will talk about later. Like the limo door. Are you adopted?"

"*What? Adopted?* No, of course not." What wild question was that? "You, unfortunately, have a dangerous amount of information about me. It'll be your word against mine about the museum, but you could cause trouble, especially after the murder. Blackmail. Is that what it's going to be?"

He didn't answer. He stopped the car in my driveway. And how did he know where I lived? Had Danny told him? He cleared his throat. "No, Katrine, no blackmail. We don't have time, but I'll try to explain. I belong to a group of families, all related by blood. We call ourselves tribes. I belong to the Fenrir Tribe. We've existed for a long time." He pulled out his phone and opened a photo. "The museum icon, that little white tile, is part of a set, a tableau that belongs to our tribe. The historians call it Calx Ossa Narratio. The words are— Latin? I'm not good there. I stayed lost in older languages. Calx…stone. Narratio…story? Ossa. I think is bones." A history in stone. But why bones?

He nodded. "Yes. That tableau, the Calx, is a set of relics entrusted to us for countless generations. They're far older than a Latin name."

The photo showed ten of the white icons, all the same size and color, side by side in two rows. Each had carvings similar to the one from the museum. He let me hold the phone. My jaw dropped when he dug in his back pocket and drew another icon, almost identical to the one I'd stolen. He offered it to me.

My first reaction was dismay. He shouldn't handle such a valuable ancient object without gloves. Damn. I should have examined the one from the museum before I gave it to Rado.

"You carried that in your back pocket?" Voice a little high, I struggled to get it back down again.

"Yes, Katrine. It's indestructible. I couldn't break it if I tried."

What? How ridiculous. I grabbed a pair of white gloves from my bag.

Garrett watched. "Gloves. You carry…"

"I'm a professional Antiquities Authenticator. Yes, I carry gloves." Ah, he gave me a sharp look of surprise. Good. He didn't know everything.

Interest had overcome common sense. I lifted the white square and drew in a deep breath. The scent…ah, I'd been there. "Turkey. North by the Black Sea, but I don't know this stone. Calx could be limestone, but if you can't break it...." I'd swear it was a composite, manmade, but...no, it couldn't be.

I studied the carvings on the surface. Proto writing, symbols, from Eurasia...what? 4,000-3000 BCE? *Could it be that old?* I laid the stone on my knee and removed my gloves. My fingers trembled with fatigue—and dread.

"What is it?" Garrett leaned toward me. His breath quickened, and his body tensed.

"I'm going to touch it." I stared straight at him. "I'm intuitive. Psychometry is the common term. I can read things by touch."

His eyes brightened with interest. Not the usual reaction on the rare occasions I speak of such phenomena. Laughter and sneers were the usual. I stared at the icon, seconds passing while I built up the nerve to do something I hated.

"What's wrong?"

I let out a breath and realized I'd clenched my jaw painfully tight. "It's difficult. Often, I don't like what I see. These...symbols are a form of writing. I recognize a few." I pointed at them, talking to put off disturbing action. "That is the mother goddess, the original eminent goddess of that time. It's common on things this old. I see symbols for birth, death, rebirth...others I don't know. I'd have to study, research. The icons, are they all different? Or is a pattern repeated. I can't tell by the photo."

"Each is unique."

I closed my eyes and carefully touched the stone. Fingers only, a feather's brush of action. Scenes—time, so much time. A world of images, animals flooded my mind—was that a mammoth? It all rolled through me…lands, mountains, men…ah, blood, knives, axes, swords. Horrific violence and if I held on, I could experience the fear, the pain. I jerked my fingers away.

"Take it back, put it away."

He did so immediately.

Drained, exhausted from the day's trauma, I needed to rest. I needed time to mourn. Touching and reading artifacts, even under the best of circumstances, could be debilitating.

"Well, Garrett, your icon may have a Latin name, but it's at least five to six thousand years old, maybe…" I remembered the scenes. "Probably older. I don't know its composition. It's not limestone, but its condition is perfect. If you have ten of them and it's a full set, there's no way to determine monetary value. They're priceless." And I had lifted one from a museum. How had it arrived there?

Garrett nodded his head and swallowed. "Yes. Priceless to the tribe. Relics yes, but our history, they're not for sale. And I only have eight. Someone stole two last year. I've been hunting them since then. I located the one in that Seattle museum. I had proved ownership and demanded its return. They refused to tell me how they obtained it, but they accepted my reward money. I was there to take possession that night we met." He lowered his voice to a soft note, little more than a whisper. "I didn't know you already had it with you, or things would have been different in that basement."

"Really? I'm damned curious. You thoroughly searched me, but you accepted the word of a thief when she told you that she left the items upstairs. That's unimaginable. You're not that dense."

He shook his head, drew a breath to speak, then let

it out in a sigh. "It's unimaginable to me, too. Something about you…"

"So, it was my fault you screwed up?"

"No, no. Just a lapse in my ability to use logic and reason in an unusual situation."

Well, for me, nothing was logical about anything that night. "You were in the basement. In the basement. Naked?"

His mouth tightened, and he waited too long to speak. He would lie, absolutely.

"I was searching in places I'd never gotten into with clothes."

Bullshit! And a hell of a lie. He continued. "There was a knife I wanted. The knife case was empty, still sealed, the alarms active. We were searching when I saw you crossing the room on the beam. You didn't see me."

"No, all I saw was the big black dog."

"It wasn't a dog. It was a wolf with excellent tracking abilities."

What? A wolf? Bullshit. "I didn't take a knife. Rado showed me a photo and asked me about it, but no, that was never my objective."

"Oh, I believe you."

"So, you happened to take a scent-tracking tame wolf with you to a museum? That is not…impossible…but totally implausible." The whole thing was getting weirder by the second. Of course, I'd torn the door off a limo with my mind. How weird was that?

"I know, Katrine. I promise you, I'll explain when we have more time."

Did I want that? Him to hang around that long. It now involved murder, not merely theft.

"Katrine, I swear this is not a set-up, not a diabolical scheme. I made the appointment with Radoslaw a month ago. I hoped he might have heard of the stolen icons and could get them for me. He said he could. I came down last night, found him this morning. And there you were."

"Yeah. There I was. So, what do you want from me?" *Everything had a price.*

"First, I want you to help me find the missing icons. We can hunt your uncle's killer, too. Who was Radoslaw's buyer?"

"Garrett, I'm an authenticator, not a finder. I spot imitations, date, and assess value. Rado was the dealer. He located objects. He has…had, ties and contacts in a world I've never touched. I have no idea who his buyer might be. He told me he kept that information for my own safety."

"Don't you want to know who killed him?" The question seeming genuine. Or was he manipulating me because of my distress. "I can tell you more about your strength, Katrine. It's a world you don't know."

"Yes, but the police have resources. Barnhouse is a total asshole, but he knows his business cop-wise. If anyone can find a killer, it's him. Don't underestimate him. He's tenacious." Unpopular but determined, he had a good solve rate. I had resources, too. I wouldn't share them with this smooth lovely man. *But he said he knew about the Push. I wanted that knowledge. He was wrong to call it strength, though. The Push came from somewhere else.*

"Detective Barnhouse has his sights on you, Katrine."

"No. He's pissed. Pissed is normal for him." Should I one day choose to commit murder, professional that I am, I would leave the site scoured clean.

"Katrine, Radoslaw's killer won't stop. If he or they think you know where that icon is…"

A large SUV pulled up to the curb behind us. Garrett's crew? Guess the limo was in the body shop.

"I still say you're making a fantastic unsubstantiated leap, Garrett. You assume that because *you're* interested in the icon, it was the cause of a murder. Over the years, Rado had an entire business built around valuable antiquities. He had enemies. I don't know what Rado did with the one I gave him. And I don't have the knife. I've lived with, and mostly controlled, what you call my strength my whole life. It's personal. Please leave me alone."

I opened the car door. He laid a hand on my shoulder to stop me. "That's a problem, Katrine. I must find those icons. This…you are the closest I've been since they disappeared."

"No. Forget about me. Ignore me and I'll go away. After all, limbo is halfway to hell."

Garrett jerked his hand away. He stared at me, eyes wide, that lovely kissable mouth dropped open. "What did you say?"

"I said, *limbo is halfway to hell.*" I flipped my fingers at him to brush the words away. "It's just an old saying I picked up from Dad. He spouted it for years when he was frustrated or angry about something I'd done. Or didn't do."

I climbed out of the car, and he met me before I could go in. "I'm sorry, Katrine."

"For what?"

"I have responsibilities. Commitments. The icon? I will do whatever is necessary to get it back." His face held an unreadable expression. Not emotionless, but something deep I didn't understand.

"Well, hell, that sounds like a threat, Mr. Dain." I wanted to kick him.

He shook his head. He gently gripped my shoulders, leaned in, and kissed me on the cheek. I froze and let it happen. My judgement, my instinct for self-preservation had deserted me. This man, physically powerful, could also be deadly. I had no doubt he could overpower me. He'd never give me time to draw a weapon.

At the same time, *his scent* almost overwhelmed *me*. No forest or eroticism this time, just a deep sense of knowing him, being welcome and satisfied in his personal space.

He turned and walked to the SUV.

I went inside to cry and console those who, like myself, endured the deepest loss and pain.

Chapter Five

The next five days passed with little rest and no relief from misery. A hundred edgy phone calls from Rado's business clients, who all asked too many questions I couldn't, or wouldn't, answer about the murder. I developed a standard line. "Mr. Radoslaw's business is permanently closed. Unfortunately, a recent fire destroyed all records. Please contact his lawyer if he owed you money...blah, blah."

Translation: Your source of illicit goods is dead. The evidence is gone forever. Get over it.

Rado once told me his will left all he owned, cash, buildings, his few personal artifacts, to Mom and Dad, then they could give it all to me. Thankfully, he made me, not Dad, his executor. Dad had his hands full with Mom.

The surprise occurred when his lawyer called with details of his estate. I knew he was rich, but not that rich. He was younger than Mom, and I'm sure he expected her and Dad to go first. Personally, I still had access to the overseas accounts—mine and his. He'd trusted me implicitly with all his material possessions, legal or illicit. What was his, was by default, mine.

Rado had begged me never to go out and procure items on my own without his help. He was always the planner and I executed those plans. One of life's chapters closed. *I would hang up my catsuit forever.*

Would I miss it? Yes, yes, I would. If I wanted my adrenalin high in the future, I'd have to take up skydiving or tightrope walking over Niagara Falls. I'd been rock climbing before. Next time I'd do it without the safety line.

Funeral arrangements had to wait on an autopsy. An event hall downtown worked well for Rado's service two weeks later. We weren't religious. Dad arranged for acquaintances to speak and say pleasant words. Several people asked to pray. Fine by me.

The turnout surprised me. So did the fact that many attendees seemed genuinely sad at his passing. Rado could be an obnoxious old shit at times. Many were grateful friends who he'd aided in their need, or those who enjoyed the company of an intelligent malcontent.

At least three hundred people packed the auditorium, all braving the intense aroma from thousands of dying flowers. Anyone with allergies had to choke. I hovered over Mom and Dad and shielded them, too. Mom had been almost catatonic since that horrific morning.

Later, after the crowd finally left, I went to the restroom. When I came out, I found Detective Barnhouse in the hall waiting for me. He wore a dressy, but ageing suit. The faint odor of moth balls drifted around him.

"Ms. Dolinski." No smile, but fortunately, no smirk or obvious hostility. Not sure I could have taken that. He'd always called me Katrine, so I guess this was another formal interview.

"Detective Barnhouse." I stood, hands together, ready to endure.

He'd questioned Mom and Dad the day after the

murder, and I know he received no more information than I'd provided. They didn't have it to give.

He glanced around the empty silent hallway, then focused on me. "I know you didn't do him, Katrine, but you know more than you say. I have questions. You should answer them. You can have a lawyer, we can deal." No threats this time, simply letting me understand the gravity of the situation, and the offer of a plea bargain.

"Well, Detective, I have a question, too. I'll trade you."

Barnhouse nodded. The cut on his head had a ragged edge. It would scar. He spoke first. "What were they looking for? Did they get it? Your place…was torn apart. Had to involve both of you."

"That's two questions." I'd tell him part truth, part plausible lie. Send him in a direction far away from me. "I don't know anything with absolute certainty. Two weeks ago, Rado told me he'd received a couple of artifacts, clay tablets, he wanted me to authenticate. They made him extremely uncomfortable. He said something about an ownership dispute, which was usually, but not always, code for stolen. He wanted to be rid of them as soon as possible since the individuals involved were… hazardous." All true.

"Stolen?" Barnhouse raised an eyebrow and winced as the slight facial movement tugged at his wound. "He wouldn't turn them in?"

I stared into his eyes. I felt a tight facetious smile form on my mouth. "No, he wouldn't. It was my understanding they came from a foreign government agent. That's always dangerous. I never saw them."

"Where would he keep them?" His narrowed eyes

and rigid jaw expressed his frustration. I understood. Rado and I had created obstacles, secure roadblocks to hinder any investigation of our lives. "You can try to look for safe deposit boxes. I'll email you with names he might have used and give permission for you to search." I lowered my voice, striving for familiarity to make him believe me. "Rado loved me. He told me many times never to get involved with his clients. I was to authenticate objects and not ask questions."

Okay, I'd tossed him a worthless crumb. "My question for you, Detective. Do you know which came first? Rado's murder or my office being searched and computer stolen."

"Murder, first. Then your office." Fast answer—too fast. Barnhouse knew something. That was scary. Rado didn't have what his murderer wanted. And someone thought I did. Garrett had assumed that it was his icon. I still wasn't so sure.

Barnhouse's brows knit, and he rubbed his chin. "So, your office. They killed him, then went there. See if you had what they wanted. Did they get it?" His scratchy voice sawed at my nerves.

"I told you. I don't know what they wanted. I don't keep anything of any value in my office, ever. I travel to my clients to see their items."

He leaned back against the wall. "Did Radoslaw have a girlfriend? Boyfriend?"

"Not that I'm aware of. He wouldn't discuss it with me if he did." I hesitated on the next part. Was I offering too much? Should I stop now? I plunged on. "Rado called the man associated with those tablet artifacts August Bremen. I never met him or saw his items but from the way Rado spoke of him, I urge even you to use caution in that area."

It was true I didn't know Bremen. I doubt he had any part in the murder, but he'd dealt with Rado. If Barnhouse dug into him, he'd start hitting government obstacles. It might also bring interference by the feds, something I'm sure he'd avoid. I wanted Rado's killer found, but I wanted to do it myself.

Barnhouse's expression turned to narrow-eyed suspicion, much as it had the day of the murder. "That man. Garrett Dain. Found the body. Can't get much personal on him. Don't like that. Suspicious, but he had an appointment on Radoslaw's books. Bought *you* an expensive lawyer." He eyed me like I would either get angry or look guilty.

Again, I needed careful words. "Danny knows Mr. Dain personally, but I never met him before that morning at the office. The lawyer he called for me was unfortunate and unnecessary. Had I been in my right mind, not in shock, I wouldn't have allowed him to do so." I started to say I had nothing to hide, but I'd never be able to utter a lie of such monumental proportion with a straight face.

Barnhouse wasn't giving up. "Dain, he watched you. I watched him. He locked on the second he saw you in that hallway. Eyes never left you the whole time. Thought he was going to snatch you and carry you away. But you said you never met him before."

A brilliant observation, Barnhouse. Shows why you're a competent cop.

"I don't know Garrett Dain. I noted his interest in me, but I have told him stay away. I don't know why he went to see Rado. I don't know what he wants. If you ask Danny politely, he might tell you more."

Did Garrett kill Rado? Gut instinct told me if Garrett killed, it would be swift and silent with no witnesses, no body, no evidence. He certainly wouldn't call the police to the scene.

Garrett had come to the funeral service with Danny and his wife Melanie. I didn't get a chance to do more than say hello, which suited me. The man appealed to me, but without a doubt he was much too dangerous. I was determined to avoid him.

****

I'd postponed my LA authentication trip, but I had to go the next day. What a ghastly ordeal. I had to wade through the client's questions about Rado and accept duplicitous condolences. The LA vases weren't antiquities. They were, however, of considerable value aesthetically and monetarily. A famous native African artist fired them fifty years ago. I found where he had signed them with his mark on the inside. One of the owners was pleased, he wanted the money, the other, less satisfied, wanted a treasure from a more distant time.

I'd driven south to LA, forced by time and weariness to stay over a sleepless night, and driven back. Oncoming twilight painted the western sky pink when I made it home to find a limo parked in the driveway. Friend of Danny's be damned. I told Garrett Dain to leave me alone.

A flash of alarm shivered along my nerves. Exhausted and furious, I tossed my bag across my shoulder and stormed into the house. I stopped short right inside the door. *Would I never learn?* I had ignored warnings from my familiar self-preservation instinct and let irritation override experience.

Marisa Trent, Garrett's high-dollar business-suit

lawyer, perched like a queen on the living room couch. Mom and Dad sat across the room, her in her power chair and him in a chair beside her. A massive man stood behind them. A second sizable brute grabbed me from behind.

The bastard locked hard hands and thick fingers that tightened like steel clamps on my arms above my elbows. He jerked me back. Immediate, immense pain blazed from my shoulder sockets and through my body.

Martial arts training is terrific. I learned how to hit hard, take a blow, and fall safely. *But in the real world, size and strength still matter.* I was not a credible physical threat to either of the brutes in my living room. I could still fight. I relaxed. The grip on my arms eased. The blinding pain eased. Not much, only enough to let me act.

I broke free—but not free enough to draw my gun. The second man stepped up and joined my attacker. Two men, too big and too strong. I fought like hell anyway. I planted a foot in one's balls. Yes, I can kick backwards with force. I'm agile and tenacious, so I managed a few solid blows. I felt a nose give way under the heel of my hand. At the inevitable end, however, they had me. Pinned down on my knees, arms twisted tight behind my back again, one had an unyielding grip on my hair. Brilliant red blood dripped from the other's face onto my sleeve then to the pale cream carpet. A fist slammed into the back of my head. More sharp pain, light flashed, and the world spun. I heard Mama cry out my name. The mini brawl was over. I'd lost. I collapsed, barely conscious.

I did hear Trent's acid voice, sharp with anger. "That

wasn't necessary."

Was she talking to me? They started it!

Trent had seen me make scrap metal of the limo door. She'd ordered a physical preemptive strike to disable me. Effective in the short term, yes, but restraining me would make no difference once I could clear my mind. Not that I could exactly control the Push, but I'd smash at least one of them, preferably her, through the wall. The brutes lifted and dumped me in an upholstered chair. I drew deep desperate breaths. I wanted to ignore the pain, but I'd taken a couple of agonizing body hits. Then I noticed. Dad...face swollen, blood on his shirt. Mom huddled, pale and drawn, in her power chair. The door on the limo was nothing compared to what happened then.

Chapter Six

The air quivered. It hummed and the low, immense sound filled the room. Like a wordless chorus of baritone voices, it pulsed as a beating heart. A thundering shudder rippled through the frame structure. Timbers groaned. Tiny chips of plaster and paint drifted from the ceiling like airy snow. A massive non-directional Push built inside me. I was going to blast the building, my home, apart. Would it tear the roof off? Would that roof crash down on top of us when the walls blew out? The walls shook.

"Katrine, stop." Dad's voice cut through the noise. He, too, had experienced previous calamities initiated by my lack of control. But I was a child, then.

Stop? I couldn't stop.

Trent and her two bullies stared around the room like trapped animals. What had they expected? That I wouldn't object to them mauling my family? I had to move. Action, a blessing, a gift, would loosen the grip of the terrifying destructive compulsion that owned me right then. I couldn't walk. I dropped down and scrambled across the floor to Mom and Dad on my hands and knees. Thankfully, the bag over my shoulder had remained during the struggle. *Oh yes.* I drew the 9 mm from its convenient little compartment.

With my concentration on movement and determined action, the chaos receded. The house thumped as if settling back on its foundation, then fell silent. By that time, I sat on the floor in front of my parents. I had the gun up and ready. No, I couldn't take all three of them, but I aimed at Trent. Not steady, my shoulders hurt too much, but that close, I couldn't miss. The gun wavered. I drew my knee up to my chest and braced my wrist on top.

Way too cool Ms. Trent shook her head. What? She was disgusted and alarmed by my earthquake show. But not hysterical. An ordinary person would panic.

"All I want today is to talk, Ms…Dolinski."

I'll give her credit. She sounded only slightly annoyed.

"Oh, yeah. Talk? That's why those big ass brutes grabbed me?" I glared at her thugs. They glared back but still looked spooked. And why did she hesitate before she said my name?

Tires screeched on the street out front. Trent rolled her eyes and had the nerve to look offended. She jerked her head at her men. "Let him in so he won't break down the door."

One of the men opened the front door and Garrett stalked in. Both men took one step back, eyeing each other like, *what have I gotten myself into?* If outrage, purest fury, had a specific face it would be Garrett Dain's. He stepped toward me. I raised the gun. He was part of this. I had no reason to trust him. His rock-hard expression instantly morphed into something unreadable. Amber eyes, perfect mouth, control, control, he might as well have been in a board room meeting. He turned to Trent. "What do you think you're doing?" I swallowed hard but lowered the gun. Board room be damned. His flat hard voice said he was going to maul someone.

"I'm performing my duty, Garrett. I'm the legal advisor and representative of the Council. I demand justice for an offence to the tribe." Trent's attractive face twisted like she had a mouthful of gasoline and couldn't spit it out.

Garrett shook his head. "We discussed the situation, Marisa. We agreed to use caution. I said I'd handle everything." I could feel his rage, not focused on me, but still terrifying.

Marisa lifted her chin. "We agreed on silence in the name of caution. I have spoken to no one. As for letting you handle things? I didn't agree to that. I'm not blind. I heard you. Saw you. I and others are concerned you won't do what's necessary. It's obvious that you've lost your mind over a piece of Serova trash. But since you're here, let's sort it out."

Garrett focused straight on her, but she held her own. The ill-tempered lawyer wasn't a coward. He turned to the two men.

"Leave." One instantly obeyed. The other glared at him. Another battle in the living room? Garrett would win. I could feel the power coiled in him like a silent cobra, ready to strike. *Why? Why could I feel something in him? I wasn't touching him. Touch. I needed touch to feel things like that. Didn't I?*

"You would challenge me, *bitîm*?" Garrett's voice sounded calm. The rage of his entry had eased. No violence—only a deadly purpose.

Trent's brute broke. He looked away. "No, *sevishtå*." He followed his companion out the door.

Bitîm? Sevishtå? I knew those words, or at least I'd heard them or something similar before. I couldn't concentrate.

I had woefully underestimated the consequences of Rado's violent death. I'd been going on with my life, hurting and missing him. I had acted as if I had time to mourn before I could form a plan to find out why someone murdered him.

Garrett kept his eyes on Trent but spoke to me. "Katrine?"

"Go away, Garrett. My mother is terrified, and those men hurt my father. At this moment I could, quite joyfully, shoot Ms. Stick-up-her-ass." My finger twitched. No hiding emotions, no blank expression for me.

Garrett took a step toward me. I raised the gun again. He stopped. I leaned back against Dad's knees. "Help me up, Dad. Can you?"

He lifted me with his hands placed under my arms and helped me to a chair close to them. I didn't lower my weapon. I did remove my bag from across my shoulders so it wouldn't encumber me.

Garrett didn't sit. He stood straight and tall, undeniably in charge. Trent opened her mouth to speak. He raised a hand and instantly silenced her. He waited until I settled, then spoke.

"Katrine." One word, my name, in a voice heavy as a granite rock. "Please forgive me, for bringing this to you in such an abrupt manner. I wanted to allow you to grieve in peace for a time, then settle other matters. Now, I'm forced to…" He stopped and hung his head for a moment, then went on. "Our tribe, Fenrir, you remember I briefly spoke of it. Blood related families? We live in Rize, Oregon."

"Rise? As in rise up?

"No, Rize with a letter z instead of an s. It's a small town deep in the mountains southeast of Portland. To get there you take a cut-off from Ascendant Highway. The Highway runs between two other small towns. Limbough and Helle."

Dad trembled. I glanced at Mom. So pale, she might faint. The knot forming in my guts tightened until it hurt, right along with my head and shoulders. I started to go to them, to comfort them. Dad shook his head. He was right. Two dangerous people loomed in our family living room, three if you count the one with the gun.

Garrett spoke in a brisk, get-down-to-business tone. No hesitation, no uncertainty, as if he could make an appalling scene less traumatic with unemotional words. "Twenty-five years ago, a man, his wife, and two-year-old daughter were traveling a steep mountain road between Limbough and Helle. He lost control of his car. It went over a drop-off and hit a tree. The wife died on impact. The man had a broken arm, and disoriented with a concussion, he climbed out and walked to get help. The little girl strapped in a car seat didn't appear injured so he left her because he couldn't carry her.

"When another driver found him, they went back. The girl was gone. She couldn't have unhooked the seat straps by herself. No sign of attack, so a wild animal didn't take her. There were no tire tracks in the dirt by the road, including those from the wreck itself. The sand appeared scoured, and all impressions erased leaving no clue that anyone had come by and taken her."

I shivered. When did it get so cold? Dad slowly rose and shuffled to the hutch in the dining room. He came back with a red cloth tote bag and a piece of paper. Obviously handmade, the empty bag had designs of different animals and birds on one side, and a howling wolf on the other. I'd never seen it before. He handed it to me along with the paper. Then he sat by Mom, his arm around her. He wouldn't look at me.

I laid the bag across my lap and held the paper. I kept the gun in one hand. The knot that had formed in my stomach released and turned to a churning pool of acid. Bile rose in my throat.

The paper was a certificate of cremation. A female child, age twenty months. Cause of death? Meningitis. It wasn't an official death certificate, merely a paper detailing the processing of a child's body. The undertaker signed it and noted he had given her ashes to her father.

Tears ran down Dad's face. He reached over and stroked Mom's hair.

"We lost her." His voice cracked. He still wouldn't look at me. "Our little one, our angel. And it hurt so much. I was driving a delivery truck. I came around a curve, saw the car, stopped to help. The woman…there was no help for her. The little girl, in the back, just like our…" He lowered his face to Mom's.

So, who was I? I'd held and presented Katrine Dolinski's birth certificate as mine all my life. I stared at Garrett. "Who do you say I am?"

He gave me a sad smile, one full of compassion. "You were born, and once called, Lisa Marie Serova."

"You're sure that's me. How do you know? You asked if I was adopted."

"First and foremost, it began with the intense connection I felt to you when we met. That instinctive recognition of our kind is a strong trait of our tribe. We recognize each other, no matter where we are. You didn't seem to recognize the same in me, but I couldn't give one of ours to the police. That's why I released you in Seattle. Our tribe, other tribes, are all about connections…I can't explain. You'll have to experience everything." His voice had lowered, and I could hear sympathy in his tone. "I remembered the stories of the missing girl who would be about your age. When you spoke of Limbough and Helle that evening, I lifted a few strands of hair from your jacket. I sent them to a private lab. The DNA report came back a direct match to the Serova family."

"Sneaky bastard, aren't you." I sneered at him.

"Yes." He answered with what sounded like regret.

Oh, I was so hypocritical. *Katrine the thief calling anyone sneaky. The many personas I'd created as a thief made deceit the sum of my life.*

I drew a deep breath to face reality. What—who— was important here? The man and woman who lost and ached for a child so much they stole one? Mom and Dad who raised me into an unusual life, but always with the greatest care and love. *Because they'd already lost one child?* Or was it the family, strangers in Oregon, who lost a child to a kidnapper twenty-five years ago? How devastated were they? Loss not only of the mother, but the child, too.

The appropriate emotion for me—the correct emotion—should be confusion and a sense of betrayal. The bindings to my life's anchors had suddenly come undone and…no, no, no. I've never felt the need for correct, proper behavior. *Master thief, con artist, selfish, so selfish, but I would not give up my life and what I loved.* I'd lost my beloved uncle, but my Mom and Dad were sitting in this room.

I went and knelt in front of them, carrying my gun with me. I wrapped my arm around my father. "For now, I am Katrine Dolinski."

"Your current consent does not negate the crime." Trent snapped the words. They cut the air. She sounded less vicious, but had her hands clenched into fists in her lap. She glared at me. Did she want to fight?

I met her gaze with my own. *Bring it on, bitch.* She froze for long seconds, then looked away. Garrett gave a long sigh that meant he'd been holding his breath.

I rose and went back to my seat. I could shoot better from there. I wasn't sure the violence had ended. I settled and placed the gun on the side table within easy reach. "As far as I'm concerned, right now, tonight, Telek and Alina Dolinski are my parents. I love them unconditionally. I will defend them. I acknowledge they have harmed others by their actions. I will deal with it at a more appropriate time." I eyed Trent. How much more cold animosity could she pack in her gaze? "Blackmail is a crime too, Trent. Name your price."

"I want the icon you stole from that Seattle museum. I want you to give it to me." She eyed Garrett when she spoke. *To me. Not to him. To me.*

"I don't have it. I gave it to Rado. I don't know what he did after that."

"I don't believe you." Trent lifted her chin and glared.

"I do." That was Garrett.

Trent bared her teeth at him like an attack dog.

I'd dropped the empty cloth tote when I'd stood to go to Mom and Dad. I picked it up.

"You had that bag clutched in your hands." Dad spoke softly. "Wouldn't let it go."

Wait? It was heavier? Something else was there. Wasn't it empty before? I laid it on my lap and shoved my hand inside. I drew out a knife.

What the hell...? Rado had shown me a picture. Stolen from the museum where I picked up the icon. *I didn't take it. How did it get here?*

The knife hilt vibrated in my hand. The red jewel on the end sparkled. The amazing runes carved on the blade flashed bright gold and cast sharp brilliant patterns across the walls. The delicate lines glowed like sunlight. I dropped it. By the time it hit the floor, the glow had ceased. It lay there, inert as an inanimate object should be.

Trent was off the couch and backed up against the wall by the door. Shock and terror marked her face. What a change. Garrett hadn't moved, but he sucked in deep breaths as if he'd run a race.

"Dad?" My little girl voice squeaked. Hadn't used it in years.

"It wasn't there." Dad held his hands up in defense. "There was nothing in the bag. Never has been. I looked this morning, Katrine. I got the bag and paper out to show you. I swear. No knife. No."

"I believe you," Garrett spoke again in his business voice again—or the voice of a man on a mission. "That knife is unique. The runes on the blade...it's called Ba'ran. My friend Lilly has one like it called Bi'ar. Bi'ar is...sentient. It comes and goes in her life as it pleases." He nodded at the blade on the floor. "That one, Ba'ran, has chosen you."

"What? Chosen? That's ridiculous. Take it away." Antiquities be damned. "I didn't steal it. I don't want it."

"That knife changes nothing." Trent lifted her chin

and sneered at me. "You will produce the icon within 48 hours, or I will go to the police with what I have, including DNA results. And I'll make sure the proper authorities know about your little Seattle jaunt, even if I can't prove you were there."

"Marisa?" Garrett's expression? Appalled. "She's tribe. That is not the way we treat tribe members."

"It's the way I treat them, Garrett. As they deserve. Especially a thieving Serova."

Garrett stared down at the knife, then back at her, as if she'd made an incredulous decision, a mistake of monumental proportions. "The goddess has decided, Marisa. She's acted. In Arizona. Now here. We're hearing her for the first time in decades. Will you defy her?"

Trent kept shaking her head. "Defy? It's time someone did." She marched out the door.

Goddess? What was he babbling about?

Garrett's face stayed locked tight with anger. It was better than the cold fury when he came in. "I'll resolve this, Katrine. I swear I will."

Resolve? At what cost, and who would pay for resolution?

Chapter Seven

I spent the next hour soothing Mom and making sure Dad had no acute injury. Mom received a dose of anti-anxiety pills, and I enjoyed a much-needed shower. Garrett asked to stay, to explain more to me. I agreed, certainly. Problem? Would Garrett tell me the truth? I had no more reason to trust him than Trent.

Garrett and Dad were sitting at the kitchen table when I dressed and returned.

"Yes, that's my basement girl," Garrett said softly, approval obvious on his face.

So, how did this man see me? I had removed the *medium-brown* girl look, clothes, contacts, and washed the brown rinse from my hair. Did I look that different? I was serious about my personas. It's not like a disguise. A persona goes far deeper. You must be the character, not just play the character. I poured a cup of coffee and sat with them. Dad started to speak. I held up a hand, palm out to stop him.

"I don't need immediate explanations, Dad." I didn't want any more confessions with a witness at the table. "You're my father. My mother is in there asleep. That's my decision for now. I truly understand that there are other people involved who have familial rights and long-standing pain. I sympathize, but I'll deal with them as best I can later. You made a troubling decision, but I will not turn on you."

Troubling decision? Appalling decision. Like the one I made in not telling Rado about meeting Garrett in the Seattle basement? Warn him that another anomaly had occurred. Would he have been extra cautious if I had? *Don't dwell on it now, Katrine. It's done.*

Garrett had a bemused half-smile on his flawless face and a taunting luster in those golden eyes. I pay attention to appearances, and I'd never seen eyes quite like his. "So, tell me, Garrett, what don't I know."

Garrett drew a deep breath. "You and I belong to a tribe by blood—or DNA as it's called today."

I nodded, and he went on.

"Our tribe, Fenrir, is part of a larger group. There are ten tribes in the group, and to a degree, each is different. We're diverse, but that DNA and culture connects us. We have shared physical attributes. Height, both men and women, average six feet. Men don't stand out. Six-foot women do. I.Q. higher than average. An extended life span. Most of us have darker skin, hair, and eyes, because we originated in the area around the Caspian and Black Seas. In our travels from our original home to this country, we did pick up a few hitchhikers from the north. That's why the occasional blue-eyed blonde like you shows up."

"Your eyes are gold."

"Yes, that happens. We can heal quickly, and there are other…gifts." He hesitated an emphasized the word *gifts*, but he went on. "Some of the tribe names are Bastet, Gaia, and Siris. We've been around and stayed together a long time. Millennia."

"Millennia?" My historical fact-steeped mind had to question that.

"Yes. That long. My tribe, and yours, most of us live

in Rize. While you and I were both born into Fenrir, inter-marriage has spread your heritage over more tribes than mine. Your mother—biological mother, Elaine—was only half Fenrir. She came from Gaia."

He studied me. I could feel it, that intense focus. To see how I accepted his tale? Or deciding which lie would be most believable. He went on.

"There are fewer than 5,000 of us in all our tribes together. We have low birthrates. And it's getting worse."

My mind churned as it skimmed years of history. "Wait. Wait. Go back. These families, tribes, they've remained intact millennia, thousands of years. I've studied history. I have degrees. I've examined hundreds of artifacts, translated old languages. Larger groups have done that, stayed together. They're usually bound by religion or geographic isolation. But a few thousand people or families? I don't know everything, and it's not impossible, simply damned implausible."

Garrett nodded. "You're right. Implausible. But for our tribes...I guess you could call it religion. A goddess, a powerful goddess, holds us together by her will. We are her personal servants, her people. We live by her laws with her blessing."

He stopped to let those words sink in. *Servants of a goddess?* My skills didn't include a lie detector. I hesitated to read him by touch, but I had certain skills at reading visible emotions. He had the intensity of a true believer.

"There's a...? You believe..." I stumbled over the words. "A goddess guiding you. Taking care of you?"

He grimaced. "Take care of? No, unfortunately we must accept responsibility for our lives, our actions. We have tribal laws. And yes. *I believe, Katrine.* I've seen too much. I've experienced the reality and lived under her authority."

"Does she have a name?"

"We've called her many names over the millennia. In these modern times, we simply refer to her as *Goddess.*"

I lowered my eyes, trying not to let his face, so attractive, or his expression, so sincere, distract me. How disturbing, this obvious conviction. Was this tribe a cult? True religious believers so often rejected all science, reason, and rational thought. Each word he spoke made me more uncomfortable. He kept going.

"The goddess gives her children various unusual and specific…gifts…when they're born. Extrasensory and supernatural abilities are among those gifts." He emphasized the word gifts. "Your exceptional talent with touch, dating ancient objects…it's as if you can touch time. The car door, your strength—"

"That wasn't strength. It never has been. It was…it is…something else." I shook my head. I couldn't explain where the energy behind the Push came from. But if he knew… "Okay, I'm different."

Dad frowned. He knew I was the best pickpocket in the game from the time I was seven years old, not to mention my misguided time as the child prognosticator. I could see how he might have believed I had mystical or supernatural powers. He'd known I was different, certainly. *He'd known I was not his biological child.*

Garrett continued his story. "The tribes were nomads across the Middle East until we immigrated to America in 1850. About 1900, drastic cultural changes roiled the tribes. The world became technical and mechanical too quickly. Birth rates tumbled further. No one knows why. Until recently, it seemed like we would become extinct within a generation.

"There was an…event…last year, in Arizona, that gave us hope. We have a new leader. A reluctant leader, with the Bastet tribe. Her name is Lilly."

I rubbed the back of my neck trying to ease the tension. What a horrible day stretching to a weary end. Garrett had more to say, though.

"Katrine, Rize is a different culture, a way of life. Oh, nothing obvious. We keep a normal face to the world. Our tribal world, however, is bound by archaic laws and customs. Unfortunately, some of us cling fast to the old ways."

"You believe, you worship, this goddess?" I had to go back to that. So far, it was, to me, the most unacceptable facet of his story.

"It's difficult to explain. We believe and we serve. There's no worship, no true official religious component. You saw the knife. She created that blade." He drew a deep breath. "Our goddess is an existent, supernatural being. I've seen proof. In Arizona, she moved the earth to help us. Oh, and there are three of them, those knives. Bi'ar, Ben'zir and Ba'ran. Ba'ran is lying on your living room floor. I wish Lilly would come here, talk to you."

"She won't come?"

"No. I suspect the goddess ordered her not to interfere, another of those archaic mystical rule things. Lilly told me that her knife, Bi'ar, comes and goes on its own. Like Ba'ran appeared in that bag. Bi'ar has been with her most of her life. She hates it."

"Hates the knife or its miraculous teleporting excursions?"

"Lilly says the knife makes it too easy to kill. It shows her how to strike, even aids that strike. She leaves it hidden in her sock drawer, but I expect it would appear at her hand if she needed it. Only someone, or something, with power beyond human could create that blade.

"You wouldn't touch it. Why?"

"No. It's a sacred artifact. No way would I put my bare hands on a knife the goddess created for a tribeswoman. Ba'ran chose you. Bi'ar for Lilly. Ben'zir hasn't shown up—yet."

No, no, no, he would not do that. "Garrett Dain, if you give me any more bullshit about my being some sort of chosen one, even chosen by a knife, I will do my best to beat you into the ground." I shook my fist at him. "Do you know how many stories I've read? From clay tablets to papyrus—and yes, by touching artifacts—all have a *chosen one* story somewhere. It's fantasy. It's not real."

The corners of his perfect mouth turned up in a tiny smile. I amused him.

"Bottom line, Garrett, what do you want from me?"

"I want you to come to Rize to meet your extended family. Will you do that? We do have to find the icon and your uncle's killer, too."

He was still associating Rado's murder with the icon. I still wasn't so sure. "I could agree, but I want Mom and Dad safe from anyone associated with your...*tribe.* No vengeance or other shit."

"I'll stop Marisa. And I'll make sure no one speaks of you until you're ready. We are tribe and we protect our own—and those they love."

I'll stop Marisa? Pretty forceful those words, and yet, less than comforting.

He reached across the table to touch my hand. I

jerked it back.

"Katrine, I understand how you feel about the chosen thing, but Ba'ran came to you. Ba'ran gives you prominence among us. Marisa, for all her words, believes. She'll see eventually."

Denial was the best emotion right then, safest until I had time to think. "That knife is not mine. Didn't steal it from the museum. Don't know how it got here. Since you won't touch it, you can get a shovel and toss it in the trash. Or put it in a box and mail it back to the museum. *I need time*. Uncle Rado is dead. Right now, I need to up protection for Mom and Dad. Give me two weeks, then call me."

"You don't need to do that, Katrine." Dad spoke up for the first time. "I'll face—"

"No, you will not. What the hell? You, Telek Dolinski, plan to become an honest man in your senior years? Is dementia setting in? Don't give me that shit." I crossed my arms on the table. I strove to let all emotion seep from my expression. "Okay. I'll keep the knife. For a while. But if anything bad happens to my parents because of Trent running her mouth, I will use it to cut out her heart. Make sure you tell her. Say it exactly that way."

"I will. You know, she challenged…" He stopped and shook his head.

"Two weeks, Garrett. It seems cruel not to let a family know about a lost child, but after twenty plus years they can wait a little longer."

"Don't worry too much about their feelings. Truthfully, Peter Serova, your biological father, is a rough, violent man. The drunk ass ran that car off the road and killed your mother. Your brothers, Morgan,

Merritt, and Randy are useless as men and tribe members. Without your mother to protect you, you might not have lived long enough to start school. Peter and his boys are the only immediate family, but there are others who will welcome you and bless your homecoming. Return to the tribe, Lisa Marie. Come back to us."

He leaned forward, and I saw the gleam in his eyes as it was when he caught me in the basement. "I can and will make the case that the goddess saved you when your mother died. That she sent you to the Dolinskis so you would survive. Our goddess lives. The more I learn about you…you are absolutely perfect."

"Why am I perfect?"

"You've accepted the goddess' gifts without prejudice. You don't deny them in a misguided religious fervor. You don't reject them as evil, the devil's work. You stand and take what you want in this world, Katrine. No guilt, no regrets. That's a trait you share with us. We are ruthless."

Ruthless? A cult of violent and deadly believers. My family?

Garrett shifted in his seat. "I need to get back and keep Marisa quiet."

"That should be easy for you. You know what she wants. It's pretty obvious. Do it and she'll calm down." The Trent woman had reeked of misdirected and unfulfilled passion. It made me uncomfortable, but no, I was not jealous. Garrett Dain didn't belong to me.

Garrett's beautiful golden eyes met mine. "Marisa is caught between two worlds. The real world and one she's created in her mind. She can't fully accept either." I heard sympathy in his voice. He did not speak to my idea of a solution to his personal problem.

He stood and I walked out with him to his car.

"Katrine, would you do something for me?"

"Depends. I don't trust you."

His smile, his warmth, washed over me like a wave. Beguiling. That was the word. *Hazardous was another.*

"You read artifacts by touch. Can you read people?"

"No." I lied. I was so not going there.

He grasped my hand and held it to his chest over his heart. "Just this once, try. Please."

His eyes gave a flash of that spectacular gold. And that flawless face? Created by an angel—or his existent goddess. His scent? Again, the deep forest. I closed my eyes and there on the sidewalk, he drew me into his arms, my face against his throat.

For the first time in so many fearful years, I let my guard down. For the first time ever, no stray thoughts, no images came to me. I received no special visions like the ones I'd had as a child reading strangers. Deep desire, a sudden and powerful urge overwhelmed me. This man was mine. Made just for me. Absolutely and completely, for now, forever. But did that mean he owned me? I jerked away. I had to escape.

"No. You need to leave me alone."

He smiled and got into his car.

I went back inside and found Dad tearing the cremation certificate to tiny pieces and wetting them in the sink. He tossed the mess in the trash and came back to the table. I could see he wanted to talk more.

"I want to say I'm sorry for what I did, honey, but that's a lie. You gave us new life. It's the only thing we ever kept from you. You know we were mostly open and honest in our family life. Our sunshine, our precious little baby. A sudden high fever. Late one night, a retired doctor in a small town diagnosed her, the nearest hospital fifty miles away. We drove to take her there but she…it was too late."

His face seemed to have aged so much since I saw him last.

"I never got a death certificate. A small cremation facility took my money. We were loners, drifters. No one knew her." He nodded at the sink. "After that we decided to leave life on the road, settle down. I got regular jobs. For a year, each day, I watched your mother slowly dying from grief. I've committed criminal acts in my life. But steal a motherless child…horribly wrong."

He smiled then, the familiar loving smile that had sustained me through the years. "You can choose to be Katrine or Lisa Marie. I won't criticize." He started to speak again, stopped, then went on. "I know you're special. Dain has spun you a fantastic tale. But no tracks in the dirt where I parked…how could that be? I was driving a delivery van with four back wheels and signs painted on the side. There was almost no traffic that day, but someone had to have seen me. I figured when I left with you, I'd see flashing lights behind me at any moment. I'm guilty, but I don't care. I love you so much, my Katrine."

****

I'd heard nothing from Garrett in the week after the showdown with Trent. I used the time to close out Rado's office and apartment. The office had little except furniture and books.

His office furniture went to leased offices in the building, and the old books to a university library. The apartment was unsurprisingly bare. Most nights he stayed at the office. There was a bathroom and shower in the basement, a couch to sleep on, and delivery for food. When I returned home the seventh day after my family revelations, I found Detective Barnhouse sitting in his car in the driveway. Mom and Dad's car was gone. Damn it. I still worried about Trent blabbing things to family in Rize, rousing ideas of vengeance. Dad had promised me they wouldn't go out without me. I'd made it a point to stay armed all the time.

Was Barnhouse waiting on them? Or to tell me he arrested them? I climbed out and he met me. He had his usual sour face on, which set me off. "Are you going to harass us forever?"

"No. Let's go inside. Just a couple of more questions." His voice sounded odd. I shook my head in disgust but went and unlocked the door. He followed me in.

We'd come in the back door, so I dragged my bag off my shoulders and dropped it on the table. I turned back to him. His usually florid face sagged, his gaze anxious under furrowed brows. Something was wrong.

"What...?" Was that my voice, high pitched and raw? "What's happened? Mom...Dad..."

"I'm sorry Katrine." Genuine compassion thickened his rough voice. "Your parents are dead."

Chapter Eight

What was he saying? Mom, Dad? Dead? He was lying to me. A trick. Shocking me so I'd talk about Rado. "Stop it! Don't do this. I've told you what I know about Rado."

"Katrine." Pity? Damn him, how dare he? He reached for me. I jumped back and bumped the kitchen table so hard it slid a few inches. The wooden legs scraped a rough sound around the room. The kitchen, the good place, the safe place—home.

"You're lying. You…"

"Katrine, stop."

No lie. Only dreadful truth. I could see it in his eyes. My mother and father were gone. The edges of my vision blurred. I grabbed at the table. If I held on tight… Barnhouse caught me. He easily controlled and walked me to the couch.

Alone. That sudden gut wrench tore a hole and left me hollow, empty. Utterly abandoned, like a child left on the steps of a church by a woman who never looked back as she walked away.

I want…I need my Mom and Dad.

It wasn't supposed to be this way. They were old, but…no. Longing, a deep ache in my chest, spread through me with each beat of my heart. I fought to shove it away and couldn't. I couldn't break through. I sat there, completely defeated, lost in a silent universe, a world of sorrow. Voices broke the silence. They crackled like frozen pieces of thin ice, shattering in spring. Angry words…Danny? Yes, he was there, holding me. Eventually, a dull numbness settled on me.

"What…" I choked and had to clear my throat.

Danny gently wiped my tears with a cool cloth. "Trine. This shouldn't happen…it can't…" Danny was crying, too. His own tears wet his face.

I had to go on. "What happened? An accident? I asked them not to go out alone. He promised. He promised. Dad's still a good driver. Did he have a heart attack? What?"

Danny glanced at Barnhouse, who sat across the room. Barnhouse wore his angry cop face again. I'd bet he came alone to tell me, because he'd hoped a shocking revelation would make me answer questions. Instead, the usually calm and cool Katrine had gone into shock.

My oldest friend slid an arm around me. "Trine, they were murdered. A group of cyclists found them late this morning by a maintenance road near the City Line Park. Their car is missing. Maybe a carjacking."

"Or not." Barnhouse spoke.

"Don't start." Danny sneered.

"Oh, yeah. Sorry, Studstill. Don't want to catch any killers, do we?" Cynicism and scorn, his usual methods of communication, had returned.

Murdered? Like Rado? Carjacking?

"No! Dad kept the doors locked. He wouldn't stop for anyone. They never went to bad places, and…wait! Why did they go out? And where? He promised he wouldn't."

My hands curled into fists. This was wrong. I had the dismal, useless urge to fight, to get to them, help them. Danny held me tighter. He hesitated when he spoke. "We...I don't know the exact circumstances, honey, no details. If we find the car..."

I cringed and hunched my shoulders as the next crushing weight dropped.

It was my fault.

From the beginning, I should have told Rado about meeting Garrett in the basement. It might have made a difference, changed something. Rado, the damned icon, Garrett Dain, Marisa Trent and her threats all focused on me.

But I had taken precautions. Despite Garrett's promise to forestall vengeance by my Rize biological family, I'd increased electronic security at the house. I'd added regular private security drive-by patrols. Dad truly swore they wouldn't go anywhere without me.

Danny took my hands and gently uncurled my fingers. I'd held them in fists so long and so hard they'd turned white. "Trine, if you know anything, anything at all, please help us. We keep going back to Garrett. Why is he so interested in you? He's been here at the house again since Rado. That lawyer, too. Why, honey? What does he want? Does it involve your parents? Rado? We need to know."

"You've been spying on me?" No. He wouldn't.

"Not him." Barnhouse spoke up. "I set up surveillance. My gut tells me you know more about your uncle's murder than you say you do. The man who found his body is still hanging around. Is it connected? Odds are looking damn good." He leaned forward, more animated than I'd ever seen him. "*You loved them, woman. Your family. You need to talk to me. Help me!*"

Talk? No talking. Mom and Dad trained me. Hold

to the silence of grifters and thieves. I closed my eyes and hung my head. Let the now dull ache spread through my body like a drug.

Barnhouse finally gave up and left, distinctly unhappy. I don't blame him. He was right. I knew little, but more than I would ever tell him. I couldn't speak without allowing him to dig too deep. My family had lived an isolated life in our own world and dealt with things ourselves in our own way. I would do the same.

Danny gave me a warning. "He's getting search warrants, honey."

It didn't matter. There was nothing in this house he couldn't see, and they'd already been through the offices. As much as I loved Danny, as much as he had learned about me on his own, he could never know the full extent of my life. I couldn't break that pattern of secrecy, of isolation drummed into me since I was a child.

Danny stayed with me that night. I didn't think I'd sleep, but he made me take a pill. He lay beside me and was there when I woke twice during the night.

"Tell Melanie I'm sorry," I told him when he left that morning. Melanie had to share her husband with his best friend. She wasn't happy, but she endured it gracefully. A good woman. I was glad he chose her. Glad he loved her enough she could tolerate me.

"Mel understands." He smiled and shrugged.

"No, she doesn't. She accepts and loves you anyway."

By the time I showered and dressed, sorrow had scoured my heart and mind clean. I would deal rationally from that point on. Or at least if the pain did break me, I'd do it in private. I remembered the spooky knife. I'd put it in a drawer, and I needed to hide it better before a search. When I opened that drawer, it was gone. My mind skipped over the possibility that it might have hidden itself.

I called Danny. How had they died? I demanded every single detail. He shouldn't have told me, but he did. They hadn't found the actual murder scene or the car. The killer left the bright blue twisted Polypropylene rope after he'd strangled them. The killer must have stunned Dad first, leaving Mom helpless. I hung up and collapsed on the floor. How terrified she must have been. I had utterly and completely failed the most beloved people in my life.

As most humans do, I eventually worked my way through debilitating sorrow to function. I called the funeral home to take their bodies after the autopsies. It would be at least a week. I sat stoically through the search of my home. The newspaper picked up the story, and the calls came, but I didn't answer. Mostly I hid in the house, staring at nothing.

I answered the door only for Danny and blessed Melanie, who brought food. She nagged me like I was one of her kids until I ate the minimum to live. I made one trip to the liquor store, bought bottles of whiskey, and drank myself into a dreamless sleep each night. I preferred it to pills. On the fifth day after their murder, the funeral home's number showed up on the phone. They had the bodies. I instructed them as Dad had instructed me. Four days later Danny, Melissa, and I stood by the three graves. Mom, Dad, and Rado. My entire world.

No funerals for Mom and Dad. Their specific instructions. I had buried them in the sphere of isolation and secrecy that had always shielded us, no matter where we went or what we did. Danny had managed to break through to me as a child, but as we grew, I had to shut him out too much. He loved me anyway.

I'd returned to the house from the cemetery when someone banged on the door. Like an idiot, I opened it without looking to see who it was.

Well, well. Marisa Trent.

She surged through the door like a wild animal, teeth bared, and eyes full of fury. I closed it behind her. I figured she wanted the icon I didn't have. Was she pissed because she no longer had Mom and Dad as blackmail material? Report me to the police. I left no evidence behind in Seattle. Her word against mine. She could cause inheritance problems for me, but I'd already hidden most of the cash.

Fists clenched, she stood staring with narrow slits of eyes. They projected so much hatred it had to weigh on her soul. "Serova bitch!" Her voice could crush stone. "Whore! Thief! You can't have him."

Oh, hell. This was about Garrett? My whole family murdered in the last few weeks, but her unsatisfactory love life was most important.

"I don't want him, Trent. Don't waste your stone-cold bitch act on me. You—and Garrett Dain—can both go to hell."

Teeth bared, Trent smiled with a joyful and hateful predator's glee at finding a victim. She punched me in the face. Fast, hard, and blinding, I hadn't expected that. Instant pain blasted away immediate thought and orientation. I staggered but didn't go down. This would be no open-handed catfight. No hair pulling, or fingernails scraping the skin raw.

She projected when she drew back to strike again. I

moved. Not fast enough. Her solid fist hit my shoulder like a prize fighter's knockout punch. Damn she was strong. I spun and slammed into the wall again. My face hit the plaster and my head the corner of a picture frame. As much as I wanted to, I would not curl up and fall. This woman didn't want to hurt me—she wanted me dead. Still leaning on the wall, the next punch took me in the kidneys. I couldn't scream because the impact drove air from my lungs.

"You will not have him!" Her earsplitting screech cut the air. "He's mine."

I jerked away, tripped over a chair, and collapsed. I landed on my back. She towered over me. A foot drawn back—she would kick me. My combat lessons? Forget them. Her attack, fast and dirty, stripped away my hours on a practice mat.

I remembered one thing, though. *Legs are longer than arms*. I kicked her in the knee. Swift! Hard! Her knee joint snapped and bowed backward. She wouldn't walk away from here.

She shrieked. Now she sounded full of absolute blinding agony...perfect. She toppled over, still screaming. I had to use the chair, but I climbed to my feet. Her screams rose in intensity. Then they deepened and morphed to a howl. Trent rolled and jerked on the floor in a massive seizure.

Damn. I'd have to call 911. I had friends who would believe me that she struck first. Blood trickled down the side of my face from where my head hit the picture frame. It blended with the stuff running from my battered nose. No real damage. Only I needed a kidney transplant. Shoulder to hip, my back throbbed. *Screw your knee, bitch! You earned it!* Now, where was my phone? Had to call before my adrenaline level fell and the pain really kicked in. I looked up to see…

Oh! What the hell? Garrett Dain stood across the room. When had he come in? Arms at his sides, perfectly still, he stared at me like a stranger.

Before I could speak, Trent made an odd noise. A moan, low and deep. It turned into a growl. She lay on her back, rolling back and forth. She…oh hell…she blurred. Not the right word, but her whole body went fuzzy around the edges. Were my eyes out of focus. A concussion?

She…changed. Oh, I'd read the books. I'd been to the movies. I'd seen the special effects of shapeshifting. *It was not real. It fucking didn't happen in a suburban living room!* Marisa Trent's distorted body sharpened and formed a wolf. Gray, brown…hell, fur and teeth. Teeth that grew…longer, sharper. It wasn't an instant transformation. I stood and watched, mesmerized. I gaped when I should have run.

She howled. Not like in the movies—but so much louder in a living room.

At least a tiny instinctive part of my mind kept working. Weapon. Where was a weapon? My bag, my gun, a knife? In the kitchen. I'd never make it. What else? A lamp? Wait. The half-inch thick glass tray full of decorative pebbles sitting on the table. Mom had loved the monster. Ten pounds of leaded crystal so heavy she couldn't lift it with her small hands. A good eighteen inches long…I snatched it up. The multitude of pebbles flew everywhere and silently bounced away on the carpet. The solid tray wouldn't break easily.

I glanced at Garrett. What the fuck? He was still standing there staring. *Standing between me and the door, too, if I wanted to run.* Marisa finished her change, her clothes hung in rags around her body. And she was...big. Way bigger than most dogs. Her dark eyes had turned to gold. Like Garrett's. Only they were not animal eyes. I stared into the sentient eyes of an impossible, ferocious preternatural creature. A creature that could slaughter with conscious logic. A creature filled with wrath and wounded desire.

I didn't wait. I raised my arms and popped her square across the head with the thick glass dish. The glass didn't break. She yelped and staggered. Yes, I'd hurt her. She still struggled with the remainder of her clothes. Clumsy wolf with no hands. I didn't dare let her get loose or she'd tear me apart. I hit her again. It wasn't going to work. Not enough weight or force. She was too big, too solid.

The blouse she'd worn remained around her neck. Her back feet tangled in her skirt. I launched and landed on top of her, knees first. If I could pin her down... She yelped and collapsed under my weight. I grabbed her blouse still around her neck, twisted and jerked it tight.

Be still, bitch.

I tightened the silky noose and held on. She twisted her head side to side. A mouth full of teeth tore into my forearms. I held her at an awkward angle, and she couldn't get a good hold. If I released her...time slowed. She kept twisting and snapping, ripping skin and flesh. Would this never end. I held on. I had to stay on top. I listened to her choke...and choke. Finally, I felt her movements under me slow.

"Katrine?"

What? Who? Garrett. He'd been standing there all along and had made no move to help me, to stop *her*.

Now he knelt beside me.

"Katrine, please don't kill her."

What the hell?

The energy of the fight, the incredible high, drained away. Pain arrived. Intense, more devastating each second. And the blood—my blood—flowed in appalling streams onto her fur and down to the carpet. Mom's beautiful carpet the color of sweet cream.

Mom...Dad...I'm afraid. I need you.

"Let her go, Katrine. You've won. Let her go." Garrett's pleading interrupted my focus.

"No. She'll kill me." My voice sounded like a rasp on metal, tortured and barely recognizable.

"She won't. Let her go. Please."

My stomach tightened into a knot like I'd swallowed a brick. The last of my adrenalin fueled strength drained away. I couldn't hold on. I released the blouse and rolled over away from them. Blood coated me. My blood. I almost killed her, but I don't think I made her bleed. I wanted her to bleed. I watched Garrett drag a pile of fur across the carpet.

Get up, Katrine. Run woman. Run.

Then Garrett was there, holding me. I hit him. My body was giving up. The blows were soft as pillows. I smeared blood over his face, his expensive suit. "You...you watched...you..."

He ignored me. He held and examined my arms. Oh, yeah. Torn, bloody mess, weren't they? I heard him call out to someone. Who else was here? Who else watched and didn't help me. Then Garrett was wrapping something tight around my arms. Pain intensified. So deep, so raw.

"Katrine?" Garrett was holding my face. "Please

listen. Do you want me to call 911? If I do, they're going to treat this like a rabid dog attack. If you tell them the truth…"

If I told them the truth, they would treat it like a rabid dog attack on an insane woman.

"No." My mind shouted, but my words came out in soft puffs of air. "No hospital. No cops. No." *My whole life was a lie. I was not Katrine Dolinski. I was an imposter. A stranger even to myself. An actor, a shadow on the museum wall.*

Bitter liquid burst into my mouth, and I swallowed. Two breaths. My world faded to a wisp of light—and went dark.

Chapter Nine

I woke in my bed. Not instantly but drifting in and out. A bitter taste lingered in my mouth. What had happened? Ah, yes. A wolf attacked me. In my living room. Garrett Dain had drugged me. The pain? Still there, throbbing, not raging. I doubted I could lift my arms. I could smell Garrett, feel him sitting beside me. I opened my eyes. Yes. There he was. The man with an angel's face. The man who had not helped me when a wolf attacked. The man who had let a monster beast have her way with me then begged me not to kill her.

I choked. The words wouldn't come. He lifted my head and gave me a sip of water. Then I could rasp words of betrayal. "You said…told me…protect you, Katrine."

He shook his head. Helpless wasn't a good look for him.

Coward. "She…changed." The image filled my mind. The first tremor, then the shimmer and blur as her body went from human to animal. It could not be real. Yes, it could. Look to yourself Katrine. Real as the scenes of an ancient time locked in inanimate objects. *Accept it Katrine! You've lived in a preternatural world all your life. Don't waste time on disbelief, on denial.* My heart rate rose, and my arms throbbed with each beat. I drew deep breaths until I calmed.

"Mom and Dad? Did Marisa kill them?" But they were strangled. Stunned first, Danny said, and strangled, not torn apart.

"No, I don't believe she killed them. But she knows something." He sounded certain. "I'm sorting through secrets and connections in Rize. I need more time." I could almost hear him plotting, scheming. There was a brazen coldness to him that seemed more deliberate, more manipulative.

"Thank you for not killing her, Katrine."

"Not killing her. Not yet. How did she...?" My broken voice betrayed me with hollow words, false courage—what a show. Oh, but the memory. The way her body, flesh and bone, impossibly rolled and reshaped itself. The teeth...I shuddered...the teeth of a killer beast.

I lifted my hands as much as I could. My forearms weren't bandaged. I had four ragged tears along the right. The arm closest to her mouth. Three to five inches, each gap neatly crossed with stitches—perfect masterful stitches. A single tear on my left, multiple pencil sized puncture wounds in both arms. My left hand was swollen so much it might burst. Most likely from hitting Garrett.

Had they taken me to the ER? What did they tell them? I needed antibiotics. What would I have said in the ER? *Oh, this woman turned into a wolf in my living room and bit the hell out of me.* Would they make me take rabies shots?

"Can you do that, Garrett?" I wanted to make an angry demand, but it came out a broken whisper. "Change...yes, you can. You were the wolf. The museum. That's why you were naked." But that wasn't the worst thing. "You would have let her kill me. You would have let her..."

"I know you don't understand, Katrine. By tribal

law, I couldn't interfere. We've established you *are* tribe, by blood, so the law applies to you. She challenged you."

"But I don't know any law. Insane. Animals…"

My whole battered body now sent out mighty complaints about ruthless abuse. Not the blinding pain of before, but I could barely think. I had to go on. "A challenge? What kind of challenge? What did I miss?"

"The challenge was to determine your place as principle or subordinate within the Fenrir tribe. If you had grown up with us, it would be determined before or at puberty, supervised, with no violence. Each family in the Fenrir tribe has a single sevishtå, as a leader. Some males, some female. But we classify *all individuals*, leaders or not, as either sevishtå or bitîm. Bitîm is subordinate." He let out a long breath.

My mind kept returning to one thought. *A woman—an animal—almost killed me*. I should go to the emergency room. Make up a story. I couldn't drive. I'd have to call a cab. If I called Danny…no. He'd drive me to the ER, then to the station to file a report. What would I tell him?

"Drugs, I need drugs. Look in the cabinet by the sink. There's a bottle of oxycontin. Mom's name on the label. Bring me the antibiotics, too."

Pills and water. It hurt to swallow, but he held me up, and I managed a few mouthfuls. I had to wet my dry throat and the chilly water eased the pills down to my empty stomach. As I swallowed, the liquid rinsed the bitterness away. It didn't take long for good old oxy to arrive, surfing on a spectacular wave. What he'd poured in my mouth before kept me out for an extended time. Long enough for someone to come in clean and sew me up.

Garrett sat watching me. I could see a struggle in his eyes. "Katrine, by defeating Marisa, you're a sevishtå tribeswoman. A leader, not a subordinate. We like to think we've outgrown bloody combat, but apparently not."

"So, I get to live—or die—by a bullshit tribal law I never heard of? Marisa tried to kill me, Garrett. It was no hierarchy game. She tried to *kill* me." I struggled to make fists and couldn't. Finally, I laid my hands flat across my chest. "And you? *Oh, well, that's life in the tribe. Get over it.* I never should have had to face a battle like that. And the fact that I won is not an issue here."

My voice had risen again, and my heart gave a couple of hard thumps before it slowed. "Since you've crashed into my life, people I love have died. And I saw, damn it! In her eyes, after she changed." I drew deep breaths. "She wasn't an animal. She knew what she was doing."

"Yes. She knew. We're not true wolves. We're something different."

Oh, I needed more drugs. No. I had to release the rage first.

"My place in the tribe? That's unmitigated bullshit. She said *you will not take him. He's mine.* It was all about you. *You, personally.* And your fucking law? What would you have done if she'd won? If she'd torn my throat out. You'd dispose of my body and go on with life in your mountains, wouldn't you?"

"No!" He jerked. "Status fights—fights of any kind—aren't supposed to be to the death."

"Bullshit! Liar! *Supposed to?* Damn you. You stood and watched."

Religious cult wingnut with his tribal law. And don't forget his true goddess, skulking around in the shadows like a ghost.

I could tell I'd disturbed him. He kept shaking his head in denial of my words. "Katrine, our tribe's blood line has degraded. Only about thirty percent of Fenrir can change shape now. If it doesn't happen at puberty, it won't ever happen. Marisa and I grew up under pressure from our families, believing we had to marry. Hopefully to produce full shifter children. I left Rize at eighteen. I lived and learned. When I came home, I couldn't do what she wanted. But if it wasn't you, eventually there'd be someone else."

"Someone else? Eventually?" I fought to keep from screaming. That would hurt too much. "And you still wouldn't intervene. Someone weaker than me, would you let Marisa kill her? All because of your freaky religious, fucking tribal dogma? I'm a thief, Garrett. What kind of a monster are you?"

He reached for me. I flinched. I couldn't move away. I didn't want him touching me. He stopped. The pain rose again.

"Katrine, you don't know my nature—or your own nature—not yet. The minute I smelled you, tasted you in that basement. You were mine. Didn't you…couldn't you feel that?"

"Yes. I felt something when I met you. But any man I choose will fight beside me, not stand and watch me get torn apart. I'll demand loyalty. A better man than you." Ah, there was emotion on that captivating face. Hurt. He had no right to suffer.

I gagged and choked on a mouthful of bile and the foul taste of the pills I'd swallowed. It ran over my lips.

He was there with a cloth and more water to bathe the burn of acid that pushed up into my throat. I'd have ulcers soon. When I could speak again, I did.

"Garrett, over the past few weeks, except for Danny, I've lost everyone I've ever loved. I've discovered I'm not who I believed myself to be my whole life. And you've been here. Involved. You brought Trent here. Shape changing? What the fuck? Something that defies the laws of biology, even physics."

"It's the gift of the goddess." His voice lowered, deepened. "Magic, miracle, anomaly, call it what you wish. And is it any stranger than your own extrasensory powers? You might deny it, but they came from the blood of the tribe—her goddess blood."

"I don't care what it is. I need to find a murderer."

"Yes, and I'll help you as much as I can. As for Marisa, I will file a protest and demand justice from the tribe. As ruthless as we can be, we don't get to kill anyone we want, or issue challenges like she did without sanction. The law says we can't turn wolf in a fight if our opponent can't turn, too."

"Sure. Your *law*. I won't hold my breath. Will a 9mm stop her? Do I need goddamned silver bullets? If she shows up again, I'll shoot first." If the swelling in my hand went down so I could hold a gun. I wouldn't— couldn't—believe anything he said. Damn, I felt bad. Was the room getting fuzzy?

"Yes, a 9mm will stop her. We heal much faster as individuals, but not instantly. Silver is a myth. Katrine, we are a violent and superstitious people living in a rigid culture. You are ours. We are yours. Come to Rize and claim your heritage. Don't judge until you've lived among us." He shook his head, and his expression was that of a man trying to explain something to a small child. "Being a sevishtå is more than a fight for hierarchy. It's a personal sense of control, a power. You defeated Marisa the day she came here and told you who you were. I saw that. You dominated her. She refused to accept the obvious defeat."

"How many people in Rize know about me?" In other words, how large is my suspect list of those who would want to punish Mom and Dad for kidnapping.

"Very few. Our tribal council, we all agreed not to speak out." *And Marisa, wound tight as a tourniquet, watching all she desired slip away, had come unraveled.*

I leaned back, closed my eyes, and then opened them. The room spun around me. "Leave me alone, Garrett. Leave me alone right now, or I swear we'll see if a 9mm will work on you."

All my strength suddenly deserted me. Oh, damn. "You bastard, you switched pills. You drugged me."

"Yes, I did. To help you heal. Sleep. I'll watch over you. I won't leave until you're up and moving in the morning. I don't think you can possibly hate me any more than you do now."

He was right. I woke once during the night, and he was sitting in a chair by the window. Sleep took me again, and when opened my eyes, first light painted the windows. The pain had eased to tolerable. Garrett came to sit by me.

"I'll leave you now. I had a doctor from a different tribe stitch your wounds. He said the tears were bad, but there was no deep muscle damage. Keep your stitches dry and they'll dissolve. I'm sorry, but there will be scars. The goddess has involved you in a scheme that goes to the heart of the tribes and our future. Ba'ran proves that." He held out a hand. "Please, touch me."

I didn't want to, but…I let the tips of my fingers brush his. My sense of awareness of him, his presence, grew deep in my mind. He was different from anyone I'd ever touched and read. I wasn't so much reading him as knowing him, being with him. How could that be?

His voice, deep and low, filled the room. "Katrine, I swear, in the name of the goddess and the blood of my tribe. If I had thought Marisa could have killed you, I would have snapped her neck like a dry bone. If she *had* killed you before I arrived, she would beg me for death for a long time before I allowed that mercy."

"And any act of violence by you would be too late for me." I pulled my hand away.

He stood and walked out. His words filled me with cold certainty. He'd spoken the truth. Another truth? Garrett Dain and his people were killers. Their goddess, their laws, the impossible nature of a beast with a conscious rational mind, such unimaginable things required preparation. I'd most certainly go to Rize. I wouldn't waltz in without defensive and or offensive weapons ready. Not immediately. I needed time.

Chapter Ten

Garrett didn't contact me in the weeks after Marisa's attack, though I did see signs someone watched me. Danny had told me Barnhouse pulled his men, so it had to be Garrett. I couldn't deal with him and his *come to Rize and meet your family* or *how I belonged to him*. If it hadn't been for the specter of shape changing and a so-called magic knife, things I'd experienced firsthand, I'd have gone to Barnhouse. He'd stir things up. My arms did heal in a remarkable time, but the scars remained red and obvious, and I covered them with long sleeved shirts.

I suffered through the required and dreaded cleanup that follows the passing of parents. I dived in with vigor and refused to consider the golden eyed man, the black wolf, who so troubled me. The profound sense of guilt and betrayal remained.

****

I didn't want my home to become a shrine or a sanctuary that would cause me to live in the past. Melanie helped me with the peculiar alien experience called a yard sale. All possessions except a few personal objects and photos went on display. Someone even bought the ancient concession trailer and cooking equipment. Good thing Melanie was there because I broke into pieces as the trailer rolled away. I couldn't watch people paw over what those I loved gathered over their lifetimes. I ran away like a gutless coward to bury my head under the covers and sob.

Then came the lawyers. Rado was stinking rich—legitimately stinking rich—property, stocks, and cash. And that didn't include the island and Panama accounts no one knew about but me. I could access them if needed. After major repairs on the foundation from my aborted Push, I gave the house to Danny and Melanie. They could live there or sell out. I added to the college funds for their kids, drew up a new will, and made Danny executor and heir of my estate. He was all I had left for family. If I were to die tomorrow, he would be a wealthy man. I wanted to give him money immediately, too, but he wouldn't accept such a gift.

I had no problems with Mom and Dad's wills. I had a birth certificate, didn't I? There was no family—or strangers—to challenge my claim. No one to ask for DNA proof. Marisa Trent didn't show her face. I kept a diligent and hopeful watch for her. *Read: 9mm carried, loaded, and close to my hand.* I hadn't finished with the bitch.

Deep inside I hoped she would arrive at an opportune time and challenge me again. The vision of my foot contacting her knee popped up occasionally. The way it bent backward at an impossible angle... What kind of damage had I done? Did changing to a wolf fix it immediately, like in the shape shifter stories that I'd suddenly taken to reading?

In any case, I watched. The 9mm would work. But I had nightmares of her and her teeth. I hadn't done the Push on her like I did the car door. A Push required a conscious effort. I was too shocked to consider that action. With the limo door, it was right in front of me and required no thought, only panic.

My personal authenticating business closed. I did keep the single room office in Senica since I now owned both buildings. I'd instructed the building manager to collect my mail, put it in boxes, and have my office dusted once a month. It could sit empty for a while. Eventually I'd sell all the real estate. I had no use for property. I had to find out who destroyed my family.

One morning I woke with the magic knife in my hands. I hadn't seen it in weeks. What the hell? I didn't take a knife to bed with me. Overnight, my mind had created an astonishing and alarming idea. Doubts, improbable, implausible, or impossible, were remarkably missing from my bizarre brainchild. Logic and reason had deserted precise, methodical, rational Katrine. *But truly, wasn't Katrine Dolinski a make-believe persona, as false as any I'd ever dressed up and painted on? Who was this new person I'd become?*

In more rational moments I considered the possibility that my mind had broken under the strain of deep sorrow and tragedy. But what else could I do? Check into a hospital? Take anti-psychotic drugs? No way. My wild and crazy idea was no weirder than my own extrasensory skills, and after what had happened in my living room? I had to try. I had to know, whatever the cost.

Right after the first winter storm hit Senica, I hugged Danny goodbye and went to the airport. I caught a last-minute private flight to LA. My name wasn't on the passenger list. I had cash and a new identity to hide behind for a while. I'd been in LA two days when a driver delivered my new SUV. In the back was a case of disposable phones, untraceable phone numbers, secret internet contacts. I was sneaking out of town.

Did I think about Garrett? Yes, and I dreamed about him. There was an indescribable longing for the man, and I desperately wished it would go away. It didn't. I had to keep busy, keep moving.

I climbed in my SUV and headed south. First across the country to Florida. I wouldn't stay in one place long. I needed time. Time to research, time to learn. Time to find a miracle. Whether I found it or not, I'd be ready to move by spring or early summer.

Chapter Eleven

April 1st, and I beheld the result of my trials and tribulations since I left Senica last fall to follow a crazy frustrating dream. I stared at the mirror in my room at the Mountain View Inn, Limbough, Oregon. Katrine Anastazja Dolinski did not stare back at me. Leslie Lee Torrence, female, early to middle forties, stood in her place. A well-worn, callously used woman, life could wring a few more years of servitude from her soul before the world discarded her to live in poverty. Leslie, the perfect pawn, disregarded as an individual.

Only a few dark strands remained in her unflattering, prematurely gray hair. Being so tall was a problem, but her permanently stooped shoulders were an attempt to minimize height. She'd hunched down by habit since her school years when she was unbearably taller than all her classmates, including the boys. Painfully thin but not totally emaciated, since her new job would require lifting.

Leslie wasn't unattractive, even with her downcast eyes and hollow cheeks. Not too many wrinkles, but enough to show her age. I designed and practiced her smile to be permanently apologetic. *I'm no threat, don't look at me.* Of course, she wore loose slacks and a long-sleeved blouse, both shades of watered-down blue, and sensible, sensible shoes.

The mirror Leslie was the result of months of work.

Appalling, painful soul searing work that challenged the impossible. I had accomplished my own personal miracle. Garrett Dain had wanted me to become a part of his tribe. I wasn't sure about that, but blood will tell, and I had found a sliver of their aberration, their perversion, in myself.

Shapeshifting had found its market niche in paranormal romances. I could find no factual accounts except certain cellular level biologicals and a few reptiles. A total body change for a human? Impossible? No. Only something not explored because logical minds couldn't conceive such. *Just keep on thinking that, Katrine. It might keep you sane.*

Garrett had said I couldn't change to a wolf because, while I had the blood, the DNA, it didn't happen at puberty. I had absolutely no desire to be a wolf. Then one night a year or so ago, I had the sudden reckless idea that there should be more practical applications for shape changing DNA. I approached it with all the determination of a bulldog locked onto a rival.

I'd changed my facial appearance before, but only by using professional makeup and special effects supplies like silicone. Excellent for a security camera, but awkward up close. My goal then was perception and deception, not radical rearrangement.

To get it, I had to fully accept everything in the deepest levels of my heart and soul. Like the children in the fairytale, I had to believe. I wanted something that suited the life I had always lived. Complete fraud. I wanted the ultimate con.

I endured three months of constant, exhausting attempts to capture and flex whatever bit of that obscene power that might be inside me. Months of constant failures battered me until one morning I felt my cheekbones shift ever so slightly under my fingers. It hurt so much I passed out. When I woke, I got up off the floor of my Florida Panhandle hotel and did it again.

I gagged, vomited, and cried in pain for weeks at the feel of my own facial bones moving, reshaping themselves a fraction of an inch under my fingers. *I'd wake up screaming from a nightmare where I turned myself into a repulsive creature and couldn't turn back.* I was in a zoo and people were gawking at me or lying on a table in a lab, waiting for experiments.

Blind determination succeeded. I'd finally achieved slightly wider eyes, modest higher cheekbones, minor, but critical, features. Makeup artists—and plastic surgeons—would understand how those tiny structural changes made a drastic difference in appearance. I spent hours eating non-opiate pain killers and applying mostly ineffective ice packs to my face.

My confidence in the skill had improved, but the moment I relaxed, the mutable features snapped back to my original face. That hurt too. Practice, practice, hours each day in front of a mirror. I finally had the ability to hold those minor but critical, facial changes with little conscious effort. At least until I fell asleep. No sleepovers or pajama parties for me. Everything else I did with aging makeup, hair dye, and body mannerisms, the same way I had managed my personas for years.

Since I occasionally woke up with the knife Ba'ran in my hands, I practiced with it too. Just throwing the weapon. A thick piece of foam worked. It simply bounced off at first, but I became sensitized to the feel of it in my hands. One other thing? I discovered that it responded to my will. If I wanted it to hit the foam point first and go completely through, it did. The way it vibrated in my hands at times terrified me. *Ba'ran wasn't alive, was it? But who knew a woman could change into a wolf.* Standing inside the Limbough motel, I was as ready as I could be. In forty or so minutes, I'd be in Rize, Oregon, my birthplace and original family home. Margret (Peggy) Balcome of Rize was expecting me— expecting Leslie, that is. Handicapped Peggy hired Leslie as a home care aid. Her new identity carried identification and references prepared by one of Rado's professional colleagues in Atlanta. Leslie had cared for her own elderly mother until she died last year. Mom died destitute, leaving nothing for her daughter but bills. Leslie had to work to live. She had references, but no official certification as a caregiver. Her skill set wasn't worth much in the world, so she worked cheap.

Peggy also expected Leslie to help as a waitress in her business, the Rize and Shine Diner, during the rush hour. Same hourly pay as an aide, but she would also receive tips as a bonus. I did spend a few weeks working in restaurants at various locations for practice. One critical aspect of my facial appearance was maintaining during times of stress. It was an uncertain area. Maybe the makeup would cover minor lapses. Leslie could observe, learn things Katrine never could on her own.

One last check and I went to my car, an older model gray sedan with a worn exterior, worn interior. It had a brand-new engine, suspension, and brakes. Looked like shit—ran like a racer. I might need a quick dependable getaway car. Leslie's bland, mediocre wardrobe, sensible shoes, and surprisingly comfortable granny panties, all fit in one suitcase. I had nothing but long-sleeved blouses because I wanted no questions about the scars on my forearms. My battle scars. My proof of triumph—or at least survival. Katrine wanted to face Marisa Trent again, Leslie couldn't.

I started the car and headed up the highway toward Helle. I'd have to watch for the turn off that would lead to Rize. Clouds of fog blanketed the road, but as the elevation rose, they turned to tattered sheets of mist. The sheets dissipated like ghosts under the growing light. Oh, such an agreeable spring day at the lower elevation. A brilliant sun graced the mountains and made me long for tinted glasses, but the masses of wildflowers along the roadside begged me to gaze clear-eyed at how they flaunted their colors. I opened the windows. Fresh, clean, infinitely breathable air filled the car.

The narrow, patched pavement needed work, but traffic was nonexistent. When I'd asked how to find the road, I learned that it was once a shortcut from Limbough to Helle. A new, lower elevation highway built eight years ago let vehicles travel faster, so few used the mountain path, unless headed for Rize.

My biological mother died somewhere beside this road. A man I loved and called father kidnapped me away from that death scene to a new life. Until recently, an intense but happy life. I never questioned the moral ambiguity of my profession. A well-trained thief and con artist from the age of six, regrets were useless. There had never been any violence involved. No violence was a fact, not an excuse, justification, defense, or apology for my vocation.

Now I was going to my birthplace as a stranger, looking for clues to murder. I wouldn't let anyone escape, not to prison nor to go free on the whim of a jury. Reasonable doubt indeed.

And there it was, the tiny worn sign that pointed the way. I made a right and headed deeper into the mountains. First came the slow twisting climb up, a slight curve down, then up again. Higher and higher, bare trees and no wildflowers, at this elevation. Whoever founded Rize craved isolation since this was the only way in or that didn't involve a cross mountain trek or an unpaved logging road.

A paved parking pullout appeared as the road reached its max altitude. A tiny official looking sign announced a scenic overlook. I stopped where a small guard rail was all that protected any foolish sightseers from a rocky cliff drop-off that plunged hundreds of feet into a forest. Altitude, early spring, small patches of snow and ice, chill frigid air gnawed at me and made my eyes water.

Rize, official permanent resident population 2,100, spread out below like a pretty illustration on paper. Set deep in a narrow valley it had swaths of new green, a typical street grid, and one lonely church steeple I could see. Did Garrett's goddess have a church or temple? I'd managed to keep any apprehension regarding his religion out of my immediate thoughts. Occasionally, though, I'd get a stray thought, something like a worm on a hook. I didn't ignore it so much as I'd decided it didn't matter. I was going anyway.

A significant lake stretched back into the mountains west on the far side of town. Ascendant Lake, blithe summer tourist destination, picturesque mountain views, hiking, boats, swimming, it was mostly five stars on the rating sites. Two lakeside campgrounds, one hotel, three motels, no less than seven B & B's, not to mention the listings for suites in private homes. No theme parks or big box discount stores. *Begone, urban sprawl.* Tight control by a vigilant City Council kept them out.

A car pulled in behind me, a City of Rize Police Department decal emblazoned on the door. Not what I wanted, but I wouldn't always be able to choose when to test my disguise.

The uniformed man who stepped out of the car smiled. Thinning sand-colored hair and pallid skin made his washed-out blue eyes appear bland as watery skim milk. He seemed mediocre, not threatening. The uniform that usually projected authority failed this one. His lean body seemed slightly stooped.

"Morning, ma'am." A high-pitched voice for a man, but still friendly. "Is anything wrong?"

Okay, Leslie, meek and mild, but don't make him suspicious. Modest cowering would do.

"Oh, no." My hand fluttered near my mouth. "I just wanted to see. The view."

"Well, I'm Sheriff Darrell Darby." Confidence filled his voice. It was an improvement. "I'll bet you're Ms. Leslie Torrence, Miz Peggy's new keeper."

"Keeper?"

"It's a local joke." He grinned. It was funny to him. "Miz Peggy's sharp. Real character. You'll like her."

I nodded, acknowledging my identity, and kept smiling. I did make shy eye contact.

He cocked his head, seemed curious but hesitant. I hoped there wasn't much crime in Rize because this member of law enforcement was pathetic.

"Well, I'm on my way to Helle, Ms. Torrence. If you don't need anything."

"Thank you, Sheriff. I'll head on down. I was just taking a deep breath before I jumped." Both hands flew to my mouth. "Oh, I didn't mean...off the cliff...literally. I mean to a new place."

He gave another laugh, followed by a bit of a frown. "You'll be fine here. Rize is a nice place with mostly nice people. We have a few hard cases, but we can usually keep them under control." He dug in his shirt pocket and pulled out a card. He handed it to me. "You call me if you have any problems."

I accepted his card with a little bigger smile. He studied me for a moment, then he winked and grinned. "I look forward to seeing you around."

Okay, Leslie had a potential boyfriend.

I managed to blush. "Goodbye, Sheriff, and thank you for your concern."

I went back to my car. I'd passed a test. Probably only a thousand more to go. I started the car and headed down into a place where every third person could turn into a rabid, mauling wolf on a whim—or a challenge.

Chapter Twelve

Main Street consisted of two traffic lights, clean roads, on-street parking, older brick buildings, nothing over three-story, nothing to cause a traffic jam. Any homeless person who made their way here was likely given a personal escort out of town. Rize presented an appealing façade, a pretty picture of how things should be but never are. Without doubt, like numerous small towns, dismal secrets and bleak stories of hate and hidden violence could make lives hell.

Craft and antique stores with flower planters in front, interspersed with small restaurants, coffee shops, and old-fashioned bookstores made up most of the Main Street commerce. Buds topped the green growth in the planters, ready to pop open and fill the sidewalks with color. Without a Chinese import big-box, local businesses survived. It was shop here or a grueling drive over the mountain to a population center. Of course, I did see a UPS truck and mail delivery.

The sidewalks sported antique type streetlights for ambiance. Typical older small town, inventing a rustic atmosphere for visitors. Large signs directed the ill and injured to an emergency clinic. According to the Rize Chamber of Commerce website, the town held three great public festivals, spring, summer, and fall. The spring festival had been the week before my arrival. Traffic and people seemed minimal, but it was ten-thirty on a Monday morning.

There it was, the *Rize and Shine Diner*. Elegant dining? The highway truck stop image would be more appropriate. A semi-white rectangular box, circa 1950, it had a façade like Ms. Leslie Torrance—worn but still serviceable.

Lifeless brown bushes filled planters along the front walk. Nothing ready to burst into bloom there. I could almost hear the building beg for a facelift—or at least a can of paint. But the spacious parking lot to the side was full, and from what I could see in the generous windows, so was the diner. A respectable omen. People will ignore numerous things to get tasty food.

I parked and checked my face in the mirror. Still holding. Show time. I'd invaded mansions, climbed through attics, crawled through duct work, and waded storm sewers with less apprehension crawling through my guts.

A rich robust fragrance whooshed across me like a cloud when I opened the door. Luscious, enticing, a multitude of scents all pronounced breakfast was on the way. My mouth suddenly filled with saliva. My stomach growled.

I stepped into a 1950's picture-book diner. Long counter with stools, all occupied, wood tables with red checked cloths and mismatched chairs filled the middle of the room. Red vinyl covered booths lined the walls. Too perfect. Soft chatter greeted me, but it slowed to silence. *Small town, everyone knows everyone and, oh my, here comes a stranger. Let's stare and make them uncomfortable. Locals. They were here first.*

A voice cut the lull in conversation like a rake jerked through rough, rocky garden soil. "There you are! Get yer' skinny ass over here and go to work."

The voice belonged to a woman *older than dirt*, as Danny used to say. My hair was chemically colored mixed brown and gray, hers was natural yellow chalk and white. She sat in a wheelchair behind a cash register. There had to be a platform because she was too high to be on the floor. She was seventy-five and didn't look a day over ninety. A well-worn, well-crinkled face, but oh, those eyes…sharp and blue as the open sky outside. *Careful, Leslie. She won't miss much.*

I started to stand up straight then remembered that wasn't part of the persona. I hunched a little more and scooted over to her.

"Mrs. Balcome?" Meek and mild, soft. *Shit, I was trying too hard.*

"Speak up woman. And call me Peggy like everyone else."

She had a smoker's voice and oh, she was irritated. Had I overdone the meekness? She tossed me an apron. It flared like an open net, and I caught it before it covered my face. "Behind the counter and help June. We can blather about other shit later."

Okay, I could do that. Working made things less awkward. I hurried behind the counter and came face to face with June. *Major intimidation.* Surely that was June's nickname. She stood at least six three. Not fat, but big. Husky was an excellent word, though giantess came to mind, too. Certainly, the largest woman I'd ever seen. A suspicious glare told me I'd be judged. Fine. Suspicion and judgement I could handle. She didn't seem inclined to beat me to a pulp immediately. I believed I could run faster than her, too. I tied on the apron and politely asked what she wanted me to do. She grunted once and handed me a box of latex gloves. "Bus tables."

My good luck. I knew I'd be waitressing and should have thought and brought my own gloves just in case. My hands were too sensitive and my sense of touch too vital to work without them.

The noise in the room had gone back to a moderate level. If the sheriff knew who I was, then many of the regulars here probably did too. And I was nobody. A servant, a helper, someone who might or might not receive a polite nod as she scampered around cleaning tables.

"Hi," the only other waitress besides June said in passing. "I'm Melody."

"Leslie. Nice to meet you."

"Yeah. Glad you're here." A plump, pretty woman with brown eyes, Melody's smile seemed genuine. Welcome words from two—well at least one— coworker.

The kitchen had two separate rooms in the back, one for food prep and the other for dishes. The dish room could double for a steam bath with its two commercial washers and the nose searing odor of bleach. A thin scowling man ignored me as he loaded one washer. I'd heard men described in books as grizzled, but he's the first I'd ever seen who fit the image. Black hair, with a gray stubble on his face that threatened to form a beard. Back bent, his arms were sticks with a few muscles. My body was lean, his emaciated. Oh, and his name was Snag.

Tubs of bussed dishes sat on a counter, untouched. I remembered my time as a waitress. I quickly scraped plates and dumped glasses. I separated silverware, too. Merely a courtesy.

June bustled in carrying a tray she'd bussed. She plopped it down on the counter and walked out. "Hurry up," she yelled over her shoulder. "Need glasses."

Snag snarled at her back. One corner of his mouth lifted to show a canine tooth.

I worked steady through the lunch hour. I ignored Snag the dishwasher and his diverse sneers and snarls. I continued to quickly clean and stack my stuff for him to easily load in the dishwasher. He continued to ignore me.

By three o'clock, the place was almost empty. The Rize and Shine closed at four. When I came out of the kitchen, I found my boss waiting for me.

"Come on," Peggy ordered. No grit in her voice this time, simply weariness. I dropped my stained apron in a hamper. At least my face hadn't let go during the day. I'd have felt that. I followed her through a door in the back of the room. Not wide enough to fit her wheelchair, she had to struggle. I automatically moved to help her. She stopped me.

"No. You only do what I can't do. You understand."

I stepped back. I understood. She valued her independence and Leslie her aide was a symbol of inevitable surrender. I'd already listened to her coarse voice for hours, past breakfast and on through lunch. A raw, tough woman, Peggy kicked and screamed her way through life. She would face the remainder of her time on earth with the same belligerent attitude.

The room we went through was spacious, but shelves stacked with gallon jugs of bottled water filled every inch. On to the next room and Peggy maneuvered her way behind a desk.

"Sit." She pointed at a chair in front of her. Then she studied me. I studied her back. I didn't want to give the wrong impression, but I had to have some self-esteem, or she wouldn't respect me. I wanted to go unnoticed, not be taken advantage of.

"You did okay out there." She nodded at the door. "Dishwasher…Snag hates everyone. Said you were tolerable. Not that he'll ever let you know."

I remembered the sneer and exposure of teeth. Yes, tolerable would work.

"June said you're too polite to Snag. Perspective, I guess. I close first three weeks in January. June goes to Louisiana to wrestle alligators. Anything less than a grizzly bear is suspicious."

Go, June, go!

Chapter Thirteen

Peggy tapped her fingers and ran them over the desk as if searching for something. "Don't smoke, do you?"

"No."

"Nasty habit. Quit last year." And not happy about relinquishing the *nasty habit* from the pinched mouth and longing in her voice. "Don't want to die too soon. Gotta keep my son pissed off as long as I can."

Oh, oh, family drama. That could make my life here more difficult.

We went over my duties. Hours weren't bad, and I'd have two days a week off. More time if needed. She seemed more concerned about my doing double duty in the restaurant than helping her personally.

"You can waitress, too." She nodded her head to encourage me. "I got a boy to bus. He's still in school. Out next week. That'll get you tips. You don't have to report the cash if you don't want to. Most use cards to pay, but leave bills on the table, too. They understand. I got good customers mostly." She handed me a small stack of papers. "Tax and insurance shit. Bring it back tomorrow."

She spun the chair away from the desk too quickly to be safe. I followed her as she wheeled out of the restaurant to a small cottage across the parking lot. Both buildings had ramps. Poorly designed ramps. Her jaw tightened with determination while she forced the chair up the incline. Such a pretty thing, Peggy's cottage. An unembellished, sturdy frame structure on the outside, but inside she'd made it a sweet, and out of character, pastel-perfect home. We passed an entire wall of photos of younger days, better days. Peggy turned her face away as she rolled by.

We entered a lace-curtained kitchen where no one had cooked or enjoyed a meal for a long time. No dish, glass, or pan was within reach of her thin arthritic fingers, even if she could grasp them. She ate her meals at the restaurant. She opened the refrigerator and pulled out two bottles of water.

"Not paralyzed," she said when we settled in the living room. "Fell and messed up my back bad 'bout two years ago." She wouldn't look at me when she spoke of the injury. I wasn't the only one hiding something. Trouble in her life. More hurt than purely physical. "Sorry I can't pay you more, Leslie. Hope the tips will help."

"It's okay for now, Peggy. This is a pretty town, peaceful, and I'm…well, I'm glad to be away from LA. I need to work, but I need quiet time, too."

"Took care of your mom, did ya."

"Yes." I didn't have to fake the sorrow in my voice.

She rubbed her eyes and slouched in the chair, revealing her weariness. "I'm a grumpy old bitch at times. Loud, complain. Got lots of problems, people jabbing at me. I'll try not to take it out on you. Try to apologize if I do."

Jabbing at her?

"Leslie…You like to be called that?"

"That's fine."

"You got a place to stay in town? It's too far to drive

over that mountain to Limbough or Helle every day. Dangerous, too."

"I saw a couple of rental places listed online. I need to call and see if they're available."

"Everyone does vacation rentals these days. Way too expensive for daily living. Summer's coming and tourists…lake's a big draw." She heaved a sigh, more agitated, I thought, than the situation deserved. The woman wanted to take care of me. Caring for others— and controlling others—was an integral part of her personality. Her inability to act, to fulfill her passion in life, had to hurt.

She went on. "Hiking, camping, lots of out-of-town folks like to stomp through the woods around here." She had a knowing cat's smile on her face, then. "Locals know better. You best stay out of them trees too."

Staying out of the woods wasn't a problem for me. But what was in the woods that the locals knew to avoid? Wolves, of course. Wolves that might prey on hikers? Now that was creepy. And highly unlikely. Missing tourists would kill business.

She plucked a phone out of a pocket on the side of the wheelchair. "Let me see what I can do." She dialed. After a conversation filled with profanities, she said "Okay, Leslie, go down the street three blocks to the old Rize Trailer Court. Roger, Roger Darby, has a trailer and little studio you can look at. You can walk here to work.

I spent an hour on Peggy's laundry and much-needed ironing while I was there. She didn't ask, but I moved some items where they were more easily accessible. She wasn't a messy person, only limited. She couldn't walk, but she could raise her body, brace it to stand, and take a few cautious steps. Sharp, crusty, she complained, but not about her obvious pain.

Before I left, she gave me a speech while we sat over a cup of coffee. "Listen. I'm a stubborn old biddy. I don't want nobody to help me. It's not personal. When I bitch, it means I'm running out of options. Don't hover. If I tell you to leave me alone, you back off. You understand that?"

I had to grin. "Be specific, Peggy. If I find you on your doorstep with a broken leg, holding your chest, and gasping for air, I should ignore it if you say so?"

She gave a rough chuckle. "Well, that's a bit much. Use your judgement. You seem pretty sensible. Just don't be jumpin' in too fast."

After I left her, I drove back to the Rize Trailer Court, a place as old as the diner. I had to decide between the two places, both slightly overpriced for Leslie, but cheaper than anywhere else. Part of me wanted the studio in a real solid house, but the trailer backed up against a pleasant patch of woods. Being an urban soul, I'd stay out of the woods, even if Peggy hadn't warned me. However, I could make a convenient escape out the trailer's back door if necessary. The only way out of the efficiency in a pinch was an undersized window.

The trailer seemed and smelled clean but needed a good bleaching. Plain mismatched olive and brown furniture, puke yellow vinyl flooring, it also offered a few cubbies and loose paneling where I could stash things.

One major challenge was personal body odors in this town where numerous citizens might have a heightened sense of smell. I'd consulted with a scent specialist by phone and email for the last few months. My reveal would be my scent if I came across Garrett.

The odds? In a town of around 2,000 or so people it might happen. I asked the specialist for something to cover my natural scent around a man with the nose of a super predator. It couldn't be a completely non-human false scent. The key had to be pheromones. I managed to get my specialist motivated, and he produced something he called generic middle-aged female. To me, it smelled like a musty abandoned house. I made up cracker size pouches to keep in my pocket, so I could pop one like bubble wrap and release a soft, invisible cloud of odor when necessary. I had no idea if it would work.

Another unknown would be Garrett's assertion that tribe members recognized each other anywhere. My only hope was that Leslie's low-key lifestyle would, at the least, confuse them.

I made a trip to the Rize Family Grocery store for coffee, cookies, and milk, the important food supplies. Used as a vacation rental, the trailer had dishes and a microwave. I never learned to cook. Fast food in college, but when mom and dad feed you until you're twenty-seven, why bother. I'd seen no sign of vermin, but two spray cans of bug killer went everywhere. I'd crawled through bug infested holes in pursuit of a pilfered prize, but I wouldn't live with them. I've been called a clean freak, but I consider it was Rado's training. Leave no trace behind, no matter how tiny. No evidence, no DNA, ensured no jail time.

I bathed, dressed in sweats, grabbed my cookies and glass of milk, and went outside. Perfect. My new home had a small deck with a couple of chairs out front, so I sat there until complete dark fell. The few security lights didn't illuminate much. Little activity around the place, but it wasn't summer yet. A couple of cars crunched by on the gravel driveway. The drivers, both men, stared.

My little porch was mostly in the dark between security lights. Something moved through the woods fifteen feet from me. I heard it, barely. I couldn't smell it since it had approached downwind. A person? Animal?

A high edge of terror ripped through me. I'd left my gun and fancy knife inside. Was it Marisa? But Marisa shouldn't recognize me, unless by odor. Oh shit. I'd bathed and hadn't reapplied my scent shield. An urge to flee almost overcame me. My heart pounded so I had to be broadcasting waves of terror. Neither lawman nor criminal had ever driven my distress level so high. I sat unmoving with my eyes almost closed. Like a fawn hiding from a predator, I didn't dare move. The temperature dropped. I couldn't take it anymore. I slowly stirred as if waking, rose, and headed for the door. My watcher didn't move. I went in, locked up, pretending nothing was wrong. I closed the curtains and sat on the couch with my 9mm beside me until I finally fell asleep. I woke as first light opened another perfect spring day.

A warm shower worked out all the kinks. Sleep erased my disguise. It takes a bit longer to put on your face when you're rearranging bone structure and conditioning yourself to keep it that way. Makeup created a carefully aged veneer over my feat of face sculpting. I chose khaki pants and a primly flowered long-sleeved blouse. White crew socks went perfect inside my lace up shoes.

I stuck my special scent packets with a needle to release tiny amounts of odor. Pinned to my granny panties and bra sides they should work. I also added a few to my pockets for refreshers. The scent specialist warned me that my crotch and underarm areas were a breeding ground for my personal odor.

What to do with my gun. It wasn't improbable that Leslie, a woman alone, would own a weapon. She'd have no need to carry it daily in a small safe town. Leslie wouldn't know about the wolves. I placed it in the drawer by the nightstand. A logical place. The spastic, occasionally glowing knife I hid behind a loose piece of paneling. At least I hadn't woken with it in my hands recently. When I left the trailer, I stuck tiny hair-like tabs on both doors, to tell if someone opened them in my absence. I approached the Rize venture with as much caution and intensity as a major heist.

The sun hadn't risen over the mountains when I walked up the hill to Peggy's place, but light spread out in gentle waves. An elevation chill made the air crisp and clean. I'm not a nature lover. I spent much of my life on the road and among noisy crowds.

A few early birds sang songs like a prayer for a prolific summer. My stomach growled. A surprise since I'm usually not hungry. Another surprise? Finding Peggy on the floor by her bed. She didn't answer my knock, but I heard her cry out. Good thing she'd given me a key to get in on my own. Had she been there all night? I knelt to examine her.

She moaned. I grabbed my phone, but a surprisingly strong hand clamped on my wrist.

"No."

"Peggy, you're hurt."

"No. Please, no." She struggled not to cry, but tears ran down her face.

"Okay, lie still a minute." I ran my hands cautiously over her, feeling for injuries. Ah, she was so thin and cold. "Peggy, I don't think you have any broken bones, but you should have x-rays for fractures. We need to be sure. Let me call an ambulance."

"Not yet. You help me up now." Stubborn old biddy.

I gently lifted her onto the bed and straightened her gown. She weighed less than a twelve-year-old. She drew quick shallow breaths, panting—or hyperventilating. Should I ignore her orders and dial 911?

She gasped. "Get me aspirin. Didn't I warn you yesterday? You do as I say."

"Yes, and I understand your need for independence—"

"It's not that. If he ever gets me helpless, they'll put me away. Say I'm incompetent. I got people helping me, but no one to fight for me up close. I'm okay. You got to be my witness. Please, please."

I stopped struggling with her. Desperation and fear had her body quivering, creating more pain. I did the only thing I could think of. I put my arms around her and held her close. She cried in long low moans for a time. She finally did what my mother would do. She stiffened her body and stopped crying.

"That's enough of that shit. I need a shower."

"Okay, I'll help you." I reached for her arm.

"No. I'll make do. You don't want to see this stinking old body."

"Why? I'm a woman, Peggy, getting older, I'll get there soon enough."

"Get rid of the mirrors. Helps a lot." She grumbled, but she let me aid her. At least she had a chair in her shower, but she desperately needed a special handicapped unit built in like I'd had for Mom.

I'd listened to Mom cry about a body she'd come to

hate. One that ached and no longer obeyed what seemed like the simplest of commands. The situation wouldn't change, and we knew it. I did want Peggy to trust me for my own reasons, but it hurt me to see her so low and helpless.

I grabbed an attractive floral dress from her closet. She had several she'd never worn because of the wash, dry, and iron difficulties. She let me help her brush her hair and draw it into a neat bun. Not too tight, but it looked fine.

"Can you do something here?" She touched a finger to the blooming bruise on her cheek. "Don't want anyone to see."

I opened my messenger bag and pulled out a jar of concealer. Not the kind you buy over the counter. I carried an emergency makeup kit to make sure Leslie stayed in character. The darkening bruise became barely visible as did a few other blemishes. I couldn't do anything for the swelling. She stared in the mirror, then back at me, but she said nothing. Yeah, she looked good. Still pale, but younger, healthier. She let me add a tiny bit of color to her mouth and cheeks.

Unfortunately, she'd whacked her arm when she fell, and I had to wheel her up the ramp and into the restaurant. *Wait, where was Mom's fancy new power chair?* I'd stuck it and a few other things in a storage unit. Things I couldn't bear to get rid of yet. A waste really. I could get it for Peggy.

Peggy drew a deep breath, sat up straighter, and appeared almost cheerful when we rolled into the Rize and Shine. She smiled at June, and June's eyes went wide.

"Over there. My table." Peggy pointed in the

direction of a single table by the front window. It had no chairs. I pushed her to one side, locked the wheels. When I turned, sour faced June had grabbed a chair. She waved a hand indicating I should sit across from Peggy. She kept staring at her. Had I done too much makeup? Or could she see the pain. I laid a hand on Peggy's shoulder. "I'll get you coffee."

"I'll get it." June snapped the words. "You sit." One did not argue with June. And she'd raised my status a bit, too. Not a servant, but closer to a companion.

Then I had time to look closer at the patrons of the Rize and Shine. I remembered Garrett's description of tribe members. Tall, he'd said, men and women close to or over six feet. June certainly fit that picture. Several of the restaurant patrons stood out, too. I hadn't had time to notice that yesterday. If I had to describe them in a word, I would say isolated. Even in pairs or more, these individuals stood apart. I could pick one simply by the way they stood and moved. Confident body language, feet apart, generous arm and hand gestures—was I like that? I'd played so many personality games in my life I couldn't be sure.

Peggy didn't say much while we ate. She ate an egg, a piece of bacon, and half a piece of toast. She needed more. I savored mine. Biscuits, eggs, and damn, such superb culinary magic.

I let out a long, satisfied sigh when I finished. "I could eat my whole paycheck here, Peggy."

"Yep. That Jim's the best cook we ever had. And you don't ever pay for food here, girl. No one who works here does. Two meals a day come with the job."

The restaurant filled. The patrons had an easy grace that said all were regulars. They called out "Morning Miz

Peggy," without looking in our direction. June came by and kept my coffee full as we waited for the morning rush to begin. June had cleared our plates when a shadow fell across the table.

I glanced up. A man stood over us, obviously trying to intimidate.

"Good morning, Mother." Such a melodious voice. With his warm brown eyes and soft mouth, he didn't look like Peggy. He gave Peggy a lazy taunting smile. "You're looking fine this morning. I heard you fell."

Alarms went off in my brain. How did he know that? Who told him what happened inside her house, her bedroom?

Sadness filled her eyes. "Not your business, Maris." She held her injured arm across her chest as if to keep that pain from spilling out of her heart.

How astounding. She accepted him, her son…spying? Of course, mothers offered irrational and unconditional love at times.

Peggy did what I hoped she wouldn't do. She nodded at me. "This is Leslie Torrence, my new aide." He gave me a quick glance. He dismissed me. A servant, nothing more. No hello, no nice to meet you Ms. Torrence. Rude asshole.

His brow wrinkled in a deep frown. "The Council is complaining about this building again. You need to get it painted." He chuckled. "Oh, but you can't afford that, can you."

"I'll get it done. Just need a good cleaning."

"But if they start fining you…" He glanced at me. "Perhaps you could persuade your new helper to wield a brush." *Such a nasty little shit standing there, obviously attempting to intimidate.*

I lowered my head and remained silent.

"Leslie?" Peggy's voice made me raise my eyes. "You should know. Not many secrets in this town. This is my only child, Maris. When my husband died, Maris, don't know how, took all the money that was left to me. If it weren't for good people in this town, people who come here, people who work for me, I'd be destitute."

The arrogant ass had an answer. "But Ms. Torrence, you must also understand, and I've told her, numerous times, I'll provide for her. She doesn't need this dump." He stared at her, not me, as he spoke. How condescending of him. And a dump? I'd just had the best meal I'd eaten since Mom and Dad died.

Peggy's mouth twisted. "Oh, he'll provide for me all right, as long as I give up my whole life and live in the prison of a nursing home somewhere outside of Rize."

"An expensive assisted living facility is not a nursing home, Mother, nor is it a prison."

"But it's not here, not among the people who count. My friends, my employees. He wants to isolate me."

This was the last thing I needed. Stuck in a family dispute over money. But I liked Peggy. I had come to respect her. I was using her, so I owed her something. She'd piqued my curiosity about unspoken things, too. His anger, her hurt, there had to be a reason.

I decided to blow Leslie's meek and mild persona to hell. I winked at Peggy. "Why would he want to isolate you?"

Peggy's eyes narrowed. Her voice went tight. "He wants everything I own that he don't already have. He gets rid of me, and he'll find a way."

I lifted my coffee cup and smiled across at her. I knew the perfect facetious and superior voice to use.

"Has he always been that greedy? I'm sure you wouldn't have raised him that way."

Peggy's eyes popped open and so did her mouth. She laughed loud and clear across the room, her voice sounding over all the morning conversation.

Maris Balcome stalked out of the now silent diner.

Peggy slowly calmed and let out a heaving sigh. "June," she yelled. "Bring me another egg. And toast. And more coffee."

Yes, she could use more food. She grinned at me while working her mouth like she couldn't swallow. "Oh, hell. I need new teeth. Need paint, need my van fixed, need—"

"No, Peggy. First you need to find out who is spying on you. You need your home searched for cameras and bugs. Which I will take care of as soon as we get back there. You and I are the only ones who should know you fell. That someone did know and didn't call for help…that pisses me off. Your son is an asshole. It's a disease and there's no cure. But beating down the symptoms can be fun."

That made her laugh again. And it made her reassess me, look closer. My meek mild Ms. Leslie failed to remain in character. *Okay, some acts offended the sensibility of an unprincipled thief like me.*

When June brought Peggy more food, she laid a hand briefly on my shoulder. Melody, the other waitress, grinned from across the room. Making friends and enemies on my first full day. I should have made Leslie the stronger female type from the start.

I made it through breakfast and lunch waiting tables and bussing without any major disasters. I received good tips and kind words from pleasant people, most of them glad Peggy had help. As I worked on fitting in, finding my place, I could feel uneasiness in voices, slight twitches, subtle body movements at times. Nothing I could pinpoint, nothing earth-shaking, but a deep and solid undercurrent of shared concern. The patrons had relaxed enough to let a stranger see inside. See. Not join them.

I searched Peggy's place for electronics later that afternoon. I immediately found the most obvious ones, the phone, and a lamp in her bedroom. A few looked like they'd been there a while and didn't appear operational. I found a live camera in the living room, pointed so that the bedroom where she fell was visible. I left it for last. Someone had been watching and listening to Peggy for a long time. I'd warned her that it was important that we speak naturally and at ease, as if no one listened. While I continued to search, I asked her about the undercurrent I felt at times in the restaurant.

"You actually noticed that?" I heard a bit of admiration in her voice. "Most new people wouldn't. I'll give you my version. You been down to the lake yet? Ascendant Lake?"

"No. I saw it from the mountain overlook and satellite pictures." I climbed a stepladder I'd taken from her garage to reach the tacky chandelier. That garage was a treasure house of tools and equipment. Peggy's Marcus had been a builder. The garage also held her inoperative handicapped equipped van. It appeared almost new. Dad had taken care of repairs on the road, and he taught me enough I vowed I'd look at the van later. Maybe Maris had deliberately disabled the engine. I might spot something if it was obvious.

Peggy smiled, a distant look in her eye. "Pretty

place, Ascendant Lake. Clear water from the mountains. City owns most of this side. Far side backs up to national forest…except for about sixty acres along the edge. That's owned by a man out of Portland named," she hesitated. "Let me get it right. Ari-steed. Only one name."

She stopped and sipped her coffee. Good. She didn't see me blink and freeze. Aristide. I knew that one. He was a contemporary of Uncle Rado. Contemporary, customer, associate, not friend. Rado referred to him as a treacherous beast, but I believe he also admired the man. And he did have two names, even if he only used one.

I'd met Aristide Dubois several times to authenticate artifacts. Rado had instructed me to wear my *medium brown girl* persona and make myself as unattractive and unrecognizable as possible. Supposedly, Aristide wasn't aware of my role as Rado's thief. I doubted that. From what little I knew, Aristide was a man who survived by knowing everything in his personal sphere.

Peggy cleared her throat. "This Aristide wants to put a big development over there cross the water. Calls it *Wolf Haven*, and honey, you never saw a more pissed off bunch of people about that." She chuckled. "Condos, bring thousands of people through town, all sorts of shit. Says Rize should grow economically."

Well, hell! Aristide. Add one more to the puzzle, another connection to Mom, Dad, and Rado. I wanted to encourage Peggy to talk.

"I've seen that situation before. Natural recreation versus theme park mentality." *Wolf Haven?* Wow, that took nerve when certain people around town might get fuzzy and sprout teeth when offended. I managed not to shudder at the thought.

Peggy chuckled. "Aristide wants to buy more land around the edge of the lake to build a road. Not too many folks buy a condo where they gotta take a boat to get groceries or a haircut. And getting materials across to build? Not happening. Problem is owners around the edge won't sell. I own almost a mile. Managed to keep that from Maris. I won't let go of it and…the tribe…" Her last words sounded distant, hollow.

Keep her talking Katrine. You…Leslie is here for information.

"Tribe? What's that?" I stepped carefully down the ladder, the chandelier bug in my hand. It seemed new. I'd planted them more than once in a competitor's office for Rado. Planted a few for myself, too, when I had a big job to do.

Peggy's situation was serious. Maris didn't impress me as sophisticated enough for such things. He was likely conspiring with someone to keep track of her. This much surveillance required a well-funded hand. Aristide looked like a superb candidate.

My employer seemed more relaxed than I'd seen her since I'd arrived. "May as well tell you. You'll learn if you stay here." She proceeded to give me the same story about the tribes as Garrett. Fenrir, blood related families, ten tribes. She didn't speak of the shape changing or wolves or the so-called living goddess. "Majority of town people are Fenrir. Their Tribal Council, call it the City Council, but it's tribe. It runs the town, too."

"Are you? Fenrir?"

"Technically. I married in. They don't like that shit. Don't happen often. My Marcus said he had to have me the minute we met. Said he'd leave them if they didn't accept me. They've got super low birth rates, these tribe folks. Want all they can to stay, marry local." She grinned, and I could look past her age. Peggy was a beauty, once. She still was if you looked the right way. A little rough, prickly, but a courageous woman, to marry into clannish, cultish, people who didn't want her. No wonder her husband had loved her.

She huffed a small laugh, low and soft, and seemed truly amused. "They do marry inter-tribe. There's too few not to. But they don't like doing that. *Incestuous*. Marcus liked that word. I called 'em that once. Pissed everyone off. 'Course I been pissing people off for years." She gripped her hands tightly in front of her. "You're a quiet one, Leslie, but don't be talkin' about what I'm telling you. I just ain't had anyone to trust in a long time." Oh, the loneliness in her voice. It made her incredibly vulnerable.

"Trust?" I let go a laugh worthy of a prerecorded sit-com audience track. "Peggy, you do realize that I'm a total stranger, don't you? You've known me for a little over twenty-four hours."

"Stranger? Yep. The one that picked me up off the floor and…" And held her while she cried. "Tell you something." She wiped at her eyes, though they remained dry. "I got lots of years dealing with people. I can trust you. Know it in my heart. I don't sense there's bad meanness in you."

Peggy's reading was incorrect. I had meanness to spare. But not for her. Not for anyone like her, either. "Peggy, you can trust me on one thing. I will never hurt you. But remember, there's always more to any individual than you see. Each person has his or her own personal motives. Right now, mine involves escape from

LA life, from sorrow that wears me down." I stared straight into her eyes and put my fingers to my lips. We had to be careful with conversation for a while.

Peggy stared. "Keep talking," I mouthed silently to her. She swallowed, but grim faced she went on. "I'm leaving the land to the city in my will. They can fight Aristide off. Town's divided. Those who want the development, business owners, not tribe. Fenrir owned *all* the land around here at one time, then got persuaded in 1960 to let others in. Trouble ever since."

I continued my search of the room. Damn, there was another one above the windowsill. It had a dab of paint over it, so it had been there a while. The information gleaned from the bugs could have well been what Maris used to take advantage of his mother.

Peggy kept staring at the gadgets, her expression one of disbelief. Tears formed in her eyes, but she kept on talking. "You go downtown, you see signs in windows. *I support the Haven.* Nasty shit. Then Aristide hired the Fenrir tribe's lawyer. Late last fall. Snatched her right out from under them. Talk about pissed. Marisa Trent was her name. Her siding with him went over like a Category Five hurricane. It got worse, too. After what happened. Everybody's upset, scared." Her voice dropped lower.

"Clue me in, Peggy. What happened?" I planned to avoid Marisa Trent just as I would try to stay out of Garrett's way. Oh, I wanted a rematch, but not yet.

"Trent? Oh. She got murdered. Out on the highway. Day after New Year's. She got the pure hell beat out of her, then strangled."

A violent shock jerked through me. I lost my Leslie face shaping for an instant. Beat her? Who could do that?

She had almost killed me. Strangled her? Like mom and dad. Again, thankfully, I wasn't facing Peggy.

"Murdered?" I forced out the word.

"Yeah. Found her lying in the snow by her car. Nasty business. Limbough cops got to her first. Wouldn't let any Fenrir around her to pick up...clues." *Wouldn't let Fenrir wolves around to pick up scents and locate her killer.*

I excused myself and hurried into the bathroom to make sure my face was okay and consider what I'd heard. Could Garrett have silenced Trent? Was that his fix on the problem? Kill her. I'd seen his fury, heard his threats. She betrayed his tribe, his people, dismissed his religion, then bolted to Aristide? I had effectively disappeared not long after our confrontation. I remembered his words the night he left me. If she had harmed me. *"In the name of the goddess...the blood of my tribe...snap her neck like a dry bone...make her beg me for death..."*

Yes, he was quite capable. And Aristide? What was his true involvement here? Resort development in a tiny mountain town? An international big shot for whom I'd once lifted a cool million in diamonds and rubies. Way, way out of character.

I forced myself to return to my search. "You have much crime in Rize, Peggy?"

"No. Occasional break in. Shoplifting, mostly tourists and kids. Oh, if you want a drink, you go to the *Ascendant Lounge* down by the lake. Don't go to the *Rize Above Tavern*. Local hang out. Bad place. Bank got robbed five years ago. Oh, a little girl got kidnapped. One of the Serova kids. But that was over twenty-five years ago."

"Kidnapped? Did they get her back?"

"No. Though I hear there's been talk about it again, lately. Heard her name mentioned in passing a table. Like she'd been found. Surprisin' after all this time. See, since I'm not blood Fenrir, and with Marcus dead, all I hear now is gossip. Now Maris, he's considered Fenrir, though he's only half. But ya know how that is. And…"

I waited for her. Sadness, sorrow, Peggy loved her son despite his actions.

"Maris hates me because he's only half. They give him all he'd have if he was full, because he's carrying the genes they keep trying to control. It was never enough for him. When he was a teenager, he was sure he was going to…" She stopped. Apparently talking about wolves and shape shifting was a taboo she wouldn't break. "Maris had a real tough time in his teens."

I'd bet anything Maris couldn't shift. Couldn't go full wolf like Marisa or Garrett. He blamed Peggy. "Maris went away for college. Somehow made a lot of money. Not that we was ever poor. Wouldn't talk about it though. How he got it. I was scared to ask. Came back when his daddy was dying and…you don't need to hear that."

Her face reflected her misery. Oh, how difficult, how dreadful. Her son. Who s*omehow made a lot of money*? That covered territory from won the lottery to gambling or a major bank heist. I'd had made a lot of money, too.

"Stop that!" Peggy snapped at me.

I jerked my head up at the steel in her voice.

"You don't go feeling sorry for me, woman."

"I apologize." She'd mistaken my introspection for pity. People's sympathy had worn me down before I left

Senica. I mourned, but recovery was easier on the beach without distractions—other than my face-changing trauma. I picked up a pad of paper by the phone and wrote out my next words.

I used to work in a security store, so I know them. I found two cameras and six audio bugs. Some look old, not operational. At least one camera was working because someone saw you on the floor. There may be more here and outside. I'll check your office at the restaurant, too. On my day off I'll go into Limbough and get something at the electronics store that will interfere with signals. They're not too expensive. They will work on most, but nothing's perfect. Newer tech may slip by, but I won't make it easy for whoever. If you don't mind, I'm going to get new locks for the doors and windows. Make it more difficult to get in. This spy installation was professional. Not cheap. You may be in real danger. Most important, when I cut the last one off, it will let the watchers know you're on to them. Will it bring more trouble? I'm willing to stand for you if you wish. Is it a battle you want to fight?

Peggy stared down at the note. I gathered up the bugs and cameras and stuffed them in a bag. Peggy crumpled my note in her fist. "I like to believe Maris isn't a bad person. I don't know him anymore."

"I'm sorry. I miss my mother so much. I wouldn't let anyone treat her like this." *Stop, Katrine. No tears to disturb the makeup.* Someone had treated my mother far worse in the end. I had to help Peggy in my mother's name. And yet how pathetic. One lousy day and I'd blown my meek mild cover. I'd also bonded with Peggy like an ugly orphan offered a home. An old woman I was selfishly *using* as a way into Rize.

On the pad, she wrote two words. *Do it!*

****

Aristide. The jewels I'd stolen for him were my fifth job over the years. Shiny rocks had more security these days, much harder to steal. Antiquities were another matter. I had obtained at least four pieces for the man over the last five years, all from private mansions. Rado was a thief and a dealer of stolen goods, but as far as I knew, he'd never condoned violence. He'd never sent me to a place with armed guards. Just be prepared he'd say. Aristide was not so circumspect. A collector of art and antiquities, he had a well-maintained reputation filled with intrigue and assassinations. When asked, Rado merely shrugged at that characterization. Certainly, arrogant and grandiose, Aristide envisioned himself an art collector.

But what did he want in Rize? A resort development in a small town by a lake? My mind briefly went to the stolen icons. Unless in a full set, the value would be far below anything I'd looked at for him. As far as I knew, his businesses rarely involved property. Import/export was more lucrative. But that information was sketchy. Aristide had called me after Rado's funeral, and I'd reassured him, as I had all the others, there was no longer a physical or electronic trail of any of Rado's acquisitions.

I went home to my tiny trailer, no food, no shower, and exhaustion dragged me to the bed. Dreams peculiar things. Disjointed, full of improbable convoluted scenes, and wrapped in fractured memories and unfulfilled desires. Clear, concise dreams are constructs that add details to a story in movies and novels because it elevated fiction. No one I know dreams like that—until it happened to me.

I stared around an endless white space. Part of me said dream, the other part said nightmare. I wasn't afraid. A woman appeared in front of me. I could see her, tell she was a woman, but details of her features lacked focus as if gazing into a foggy mirror.

"Who are you?" I asked...or think I asked.

"My people, my tribes, once called me Cybele. It's not my name, but the tribe always had to blend in and work within the times. Cybele was a popular deity when I joined them."

Ah, the source of my dream. "So, I'll bet you're Garrett's goddess. His existent goddess." Did goddesses understand sarcasm?

I could feel her pleasure vibrate around me as if it were my own. Now that was unusual for a dream though less unusual than the clarity of the unfolding scene.

"Yes, he makes me stronger, and I need more like him. Goddess is a label, though, not necessarily accurate, either. I'm not omnipotent. There are rules. I'm only permitted to take specified actions. Even here in this place, this gathering of men and women who respect me, the Earth alone is mine to physically command.

"You must understand, Katrine. Communication with my tribes, with any human, is one of my greatest problems. Last year, I gained a follower of a different sort. Having her has made me much stronger. Once she accepted me, I could directly speak to her. I can speak to you, but only when you sleep. Your adoptive father was a less than perfect solution for you. I stood over his shoulder there on the side of the road. Somehow, I found the strength to urge him, encourage him, to take you. He

knew it was wrong, even for love. I don't know who killed him and did not have the power to save him.

I had a problem with her narrative. "And Telek Dolinski had to be encouraged by you to steal? That's unbelievable."

"No, it is not. He was a thief, not a monster. He knew the difference between a living child and a shiny trinket. It drained much of my available strength to shove my words into his mind and erase any trail he left behind. He's not tribe. To recover, I had to become inactive for more than five years."

"Why? Why did you do that?"

"I felt it when you were born. You were destined to be a powerful member of the tribe. The old gifts run strong in your blood. I saw, felt, your mother die. If you had stayed here, without protection, your biological father would eventually have killed you."

"Well...thanks. I think."

"Now, this is important. Ba'ran, has accepted you. Always carry it with you, and it will guide you and help defend you."

"From what?"

My phone rang. I woke instantly. Damn, what a dream. I wanted to go back and...what? It was a dream.

Chapter Fourteen

I had four phones, all with different numbers. I grabbed the one that buzzed and checked the caller. Danny.

"Morning?" My voice sounded weird. A dream hangover?

"Trine?"

I cleared my throat. "Yeah, Dan, I'm here. Had to wake up. What time…?"

The clock said six a.m. I'd been planning to call him but wanted to go out of town in case someone monitored me. Danny was always one of those aberrant creatures they call *a morning person.* Bless his heart. Like most of his kind, he sounded happy way too early.

"Too early for you. I know. Just checking. As long as you're okay. Oh, Barnhouse wants to know where you are."

"Not in Senica, Dan." I had sent him the occasional post card from various Florida beaches.

"Okay, Trine." No, he would not ask. He might be worried, but he respected me.

I sat up on the edge of the bed, rubbing my eyes while I asked about his family, trying to change the subject.

"I called to tell you we've decided to sell your house," he said. "Do you mind?"

"Danny, it's yours. Sell, give away. Drop the

insurance and burn it down."

"Well, at least I have options. Trine? You're not doing…Rado…his business…"

Okay. So, Danny knew more about me and Rado, and let that knowledge skim across his mind without acting.

"No, Danny. Rado's business is gone. That fire in the office basement destroyed all records." I didn't add the words, *thank God*, but…yeah. Thank God. Or even Garrett's goddess.

I couldn't tell Danny I was now dealing with a beleaguered old lady's family problems while attempting to infiltrate a weird cultish society. I didn't dare mention Aristide.

He laughed. "Now my news. I had a job offer from Portland. Detective, but a higher grade and working on a special project. I start next week. Melanie agreed. Selling your house will get us a place to live in a good neighborhood. It's expensive there. Melanie wants to go back to school to get her Master's."

"That's great, Dan. And if you need more money than the house brings, you go tell my lawyer. I told him to give you whatever you want. There's plenty for both of us. I know we lived modestly, and Mom and Dad always did the *one step up from absolute poverty* routine, but they misled me. Not sure why. You're my only family now, Dan. I love you and Mel. I want to share."

"Share? Like we did lunches in school? You felt sorry for me and traded your chocolate for my peanut butter and crackers. You always had chocolate."

"A simpler time, Danny. You'll have to buy your own sweets now."

"Trine?"

"Yes, Danny."

"Do you believe Garrett killed your parents? Barnhouse is stuck on him. I hear Garrett's name sometimes when he's on the phone. I don't know if he's found something or run into a wall. You know how tenacious he is. I thought he'd say you and Garrett conspired on Rado. He knows how much money you inherited. But he's more focused on Garrett."

I hesitated. How did I answer that? Garrett was, in some mysterious way, connected to all three murders. The big questions were how and why. And what info did Barnhouse have that Danny couldn't get? I hesitated too long.

"Trine?"

"I'm here. Dan, I don't know Garrett. I've only been around him a couple of times in my life." And each time was a catastrophe. "Yes, he's intense. He's capable, but I don't think he would leave bodies lying around. And what's his motive?"

"Capable? Yeah, I've seen him in action in the service. Motive? I haven't contacted him. He called and asked where you were, but I didn't tell him. Was he stalking you? Is that why you left?"

"No, he wasn't stalking me. I told him to leave me alone and he did. Garrett belongs to some weird religious crowd. That sort of thing scares me."

"Like a cult? And you're going to stay as far away from the cult as possible, right? How did you find out about them?"

"Garrett himself told me. Before I left for the beach, he gave a recruitment pitch. It didn't sound...enticing."

He didn't answer for a moment. Then, "You will call me if you need help, won't you?"

"If I need help with anything you can do, I will." *No, my dear friend, I will not call you. This is a deadly game with supernatural performers. I was born for this. You are not qualified to play.*

We talked a little longer, long enough he could trace my call and pinpoint me if he wanted to know where I was. He respected me more than that. Him living in Portland? Uncomfortable. *When Peggy had said Aristide's name, told me his plans, it squirmed like a tiny cancer, blooming in my mind.*

The dream I'd had concerned me. My usual dreams, those few I remember, are chaotic scenes, often repetitive, drifting in and out and making little sense. I remembered every moment of last night's appearance of the so-called goddess. A bit fuzzy on the visuals, but excellent sound. Should I consider it a delusion? I'd lived with extra sensory perceptions all my life. I'd accepted the wolf and my own minor shifting ability. Then there was the glowing knife that wanted me to kill things. A goddess? Why not?

I fought all emotion down and tried to be rational. In seconds, I gave up and fought the desire to go back to bed. No way. Time for a shower. Today would be a busy one.

I washed sleep away in the shower, and despite my efforts to suppress all such thought, I kept going back to my amazing, vivid dream. Garrett's goddess talking to me about my parents. My dad specifically. Was the confusing idea a subconscious attempt to absolve him of his kidnapping crime? A goddess made him do it?

Today was my day off and Limbough was the largest town close to Rize. I doubted I could find what I wanted there. My best bet would be Oregon City. I could make it there in an hour.

The greenery in town, bathed in sunshine, sparkled with the dewy remains of a gentle shower that had fallen unobserved in the darkness. A fitful breeze with only a hint of a chill made a promise—*Summer is coming.*

I needed gas, so I had to pass the diner. I saw Maris Balcome entering. I calculated, considered action—and nonaction. By the time I finished filling up, I'd decided. Meek, mild Leslie was going to get assertive. I had doubts. It was likely a mistake. I just couldn't get over finding Peggy lying on the floor in pain. The idea that someone knew and hadn't called for help...no one deserved that.

I parked in the Rize and Shine lot and walked in the front door. Good. Peggy wasn't there. Maris was sitting in a booth with a couple of men I knew were locals, even if I'd never met them. All chatter eased to silence when I marched up to the table. I had all the electronic bugs and cameras in my hands. I tossed them in front of Maris. They clattered on the table, but one smacked down into his eggs and another splashed in his coffee. He jerked and gawked up at me.

"Tell me, Maris. Did you enjoy hearing your mother lying on the floor crying in pain? God forbid you should call for help." My voice rose. "I'll never have kids. If I had one like *you*, I'd drown him in the bathtub."

I turned and marched out to my car. I climbed in in time to see Garrett Dain go into the diner. He's the one person I didn't want to hear my voice again or smell me. With Marisa Trent dead, he was the only one here who might see through my disguise.

I wondered if Peggy would call and chew me out, fire me. She didn't. She did know how to text. Twenty minutes later, a few words only. *WTF! Go Girl!*

Peggy was a fighter like my fearless Mom before cancer. My rational mind told me I was using Peggy's trials to compensate for loss and guilt. Not healthy, but not the worst thing. Maybe I should see a doctor. I wonder if one would believe me about the wolves. Most likely they'd hand me drugs and suggest a few weeks in a *facility*.

I had a good day. The face shaping went as soon as I left Rize. No longer forced to be conscious of my looks or my actions, I never enjoyed shopping so much. I almost forgot to shape Leslie to go back. When I did return, I discovered the tiny little tags on my door were gone. Someone had been inside. Whoever opened it locked it back. They had a key. I waited, listened, but no sound, no sense of presence came. I unlocked and opened the door carefully, ready to jump back and run. Everything appeared in order. Until I started looking closely.

Searched. Carefully, with no mess, only tiny misplacements. A cushion on the couch with the pattern turned the wrong way. I glanced at my hidden spot where I'd carefully peeled and replaced the paneling to store things I might or might not need. Not disturbed. Nothing terribly incriminating in my hidey-hole, cash, and extra ammo, but I'd rather no one examined those.

In the bedroom, I opened the nightstand drawer. The 9 mm lay in its place, but it too, slightly repositioned. Whoever ordered a search, would show themselves soon enough. I'd already instigated enough trouble they had to pay attention.

I found two audio bugs, one in my living room and another in the bedroom. I didn't remove them. I'd keep my mouth shut and go out to make any calls.

I'd hidden Ba'ran in another spot. It too, was safe. I'd bought sheaths that would allow me to carry the knife concealed if I felt the need. I didn't like the light show. It vibrated at times, too, as if urging me to kill something.

I'd had knife fighting lessons. Rado's plan to be sure I could defend myself. The first lesson? The best defense? Avoid confrontation. Running away, not aggression, would always be the preferred and safest option. Fight only if I couldn't escape. In desperate situations grab the gun first, not a knife. With my lean athleticism and martial arts skills, I was better than 99.99 percent of the rest of the world. *Unfortunately, that 99.99 percent would never attack me.* The remaining .01 percent, professionals all, had deadly skills far beyond mine. I'd met a few with frightening regularity when I had walked in my former world.

My trip to Oregon City had been a success. I bought a couple of jamming devices for audio bugs, one for the house and one she could carry with her. Added to that, were three surveillance cameras that would send digital recordings to a file on her computer. Two outside, front and back, and one inside should cover things. Then all I had to do was convince Peggy that they were cheap. I told her most of the expense was in installation, and I could do that.

While I was out, I called and arranged for experts to refurbish mother's power chair in a specific way, then shipped to Rize. It had to look used, but not worn out, although it was less than two years old and in immaculate condition. I'd have to convince Peggy it wasn't charity.

I installed my security purchases on her house the next afternoon after the diner closed. I'd studied many devices in detail for years to escape detection on a heist. Type, function, location, how to secure such in obscure but vital areas. Most importantly, I had installed them myself when I needed information so Rado could plan.

"You sure you're okay up there." Peggy wheeled around her small deck so she could watch me work. I stood on a ladder installing a camera at the back corner of her cottage. I'd already been in her attic to run the necessary wiring and add battery back-up. The unit in my hands was tiny compared to some I'd encountered.

Peggy's husband was a craftsman. Her separate barn-like garage contained a wealth of tools. Dad taught me about construction and repairs. Every winter when we left the carnival and festival circuit, he would find employment at different jobs. I could swing a hammer, measure, and cut a board. I knew the basics of plumbing. A most practical thief, Dad always said I couldn't get into or around a place unless I knew its construction. I used that knowledge often.

With only one door to go, I pushed on to near dark. I popped the pins on Peggy's back door, and had it laid out on two sawhorses. There was no provision for the dead bolt lock I'd purchased, so I had to drill a hole in the door for one and install a new plate on the doorjamb. I'd finished when Maris walked up. He immediately puffed up with wrath. He focused on me.

"What the hell are you doing? You're destroying my Mother's—"

"Shut up, Maris," Peggy shouted from the porch. "She's looking out for my safety. You won't. I asked you to change my locks. You told me to call a locksmith. You know damned well I can't afford that."

He pointed a stiff finger at the door. "She can't do

that. She's not—"

"Yes, she is. Go look at the front door she finished if you don't believe me."

"But…but…" He stuttered. His arms flopped up and down as if he wanted to act but couldn't. "You need a permit." He suddenly sounded so desperate. He shook his head and bit his lip like a desperate child.

She rolled closer to him. "To replace a lock? Don't be ridiculous. Unshed tears puddled in her eyes. "Maris, son…" her voice fractured. "Why are you doing this? Talk to me." She drew a breath that ended in a sob.

Maris stared at her for a few moments, then crumpled like a heartbroken little boy. His face folded into a mask of misery, one so palpable I'd say he'd never smile or laugh again. He turned and staggered away. Just before he went out of sight he fell to his knees, then scrambled up to go on. *What the hell? Had my little scene in the diner affected him that much?*

Peggy's desolation changed to fear. Her voice wavered like a thin stream of water in a drought. "Leslie, what's going on? What can I do?"

"I don't know, Peg. I don't know him. But guessing? I'd say someone has him by the balls. He's in trouble, bad. I don't think there's anything you can do. Sorry."

"Damn it! They want my land. They're *making* him pressure me. That blasted Aristide, I'll bet."

"Be careful. That's speculation."

"He—whoever—can have it. It's only land. I want my boy back."

"I understand, but I don't think it will work that way. Too easy. You could lose *him* and your land. I'm not finished here and…" I winced. I'd said too much.

Quick minded Peggy jumped on it. "It's okay,

honey. Won't ask questions. You're strong and you been good to me. Please, please be careful. Don't push too hard. People here can hurt you."

Don't push too hard? Not going to happen, Peggy.

****

I'd had to play sick during lunch the next day when I spotted Garrett coming in. My disguise would hold, but my scent, with my little aroma packets, might not be sufficient. Dodging him hadn't been a problem so far. And yes, I'd thought about him. Erotic fantasies kept popping up at the most inopportune times, too. Freezing cold rage wiped them away when I remembered how he watched Marisa try to kill me. Marisa murdered so callously and left lying there like roadkill.

Garrett's sincerity, his belief in his goddess troubled me. Everything about him troubled me. It had to. What he would allow—or do—in his goddess' name and his tribe's law. Imagination or not, I had decided to take my dream goddess' advice and now carried Ba'ran all the time, hidden in baggy pants or a jacket.

I'd been in Rize several weeks and took pains to work my way around town. I learned names and positions of quite a few people, but it would take the whole summer to go through it all. I wanted to become a familiar sight. My brain kept a running dialog of questions. The new bits of information—and they were bits—clarified nothing.

One thing became obvious. Peggy would be my only source of information. Peggy, whom they shut out when her husband died. *For all my work, my way to the inner sanctum wasn't going to come through Leslie. I needed a new plan.* Unfortunately, except for dodging Garrett and the regular pain of changing my face I'd come to enjoy being Leslie. Leslie found casual friends and laughter at the diner and a comforting peace alone in her little trailer by the woods. Yeah, Leslie sought and deserved peace and friendship—banalities that would doom a Dolinski outlaw.

Did Garrett kill Rado? Marisa Trent? My parents? I could see a minuscule possibility with Rado. It was a far greater possibility that Garrett did Trent. Helpless old people? He had no reason. Unless it was to uncomplicate things. He wanted me in Rize. I would have no familial ties to keep me in California. No, I'd bet he was far too serious and determined for such a convoluted plan. Garrett would cut through in a straight line.

I walked downtown one evening, planning to have dinner at a small restaurant on the lake. The best thing about Rize was its walkable size and safety. The sun had fallen behind the mountains, but the clouds, reflecting its golden light, were deep lustrous pillows in the sky. A cool idle breeze drifted from the lake and flirted with the trees.

Shops stayed open later to take advantage of the lengthening daylight and the arrival of the season's early tourists. Many of the window displays carried made in China items. Pretty, but cheap and tawdry after I'd held magnificent pieces of jewelry and significant artifacts. I'd schooled myself to give those beauties up. Rado warned me constantly of the danger. Don't keep stolen property. *Take it, sell it, then buy what you want.*

Walking with an easy stride I realized I could become addicted to my—Leslie's—loose khaki pants and comfortable shoes. The light jacket I wore had an inside pocket that easily and comfortably carried Ba'ran.

I had decided earlier in the week that I needed more

exercise. In the mornings, right at daylight, I would run through the park and around a track. Paced by a few dedicated strangers, I was back up to two miles.

This evening I'd let my dyed brown, gray streaked hair loose from the band I wore at the restaurant. It touched my shoulders, longer now than it had been in years. I'd need a trip out of town to find a salon for a touch up soon.

Footsteps scuffed on the sidewalk behind me.

"Hello, Ms. Leslie." Sheriff Darrell Darby stepped up. He had a grin on his face that said he was a man interested in a woman. I returned his smile, but not his enthusiasm.

"Good evening, Sheriff."

"Oh, it's just Darrell. I'm off duty for a while." He lowered his eyes. He seemed a little too shy and self-deprecating for a professional law man. The weak pose didn't flatter him.

His thin hair, the color of baked meringue, professionally styled, gave the illusion of fullness. Stiff with hair spray, at least he eschewed the dreaded comb over. He matched Leslie in attitude. If I was drab Leslie, I'd be delighted. I had no intention of entering a relationship. Leslie was an absolute lie, a complete con.

"Tell, me, Darrell, is your job challenging? Rize seems so peaceful."

He blushed. "Well, tourists take up the most time for me. Misplace stuff, sure it was stolen. Kids shoplifting. Have a few domestic type arguments, mostly loud, occasionally physical. Anything bigger, more serious, I would call in OSP." He lowered his voice as if spilling a secret. "That's Oregon State Police. They have resources. About all I can do is ask questions, fingerprint, and lock up for a few days." He stopped and caught my arm at the elbow. "We should walk back this way, now." He tugged at me, drawing me away. Concerned? Why?

We were standing beside the Rize Above Tavern.

"Oh, Peggy warned me not to go to that bar. Not that I go to bars anyway." At least Leslie didn't. My excellent hearing perked up at the crash of glass and furniture. I turned to go with Darrell when Garrett Dain kicked the tavern door open and dragged out, with apparent ease, two bloody, barely moving men. He had one by the arm the other by long black hair. With a combination of force and grace, he dropped them on the sidewalk. He immediately stalked back inside.

Chapter Fifteen

I knew Garrett was strong. In a T-shirt and jeans, not just an expensive suit, or wonderfully naked, an aura of power spun around him like a cyclone. Men would step out of the way if they passed him on the sidewalk. Women's imaginations would perk up and they would want to throw themselves at him and beg him to take them. I remembered how it felt to be in his arms, if only for brief moments.

Stop, Katrine. Just stop. He stood back and watched while you fought for your life.

Darrell laid a hand on my shoulder and moved closer in a protective, but pathetically ineffectual, posture. "Sorry you have to see this, Leslie."

Garrett came out hauling another man. Younger, not bloody, still on his feet, he didn't resist. He pointed to the two prone men and the still conscious one dropped to sit quietly beside them.

Garrett glanced up at Darrell and me. And stared. This was the brutal Garrett who threatened Trent's bullies at my—Katrine's—house. Standing there on the sidewalk, eyes narrow, feet spread in a fighter's pose, he was breathtaking.

He stepped closer, slowly as if we were waiting for him. I swallowed hard. Major test time. My secret was in grave danger. I slid my hand in my pocket and popped two of my concealing scent packets. I drew it out and used my fingers to smear the miniscule bit of fluid across my shirt. Food odors from the diner should have clung to me and wonder of wonders, I was down wind. Ba'ran pulsed like a beating heart, silent and deadly. Responding to my stress level or the magnificent man standing before me.

Garrett's expression had turned to unfriendly curiosity. Unfortunately, that curiosity focused on me. Probably because of Maris and the bugs. He had to have heard. A spot of blood marked the corner of his mouth, and a slight red swelling ran down the side of his face. I could see blood on his hands, too.

Oh, hell! How can a man be so desirable and petrifying at the same time? How can I forget that he…stop, Katrine. Focus. Focus on Leslie.

Darrell fumbled with words and introduced me as Peggy's nurse. Garrett made Darrell uncomfortable. I understood. He was a half-grown puppy facing down the wolf. He stared at the sidewalk and shuffled his feet, obviously wishing he could run.

The wolf ignored him.

"I heard what you did for Peggy." Garrett's voice carried a weighty tone, like a hammer about to fall. Since he was upwind, his scent almost overwhelmed me again. The woods, the land, the forest—and the deep taint of blood on his body and clothes.

Danger, danger Katrine. You're not supposed to know him.

I—Leslie—barely made eye contact. The sheer weight of that gaze bore down on her. My voice shook. "It seemed appropriate. Peggy was hurt."

"And you found those devices. Installed cameras for her. How?"

The question wasn't unexpected. I'd already answered it a couple of times. I'd practiced the Leslie tremulous voice for hours. "I worked three years at an electronic security company in LA before they went out of business. Technical sales assistant. People quit, I helped install. I learned a lot." My answer was far too complex for a lie. The key to successful lies was simplicity. I should have left Maris alone. Paying someone to falsify employment records of a defunct security company on short notice had cost a fortune, too.

Thankfully, a tank of a shiny black pickup truck pulled up and parked at the curb. It drew Garrett's attention and interrupted his interrogation. I choked down a sigh of relief.

The driver who climbed out of the truck claimed my attention. Easily as tall as Garrett, he had the efficient grace of a distance runner—or a wolf racing across a meadow in pursuit of prey. A hard granite face, dark hair, he could be Garrett's equal in strength. No doubt he would match his ferocity, too.

Garrett stepped toward him. "I told you to keep the boys at home, Serova."

Serova? Peter Serova? Was this my biological father? The sight of him stirred something inside me. Not a memory. More like a recognition.

Peter and Garrett faced off. Adversaries, determining whether to battle? Or wait for a more fortuitous time. Peter glanced down at his sons. Yes, they would be my brothers whom Garrett had beaten down. He shrugged, as if to brush away Garrett's presence. He wasn't backing down, but he wasn't going to fight—this time.

The older man opened the back door of his four-door

truck then and he and the conscious son loaded the other two. They were moving by then but required help. I noticed trivial things. Peter seemed rough and careless handling his sons. Not so. He took care not to twist an arm or leg wrong. He gave each a brief, casual examination before he moved them. My biological father and the youngest one climbed in, and they drove away.

Thankfully, Darrell caught my arm and led me away before Garrett could continue questioning me. "Don't mind Garrett." He spoke softly. "He's not as tough as he sounds."

What an utter lie. *Not as tough, my ass. More like a tightly controlled savage. And he certainly spooked Darrell.* I desperately wanted to ask about Peter Serova and his sons, but it didn't seem wise. Odd situation though. "That fight, don't you have to take notes, write reports, and stuff for that?"

"No, that one's not my jurisdiction. I'm responsible for regular people."

I didn't have to pretend to be confused. "Regular people. As opposed to…?"

"Tribe people. Did Peggy tell you about the people who live here? Fenrir?"

"A little. A large blood related family. She said her husband was a member. And Maris."

"Tribe people own most of the town. They take care of law enforcement for themselves. I do the rest. Regular locals and tourists." He glanced around. No one was close. "Only a few of the tribe people ever cause problems. And they have people that officially handle them. Garrett does personal things when someone asks, though. The bar owner or someone says the Serova boys caused trouble or stole something." He blushed. "They fight a lot, these tribe people. Or so folks tell me."

So, the sheriff was little more than a security guard for tourists. "Darrell, I have to ask, are you okay with that arrangement? Two jurisdictions in one town?"

"Yeah. It's cool. We work together."

Darrell puffed up a little, a silent repudiation of the *work together.*

"What exactly does this Garrett do? Just beat people up?"

His jaw tightened, and I could see a small vein throbbing in his neck. "No. Not always. He's a lawyer, too. Takes care of tribe business. You see him like that back there, then you see him in a suit and he's a big shot executive. Tribe people are mostly careful. Keep to themselves. They don't like anyone messing in their business, though."

"Peggy said the same thing."

"Smart woman, Miz Peggy."

"Was I messing in their business? Taking out those bugs?"

"Maybe. But you did right. It's wrong to spy on her like that. Let her be hurt. I shouldn't be talking about this. You shouldn't either."

He brushed my hand with his. Merely a touch, enough to get my attention. "Listen, there's a bluegrass concert Sunday evening in Limbough. You can take chairs or sit on the grass. Would you like to go? If you like that sort of thing."

Now what do I do? I waited too long to answer.

He hung his head, dejected. "I'm sorry. I guess I shouldn't have—"

"Oh, no. Thank you for asking." I looped my arm in his. Then I could tell the truth. "My mother passed away last year, and she loved bluegrass. I was thinking of her. I'm not ready for music yet. You didn't know." He was giving me valuable information, but I had to avoid any relationship. We walked on. He stopped and grinned at me, nodding his head to the right. "That's the station. I better go back to work.

"Ah, yes, of course. I shouldn't be curious after you warned me, but what will happen to those men, if you have no jurisdiction. I've never seen them around town."

"Depends on the damage. Mostly they stay out of town on that farm they own off the Limbough road. They come into town, Garrett takes them down, calls Peter. Peter comes for them and pays damages." He chuckled. "Now there's a nasty dog, that Peter."

An irrational impulse to defend Peter, a man I didn't know, surged. I fought it down. Darrell kept smiling, but it seemed so artificial, so forced. "Someone's going to kill one of them one day. Just you stay away from them. They happen to come in the diner let June have them. They're scared of her."

I shivered. "I'm scared of June. Love her, but she can be terrifying."

I said goodbye and walked on. My trailer door was slightly ajar. I pushed it open. I had a most unusual visitor. Maris Balcome sat on my couch, holding my 9mm.

I had two options. Run or confront him. I wasn't going to run. Oh, he could be dangerous, but I'd committed myself to this path and would go on. I went in and closed the door behind me.

"Be careful, Maris. Don't shoot yourself and try to sue me."

"I know how to handle a gun." He gazed down at the

weapon, not at me.

"I'd have thought Peg would teach you better manners than to break into a woman's home and handle her personal things. But I guess it's not much, compared to spying."

At least he hadn't questioned the fact that I carried serious fire power. I laid my bag on the kitchen counter. Ba'ran, still in my inner jacket pocket, vibrated against my breast.

He turned the gun in his hand. Careful, skillful, his fingers caressed the barrel. "You need to leave Rize." A firm masculine voice, serious but with no malice.

"I beg your pardon?"

He gently laid the gun on the table by the couch. I relaxed the tiniest bit. I had the magic glowing knife close to my hand. It was satisfactory for surprise.

Maris didn't move. He stared at me for a moment, then a frown formed on his forehead. "Okay, Ms. Torrence, how much? To leave town. I'll pay."

"I don't want to leave town. I like it here. I like your mother. My own died last year, and I know how *very precious* mothers are. That's something you've forgotten—if you ever knew at all. I'd give anything to get mine back, if only for a few days." My voice broke in true sorrow. "Then I could tell her all the things I never got around to saying." He suddenly wouldn't meet my eyes. "Peggy loves you despite the way you act. How much you hurt her."

He squeezed his hands into fists, frustrated, like a dog on a chain. Unfortunately for him, the dog would be a cocker spaniel, not a pit bull.

"What's with you, Maris? I sense you love your mother, but you're breaking her."

"I'm trying to protect her." His jaws clenched, and he shook his head. "I'm afraid she's going to get hurt. She needs to sell that property on the lake. Get out of the way and be safe. Damn it, I didn't bug her house. And now it's like you publicly declared war on her behalf. She can't win. You can't win." He sounded as if he'd already given up a fight.

"Declared war? And to whom have I made that declaration. It's painfully obvious it's not you. Maris, I agree I made a mistake. I shouldn't have tossed those bugs in your face. It wasn't necessary. But finding her on that floor, crying in pain, no one to help her, offended everything in me that I consider human."

He gave a wild shake of his head. "Are you a cop?"

"No." I stepped back. "That's ridiculous." Uh, oh. Trouble. *The listening devices in the trailer.* "Do I act like a cop?"

"Sometimes. I've seen you watch, pay attention to everything. You listen." He leaned forward, completely focused on me.

So, did a cop and a professional thief act the same? Interesting concept.

"No, Maris. Not a cop. It's only vicious experience. Violence was a way of life in my LA neighborhood. I grew up where some thug could gun you down in the grocery store. You've got to know all the exits when you run."

"You see your mother in mine?" He touched his ear, then waved his hand around, warning me my place was bugged? "So, my mother is Leslie Torrence's grief therapy."

"Yes, if you want to call it that. I don't care. I'm an employee. An aide. I'll try to protect her from accidents and keep her safe. I'd do that for anyone. I'll use my experience to comfort her when I can."

"You could help her by listening to me, making her listen, and getting out of Rize."

"And what would that accomplish? She's not going to sell that property to that man in Portland. She's adamant about that. You aren't going to change her mind. I can't either."

He stood and motioned for me to follow him out the door. I did, and we stepped away from the trailer. He stopped. "Can you use the gun?"

"Of course. I told you. LA neighborhood home."

He studied me with eyes exactly like Peggy's. "Keep the gun with you all the time. In your purse, your pocket, keep it ready." He walked away. He reeked of sincerity—or he put on a good act. Maris Balcome was a man in trouble and not strong enough to beat his way out. I didn't want to carry the 9mm all the time, though. All my permits were in Katrine's name and getting one for Leslie might focus too much attention on her. Ba'ran would do for now. I went back in the trailer, determined to rest for the evening.

****

I was in the white space again. Of course, my mysterious visitor was there. And annoyed.

"Try not to wake up too soon this time."

"Okay. If you say so." I wanted to say she sounded like a harpy. Harpy? Why did I think of that? "So, Goddess, I held a piece of an Assyrian tablet once. It gave me an image of a bird with a human face. The face screamed."

"Many things screamed when the Assyrians were around. They were not a pleasant people. That gift you

159

have for touching things, reading them, reading the past, hasn't shown up in one of mine for five hundred years. We must talk about now, not history. If we settle this, I'll give you all the history you desire."

Promises, promises. In a dream, no less. "So, you're a goddess. Everybody wants something. Tell me exactly what you want. I warn you. You'll need a fantastic sales pitch. Did you see me fight the bitch wolf? Am I losing my mind? Are you my imagination?"

"Don't worry. You are quite stable in mind and body. I did not see but heard the tale of Marisa's challenge. Be proud of your scars, warrior. They're the price of survival. You remember that I told you I'm not omnipotent. Let me simply say I, too, have rules that I must obey.

"This is a dream for you, Katrine. I'm much stronger since my servant in Arizona came to me. I could only speak to her in dreams until she accepted me. To form that permanent contact, I grant a tribeswoman, one with a specific set of genes, a boon, a blessing. She will, in turn, serve me. Then I can contact her at will and offer her aid."

"A woman?"

"Yes. I am female in nature. There are others like me in this world who are male, but not among my people."

"And this boon/blessing? The one that allows...ah, stuff to happen?"

"Boon? Blessing? I will save my tribeswoman's life or the life of someone she loves. She, in turn, serves me."

"That sounds...controlling. A puppet show."

"Yes, it is in some ways, yes. My people are...mine. Often, events in their lives are set, staged. The outcome

of that staging is not. Katrine, I'm fighting to survive. When the tribal blood in my people thins sufficiently, I will die with them. You and the others like you are a part of me. I am a part of you."

"Again, what do you want from me?"

"For now, you follow your plans to find murderers. But exercise the powers your blood, your genetics—gave you. You are an agent of change. Ba'ran came to you. Damn, you bitches were easier to handle when you dressed in animal skins and popped out a baby each year."

I laughed. It was all I could do.

"I know you're not ready, Katrine. I'm begging you to—"

My clock went off. She might be a goddess, but she had incredibly poor timing.

Chapter Sixteen

Peggy created a minor fuss when the delivery company, per my instruction, dropped off the power chair. She complained the entire time she enthusiastically examined every inch. I expounded on the multiple comfort functions. The people I'd paid to work on it charged mega dollars but had done an excellent job of making an almost new machine appear moderately used. Distressed leather, patched in a few discrete places with duct tape, it was narrow enough she could make it through most doors with ease. It would lift and lower her, and change multiple arm, leg, and back positions to aid in circulation. Then there were the built-in massagers.

I lied and explained three times that the chair was a charity donation to my mom. I said it was in storage, and the only thing she owed was the delivery fee, which she could pay when I received the bill. Of course, once I got her comfortable, the contraption hooked her like it had Mom. *Senior empowerment in action.*

"Want to take it for a test ride, Peggy?" It was afternoon of the day after delivery, and the restaurant had closed.

"Sure. Let's go down to the lake, that's two miles. Ain't been there in ages. We can call June if we run out of juice."

"The batteries are almost new, and it's fully

162

charged. It should do that." The range was closer to fifteen miles on a solid surface.

Floral decorations adorned the town in preparation for the Summer Solstice Festival. I'd rented a power washer the week before and cleaned the Rize and Shine to keep up with the trend. June helped me plant new landscape bushes out front. She procured them and I did not ask their source. Not perfect, but we painted the trim around the windows, too. June held the ladder while I had touched up the wooden sign that hung over the door since the day the diner opened.

Peggy played with the chair controls as we walked along, making minor adjustments. She'd become a far more proficient operator than Mom.

"How come you're so good to me, Leslie? I know I pay you a pissy little bit of money. I do understand about your mom. How you feel. But you know, you could sell this chair if you need money." Peggy slowed so I didn't have to walk so fast. She raised the seat to place her on a more comfortable level to talk. While impressively mobile, I quickly realized the chair was far too zippy. I should have had a speed governor installed.

"Call it payment for healing. I'm working, made a few friends, and having fun occasionally. I truly needed that life change. It's good."

"Okay. I been watching people for a long time. Please. Ain't nobody around to hear. Talk to me, girl." She held up the portable bug detector to show no one monitored us. Peggy had taken to the spy game with zeal. She kept her computer hot plucking every bit of information she could find. She meant me no harm and maybe a little honesty wouldn't hurt.

"Peg, everything I said about you and Mom is true.

I swear it is. But I'm looking for something here in Rize. I'm desperate. I'm using you. And yes, I feel guilty. I should give a little in return. I do like you very much. I respect your courage."

"You a cop?"

Wow, second time for that question. "No, not a cop. I'm a victim of a vile theft. What I lost is gone forever, but I believe the thief is here in Rize. I want to kick ass."

"How you figure you're using me? You help me, I pay you. But I feel bad, too. I can't pay you enough for what you do. Or this fancy chair. I looked at them online once, wishing I could get one. Round about eight, nine thousand dollars new. Five used."

I should have known Peggy wouldn't miss that.

"It *was* my mother's. It had cushion covers with pink roses on them. She loved it. A real speed demon, my mom. She…" I had to stop and swallow. *No crying, Katrine. Don't screw up your makeup.*

Peggy rolled on without speaking, except to greet an occasional passerby. It was dinner time and most park users had headed home. The paved path we followed trailed through the deeper wooded area of the park where I ran early in the morning. Less light, but still enough to see everything.

Peggy reached out and touched my hand. "I hear a lotta sadness in you, Leslie. But exposing those bugs and cameras… Like the spy shows say. You blew your cover. Showed a lot of skill."

"My cover isn't exactly what you think it is." My cover was an impossibly altered facial structure. "You were hurt, someone knew. They left you there. Maris learned about it too late to help. He cares for you—but he's scared."

"But he won't talk to me." I could hear her heart breaking in her voice.

We continued on in silence. I glanced at her occasionally. I could almost see and hear her mind churning. She drew a breath to speak, stopped, then went on, "Listen, girl, those things in my house were illegal as hell. I noticed you weren't in no hurry to call the police, make a report. Most would have done it first thing. Not that it would have done any good. This is Rize."

"I know. Darrell Darby walked with me downtown a few days ago. We saw a fight, and he didn't interfere. He told me his unusual enforcement situation."

"Well, tribe knows what happened by now. What you did. I ain't heard nothing from them. Sheriff Darrell's a nice man, but he's got his own issues. Him and Marisa Trent had something going hot and heavy once. It kind of broke him when she was murdered."

Darrell? And Marisa Trent? Talk about an odd couple. But Marisa was almost insane with desire for Garrett? What would she do with Darrell? She could use him, manipulate him. That fit her character. Poor man. I shouldn't be surprised.

"Leslie? I don't see nothin' ever relaxed in you. I see a woman sharp as a pin, calculatin' every single move, every word. You're on my side. Right?" She gave her witch's cackle. "We can plot evil deeds, together. You know how, I bet."

"Evil deeds?" My whole life was an evil deed. "Oh, Peggy, you have no idea. And yes, you know I'm on your side. Wait. What evil deeds do you have in mind?"

"I'm still thinkin' on that. You need help, you come to me. Except money. Got no money." She expertly guided the chair around a hole in the sidewalk. "Now, I don't have a nose like a Fenrir, but Snag says you smell…funny."

I laughed. "Snag smells like a wet dog."

"Oh, sugar, don't be callin' no Fenrir a dog. They get mightily pissed about that."

"I'll bet they do." Since she providing information… "Peggy, is there any talk about who did kill Marisa Trent? Or why."

"Some—more than a few—say Garrett killed her."

"Darrell told me a little about him. I'd say there are people in this world you should step back—or run from. He's one of them."

She nodded her head. "You remember I told you about Aristide? Marisa went to Aristide's side. Gave her family and their so-called Council a royal finger. Told him secrets, too. These Fenrir people are awful strange, even the nice ones. She's a traitor to them. I've known Garrett since he was a baby. Hate to think it about him killin' her, but it might be."

A traitor? And had Garrett executed her. I had to face the possibility.

Peggy stared around. No one was within a hundred yards. "Let me tell you about the plague they call the Council of Rize. You need to know to stay out of trouble. Three people lead Fenrir—and the town, too. And believe me, most members fall in line behind those three. There's Isabell Anext, she calls herself a priestess for the…goddess. You know about…?"

"I've heard stories, Peggy."

She eyed me. Clever old bitch. Oh, I did like her.

"Well, people, some people, get mighty twisted about Isabell. Her title is Tribe Priestess, and she's supposed to be a counselor, settle complaints. She wants more. She wants to run the tribe her way. After Isabell there's Ted Balcome, my former brother-in-law. He's the money man, the accountant. Brain smart and common-sense stupid. Mostly he follows Isabell. Fenrir has a lot of money. Every tribe member gets a share. I get a share because Marcus left me a widow. Maris managed to take that, too." She drew a deep raspy breath, her years of smoking showing in decreased lung stamina.

"Then there's Garrett. Don't let Garrett's pretty face fool you, honey. I watched him grow up. He was a wild but good-hearted boy when he was young. He's a cold one now. Hard and mean at times. And arrogant. He'd stare down his nose at you like everyone did me when Marcus married me."

"Darrell suggested he was an enforcer." I told her about my encounter in front of the tavern.

"That's a good word. Darrell's a good man." She stopped to make several deep coughs. How long since she'd been to a doctor?

"Peg, you said you heard Garrett killed Marisa Trent? Kill her and leave her body by the road? That's sloppy. I've only seen him, don't know him, but I doubt he does anything sloppy."

"Maybe he wanted to send a message. Traitors die."

A message? To whom? If I dreamed of their goddess again, I'd ask. Was I taking those dreams seriously? At this point, all I'd seen, all I'd felt, anything was possible.

Peggy slowed the chair over a rough spot on the sidewalk. I'd almost tripped there during my run yesterday. She sighed. "This law the tribe lives by and their goddess...damn, they're dangerous." She fell silent for a moment, then, "Leslie please be careful...well, you know how it is with religion. My religion, my god is the

167

only god, and I can do anything I want to non-believers."

"Peggy…never mind. Let's talk about something better than the Fenrir Tribe." I needed to get my hands on a copy of that tribal law.

Ascendant Lake Park did shine. Beds of flowers, fountains, cool paths among tall forest trees, said the city planted the taxpayer's money here. A sign solicited funds for a future botanical garden. Things changed when we reached the lake. The stink of dead fish burned my sensitive nose.

"Damn Eckhert," Peggy snarled the words. "He's done it again. Son of a bitch has a fish cleaning station with a tank he's supposed to have pumped out. He keeps *accidentally* spilling it into the lake. Bastard!"

I was taking shallow breaths, trying to keep my hand from my nose. "I take it he's on the anti-development side. Keep the tourists away."

"Yep." She handed me a small jar. "Put a tiny bit of this in each nostril. Careful. I got a herb lady who makes it for me."

Careful indeed. It almost knocked me off my feet. But it did ease the eau-de-Pisces aroma.

We walked deeper into the woods, and the smell faded. Twilight began under the shade of the trees. Quiet, peaceful—if Ba'ran hadn't suddenly vibrated like a small earthquake.

Two men came around a slight bend in the path. Suits and ties, too well dressed for locals or tourists, they strode toward us with steady determined steps. Both had pistols in hand.

It was over before my mind could form a thought and act. I didn't decide what to do. I just did. My hand shifted and snatched Ba'ran. I hurled the blade. No aim, only throw. A dense solid thunk and Ba'ran's hilt appeared one man's chest. The single jewel flashed scarlet light.

The other man stumbled when his partner fell. He recovered and raised his gun. He pointed it straight at us. I did the only thing I could. Like that limo door, I pushed. Time stopped. My heart gave a single, dreadfully long beat. This man flew off his feet, straight back, and smacked into a massive oak tree. He hung there for a second. Then slowly slid down. On the ground, his body folded into a dreadful shape.

I forced oxygen into my lungs. How utterly horrifying. The red stone on Ba'ran's hilt faded to a dull glow. A barely aimed throw, an incredible strike, had impossibly cut through bone. I had killed them.

Peggy's voice broke through my stunned mind.

"Leslie? You moved so fast." She gazed up and wonder filled her eyes. "Like in the movies where they speed things up." She looked at the men again then turned her face away.

I straightened. People had seen Peggy and me walking around the park. Bodies found on the trail would cause questions. Self-defense, but demands for details would abound. Those demands would make me lose Leslie. Her persona would not hold against a concentrated professional investigation.

I used my rapidly fading adrenalin rush to go and jerk Ba'ran out of the body. No blood clung to it, so I return it to my pocket sheath. It slid out so easily. *Was its desire sated? What manner of weapon from hell did I carry?*

I dragged its victim back into the forest, out of sight. Damn! I was playing a deadly game without knowing the rules. The man I'd thrown against the tree? Blood? Only a trickle from his nose and mouth despite crushed bones in a skin bag filled with soupy liquid. He sloshed. I didn't hesitate. I didn't falter—except when I threw up on a bush. A desperate effort got the men deeper and farther away from the path. *Hide them, supernatural freak that you are, Katrine.* Eventually, I would have to examine the specter of murderous intent blended with supernatural magic.

Finally, we were far enough from the path that no late walker would see them. We'd be okay if no wolf came along and smelled death. Preternatural eyes would see there had been a swift but lethal struggle.

I motioned for Peggy to follow me out of sight. The chair's larger tires easily negotiated the terrain. She stared at the bodies and appeared dumbfounded. At least she wasn't hysterical when she spoke.

"They were going to kill. Maris wouldn't…" Ah, now came the break down. I had to head it off.

"No, Maris wouldn't." I clamped a hand on her shoulder. I had bodies to dispose of and I needed help. I'd been running on instinct for a while. Might as well keep going. Garrett…no, not Garrett. "Dial Maris and give me your phone."

Her brow wrinkled in confusion. "Maris and I had an interesting talk, Peg." And I was going to take charge of his ass.

She called. Maris picked up.

"Mother?"

"This is Leslie, Maris. Don't talk, listen. You remember that conversation we had? Peggy needs your help. Right now. You, alone. You understand."

He went silent, but not for long. "Where?" That was

the right question.

Good boy.

"Peggy's not hurt, but please don't let anyone see you coming down here. Mom will be proud of you." I gave him instructions.

I'd thought Peggy would ask questions, but she didn't. She sat with her hands in her lap, looking lost. She'd married a wolf and he was her shield. I'd never killed anyone, and except for Mom, Dad, and Rado's murderer, never wanted to. I couldn't even kill deadly Marisa when I had her down, though I might have had Garrett not intervened.

Peggy had a box of tissues and I used them to carefully search the two men for ID. Portland addresses on their driver's licenses and credit cards. I found only the usual pocket shit, and the keys to a rental car. I watched for Maris and called him into the woods. Thank God, or the tribe's goddess, there was no more traffic on the path. I motioned him back into the shrubbery. His nostrils instantly flared at the odor. He might not turn wolf, but he was Fenrir.

"What's wrong?" He immediately went to Peggy and knelt beside her. I'd made an excellent choice on whom to call. "There's blood? Are you hurt?"

Damn, Peggy sounded calm now—if a little stressed. "We got attacked. They were going to kill us. With guns. Leslie took care of it. I think you need to help her hide the bodies."

Maris froze. He stared up at me. I motioned toward where I stashed the two would be assassins. His mouth dropped open. Recognition came in his eyes.

"You know them, Maris?"

"Yes. They work for Aristide." He rubbed his hands

over his face. "Oh, Goddess."

I sighed and shook my head. "Yeah. Goddess. Bitch has been busy."

I held up our attacker's car keys. "It's almost dark. Peggy should be able to make it home alone. The chair has safety lights. If we can find this rental car, ditch it and the bodies, no one will know exactly what happened. Is Mama's baby boy up to that?" I made a guess, searching for more information. "You're in trouble, Maris. This Aristide fellow is running out of patience with you. Whatever he's got on you, he's probably going to expose you soon."

His expression said I'd guessed correctly. Maris gazed at his mother. She sat, hands on her lap, head lowered. He held out his hand. "Give me those keys. You take Mother home. I'll take care of things here." He stood straighter, taller. He had found the courage to act— and accept the consequences.

Relief. Disaster resolution was rarely this easy. "Send a text to her phone when things are clear. We'll talk later. Wipe everything you touch and see if you can find and disable the GPS on the rental car. Most of them have them these days. It will buy a little more time."

"Maris?" Peggy reached out and grabbed his hand. "I understand you're in trouble. Son, what did you do? Was it so bad…?"

He went motionless, like prey with the predator looming over them. Then…

"Aristide…It's not about the land. Not now. I stole one of the Tribe's Calx icons, Mother. And I sold it to Aristide for a million dollars. I had a debt to pay. In Las Vegas. I traded one set of threats for another closer to home."

Peggy frowned. "You mean all you did was lift one of those fancy bathroom tiles? Well, hell. I was scared you'd hurt someone or done something bad."

His mother had her priorities. The Fenrir tribe's precious art collection wasn't among them.

"Mother, the Council will send Garrett to kill me if they find out. Now Aristide wants the rest of the icons. He's obsessed. It's like a curse." He rubbed his hands on his pants. "Killing you would be a warning to me. I'm not going to escape. I want you safe, out of the way."

She smiled up at him. "That's okay, Leslie will take care of it. Just you wait and see."

How appalling. "Peggy, I'm still a stranger. You still don't know my motives. You don't know what I want here."

"Neither do I." Maris's voice carried sharp bristles. He gazed at the bodies. "But whoever you are, you killed to save my mother. If you have the guts to take on Aristide, I think I'll be on your side."

Maris did gawk at the limp tree smashed body. More fluids had begun to leak out of orifices. He stared at me, his expression begging for an explanation. *Sorry, buddy. That's not even remotely possible.* He finally shook his head. I thought I could trust him to get the job done. But I'd blown my meek Leslie persona again.

We didn't talk when I walked home with Peggy. It was full dark by the time we got there. She asked me to stay the night. Then… "You did that. That man. The tree. How? You got to tell me."

I did owe her that. "It's called telekinesis, Peggy. Moving objects with the mind. I don't understand it. I've done weird things like that since I was a kid. When I get scared, under stress, I lose control. But all I can do is push things away from me."

"It's…" She stopped. "Lots of scary shit around here sometimes. Most folks don't even see. You ain't the least of it. I'm a little less scared for you. Still glad you're on my side."

I couldn't sleep. Nothing was going to cancel the sound of a human body hitting that tree at…how fast? How fast had I drawn Ba'ran from its sheath? It gave a tiny shiver.

I'd always endeavored not to touch and read weapons. Disturbing visions would appear, visions of slaughter. Ba'ran didn't offer shit. And the tree man? *Telekinesis?* I wanted him gone and he went—only he met an intractable oak tree on the way. And there was absolutely no one I could talk to about either action. Unless it was my dream goddess who was unenthusiastic about explanations.

One thought did spark curious ideas. Maris said Aristide was *obsessed* with obtaining all the icons. It added a new angle to the mystery around this place and these people. Aristide, icons, wolves, and murder. A puzzle I had to solve.

At 4:30 a.m., Maris sent a carefully worded message to Peggy's phone that he had resolved the problem. That was suspiciously fast, but I'd take what I could get. I finally fell asleep on Peggy's couch. I didn't want to dream. No such luck.

Chapter Seventeen

The white space around me quivered.
"Are you there?"
"Yes, Katrine. I'm here."
"I killed two men."
"I saw you. This land here is mine. You are worthy of the Fenrir Tribe. So fierce."
"Ba'ran took over. For the time, for a few seconds, it owned me. I've had knife training, defensive mostly, but this wasn't a fight. I threw, and the knife did the rest."
"There are three of the blades, each carries the spirit and will of a remarkable warrior. What you felt was that spirit. It is an unfortunate side effect of the blade's nature. Bi'ar's guardian had it in her possession all her life. She had time to become familiar. In time, you will gain control."
"To what end? What is its purpose?"
"Protect its bearer, the one chosen to carry it."
"Chosen. Do you know how much I hate that word? Does being chosen contravene the idea of free will completely?"
"Free will?" Can a goddess sound petulant? Absolutely. "Katrine...Lisa Marie, you are a full-blooded member of the Fenrir Tribe. You have free will, but you have built-in responsibilities. You'd understand if you'd been raised among my people."

"Why didn't you pick someone like that?"

"I made attempts, years ago. It didn't work. Born in the tribe. They want to worship me, like that Anext woman. I do not want worship. I need someone to guide, not give orders."

"What about the other man? The tree? I wanted him away from me and…"

My stomach churned. I poised on the edge of waking.

"Unfortunately, I couldn't select the traits you would possess. Perhaps you should go somewhere quiet and try to learn control. As I've told you before, I'm not omnipotent. I know so much, but I'm not an all-seeing eye. I will help you as much as I can, Katrine. Truthfully though, now I'm depending on you, Lilly, and other women I have yet to contact. It's incredibly important. Each one that I gather in makes me stronger."

"You watch me all the time?"

"No. I watch you more right now because you are coming into a critical period."

"What are you? Really a goddess?"

"You seem to be fixated on that concept. How do you define a goddess?"

"I have no definition. I don't…didn't believe in them." Restless energy filled me. I was on the verge of waking.

"Creation and perfection are powers infinitely greater than mine, Katrine. I, and others like me, are a part of this world. We're hidden, guided by rules that say we must stay hidden from all but those we claim. Our own people. And no, you don't need to know who makes the rules.

"Thousands of years ago, I had a physical presence.

I found a group of humans and walked among them. Lived among them. They fascinated me. Hunter-gatherers, they had a nature far different from the others. Bigger, stronger, another race altogether. I came to love them. They were dying, slowly, locked in primitive and destructive ways. Their religion, like all human religions, was a curse they couldn't break. I gave them a new one, a goddess, centered on myself. I even bore children among them. Every living tribe member carries some of my original physical self.

"I battled against vast odds." She hesitated, then, "I gave up my physical presence in this world to do so. My few loyal followers and the land they claim is all I have now."

"You gave up your body?"

"Yes. And my people survived, prospered. But that set up my communication problem."

"Tell me again. Once a tribe member, a sucker like me, a specific conscious mind, accepts you, you can talk directly to them? No exhausting dream walking?"

"Yes."

"Can you then compel obedience?"

"Yes."

"So, someone becoming your...direct conduit to the Fenrir Tribe...creates a slave?"

"But not a mindless slave. A willing slave."

"Excuse me, goddess. But the words slave and willing are not congruent anywhere in my world."

****

I woke weary and unsatisfied. I had a few answers that didn't come close to what I needed. I helped Peggy rise and showed her the text, then deleted the words. She was quiet, and I wondered if I'd lost her. Then she grabbed me and hugged me tight. I went home to lie down for the rest of the morning, but I couldn't.

Control? I had it once, long ago. Moving things with my mind? I did remember pushing Danny on a swing while I sat under a tree reading a book. I remembered tumblers and pins falling into place in various locks. Had I picked that lock with my tools? Or had I fumbled around and let my mind work?

The next day brought another crisis. As if a murderous attack wasn't enough. Recent events traumatized me to a degree, but Peggy had recovered like…well, like Peggy. That damned power chair! Why the hell hadn't I just bought her a better wheelchair?

"Peggy, please slow down before you run over someone." I raced down the sidewalk after her. There were houses off Main Street and all had neatly trimmed grass lawns. She didn't hesitate to tear corners across the perfect green.

She made a sharp right to avoid Darrell Darby who nimbly danced out of her way. That caused her to hit the grass again and immediately slow, but not fast enough to miss a lovely flower bed. The wheels dug in. They spun, digging ruts and spewing plants and dirt before they gained traction. She was off again. Darrell and I raced after her. Damn, that chair earned the word power in its name.

"How do you cut that thing off?" Darrell huffed out the words.

"There's a switch on the arm. She's got her hand over it."

He wasted a few precious breaths and then shouted. "Miz Peggy, I'm going to arrest you for reckless endangerment. You can ride that darned thing right down to the jail."

Where did Peggy fall in the halls of justice around here? She wasn't tribe by blood, only by marriage. Was she one of the *regular people* in Darrell's jurisdiction? If both rejected her, she would be untouchable—or in deep, deep shit. Of course, I'd be standing beside her.

Damn, I was sweating. I discreetly reached in my right pocket and popped two of my scent packets. What had Darrell called me on that first day? *Miz Peggy's keeper.* Oh, yeah.

Peggy leaned forward, focused on her path, and raced on. She used her right of free explicit speech to burn her opponents. "Bitches and sons of bitches and all their fuzzy little bastards crawling on the floor." We again struggled to keep up. She continued to vocally express her rage. "Tell me about a meeting where they're gonna talk shit about me. They figured I'd be pushing my old wheelchair up that hill. Or waitin' for a car. Be done before I get there."

An envelope had arrived during the busy mid-morning hour. A young man had burst in the diner door. His eyes wide with terror, he dropped it in her lap. Peggy opened it, skimmed down it, breathing faster as she hit each line. She spun around, was off and down the ramp and on the sidewalk like a drag racer with a green light. I dashed out behind her.

The imposing gray stone Council building, obviously built in a previous century, stood like...okay, a Greek temple. Two blocks off Main Street, I'd not been by it before. Ionic columns held the roof over a wide porch, tiled with marble, wide steps led up to large ornate...were those gothic carved double doors? Talk about eclectic historical. Per federal law, it did have a handicapped ramp on the side. The expensive power chair conquered the incline with proficient ease. Clever Miz Peggy had practiced her motoring skills. She rolled up to a side door and banged her fist on the plate that was supposed to allow automatic opening. Locked. She screamed in rage.

My Mom's aim and motor skills were not expert, and I'd had the front of the chair reinforced with bars to protect her feet. Unfortunately, it made the high-power chair, now occupied by an adroit operator, an effective battering ram. She backed up the chair and rammed it forward. It hit the wooden door hard. Like a bat hitting a ball. Everyone inside had to hear. Back up, crash, back up, crash.

Darrell suddenly laughed like a giggling little girl. I didn't deem it funny, since everyone knew who had provided her with such a formidable weapon.

On the fourth charge, the door opened. She shot inside. A sharp yelp followed. Oh, hell, I'd created a monster. I jumped in after her. "Peggy? Are you hurt?"

The man who had obviously opened the door stood back, rubbing his knee. "No. She's not hurt."

I hurried past him. During her myriad of complaints, Peggy had told me that only a few meetings in this building were open to the public. Non-tribe landowners complained mightily about decisions made for the whole town without their inclusion in the process.

We entered a single, large high-ceiling room. No chairs here. Most of the audience sat on three tiers of wide wood steps, built around the circle. A mini amphitheater, or like a kiva from the desert southwest. The floor, polished, shone like a basketball court, and had a weird design inlaid in darker wood at the center.

Easy to see all the audience was tribe. Damn. I was standing in a circle of wolves.

Three people sat behind a curved desk overlooking the empty circle. A man and a woman I didn't know, and Garrett Dain. Garrett at least was smiling. He was also back in his fancy tailored suit.

Peggy wheeled herself through an opening in the spectators. They quickly moved to make room for her. Fortunately, the floor was smooth. Unfortunately, the blanket she'd covered her lap with was caught up in a wheel. I rushed to snatch it out of danger. That put me in the middle of the circle with her, facing the dais. To lower my profile, I knelt beside her and worked the material free. I also popped two more scent packets, the ones I'd positioned by my armpits.

Her bony body quivered, and her left leg visibly twitched.

"Cowards!" Peggy waved the paper at them. "You don't have the decency to face me?"

The woman, a plain obese creature draped in a white robe sneered. She had tiny black eyes set in a full puffy face, and her body jerked as she smacked her hand down in front of her.

"That's because you waste our time arguing with us, Peggy. We're tired of your nonsense."

"*You're* tired of it." Garrett spoke softly, but everyone heard him. I'd noticed that about Garrett. He would never have to shout. People automatically listened.

I managed to get the blanket out of the wheel and tucked it around her legs. She handed me the paper. I quickly skimmed the contents.

"Condemned?" I'd had no intention of speaking out,

but this shocked me. Everyone in the room gasped. I'd call the Rize and Shine a bit rundown, but not dirty or unsanitary. I took my turn cleaning the bathrooms, too.

The spectators shifted on their seats and murmured to each other. The combined voices warbled in a tone of dismay and anger. The Rize and Shine had the enviable position of a beloved institution. The gathering place for the locals to share gossip over a pleasant home-cooked type meal. Outstanding food didn't hurt its reputation, either.

Ms. Plain and Obese's face flushed. "There will be no discussion. A majority has voted." Her voice had a chainsaw edge. She had to be Isabell Anext, the priestess wan-a-be referred to by Peggy and my dream goddess. She nodded at the man next to her. I'd bet he was Ted Balcome, Peggy's brother-in-law, Maris' uncle. He seemed embarrassed. Oh, a majority of two votes, Ted and Isabell.

I glanced over at Darrell who leaned against the wall, out of the line of fire. He had his fist near his mouth like he was chewing on his knuckles. In character for him, but worrisome. He knew far more about these people than I did.

"I don't remember any discussion about closing Peggy's place." A man's voice spoke from behind me. I still knelt to keep a low profile. I couldn't turn to see who it was, damn!

"No discussion is required on a health issue." Anext snipped the words to sharp points.

The man spoke again. "Saoshyañt Anext, if there were health issues at the Rize and Shine, over half of us in this room would be in peril. Therefore, I believe discussion is in fact, mandatory."

Saoshyañt? My mind skimmed through my inner dictionary. Garrett had explained sevishtå and bitîm, top dog and second. Now this man used another word, one extraordinarily close to Avestan. Language morphs with time and use. It breaks off pieces of words, mixes them with colloquial slang inventing new descriptions or actions. *Possible textbook translation? Benefactor, strengthener, or a religious leader, a prophet?* Peggy called her a priestess.

The man behind me spoke again. "I request that the matter be placed before the Council."

"No." Anext snarled the word.

"Yes." That was Garrett.

Both stared at Balcome sitting between them. His mouth twisted. He shook his head like he meant no, but he couldn't make his words cooperate. "Yes. We should have discussion. It's inevitable. Clear the room."

"What?" Peggy shouted. Her voice approached a screech. "You fuckers gonna talk about me and I don't even get to hear? If Marcus was here…" Her voice broke.

A tiny bit of applause came from the back. "Let her stay," a brave fool shouted. Others around the room murmured in agreement. Peggy, grouchy, mouthy Peggy, had friends. *"She's helped a lot of people," June had told me once.*

"Harat! Clear the room." Anext shouted the words. Every person there sucked in an audible collective breath. Ba'ran, hidden its sheath in my pants, vibrated like a silent cell phone. Danger closing in. It expected violence.

A man, a thick heavy bodybuilder type, came from the side.

Ba'ran vibrated hard against my leg again, demanding my attention. Warning not required—I could see the intent, the hatred. This one liked hurting people. No uniform, only a button up shirt and slacks. He kept glowering eyes steady on Peggy. He meant to move her by force, and he'd love doing so. He hunched his shoulders and curled his hands into fists.

Wait! They were going to allow this? Would Garrett again stand by while violence raged? No need for a blade. I'd push Harat through the fucking wall. That would destroy my Leslie persona, but he would not touch her. I rose, drew a deep breath, and stepped between him and Peg. When did I get so brave? Was it when I killed two men?

Darrell was suddenly there with me, hand on his gun. To the Rize Sheriff, I was what he called *Regular People*. Not tribe, but those in his jurisdiction. When did *he* get so brave?

"No!" Garrett stood. A single word and Anext and Balcome were looking at him like they wanted to run. Even the Harat brute stopped so fast he went to his toes.

Garrett projected an aura of incredible leashed violence. If he was a CEO of a corporation, staff meetings must be from hell.

He stepped from behind the desk and came toward us. Another scent packet in my pocket made a tiny pop when I mashed it. Tomorrow I would order a gallon of the liquid concealer. The big bully threatening us backed away. Garrett knelt in front of Peggy. He laid a hand over hers.

"Will you allow me, trust me, to act as your advocate?"

She gazed at him for a long moment, then let out a

breath. "Yes, Garrett. I will trust you." For a brief second, her face filled with sadness I knew so well. I wanted to hug her. Peggy had agreed that Garrett might have killed Marisa—but she trusted him anyway. Could I do that?

She turned her head to scan the room, then powered the chair toward the door leading to the ramp. Darrell and I followed. By the time we got there, she was down the ramp and a hundred feet ahead of us. Not racing, but we'd have to walk fast to keep up.

"And who was that Harat guy?" I asked Darrell as we followed Peggy.

"Harat—Jacob Harat—is a kind of bouncer for meetings. Isabell's…I don't know what he is to her. Maybe lover. Most people don't like him. I can't attend the tribe only meetings. Sometimes terrible meetings I hear. Bad blood, violent." He shook his head, eyes narrowed and jaw tight. "Leslie, please try to avoid any Fenrir. I've seen them go out behind the building and batter each other bloody until one goes down. They do it other times, too. *They fight all the time*. It's not my business. Most I deal with is a fight two fishermen get into over the same rental boat."

"And they have their own laws?"

"Yeah. They make their own rules. Evil rules. Who can get married, who they can date. Marisa was different."

"Marisa?"

He didn't speak for a moment, "She was a friend of mine. In the tribe." His expression softened, and he stared at the ground. When he gazed up again, tears had formed. "She wasn't like the others. She died." He straightened. He wouldn't say murdered.

"You stood against them for Peggy today, Darrell. For me, too. That was so brave." Out of character too, but he had tried. "If a tourist comes up against one of the tribe's people, you stand for them."

He expression of sorrow faded. "Thank you. Not really courage. Fenrir people consider themselves stronger than everyone else. So, their law says they're supposed to make allowances for the lowly regulars like us. Mostly they do. Good thing. No way could I stand against Harat.

"Lowly regulars? How arrogant."

"Yep, arrogant describes most of Fenrir." He chuckled. "I ought to arrest you, Ms. Torrence."

"Me? Why?"

He used his hand to make an exaggerated point at Peggy's back. "You've empowered a holy terror rolling down our sidewalks."

"No, Darrell. I simply believe in enabling and encouraging senior citizens to be mobile." I punched his arm lightly, too late realizing he might see it as flirting. He grinned but wouldn't meet my eyes.

"Miz Peggy gets any more power...don't believe Rize would survive."

"I need to see that paper they sent her. Condemned might mean unsafe building, or it might mean unsanitary conditions. Unless the floor's about to fall through or the roof collapse, it can be fixed. Could it be sabotaged?"

"Maybe, but I think they've decided to use things they've ignored for years." He didn't sound hopeful. "Some of the old pipes are lead. Drains are asbestos cement, too. But with Garrett on her side, she'll be okay for a while." Okay, that solved the mystery of why Peggy spent a fortune on bottled water for cooking and serving.

Nothing came from the taps except dishwashing. She cared for her guests.

Chapter Eighteen

Everyone was waiting at the diner. I gave a quick summation of the events. We made it through lunch then Peggy and I sat at her table. I was finally able to read the *official condemnation notification.* It did indeed describe lead pipes and asbestos. Faulty wiring, overloaded electrical panel, according to them, the Rize and Shine was in its death throes. Though inflated and rudely administered, the complaints were mostly legitimate. Peggy was living in denial. "Peggy, this place is still on a septic tank. Aren't sewers available? What about the electrical?"

"Septic tank works fine long as I have it pumped every six months. You know how much them bastards want from me to hook up to their fancy sewer pipes? Tried to get the electrical fixed but they wouldn't let me."

June towered over us blocking the light. "Sewer costs less than having the tank pumped." She set another pot of coffee on the table. "And no, they wouldn't allow the Tomlin boy, who learned a little electrical shit in high school shop, to do the wiring. You just like fighting with them. It's entertainment."

Maris marched in. His expression was like a thunder cloud, looming over the world. He held out his hand for the letter and I gave it to him. He scanned it, bent, and kissed his mother's forehead, and without a word, stalked back out. He feared Aristide, but he'd take on the Council for her. I wondered if my actions on Peggy's behalf had empowered him.

Peggy sighed and smiled. A tear formed in the corner of her eye. "I need to go home and rest. Leslie, you can take off. I'll call if I need you."

I stood. She sounded like she wanted to be alone. "Make sure you charge your phone, Peg. Keep it with you all the time. I'll see you tomorrow."

She caught my hand in bony fingers. "Thank you. I don't…" She released me. "We'll talk later."

Before I left, I endured the terrifying sensation of June enveloping me in her massive arms. I think she meant it as a hug, but it felt a bit like she buried me alive.

****

"Tell me, goddess, what's with the mix of languages, Greek, Latin, your tribe keeps spouting. Today I heard a word that might possibly and originally been Avestan. Saoshyañt. I've studied artifacts but didn't go deep into the language translations."

"Saoshyañt is one of the ancient titles for leaders. Language evolves. It transforms. I'm amazed that anything original remains.

"My tribes moved all through Mesopotamia, through Greece then eventually across the ocean to America. An onerous journey of numerous generations. And they added fascinating bloodlines along the way. The shapeshifters, the cats and wolves, are two that remain mostly pure. They joined the tribe in what's now Turkey. I have no idea where they originated. Mesopotamia…I'll tell you things that will surprise you someday. You, because of your travels, will appreciate them."

"I would appreciate things here better if I had more information."

"Well, here's something tangible for a modern woman. DNA. Now that's a fine innovative word. Or compilation of words. It's much more specific, but less poetic, than simply saying the bloodlines. Inconsistent in results, but bloodlines can be combined and recombined through mating to focus on certain traits."

"You breed us? Like lab animals?"

"No...yes. There are worse things. You all get your height from a band of Amazons who joined the mix a thousand years ago. The shortest was seven feet, giants in any time."

She was right. There were worse things. Like the uncontrolled breeding of humans, spurred on by religion, that would eventually destroy our habitat and lead to extinction.

"I keep my tribes healthy by inserting non-tribe blood occasionally. Allowing them to intermarry more often helped the cohesiveness, too."

"Like Peggy?"

"Peggy inserted herself. She captured Marcus and never let him go. But she has excellent genes. Vast courage there."

"Goddess, religion, worship, priests, holy warriors, are a way of controlling people. Isn't that what you want? With me. Contact and control of your people?"

"Of course. I know you don't like it, but when you accept, you will be my official priestess for Fenrir."

"I will?"

"If you don't like the word priestess you could use Âthrava Nâirika. The actual title isn't important. It's about continuation and strengthening the gifts."

"When it comes to my being your priestess, will I have a choice?"

"Oh, yes. It will come to you under duress, but it's a choice just the same."

"One thing, do they, Fenrir, fight like Darrel said?"
Silence.

"You still there?" She was, I could feel her.

"Yes. Fenrir enjoys those battles. It's the wolf in them I suppose."

I woke with a start. She'd kicked me out of my dream. I considered her an unreliable source of information, and the goddess' desire for communication with me left me exhausted in the morning.

****

Leslie was learning about Rize, but consistently remained on the outside of the tribe. I'd learned nothing that would connect anyone here to Mom and Dad's murder. I hadn't expected anyone to give information for free, but I'd hoped for more gossip. The extraordinary cohesiveness of their society kept me away. I'd never penetrate as Leslie. Something had to change. And it did. Garrett caught me. I suppose it was inevitable.

The third building on Peggy's property, more like a small barn, had physical therapy equipment made to accommodate her injury. She couldn't use it without aid and supervision, which, thanks to Maris, hadn't been available. I'd moved things around to clear the area. There was also a weight bench and an array of weights I could use. My routine of running, stretching, and push-ups wasn't quite enough.

Peggy had a long set of hand-high parallel bars with a harness to hold her up while she walked along. She'd never walk unaided again, but the exercise eased her pain. The more she moved, the easier she could move.

"You didn't have a stroke, did you?" I checked her harness to be sure it was snug.

"Nope. Tripped and fell down the steps."

"How long since you've been to a doctor?"

"You startin' to sound like Maris. At my age, all them big-headed ghouls want to do is shove pills down me. Or cut me. One was gonna run me through one of those pipes like a coffin. Don't like doctors."

Of course, she didn't. But she now smiled when she said her son's name.

The weather had warmed to the point where I had both doors open. The barn sat back away from the diner. I had on black leggings and a white tank top, and I'd worn a long loose shirt over them outside the building. I kept it nearby in case I needed to cover up fast. My body, my figure, a firm, slender younger woman's shape, would raise suspicions. Peggy had said nothing, but she'd already come to accept that my projected image was not a true picture. I was on her side and that was all that mattered. She was walking in her harness while I sat astride the bench and lifted arm weights. I'd worked up a steamy sweat when Garrett walked in.

"Peggy? I've settled your—" His head jerked up, eyes wide, confusion on his face. He stared around the room.

Oh, shit. Game over.

I reached for my shirt to cover up and break one of the scent packets I always carried. Too late. His eyes lit up like he'd turned on a switch. He followed his nose. No way I could disguise this sweaty stink bathing my body. I had straddled the weight bench, legs wide. In an instant, he was there, straddling too, sitting with his knees against mine. He grabbed my wrists.

He leaned forward and stared intently into my face. "What the hell?"

I looked away. If I gazed into those golden eyes…

I twisted, but as in the Seattle basement, I couldn't break his hold.

He shook his head in denial, still not reconciling my face with my voice or odor. "How did you…? I've searched all over hell for you! I had the best PI's and computer geeks in the country looking for you. They broke into your lawyer's office. Danny wouldn't tell me shit. Just that you were okay."

"Danny's my good loyal friend. I told you to leave me alone. Didn't I? I told you I needed time. I can't trust you. You know that, and you know why." My breath hissed through my teeth. I jerked but he still gripped my wrists tight. I went on the offensive.

"Did you kill Marisa?"

He released me. "No, Katrine, I didn't kill her." His voice was heavy with resignation. "She betrayed tribe and the goddess. It would have been my right. My duty. She gave Aristide secret information." He drew my hands to his mouth to kiss them. Brave of him. I could scratch his eyes out. I didn't want to. I wanted the truth.

"Mom and Dad? Did you…" I almost broke on that one. Stupid, he wasn't going to confess to that. *Oh, no. I was crying.*

Then Peggy drew out the courageous woman who defied culture and tradition to get her man. Somehow, she'd wiggled out of her walking harness and back to her chair. Before I could blink, she zipped to us. She had a gun, a small but deadly pistol, drilled into the back of Garrett's head. She gasped from exertion, but the gun remained steady. "Now you listen, Garrett Dain. I changed your diapers and fed you at my table right beside my own son. Fuck your laws, fuck your goddess. You will not hurt Leslie."

Garrett sat perfectly still, his eyes on me. Oh, that exquisite face, that so appealing kissable mouth. He spoke softly and with a soulful tone that touched me deeper than I believed possible. "Katrine…Leslie…I swear on my mother's life, the tribe, and the name of the goddess, I did not kill Marisa, Radoslaw, or the Dolinskis. And I swear on the same I will never hurt you."

I glanced at Peggy. "Is that enough?" I had no idea. Instinct failed me here.

Peggy lowered her gun. "Well, it's a damn good oath, cause he really does the goddess thing. Loves his mama, too. But then I guess I *want* to believe him." She stuck her weapon back in the chair's side pocket. "Seems like you want to believe, too."

I wanted to believe him. My life's experience told me that except for Danny, all the people I could trust were dead. And I wanted Garrett Dain, despite my doubts, I wanted him. Trust him? Not yet.

Garrett released my wrists. He laid his hands on my cheeks. His thumbs wiped at my tears. I remembered I was wearing Leslie's face.

He frowned and leaned closer to study me. "Did you have surgery?"

"No surgery. I learned a few tricks. You know. Like sit or roll over and beg."

He ignored my dog references.

He kissed me, softly on the mouth, and I wanted to drag him closer.

I relaxed and let my face go back to its natural state.

"How?" His eyes grew brighter, and the gold shined.

"Just a tiny bit of shapeshifter DNA. I think. Don't know for sure."

Peggy gasped. Garrett grinned, and excitement filled his voice like a kid offered a long-desired toy. "That's amazing. When did you learn to do that? I've never heard of anyone who could. It's on the list, but—"

"List? There's a list?" Oh, shit. I leaned back but couldn't escape the hands suddenly gripping my shoulders.

"Not exactly a list. It's tribal history, Katrine. Shape shifting, supernatural, mind driven skills like healing. They're so rare now." His hands slid down my arms to hold my hands in his. I couldn't decide if I wanted to pull away or get closer, so I rushed an explanation of my daunting task.

"I got a wild crazy idea last fall." Or, according to the goddess, she gave it to me. "I didn't think it would work. I needed to learn about this place. My face? It still hurts. Every morning. I hold it all day. And this little bit is all I can do. All I want to do, ever." Deep in my heart—or because of Marisa's attack—I did believe that shape changing of any kind was a perversion of nature.

Garrett glanced at Peggy. "Isn't she magnificent?" He didn't wait for Peggy to agree or disagree. "Okay, what do you want from me? I've begged you all along to let me help you."

"For now, it's the same. Leave me alone. And tell me what you know about Aristide's dealings here. Gut feeling? An out-in-the-woods tourist development across the lake? No way. He's too big for that." I knew what Aristide wanted, but I wouldn't betray Maris. "My contacts with him have always been through Rado."

Garrett shook his head. Sadness filled his voice. "You should assume Marisa told him everything she knew about Katrine's story." His voice grew hard and cold.

I shared a bit of information. "I told my lawyer to give Aristide a phone number. Maybe he'll call me, and I can learn—"

"No! You stay away from him. You don't know—"

"I don't know? Rado…" *Stop it, Katrine. Just stop.* I jerked my hands and this time he released me. "I will do as I please, Garrett. If you bully me, I will leave and never see you again." I decided I'd offer a little more information—and a tiny gift—to see how he reacted. "You're still missing two icons. Aristide has one of them." No, I would not speak directly of Maris' theft. "Once I find where it's hidden, I'll go in and get it for you."

Garrett grasped my thighs above the knees. "No. I had him watched. The way he lives…security, armed security, cameras, a fortress, not a museum." His hands squeezed tighter. "You don't have to risk that. For a piece of old carved rock? I don't believe the goddess requires such material things."

"I don't either, Garrett." No, his goddess was more concerned about her communication problems. His hands kept gripping me, restraining me…not good.

"Your tribe cares."

"Our tribe, Katrine."

"Okay, our tribe. Garrett, they care big time. Right now, I care nothing for the tribe. I care about what happened to people I loved." I noted that he hadn't seemed surprised that Aristide had one of the icons.

Maris must have told him.

The large shirt I'd worn over my outfit lay on the floor beside me. I reached down and jerked Ba'ran out of its sheath where I'd covered it to keep it out of sight. It slid into my hand with an instant touch. A soft glow of golden light wove through the runes on the blade.

Peggy gasped. She remembered what I had done with the knife.

"Garrett, I can't get rid of this. It keeps coming back." I lifted the blade. "This gaudy piece of bling tells me how to kill people. It tells me how much fun killing is. It likes the taste of blood. Then there's the cryptic nonsense I get from a pompous bitch who says she's your goddess. She haunts me in exhausting dreams. Believe that or not as you wish. I won't have peace or rest, until I see this thing through."

He sat unmoving, then let out a long sigh. "Sheath Ba'ran, please. Someone might see."

I sheathed the blade.

Garrett touched my hair. "The goddess? She talks to you. Has this turned white yet? Did you dye it?"

"Turn white. No. Why?" What was he talking about?

"I have to go." He stood. "I dream about you, Katrine. I think about you all the time. If I stay here longer, I'm going to drag you out into the woods and keep you. They'll hear us howling all over the mountain. Please be careful. Please."

He stroked my cheek, bent, and kissed me softly, smiled at Peggy, and walked out. I wanted to stop him. Demand more information. Same old bullshit. Only no one died this time.

I shook my head. "He seems mighty sure I actually

want to go howling with him, doesn't he, Peg?"

"Most women in Rize would give a lot for that." Peggy rolled closer. She stared at me with profound intensity, donning her glasses to see better. "Katrine? Leslie? Who is…who are you? You got to tell me."

I had to tell her. I owed her. Fearless, she'd risked injury to jump in and defend me from a dangerous man. I leaned back to watch her expression as I told my tale.

"My official name is Katrine Dolinski, but I was once known as Lisa Marie Serova. When I was about two years old a man named Telek Dolinski kidnapped me from a highway accident halfway between Helle and Limbough. Telek had lost his own two-year-old daughter to meningitis a year or so before. They raised me as their own. My father, my mother, and Uncle Radoslaw were murdered last year. I don't know by whom or why—yet. All I have is clues. I know the missing Calx icons, the Fenrir Tribe, Garrett, and even Aristide Dubois, are all mixed up in a massive puzzle." I wiped my hand over my face, and it came away smeared with makeup and concealer. "I hate it when I cry."

"Well, that's a mighty fine face you're hiding." She laid a hand on my cheek. "I 'member the night Lisa Marie was born. I drove your mother, Elaine, to Limbough to the hospital. That sorry shit of a husband was out drunk somewhere. I got a picture of your mama and you. I'll give it to you. Damned if you don't look most exactly like her." She cocked her head to study me. "Anybody in the tribe who knew her, sees this face would know. And your Dad's name is Peter. You got three brothers. Morgan and Merritt, they're a couple of years older, and Randy, he's younger. Lotta trouble amongst them."

I had already seen, if not met them. I did want to meet them before I made judgements.

Peggy's curiosity remained strong. "How do you do that? Your face. I'd seen the wolf change. Marcus did it. But this…"

"I'm not a wolf. This face is all I can do. Right now, I don't know Lisa Marie. She only exists in my DNA. Right now, I'm Katrine Anastazja Dolinski—a.k.a. Leslie Torrence."

She leaned back, relaxed, smiling broadly. "So exactly who is this Katrine Anastazja Dolinski. Anastazja. I like that name. Tell me true. No stories. Leslie's a damned fine liar, but now I need something more."

"Peggy I'm so sorry I had to lie to you." *Tell her true?* "Katrine Dolinski is a corrupt and immoral individual by civilized cultural standards. The Dolinskis, a pair of life-long con artists and thieves, raised her that way. Mom and Dad's smart, sweet little girl cleverly learned to use her innocence to prey upon those who let their guard down. Those with human kindness and basic decency. She could charm and pick pockets by the time she was seven and shoplift not long after.

"And her mother's brother, her uncle Rado? He started her on B & E training when she was nine. Small kid to get into tight places. She grew up to be one of the most prolific cat burglars in the multi-million-dollar jewel and artifact underworld for the last ten years."

Peggy's eyes went a little wild. Her hands twisted in her lap, but she quickly relaxed.

"Your mother? Murdered?"

I nodded.

"Oh, darlin,' that hurt is… And Garrett knows all

that."

"About the murders, yes. And he knows I'm a thief. A successful thief. I doubt he understands the true magnitude of my long life of depravity. I'm not sure of anything anymore, Peggy. I'm lost. I've mostly shed my life as Katrine Dolinski. I'm not Lisa Marie Serova, either. Even Leslie is a disguise, a con."

"And you said…the tribe's goddess talks to you?" Ah, the first skepticism. That was fine with me. Sometimes I wanted it to be a hallucination.

"I dream about her. But it might be Garrett's desire for her to be real—or my imagination. Tell you something else." I gave her a big grin. "You hear about the tribe's icon that was in the museum in Seattle?"

She nodded. "Maris told me."

"Garrett went to lay claim." I winked and laughed. "I snuck in and got it first."

Peggy sat still for a moment, then laughed. Low chuckling at first, then it burst into a joyous note that made me incredibly happy.

Chapter Nineteen

The next morning, Sunday, I stepped out onto the deck just after dawn. I'd made a habit of sitting there and drinking coffee to begin my day. For a change I dragged on my jeans and slid a soft T-shirt over my head. Leslie's plain tasteless clothes weighed on my mind. They grew heavier each day. The trailer park would remain quiet until noon, so I didn't need my Leslie face yet. Making and holding Leslie's face still caused nightmares of it freezing in that shape.

Sitting on my deck with coffee, I'd decided that Oregon, like Northern California, was beautiful. I've never been much of an outdoor person, but I could appreciate it from a distance. I'd finished my cup when I heard a soft whining noise.

Garrett—the wolf Garrett—watched me from the shrubs and trees. Deep black with the silver on the sides of his head—beautiful creature—he could be no one else. What an utterly alien sensation. Comprehending an animal with a reasoning brain.

He stared until I acknowledged him, then turned, stopped, and turned back. Oh, he wanted me to go with him. Why not? I nodded agreement and held up a finger to tell him to give me a moment. Back inside the trailer I put on my athletic shoes and slid Ba'ran in its sheath. I'd carry it on my belt. As I left, I stuck my tiny tape across the front door. No one had gone in to search since that first time, but I had to keep my guard up.

Garrett waited for me at the start of a narrow trail up a mountain. I laughed. How preposterous, like an old TV show.

"Lead on, Lassie. We'll find and rescue that kid trapped in the well. Oh, yes, we will."

His low rumbling growl made me giggle like an adolescent meeting a rock star. I guess he didn't appreciate my humor. He trotted effortlessly ahead. Before long, I trudged up a brutal incline. It's a good thing I'd exercised. The trek presented a true challenge for my stamina and athletic abilities.

I stopped at an infrequent level spot to rest a moment. The scent of pine grew stronger here, as did the deep loam of the earth. The same scent that spun around Garrett in an invisible cloud. It marked his home.

The trees towered like sentinels over us. Patchworks of green brush stippled the ground where sunlight forced its way through and around the dense canopy. Even a city and highway girl like myself could revel in the wild green beauty of these woods. Small streams over rocks that created miniature waterfalls and pure air cleansed by the forest trees.

How completely stunning and beautiful—and surprisingly quiet. I understood. Two predators walked through the sanctuary. Garrett stopped and stared back at me, questioning.

I plopped down on a handy fallen tree. He came and rubbed up against me. His fur, so soft, I wanted to hug him, pet him, but wasn't that treating him like a dog? Argh, I needed a quick course in Wolf Etiquette 101. He licked my face, right across the mouth.

"Ewww." I pushed him a way. "You haven't had

that tongue anyplace nasty, have you? I've seen what you canines lick." He shoved me over backwards and pounced on top of me. He swiped that long tongue across my face furiously until I made a laughing apology. I stared into those golden eyes. Like Marisa's, they were not animal eyes. The same preternatural intelligence glittered there. His body, easily the same weight as the man's and those teeth…my wolf.

We went on and came to a tiny cabin hidden by shrubbery and built into the mountainside like a cave. The door stood open. Garrett rushed on, leaving me behind. I followed more slowly, and he was standing there waiting. He'd changed shape and donned a pair of jeans. Disappointment—and gratitude. I wasn't ready to see him naked again, no matter what I wanted.

Ah, he opened his arms and folded them around me. His warm male body against mine, his mouth on mine, this was perfect. His touch overwhelmed me once more. *That deep inevitable and undoubtable sensation that he was mine for a lifetime trapped me again.*

I knew he thought I should abandon my search for murderers. And if I did, who would I be? I already had enough identity problems. I leaned back with my hands on his hard chest. Seeing him like this, feeling his sleek golden skin under my fingers… "I thought about you, wolf. When I traveled, when I rested."

He shuddered. "I thought you'd hated me." His voice sounded thick and heavy, filled with longing.

"Not hate. Anger. And disappointment."

"I understood how you might think I killed Radoslaw or your parents. You couldn't discount the possibility."

"Except I haven't discovered any reason why you

would. My parents anyway. Rado was prepared for trouble. You had an appointment. Was he prepared for you? If not…"

"Who had he expected?" He released me and closed the door.

The cabin, a rough primitive construction, had spaces between the boards that allowed soft light to flow across an eight by ten room. Even with a single chair and blanket covered mattress it seemed barely habitable.

"Wow! Garrett, you have scored the ultimate bachelor pad."

"Sit with me." He drew me toward the make-shift bed. "This is the place I come to when I want to be alone. It clears my mind. The wolf has my surface thoughts and wishes, and he's at peace here. His needs are elemental and unsophisticated."

"You consider the wolf as a separate entity? A separate personality?

"No, we are the same, always, but the…thought process…is different. If I'm hungry, the man says go get a steak. The wolf says let's kill something."

I sat beside him, but he immediately drew me down, so we could lie face to face. The blankets under us smelled of fabric softener. They hadn't been stuck in this woodsy shack for weeks. He'd thought of me, my comfort. He folded me in his arms and stroked my hair.

"Katrine, I failed you horrendously with Marisa, and I most humbly beg your pardon. I recognized a tribal challenge. When she attacked you, the rational part of me demanded I intervene. But the tribe…I've lived with its law all my life.

"But she changed shape in the middle of the fight. When a challenge is issued, the combatants are supposed to fight human on human or wolf on wolf. I hesitated and then you were on top, killing her."

"Oh, yeah. I was chewed all to hell, but I wanted her dead. Something I never felt before. Wanting to kill." I put my head on his chest and listened to his heartbeat. When he spoke again, the words came softly to my ear.

"I'm afraid, Katrine. Deeply afraid. I haven't felt such terror since I was a child. I hate it. You're digging into things that will get you hurt—or killed. I can't bear it. The family of your heart has fallen victim. Yes. I believe it's all connected, too."

"I…we…need to get those two icons back. I think it will solve four murders. And then there's my biological family. I don't know any of them except by reputation. And what I saw when you beat the hell out of them."

He chuckled softly deep in his chest. "Peter and all three of his boys can shift. That's rare, close to a miracle. Everyone had hopes for the boys. They were promising before their mother died.

After that, Peter let them skip school, let them run wild. He defends them. Guilt, I expect. The accident was his fault. He was so drunk." He sighed. "The Serovas are a challenge. They start fights, they steal, and most of the girls follow them like puppies regardless of parents, boyfriends, or husbands. I take them on personally because I'm afraid anyone else might kill them."

Confusing. The man was…what? Enforcer? Executioner? Protector. And I'd watched Peter Serova handling his sons. Not a gentle touch, but he cared in some masculine, non-demonstrative way.

I rubbed my hand down Garrett's arm. Everything in me demanded that I get closer, touch him, taste him. Not yet—not yet. "Garrett, all the pieces of the puzzle point to the icons and Rize. That's why I created Leslie and came here. Please, if I mean anything to you at all, help me."

"You don't have the skill to take on Aristide."

I rose to gaze down at him. "You believe that. I have life as a successful thief among many thieves. You don't know a fraction of what I've accomplished."

He stared at me, and I realized I was as much a confusing stranger to him as he to me.

"Katrine, one night, not long ago, I helped Maris Balcome dispose of a car and the bodies of two of Aristide's men. He said he'd learned they were going to attack Peggy, and he killed them. One was knifed through the heart and the other had most of the bones in his body broken or crushed. Maris said he fell during the struggle. Maris is physically strong and skillful enough to kill like that, but he is not, nor has he ever been, a fighter."

Now what did I say? Admit Ba'ran had jumped from my hand into a man's heart? That I mentally snatched a man up and bashed him into a tree? That I killed human beings. I had no idea what Maris had told him.

"Yes, Garrett, I was there. We were attacked. Why did Maris call *you*? Peggy said you and he were…estranged."

"He wanted to confess to a theft and tell me that Aristide owns him."

"He broke your law. But you helped him anyway."

He shrugged, but it was tense. His shoulder muscles tightened and stood out. "Maris and I were close friends once, until I turned wolf and he couldn't. Most important? He's tribe. Aristide is not." He lowered his head, then raised it to gaze into my eyes. "I'm trying to get him out of Aristide's reach for now. I wish you would let me do the same for you."

"You mean leave? Hell no. But Leslie is finished here. She's learned all she can. Katrine will come back in her place. Garrett, why do you not understand? Your so-called goddess is leading me on. I don't know why. She's urging me to fulfill my goals. To find a murderer— or murderers. She keeps telling me how helpless she is. If you believe in her, why can't you do the same for me?"

He squeezed me tighter. "I believe in her. I believe *she* is using you for her purpose, not your welfare."

"And you are? Looking out for me? Or are you pushing me out of the way, so I'll be safe? Then you don't have to bother about dealing with me and my problems."

All tangible items had a price, every stolen antiquity, every shiny stone. I would find out who killed my parents no matter the cost. Garrett Dain was a distraction. A beautiful, desirable distraction, but I would sacrifice any relationship to know the truth.

"I'm always on your side, Katrine. Even if I don't agree."

"And even if I'm a Serova?"

"No one's perfect." He pushed himself to his feet and offered me a hand. "I need to change and lead you back, so you won't get lost. You probably don't want to watch."

"No. I'll cope eventually. I was sick for days after I watched my own face change." I had to ask. "I was afraid once I changed it, it wouldn't go back. Did you ever…?"

"The first time I shifted, I was afraid that I wouldn't want to go back. That I would give up humanity altogether. Running wild through the woods, running free. Total addiction. The ultimate drug. My mother, she was the wolf in the family, she had to use food as bait to hunt me down and drag me back home a few times."

"I hate the change, small as it is. It requires too much energy to maintain."

"But you are so adept. You covered your scent, too. If you hadn't been sweating in Peggy's barn, I wouldn't have known."

"Leslie is a servant, a lowly helper, you had no reason to pay attention to her."

"I'll admit I was curious when I heard that you confronted Maris. It confused me, but I couldn't pinpoint why. But it's a lesson. Pay attention to everyone. Dismiss nothing because it's common or ordinary."

He kissed me then, kissed me, deep and long. My body responded, my mind responded, I wanted to cling to him, keep him close to me. I couldn't. Not yet.

He opened the door and stood behind me. I heard his jeans slide off and had another moment of regret. I would like to see him again, hold him again. The wolf's heavy body brushed by my leg, and I followed him out into the woods.

When I returned to my trailer, I shaped my face. I walked downtown to the Nikos Deli, bought a sandwich, and went to sit in the park to relax and try to get my mind straight. I'd already had my daily exercise mountain climbing.

****

"Why are you not practicing your other Gifts?"

White space again, another conference call from…where? My own mind?

"Goddess, you do know that I don't rest when you do this, don't you? And I don't have other gifts. I can

read by touch and shove things around. That's it."

"Ba'ran pressed information directly into your mind when you fought."

"No. It jumped in and took over. Reflexive action. Too fast for me to form a thought. Too bad you can't do that. Shove the info up my ass. I'd probably have a few more answers."

"No, you'd have a room in an institution. No matter how much I love and envy my people, I'm not human. I have never been human. My thought process would eradicate most of your brain cells. Not that you're using them anyway. Practice, Katrine. You must."

Chapter Twenty

I was in Oregon City treating Katrine to a mani and pedicure when one of my four phones rang. The nail technician working on my feet grunted in annoyance when I started pawing like a puppy in my seeming boundless messenger bag. Of course, the one I wanted was on the bottom. It was the phone I used to call my lawyer. By our arrangement I always called him. Instinct fought the pitched battle in my mind. Impulse said answer it, it's important. Logic said it's trouble, let it go. As usual, impulse won.

"Good afternoon, Katrine."

Ah, I knew that satin smooth voice. *Aristide.* Cultured and seductive, sexual without being cloying, it demanded obedience and offered pain and pleasure. A sensual wave coiled in my core. It made my skin feel hot and cold at the same time. But according to Maris, that same velvet voice had sent men to kill Peggy—and I had thwarted the assassins. No, Leslie thwarted. Leslie who could disappear in an instant if necessary.

"Good afternoon, Aristide." The net around me grew tighter. *Coincidence be damned.*

"Are you well, my dear? I endeavored to contact you several months ago, but your lawyer said you were traveling."

"Yes. Recovery time. I sat on a warm beach for the winter."

"I'm sure. Healing from such an ordeal as yours takes time. Perhaps I shouldn't ask, but do you know any more about your parents' passing. It was devastating, I'm sure." Oh, that smooth, smoky tone, so perfectly pitched to console.

"You mean their murder?" The young woman working on my feet jerked. "Call it what it is, Aristide. No. The police won't tell me anything."

"They can be difficult, I agree. You know, of course, I did business with your Uncle Tulmic, but I also knew your parents quite well years ago when we were all young."

What? Shock slapped me like a hand grabbing a live wire. I drew a quick audible breath and he, of course, knew he'd surprised me.

Be calm, Katrine. Pretend you're on a mission to relieve a millionaire of his treasures.

"Really? They never spoke of you." Rado had dealt with him and all I'd heard were warnings. *Stay away from him, he's evil.*

"I'm not surprised, my dear. It was unfortunate, but your father...let us say that Telek and I had a fundamental disagreement when you were barely a toddler. After that, I only dealt with your Uncle Tulmic." He paused dramatically. "Looking back, I have regrets. At times, we fervently desired to change past events, to reverse our mistakes." That beguiling voice begged me to believe his story. "Until our disagreement, Telek and I were close. I could tell you stories. Telek, Alina, Tulmic, and myself. Oh, yes, it was a delightful time to be young."

The technician lifted my foot and carefully dried it on a soft towel. Ah, the luxury calmed me a bit. The puzzle of murder and theft suddenly became more complex, and the abhorrent mine of lies burrowed deeper. He went on in the same condescending voice. "Are you back in Senica, my dear? I have a new project you might be interested in. It involves a few unusual antiquities."

Walk carefully, Katrine.

"I don't stay in Senica. Too many memories. The future? Emory has a significant doctorate program—if I can get in. Or travel to the Middle East again—if I can find a place where there isn't a war in progress." I carefully hesitated, to tease him. "We could talk, though."

But no, Aristide, I will not tell you where I live. He might already know, but I'd play the game.

He and I were feeling our way around, trying to offer enough information to get what we wanted. I knew my motives, my most imperative goals. What were his? He continued to probe. "I understand your police officer friend is now in Portland. In fact, I saw him the other day. An award they gave me for a recreation center I funded to allow delinquents a safe place to plot their next crime."

Okay, now the threats. No longer pretending to be a nice person. And he'd been tracking Danny. *Enough with the games.*

"Recreation center? How civic minded of you, Aristide." Just a tiny touch of sarcasm to show him he wouldn't fool me. "So, you're in Portland?"

"For now. I would like to see you, Katrine. You understand things in life that would escape others. I grow more nostalgic as the years pass."

"You're not that old, Aristide, I remember you."

Okay Katrine, flirt with him. "You looked as if you had defied time when I last saw you. Rado agreed. He sounded envious."

"And I remember you, lovely Katrine. The dowdy disguises you often wore might have fooled your clients and professional colleagues, but not a connoisseur of beauty such as myself."

A connoisseur of beauty? Oh, boy. And a consummate liar. Did he think I never looked in a mirror? Vanity, except for my status as a master thief, never touched the personas I created. True beauty? Could I attain that pinnacle if I shaped my plain ordinary face as I had with Leslie? It would be just another mask.

"Thank you, sir. I've closed my authenticating business. I no longer need professional disguises to increase my credibility." I quietly laughed, warm, friendly.

"Wonderful. May I use this number to call?"

"I love cell phones. I have a collection. At least twenty. It's hard to keep track at times. Do you have a number where I can leave a message?" *And how did you get this number from my lawyer? No, don't challenge him Katrine, not now.*

He laughed at that. "Oh, Katrine, Tulmic, Telek, and Alina would be so proud of you. They created perfection. Very well, my dear. Call Sedalis Imports, in Portland, and speak to Ms. Harris, and she will give me an immediate message from you."

"I will do so. I look forward to seeing you again, sir."

"And I you, clever and most amazing lady."

Clever and amazing. Oh, yes, that was a tiny bit closer to the truth than the clichéd beautiful.

Aristide. How old was he? Rado's age? No, younger. Middle to late forties, I'd bet. Physically fit, he had appeared barely thirty-five when I last saw him. He must have been in his early twenties or even teens when he knew Mom and Dad. If he knew them. I had no way to verify. I'd scanned all the papers stored in the basement. Other than the cremation certificate Dad destroyed, none had gone back to the time of my...or unfortunate little Katrine's birth and tragic death. There should have been more. Dad's meticulous nature and Mom's tendency to hoard would have gone in that direction. Maybe the important things had been in Rado's safe when it burned.

And the specter of Marisa Trent remained. Had she told Aristide about the deception around me? Did she say that I was a replacement, a changeling for an ill-fated daughter? Only one way to find out. I had so much to think about on the drive back to Rize.

****

Preparations in Rize escalated as the calendar rushed toward the Solstice Festival, though it was a month away. Even the crabbiest of individuals hinted at excitement during upcoming events. Peggy grumbled, but let June decorate the diner with flowers and odd objects no one would explain. Weird rune-like metal ornaments hung in the windows and colorful weavings covered the walls.

Wolves: statues, pictures, stylized, and impressionist, were everywhere. They reminded me of the red bag, the only thing Dad had stolen from the wrecked car besides me. The one in which Ba'ran first entered my life.

The restaurant patrons' excitement raked my nerves.

Peggy suggested it was because I was, as Lisa Marie, a part of the tribal consciousness. Only she didn't use words like consciousness. She had a more colorful vocabulary, but I got the idea. I asked for, and was granted, a few days' reprieve.

I left town. I had a plan.

I had a couple of fun days with Dan, Melanie, and their darling twin girls. The warm hominess of their new northwest home surrounded by mature evergreen trees relaxed me more than I thought possible. It had to end, though. I'd called and left a message for Aristide. He promptly returned the call. *Come to dinner with me, Katrine.* He would be sending a car. He didn't ask Danny's address.

I'd purchased a black sheath dress. Expensive, fitted, feminine but not terribly seductive. Hem barely above my knee, modest cleavage, and long sleeves, I went for sexy without brazen. I wore a pearl necklace supporting an emerald the size of my thumb, surrounded by diamonds. An incredible gift from Rado. I was never inclined to buy such myself. Leslie might have, but of course, hers would be fake costume jewelry. I needed to cover my scarred forearms, too. I'd managed to keep Danny from seeing them. The skin tears could have come from any accident, but the bites, the parallel rows of punctures, were far more obvious.

Almost time to go and I stood and admired myself in the mirror. Melanie screamed. An alarming shriek of terror followed by the sharp clatter of smashed crockery. I grabbed Ba'ran and raced for the sound.

Melanie lay on the kitchen floor, unconscious. Broken shards of pottery scattered across the floor in front of her. Danny had arrived first. Gun in hand, he focused on a naked Garrett, sitting on the floor.

"What the hell…?" Danny shouted.

Garrett threw up his hands. "I'm sorry. I didn't mean…shit!"

I rushed to Melanie, dropped to my knees beside her. "Dan, either shoot him or come help me. Or both."

Danny holstered his gun. No problem. I now knew I could shove Garrett through the wall and out to the street if necessary. We couldn't find any obvious injuries, so Danny gently lifted her from the floor and carried her to the living room couch. I turned on Garrett, still sitting on the floor. I almost kicked him. "If anyone is watching this place and saw you…"

"No one saw me. That's why I came in the back door disguised as a dog. It's concealed and I can pass for a German shepherd or husky most of the time." He shoved his legs in a pair of sweatpants he must have carried with him. Right. A dog trotting down the street with a pair of pants in his jaws. So inconspicuous. I think—I hoped—he'd come through the small forest surrounding the house. He could manage that with ease.

Danny was tending to Melanie as she revived.

"I fainted." Melanie stared at him, her hands twitching and pulling at his shirt. "I never faint. I…it was a dog then…I thought it…what happened?" She froze. She'd noticed Garrett leaning against the door jamb watching us. He at least had the grace to say, "I'm so sorry. I didn't see you, or I would have waited."

Danny had his arm around her, and she buried her face in his shoulder. He kept murmuring softly in her ear. Finally, she straightened. She was a mother and a cop's wife. She'd overcome shock and moved to survive and protect what she valued.

"Melanie, please accept my apologies, too." My apology was sincere. "I should have checked into a hotel and visited. This was supposed to be simple. Come to Portland, visit my friends, go on a date, and leave." At least the kids were away with their grandmother. "He's not supposed to be here." I glared at Garrett. "Obviously, he's stalking me."

Melanie shrugged and gave me an unconvincing smile. "I asked you to stay here, Katrine. It's been fun until…did I see…oh, hell. What did I see?" She started shaking again.

"You saw him change." I shivered. "Yeah. It's stomach-turning. I've only seen it once. It freaks the hell out of me, too."

Melanie glared at her husband. "You're not surprised."

He hung his head and pulled her closer. Danny had chosen well for a wife. Such an incredibly strong woman, her initial reaction to shape changing seemed calmer than my own. I patted his shoulder. "Come on, Dan. Couldn't you have wounded him? Get him the hell out of my way?"

"Tempting. I know what he is. I saw it once in Afghanistan. They trapped us, and he changed and got out to bring help. I swore I wouldn't tell anyone. How, when did you learn, Trine?"

"I learned in my living room, but not from him."

"Go on a date?" Ah, Garrett had caught up.

"I have a dinner date with Aristide tonight, where I hope to obtain information. He dealt with Rado extensively. I'm hoping I can—"

"No!" Danny and Garrett spoke at the same time.

"Katrine, you will not go to him." *Garrett Dain*

217

giving me orders?

Danny was not any better. "Katrine, that man is a dangerous criminal. The special task force I'm on…" At least he made it a plea, not an order, but then he knew me. And Aristide was the focus of his new job in Portland, the one he hadn't talked about. *But Aristide knew about him, why he was there and where he lived.*

I stood and faced Garrett. "Now you want to protect me? From one man? I was fighting for my life and you…" *Stop, Katrine. Let that be and go on.*

Rado had trained me well and had moved me from a small-time thief to star cat burglar. Overconfident? Oh, yes. But murder and vengeance were never games for weaklings.

"I'm going to dinner with Aristide. If either of you follow me, you could put my life, and other lives, in danger. If he sees Garrett…"

Garrett's arms were at his sides, fists clenched. "I can keep you here. I can expose your charade in Rize and—"

"Restrain me?" I was on my feet, ready to fight. "You think you can—"

"What charade? What's Rize?" Danny's distress shot up and out the window like an escaped canary. He drew Melanie closer, but his free hand was on his gun.

I had to get out of there. "Talk to Danny while I'm gone, Garrett. Tell him whatever you wish." I laid a hand on Danny's shoulder. "Listen to him. But I warn you. He might not lie, but he does withhold important, even critical, information. Believe it as you will. No judgements until you hear my side."

I faced them and forced myself to be calm. "I have every intention of finding out who murdered Mom and

Dad. And why. Aristide knows something." I eyed them closely. "Danny, I love you dearly, you know that. But if either you or Garrett interfere with me or my plans, I will leave and never see or speak to you again. I don't know if my leaving would matter to you, but…it would devastate me."

Garrett groaned softly under his breath.

I picked up the soft purse I intended to carry. Wait. Why was it so heavy and lumpy? I opened it and snatched out Ba'ran. I'd laid it on the kitchen counter to help Danny with Melanie. Ba'ran flashed its usual golden blast around the room. I had no intention of carrying a weapon. It had other ideas.

"Why the hell can't you stay where I put you?" I shouted at the knife. Then I realized Danny and Melanie were staring, wide-eyed. I winced. "Sorry. I can't quite control it—yet."

I raised Ba'ran. It flashed one last time. I pointed it a Garrett. "And while you're at it, wolf, why don't you tell him about this, too. He's my family, my brother. He saw enough from me as a kid to believe you. Melanie may take some convincing, but eloquent ass that you are, I'm sure you'll manage." I glanced at her, into her now curious eyes.

I immediately regretted ordering Garrett to give Danny information without specific instructions. It was a mistake that would only complicate things. Too late. I'd deal with it later.

A limo drew up out front. I shoved Ba'ran back in my purse. If it wanted to come, I couldn't stop it. "Melanie. I'll be gone tomorrow. I had no intention of bringing this on you."

"What?" Ah, Melanie had recovered. "You can't

leave until I know what's going on." She cast a skeptical glance at Garrett.

I shook my head and laughed, not in amusement, but irony.

When the driver came to the door to politely inquire about me, I followed him out and slid gracefully into elegance.

Aristide's place in Portland sat in the Pearl District, an area of mixed-use buildings with attractive street trees. I'd located it long before I'd agreed to dinner with him. The three-story structure had an art gallery on the first floor. It also had underground parking.

My mind measured, calculated, and plotted. How to get in and out undetected. Nothing presented itself immediately. I'd already checked. The storm sewers were too small for me. A steel gate had come down behind the limo as we entered the garage.

The driver stopped and an incredibly sturdy woman met me and escorted me to an elevator. She had sharp watchful eyes. A heftier version of my *medium brown girl* persona, she carefully and obviously scanned my body, looking for weapons. Not that the figure-hugging dress would allow anything. She didn't ask to search my purse. It was fabric and too small and narrow for a gun. And Ba'ran? I thought it was metal, but it didn't set off the obvious detectors as we stepped into the elevator.

The elevator quickly carried us up where Aristide stood waiting for me when the doors opened. My escort held the door as I walked out. She quickly stepped back and cast her eyes downward as the door slid closed.

Oh, my, such an elegant vestibule with marble floors, heavy floral wallpaper of flocked velvet, and ornate, gilded fixtures. Gilded?

Aristide chuckled as he gracefully took my hand, lifted it, and kissed my fingers. "Yes, Katrine. I see it in your eyes. The previous owner of this building enjoyed baroque fantasy. I have not remodeled this little room yet. I enjoy the expressions on my guest's faces when they enter." He had a finesse that said he was far superior to you—richer, better looking, and impeccably mannered.

Aristide was not as tall as Garrett or others I'd met since moving to Rize. I could stare him in the eye. He stood slim, straight, and elegant. Every time I'd seen him, he had a half-smile on a delicate mouth. So suave in his outrageously expensive black suit, his jet-black hair trimmed in a classic cut—and handsome if a woman liked the slick, smooth, super-spy type. When he turned those shining dark eyes on you, you felt like you were the only person in the room.

He brushed fingertips over the palm reader on the wall by the door. No cameras here, though I had spotted them in the elevator. I could be as facetious as anyone. "You have excellent security, Aristide. It must comfort you to know your acquisitions are safe."

"It does. However, it comforts me more to know that my immediate person is safe. I enjoy my trinkets, but I have priorities."

Was he bragging? Or warning me. I started to ask him who would violate his immediate person, but I didn't have time for a lengthy recitation should he choose to answer honestly.

"Ah, Katrine, you are as beautiful as ever."

"Thank you." I made eye contact when I smiled. Not exactly spell-binding charm, but it would do. I wasn't there to seduce him. *But you will, Katrine. If necessary.*

Aristide led me into a sitting room. Contemporary and stylish, decorated in pale blues and grays, it ended at a wall of windows overlooking glittering city lights. The dining table would take advantage of the panorama. Sparkling crystal and candles complemented the scene. The gentleman held my chair as he seated me. Rarely in my life had I dined so formally and in such luxury. I'd managed to avoid social situations except when wearing a persona to get what I wanted. Yes, a false woman acting in a play.

While Aristide poured the wine a silent, silver-haired man in a black suit entered, pushing a rolling cart before him. What a meal. The salad appeared so fresh I'd swear they plucked the greens from a garden only ten minutes before. Beef Wellington cooked to perfection, vegetables that would tempt the most voracious of carnivores, and of course, accompanied by the perfect wine. We savored our meal with only small talk, as in the view and my compliments on the food.

One thing did come to mind. I was rich. I could afford expensive food. Why bother? I cherished the delightful meals of the Rize and Shine Diner, served in friendship, as my parents had served me with love. I valued those far more than any gourmet feast from this sophisticated and evil man sitting with me at the table. When we finished, the silent man returned and cleared the table, leaving only our glasses and wine.

Aristide, appearing totally relaxed, began. "I'm having a particular and private reception in the fall. I've acquired a few rare pieces from Syria. They're selling whatever they can loot and carry to buy guns. Would you like an invitation?"

I nodded politely. "Yes, it sounds interesting."

He frowned, as if he wished to say something that troubled him, or something he didn't know how to say. Unsure? Aristide? Bullshit.

"You may say or ask what you wish to me, Aristide. You and I can avoid the games. They waste our time."

He cocked his head, studying me. The city's lights made a perfect display in the windows. The candle's flame reflected in his eyes like the fire dwelled there, too. "I told you I knew your parents before you were born."

"Yes, I remember."

He had his elbow on the table and his fingers briefly covered his mouth, then dropped away. "Twenty-seven years ago, I stood on a bridge with Telek Dolinski as he cried and scattered a tiny box of ashes. His young daughter. They went into a river leading to the sea."

"I'm sure it was a sad occasion. He was always a loving man."

He kept his intense gaze focused on me. "Imagine my surprise when I met him two years later, and that unfortunate little girl had been resurrected."

"I can assure you, sir, I don't have to *imagine* surprise."

"I raised an eyebrow when I first saw *you*. You were four years old. But Telek begged me ask no questions, so I left it there. We were still close at the time. Telek and Alina did an amazing job raising you. They molded you into their image. Born and bred thieves, those two. Con artists extraordinaire." He cocked his head and frowned. "Petty operators, though. Unlike your Uncle Radoslaw, your parents never gazed beyond or rose above the narrow confines of the road before them—or the pocket of the next mark. It certainly pleased me to learn your uncle had taken over your education."

Insults to Mom and Dad wouldn't move me. I gave him a saccharine smile. "Did you gaze down upon my parents for their pettiness—or envy them their freedom."

He shrugged. "Both, but I watched you with curiosity. I did wonder if they would have taught you as they did, placed you in such peril...used you...if you were theirs by blood? Would they have treated you differently?"

"I don't know. I live in the present and won't waste my time on speculation."

Used? Mom and Dad loved me. I never felt in peril. But I now knew a true daughter of their bodies would not have had the psychic or athletic skills of a Fenrir tribeswoman—a child of the goddess.

"So, tell me sir, is Aristide, the notable philanthropist and collector of antiquities judging the Dolinski family for their uncommon child nurturing skills? Or does he judge me?"

"I judge no one, Katrine. I simply measure them by their usefulness."

"And...?"

"You and your uncle have been most useful at times. He had vision. He certainly raised your values and expectations beyond low-life carnies and trailer-trash pickpockets peddling imitation Polish food."

Oh my. Rougher insults now.

I smiled and lifted my glass in salute. "How observant of you. Now, here's a crude little memo from the trailer trash. Fuck you, Aristide. Now, what do you want?"

Yes! I had maintained a perfectly calm voice and a smile. He laughed, a thrumming sound that came from deep in his chest, odd in such a slender man. When he settled, he picked up his wine glass and sipped. "Come, let us go to a more private and secure room."

"If you wish." I rose. "Do I have to remind you that the *fuck you* was rhetorical?"

"No. No reminder. Certainly, you are desirable, but quite frankly, your professional abilities, your clever hands and exacting eye, are far more attractive to me." His eyes scanned my body. "Although, should you be willing, you would be welcome. I believe you would have no regrets." He held out a hand and gestured toward a door.

We entered an elegant room, a library of sorts, with heavy wood furniture and an old ornate bar across one wall. It didn't match the modern sophistication of where we dined. It reminded me of Rado's heavily curtained office—minus the dust and mold. I did note that he laid his hand upon another palm plate beside the door. Security, security, required by a man who surely had much to hide.

I sat in a chair with a firm high seat, not the couch. I could rise quickly, and he couldn't sit too close beside me. I'd picked up my purse, so at least I had Ba'ran.

I refused an offer for more wine. He picked up a folder from the bar and sat in a chair beside me. A dramatic pause, then, "Several years ago, I acquired an investment property in Rize, Oregon. It's in the mountains south of here and was payment on a debt. I examined it and decided it would make an excellent resort. I handed it off to my developers. I rarely deal with such in person. My developers, however, encountered problems. I explored the situation, and other prospects came to light."

Chapter Twenty-One

Aristide handed me the folder. Photographs. A series, the first a path leading into a triangular opening in a natural rock wall covered with sprigs of vegetation. Oregon forest at its best. The photos continued into the cave, well lighted, with mesh steel ramps and rails to ensure solid footing. Low lights cut into darkness and a wide set of steel stairs led down into the deeper earth. Another steel mesh bridge swung across a well-lighted, brilliant blue pool of water, then up to another open space. More lights there, exposing stalactites hanging from a far ceiling. A waist high rectangle of stone came next, as if someone had carved a table out of the floor. He handed me more photos. Garrett's tableau of ten icons lay on that table. These were exquisite in detail and in perfect high-resolution focus.

Aristide chuckled softly. "Carved white stone icons. Supposedly ancient. There are ten. I have obtained one. I understand that you, at one time, had another. Eight remain in that hole in the ground. I want them. All of them." He spit out the last three words in ferocious spikes. Calm immediately returned. "That cave is a temple of sorts. It belongs to a cult called the Fenrir Tribe. Zealots. True believers of a demanding goddess."

"Let's save time, Aristide. I have been apprised of the goddess mythology and my supposed familial connection to Fenrir people, the Serova family in particular. I know my birthplace and how my father obtained me. I have not been to Rize, which sounds more like an asylum than a town. I don't plan to go there. I'll consider it in a few years. I've lost the only family I knew. The only family I want."

Aristide gave me an optimist's smile. "It's so peculiar. Two of those ten icons went missing almost a year ago. I purchased one icon from a thief, who swears he only took a single piece. The second missing icon suddenly appeared in a Seattle Museum. I've been unable to determine how they obtained that piece.

"I had asked Radoslaw to get the museum icon for me. He agreed. He called me one night to say he had obtained the desired object. I left Portland immediately, arrived at daylight, just as the police swarmed the building. I had to leave." Aristide watched me closely, as if he thought I would offer a bit of information.

"This is interesting, Aristide. But what do you want from me?"

"I know about the museum, Katrine. How you met Mr. Garrett Dain. My contact in Rize was quite vocal. Quite disturbed. She believed you were holding that second icon."

She would, of course, be Marisa. I stared at him with what I hoped was an honest expression. "I don't have that icon, Aristide. I gave it to Rado and went home. I don't know its current location. Certain people have chosen not to believe me. Their disbelief changes nothing."

Aristide raised a hand. "I believe you. However, that changes nothing for me either. Now, I was informed Mr. Garrett Dain, an important person in Rize, is quite smitten with you."

I'd bet Marisa had told him nothing about the wolves and actual shape changing. I'd bet she held back to keep one element of surprise—or didn't want him to assume she was a nut job fabricating a wild story.

I flipped my fingers casually, to dismiss his idea. "Regardless of his illusions, I am not smitten with Garrett Dain. I've told him to leave me alone and so far, he has."

"Or, like myself, he couldn't find you." His dark eyes sparked with tiny fires. "However, considering my information, it is possible a long-lost child could go to Rize and claim her heritage. And obtain other valuables."

I struggled not to laugh. It bubbled up anyway.

"Oh, my God, Aristide. You think I should go to an insignificant town in the mountains, fuck Garrett Dain, make nicey-nice with the relatives, so I can thieve for you? From a cult, even. True believers, religious nuts in the woods…caves…and with snakes and wild animals. And bugs?"

He accepted my amusement with a gracious nod of his head. "Katrine, there are no guards in that cave. The path to them is clear across stone and sturdy walkways. My source informed me the tribe believes their goddess dwells there and keeps watch. Superstitious garbage, and exactly the reason they went missing. Though I don't understand why a thief would take only two. The complete set would be easy enough to carry. I'm offering you a significant award."

Now was the time to bargain.

"Reward? Oh, yes. Everyone desires something, Aristide. I suppose it depends on what a person is willing to pay to attain that desire." I leaned back and tried to appear inscrutable. "My desire? To know who killed my mother and father. I will do—or steal—whatever is necessary to get that information. Dysfunctional as they were, my heart holds them dear. Do you know who killed them?"

He hissed a shallow breath through his teeth. Surprised? If so, it quickly faded back to amused arrogance. "Do you not want vengeance for Radoslaw?"

"Rado dealt with so many heinous people. I don't know if someone killed him because of the icon or some other reason. But why were my parents murdered? They had nothing like artifacts or jewels. Rado kept his and my business as far from them as possible."

"As a heinous person who dealt with him myself, I would agree." He opened a desk drawer, lifted out, and offered me a hand-sized slab of carved white stone. The second missing icon, of course.

I shook my head. "I don't handle things like that without gloves."

"I have gloves. Will you at least look at this one for me? Tell me it's real."

Motivated by curiosity, I slipped on the white gloves he offered. While the icons might appear the same at a distance, this one was moderately different from Garrett's. "It's genuine. Old, but not exceptionally old, one to two thousand BCE. The symbols are from that period. The mother goddess, rain, flood, death…no, not exactly death. Plague."

I raised it to my face and drew in a breath. I didn't say, but I knew it came from the south. Egypt? Sinai? Garrett's had come from Turkey and was far older, at least by 2,000 years—and carved of the same mysterious stone as the one I'd taken from the museum.

"And its value, my dear?"

"It's a piece of beautifully carved art. I'd say half a million or so. You know how that works. A buyer's desire sets the value. The set as a whole…millions."

"I have millions, Katrine. Now I want the things I'm told I can't have. These," he raised the icon, "and others like them, are as gold to me." He laughed, barely a huff of breath. "And yes, my dear, I need you to use your skill and fortuitous connections to collect the remaining icons in that cave." He lifted his glass and sipped his wine.

"Aristide, I have stated my goal. If you have information…"

"But, my dear, I have other things to motivate you."

"I see. Now comes the threats of dire consequences if I don't do your evil bidding."

He laughed again. Genuine amusement. I suppose I was his entertainment for the evening. I could kill him. Ba'ran would instantly come to my hand.

"Very well, Katrine. I've found a few Dolinski and Radoslaw relatives who might be interested in the inheritance that is theirs. You were not legally adopted."

I'd already moved my money—and what Rado had—to more secure facilities. New accounts, closed accounts, Rado had taught me to do that often. I was as secure as possible there.

He continued. "More significantly, I have proof that a few valuable items in my own collections are stolen. Regretfully, if discovered, I'd have to return them to their previous owners. I'd make that sacrifice for justice's sake. And I would, of course, name the person who acquired them for me."

"Regretfully, Aristide, you're full of shit. Fuck the Dolinski and Radoslaw heirs. Go for it on that one." I'd left no evidence behind in my jobs. It would be his word against mine, his tarnished reputation against my sterling professional standing. I could play the game, though. I stopped smiling and stared straight into his eyes.

"Aristide?" He wasn't that stupid—was he? "You would turn me in for stolen property? That's a small crack in the ground that could bring on an earthquake. My arrest would make Rado's prominent international clients incredibly nervous. What confession might I make to get a lighter sentence? My advice? Don't do it. You'll get us both killed."

Rado never named his clients, but he said certain people had armies and the equivalent of the CIA behind them. Aristide? He was a small fish in their sea, and he was intelligent enough to know the danger. He wouldn't take a chance on stirring things up.

"I told you my price, Aristide. Otherwise, we have no further business."

His mouth twisted as if part of him wanted to smile, and the rest wanted to remain somber and threatening. "Yes, Katrine, I can give you what you desire."

I drew a deep breath. I had a knot in my chest, and my hands were suddenly wet with sweat. He walked to the bar, grabbed a bottle, and filled a glass with amber liquid that was probably much stronger than wine. He lifted the glass to offer it to me, but I shook my head. He quickly swallowed and poured another.

I was close to getting what I'd come here for.

"So, what do you offer?"

He returned to his chair. "I have a recording, a confession, an admission of responsibility for your parents' murder and naming the actual killer. I will give you that for the remaining icons. Payment on delivery."

Covetous Marisa, her desire for Garrett, had given

me a path by going to Aristide. I didn't know where it would lead, but I had a deep feeling it was right. As a hoarder of stolen antiquities, Aristide was among Rado's peers. He kept his bargains among peers as far as I—and Rado—knew. If he tried to swindle me, I'd have no qualms about killing him, like the men he had sent to kill Peggy.

"Very well, Aristide. I agree to the terms. I give you the icons, you give me my parents' murderer. However, I must warn you. These multiple random events around us, connecting us, are creating a hellish set of coincidences that could result in epic failure. We could both die for our sins. Rado, if he were present, would tell me to run like hell."

He nodded his head and lifted his glass. "The coincidence disturbs me too, Katrine. But I've always lived on the edge. I've survived."

"As have I. However, it *will* take time to plan. Showing up in Rize and shouting 'here I am' will not allow me to breech the inner sanctum. If they're as cultish as Garrett Dain, they won't accept me immediately. They could just as easily turn on me. Love and lust, while formidable, are not unalterable or eternal."

"And yet, you will prevail."

"Yes, Aristide. I will prevail."

I left in his limo not long after that. I'd played dangerous games in Aristide's world before. With Rado's help. This time I'd be on my own.

Danny was waiting for me, questions in his eyes.

"Tomorrow," I said. "Please."

He nodded. I went to my room and found Garrett lying on my bed. The only light was a tiny lamp. He wore the sweats from earlier. I grabbed an oversized T- shirt from my suitcase, stripped down to my panties, and pulled it on. I climbed in beside him, and he turned out the light. I moved against him.

"Talk tomorrow," I whispered, my face against that solid chest. I slept in his arms. What obscure facet of his laws and customs would cause him to act—or not act—in my best interest? I couldn't allow him to stand in my way. That would destroy both of us.

Chapter Twenty-Two

Melanie and Danny pinned me down over coffee the next morning. Garrett had clued me in on what he had told them. His version of my story started when he met me at Rado's murder scene. He explained that when I casually said, "Limbo is halfway to Hell," he became suspicious about my identity, and checked my DNA. That led to the story of my infant kidnapping. He hadn't spoken of my theft of the icon, my identity as Leslie, or the doomed Marisa Trent. Sanitized was the word for his version. Enough truth to work through things, but not the whole story.

Garrett did talk about his own desire for me to rejoin my biological family in Rize. Thankfully, he didn't touch the culture and the goddess. He said his shapeshifting was an anomaly, but some of the tribe could do the same. He told them of Aristide's desire for the lake front property in Rize. Not a first-rate story. Danny was super smart, and he wouldn't buy everything. His taskforce would have much more information about Aristide.

To my surprise, the fact that Dad kidnapped me didn't weigh heavily on Danny. He was mostly pissed that I hadn't told him about it right after I knew. He began a litany with, "You should have talked to me, to Barnhouse." He clenched his hands into fists on the table. He was rarely that demonstrative, but I'd pushed his limit hard. "Did you not consider vengeance for your kidnapping by your biological family? You took Garrett's word that he would deal with things? We could have protected them, Katrine."

"No, Danny, you—Barnhouse—would have *arrested* them. Jail is not protection for an old man and frail old woman. After losing Rado...I couldn't endure that. It would have broken me." I shook my head. Oh, the hypocrisy. "Right now, you know a man who turns into a wolf—or at least a supernatural being shaped like a wolf. Barnhouse...how would he deal with such?"

He rubbed his hand over his face. His life and mine had stretched an incredible distance. "Katrine, I remember. The summers I went with you. You toured the country in a carnival of thieves. No. Not toured. Participated. You gave a universal shrug to all when I asked. I loved you and needed your friendship too much, so I let it go. I chose complicity and hoped for the best. Until now, I had the best."

A tear formed in my eye. I was going to lose him. Mom, Dad, Rado—Danny was all I had left. I started to rise. He grabbed my hand.

"Sit down, Katrine. Twenty years of complicity is a hard habit to break. But too many things are out of my control." Danny held my hand tight. "Listen to me! I came to Portland to help take Aristide down. Rado is listed in the files as Aristide's close associate and probable accomplice. Rado dealt with stolen goods. No proof, he was too slick."

I drew a breath to speak, and he squeezed my hand tighter. "*But your name is in the files, too, Katrine.* As of now, there is no evidence you were involved in anything. You had to have handled stolen things, authenticated them. The question would be, did you know what they were."

I stared down and couldn't meet his eyes. "Trine, you worked. Your income was appropriate for what you did, you lived moderately, caring for elderly parents. That's good. But you're Rado's niece, now his sole heir. Eventually, they're going to question you. Specifically, about what was in his vault and computer that mysteriously burned. You're already too close to Aristide. You must stay away from him. Don't talk to him, don't associate with him. Go to Rize with Garrett or go back to Florida and sit on a beach. If you get involved, I can't help you."

I desperately wished I didn't have to lie, but too much depended on this. "Danny, my only direct involvement with Aristide over the years has been authenticating pieces in his collection, like I did for Rado and other clients. I had dinner with Aristide last night because I wanted to know if he knew anything about Mom, Dad, or Rado. You know what he wanted from me?"

Danny shook his head.

I swallowed hard. *Lie, Katrine, like a dead dog in the street.*

"Aristide has discovered my link to Rize. I don't know how. He wants me to go to Rize and use any family connections I might have to pimp his shitty resort development. How sleazy is that? I've found no clue that he's involved in murder. I'll do my best to stay away from him."

Danny sighed. "Garrett—"

"Garrett is an asshole who has fought me at every turn, misled me—"

"Trine. You slept with him last night!"

"But I didn't…never mind. I'll deal with him."

Danny wasn't happy. *Oh, it hurt so much to lie to him.*

"Garrett says he's protecting you. That's fine with me. I do love you, Katrine. I've said too much. I've compromised a multi-agency investigation. Be careful." He stood and walked out of the room.

****

Garrett and I sat in Danny's basement. I tried my usual defense, sitting in a single chair. He grabbed my arm, pulled me to a couch, and down onto his lap. Okay, that was comfortable. I laid my head against his chest. At least he'd borrowed a T-shirt to cover his skin. Briefly I wondered where all the hair went when he changed shape, but my mind rejected the mechanics.

"Garrett, I must make my own plans and decisions. Whatever relationship we have…shit. Last night you said I couldn't do something you didn't like and then offered to restrain me. I can't trust you."

He shrugged. "I can't stand back and watch you get hurt. Or killed."

Had he forgotten that Marisa tried to kill me, and he stood by and watched because of a tribal law about challenges to hierarchy? I should try to let that pain go, but I still couldn't.

"I have a plan, Garrett. If you can't or won't aid me, you need to leave me alone."

Garrett remained quiet, staring across the floor where children's toys, evidence of Danny's life as a family man, lay scattered around in a haphazard pattern. The room might be a man cave someday, but Danny valued his family more at this point. I so wished he had a safer job. I wished he'd accept the money I wanted to give him. He wouldn't have to work.

"Okay, Katrine. Tell me. What do you want me to do?"

"For now, go back to Rize. I have arrangements to make. Tell Peggy to make excuses for me, and make Maris take care of her. I...Leslie will be back in a few days."

"Make Maris?" He sounded amused.

"You know where he buried the bodies, remember. He is susceptible to pressure. Just don't break him."

"No, Katrine. This, the icons, Aristide, murders, it's too much. It can't all be yours."

Garrett the enforcer, sentinel, holy warrior—his tribe had charged him with upholding his goddess' rules. In some ways, he and others like him probably served his tribe with far greater proficiency than her power allowed. I hated it, but I had to consider him an obstacle. I couldn't go over him, so I would go around.

That evening, Garrett slipped out in wolf form. I was concerned with Aristide watching the house and wanted to get him away as soon as possible. I needed to get out, too. I left and checked in to a hotel. I spent a day and night making phone calls on multiple phones, setting up complex and fragile plans. To my amazement, things fell quickly into place, eased by money transfers of course.

My last call went to Aristide. He'd given me a personal number. He answered first ring.

"Yes?"

"Are we secure?"

"Yes. I'm paranoid about security, remember. You may speak."

"I need all those photos of the icons you showed me, in as high of a resolution you can get them."

"Of course. Anything else?"

"Yes. Don't push people in Rize. Don't take any action that will get them upset. When people get upset, they're unpredictable. I'll need a degree of control there. Just be cool for a few weeks. And here's advice you probably don't need. Watch your back in Portland."

He chuckled softly. "I have that little taskforce of your friend's under control."

"I don't want Danny hurt. You don't want that either, Aristide. I'm sure you'll get an excellent laugh out of my piss-ass threat, but you don't truly know me. You have no idea what I can do." *Like throw you into a concrete wall without touching you and smash you to blood jelly.*

His breath caught as he hesitated. Had he realized I spoke the truth? "Yes, Katrine, I understand. It's a small thing for me. Your friend is safe."

I'd check the phone occasionally but kept it off with the card always removed. This part of my plan was complicated, and not fully formed, which was good, because things were going to change. Chance events could easily skew my world to hell.

I received the photos, sent them on with detailed instructions on what I wanted, and a promise to call with more information. Then Katrine Dolinski morphed to Leslie Torrent. Leslie headed home—home to Rize.

To move forward now, I needed to be a part of the tribe. Small communities create complex interpersonal relationships and the specialized functions of individuals, i.e., mechanic, café matriarch, doctor, maintenance man. In the case of Rize, there were two distinct communities. Tribe, and what Darrell Darby called *Regular People*. Leslie the caregiver to the elderly had outlived her usefulness and served her purpose. She'd let me learn as much about Rize as a stranger could. It was now time to go native.

****

The white space around me shivered.

I groaned. I'd driven through the mountains and arrived in Rize at 3:00 a.m. I needed rest. I needed other things more. I'd have taken a sleeping pill if I had to. She was there, waiting.

"Okay, goddess, let's talk communication. You urged my dad, who was not tribe, to take action."

"Yes. And it drained me dangerously for a time."

"Can you simply make suggestions to someone, not tribe, without including heavy compulsion? Is it any easier? What if that someone wanted to do something, but only needed guidance?"

"Yes. I could do that with modest effort. And within the rules. Suggestions, not commands. It will weaken me, but not completely drain."

I told her my plan, which was far from complete, and what I needed from her.

"That's brilliant, Fenrir tribeswoman."

"It's shit, goddess. Too complex, full of holes with a dozen things that can go wrong. It's all I have."

****

I rested in my trailer for a few hours, then packed my car. Leslie had an emergency and had to leave town. Peggy cried when I told her, but Maris had finally stepped up and helped her. He had her van in the shop for repair and hired a woman to come in once a week to clean and do laundry. He even ordered her ramps rebuilt for safety. I assured her I would be back as Lisa Marie and reminded her we had a connection through my biological mother. She and Peggy were friends, so it would seem natural to connect. Peggy would send me, as Katrine, word about pictures of Elaine she wanted me to have. I could visit the restaurant often, then she and I would become friends, too. Oh, yes. I already missed the food.

Peggy thanked me profusely for helping get Maris back, but she gave me too much credit. Maris did love his mother. He was ready to break. I simply helped him fall in the right direction. He knew he'd done something evil and finally had the courage to act and hope for forgiveness. Now he only had to stay away from Aristide.

I gave myself a week after I left. Leslie drove a nondescript, ordinary car. Katrine drove a brand-new black BMW sedan that zipped around the tight curves of the mountains with the ease and grace of a snake climbing a tree. My now platinum blonde hair was a cap that curled in a decidedly feminine way on my neck and ears. I had expensive designer clothes that flattered my body, exposing enough skin to be sexy, but not enough to be tasteless. Excellent slender body, slightly attractive face, I still wasn't a stunning beauty.

Leslie had wanted to go unnoticed. Katrine would jump in and strive for results. Besides, if I wanted *unnoticed* all I had to do was stand next to Garrett. And yes, I'd been thinking about sleeping in his arms that night. It was a pro and con thing. Pro? Beautiful sexy man, desiring me. Con? He could screw up my plans big time. Did any of that fall within the parameters of true love?

Leslie had been gone for a week. I would have preferred to wait longer, but I didn't have that luxury.

Despite his words on patience, Aristide would get restless soon. I needed to find a way to explore that cave where the icons were located. And I had to find a guide besides Garrett. Given a chance, he would interfere as he had at Danny's. I had to admit to the loneliness and bitter depression during the time I was alone on the beach. I thought of love and companionship but beautiful men like Garrett simply didn't choose plain girls like me. I wanted Garrett, adored being in his arms, wanted him naked…not yet. It would be one hundred percent or not at all.

I arrived late. Sunset failed to show as gray and black clouds boiled over the mountain tops like giant errant balloons. A storm threatened. The drive through Rize and passing by the restaurant hurt a little. I missed Peggy, June, and the rest of the gang. Maris had told me I was using his mother as grief therapy for the loss of my own. Logical, I suppose, and it was a natural human way to ease the pain. I did talk to Peggy a couple of times on the phone, and she was a source of information.

According to her, gossip at Rize and Shine focused on the kidnapped Serova girl Garrett Dain had found. She would be returning. I would make no assumptions about who knew what. I figured I'd ride into town in my expensive chariot and let the proverbial shit hit the fan. With my bloody magic knife, barely controllable extrasensory Push and, if necessary, the deadly 9mm, I could do a lot of damage. Again, I cautioned myself against overconfidence. Even with all my weapons, I'd be vulnerable. I'd spoken to Garrett before I arrived. I let him know when I'd be there, but I'd again asked him not to crowd me.

I would have to settle in and become familiar with

the place in a different context. Summer tourists had booked all the quaint Bed and Breakfasts for the entire summer, so I had to take a room at the Sun Rize Hotel. Constructed in the 1890s, the four-story rectangular, red brick structure appeared modest and sturdy. Stone gargoyles perched on each corner stood as guardians and the only adornment. I'd never been inside with my Leslie persona, but the place had a reputation as luxurious, and expensive for a small town. It didn't have a portico or a valet so I parked by the artfully painted sign that warned of towing if you were not a hotel client. I grabbed my suitcase and another bag to carry inside.

The hotel lobby was old but amazing. It earned the luxury rep. The second I walked in the door I fell into another age. Museum quality Art Deco, the architect had copied from the Chrysler Building. Sculptured reliefs in brass, glass, and wood, fawn colored burnished marble floors, it had the eye-catching zig zag geometric patterns popular in the 1920s and 30s. Art and photos on the walls begged for closer inspection.

The lounge to my right was an extension of the lobby, filled with crafted wood furnishings, and anchored by a massive stone fireplace. The dining room to my left, called the Sunset Brasserie, had upholstered dining chairs and white clothed tables set with crystal and silver. Each table had a small vase filled with fresh flowers. Complete opposite of the Rize and Shine Diner with its 1950's midcentury truck-stop panache.

I approached the reservation desk, a finely polished wooden monolith with exquisite inlays of herons walking in a pond of cattails. The middle-aged woman who accepted my credit card cast furtive glances at me when she thought I wasn't looking.

I received no "Welcome to our splendid hotel" speech, either. Okay, silent I could do. I registered as Katrine Dolinski, not Lisa Marie Serova. Five people stood around and stared. Nothing like being the center of attention. Good thing I wasn't shy. Only one who didn't ogle me was the ancient man who shuffled over and silently demanded control of my luggage. Stooped with age, he stared at nothing but the floor while he plopped my not excessively heavy bags on a rolling cart.

He led me to an elevator that matched the lobby. An ornate open cage, it personified a long-gone age. I laid my hand on the polished brass design. A mistake. Unbidden, it slapped me multiple images of past events. The cage had not aged gracefully. It witnessed acts of violence, blatant sex, and once fell two stories to crash in the basement. I sucked in a breath and snatched my hand away. The lift mechanism clanked and whined, protesting every inch of the ride. I'd vowed to use the stairs for my stay at the Sun Rize.

My second floor room was spacious, a rustic-country style, and distanced from the Art Deco first floor by a hundred years. I'd sleep in a genuine cast iron bed, store my clothing in a finely polished wardrobe from another century, too. A multi-hued handmade quilt spread out on the bed to keep me warm, and a riot of flowers bloomed on the wallpaper. Stare at the blooms too long and they'd bless you with a migraine. And was that a tree right outside? It would be a stretch and I wouldn't be able to get back in, but escape was escape.

I'd arrived the week of the Summer Solstice. Rize hosted a three-day festival for the event. Vendors reserved the park and lakefront for the actual Solstice celebration. They promised fireworks, too. I unpacked, hung up my clothes, and went downstairs to the restaurant with the five-star reputation. The storm that threatened on my arrival broke over Rize. Rain, lightning, thunder—other storms would come and inflict far more damage than the weather.

Chapter Twenty-Three

When I woke, the night's storm had passed. An unsullied pink-sky dawn painted the scene outside my window. I'd slept well. I rose, showered, and dressed in three-hundred-dollar designer jeans, a silky soft silver-gray blouse, light jacket, and the comfortable shoes that were Leslie's addiction. I seriously considered never wearing heels again. I'd discarded every stitch of Leslie's clothing, as I'd disposed of my catsuits after each heist. A much lighter, crossbody bag of exotic, sapphire blue-leather carried Ba'ran and kept my hands free. I might carry the 9mm later, but not today. Katrine Dolinski, a.k.a. Lisa Marie Serova had arrived. And she was hungry. Last night's meal in the hotel restaurant was edible but wasn't real food to me.

I headed out on foot into a cool dewy morning, awaiting the sun to rise over the mountains. This was the time I missed, the time I'd loved to run from my little trailer down to the lake and back.

Darkness claimed spots under larger trees, but the anticipation of dawn engendered the belief that the coming illumination would dispel all danger. No running today. I'd have to find a different route, not Leslie's usual path. Being Katrine, not Leslie, could be as difficult as being Leslie, not Katrine. Had to keep my personas straight.

I'd called Peggy and she was expecting me. She'd

told everyone I was coming, as a friend of my mother's she wanted to see me. She would have photos ready for me and I was anxious to see them. If asked, Garrett would say he got us together because he wanted me to meet Peggy first and be welcome here. Maybe he wouldn't screw me up there, too. His words of advice? *Try to look innocent.* I could do innocent. Played the character with ease various times. Peggy, who had probably never looked innocent in her life, caused him some trepidation.

When I walked through the door of the Rize and Shine all conversation ceased, as it had for Leslie. Whereas Leslie had stopped, cringed, and meekly avoided all eye contact, Katrine stood tall, smiled with bright-eyed sincerity, and gazed around the room. She also stared them straight in the eye. It was a challenge of sorts. Not to fight, but to say here I am, pay attention people. Most turned away and went back to their food or coffee. Others gave blatant and suspicious stares.

I spied Peggy at her usual table. I went to her. Oh, no, she was crying. I knelt beside her chair and—shit. That's what Leslie did when she interrupted the Council meeting and many other times. Too late. I was there. Peggy took over.

She wrapped both arms around me and dragged me as close as the chair would allow. "Oh, I'm so glad to see you. You were a baby when…" She released me. "Have breakfast with me, please."

I rose and sat in the chair across from her. A most welcome thermal pot of coffee waited on the table. Before I could pour a cup, June suddenly towered over us like a rockslide poised to crash down on unsuspecting hikers.

Peggy eyed her then glanced at me. "June, this is Katrine. Elaine's daughter. You remember Elaine."

June sniffed, wrinkled her nose, and stared. I smiled pleasantly and said how happy I was to meet her. She grunted and walked away.

I glanced at Peggy. Peggy shrugged.

Peggy and I had a quiet conversation about my journey to Rize and my accommodations. She was particularly interested in the hotel restaurant. And a bit contemptuous. "Didn't know you'd be stayin' there."

Not long after that, June returned with full plates of food balanced on her arms. I hadn't ordered. Peggy's was her regular toast and eggs. Mine, damn it, was Leslie's regular eggs, muffin, and a bowl of fresh fruit. I glanced up and I thought she might have almost smirked. Peggy laughed. Yeah, it was funny. I certainly hadn't fooled June, but we had worked side-by-side as we served meals. She certainly wasn't one to spread tales. She would question Peggy later, of course.

I almost cried as I savored each mouthful. The cook's complex special seasoning on the eggs, velvet fresh butter sliding over my tongue, I would commence anew the unholy trinity of eat, heart pounding exercise, and eat more.

"I'm home." I spoke only to Peggy. "Not the town, not yet. I'm here at the Rize and Shine."

Peggy gave me a smile so loving I wanted to cry. My loss, combined with her loneliness, had created a formidable bond between us.

Please, please let me keep that feeling after I finished my task here. A prayer? To whom? Not the tribe's goddess. Her ability to aid me bordered on non-existent.

June cleared the table and returned with a shoe box for Peggy. Family photo time. The pictures were interesting, seeing my bio-father, mother, and brothers. I hated the explanations that accompanied each. I might be interested in the people, their lives, but not intimate details of the past. I felt compelled to ask questions.

This went on for an hour. At least the pile was getting smaller, and most of the early morning diners had gone on their way. She was right about one thing. I looked so much like my mother I'd call it spooky.

Peggy offered me another one. "Your mother didn't like this one, but I did. I snapped it right before…" Right before my biological father ran the car off the side of a mountain and into a massive unforgiving tree.

My obviously pregnant mother sat in a chair, smiling. The two-year-old standing in front of her was not. A little blonde girl marched toward the camera, eyes narrowed, fists clenched in a head-on full attack. The expression? I laughed. Such a fierce little thing. Was that me?

"Oh, yes, you were a fighter." Peggy chuckled too. "Your brother, Morgan, he was four, had stolen a toy of yours and you were on your way to take it back. He thought he was hidden behind me."

"Did I get it? The toy?"

"Oh, yes. You punched him in the eye and bloodied his nose. I'm not saying this to insult you, but you always acted Serova, not Dawkins like Elaine."

"I suppose I'll meet them all eventually."

"Yes. I'm worried. They're…"

"Not nice people. I've been cautioned. Don't worry. Regardless of my strenuous objections, Garrett said he spread word and appointed himself my personal guardian. He says they're afraid of him."

"No one's afraid of Garrett unless they've pissed him off." She suddenly frowned and shook her head. "Them Serova boys do a mighty job of that."

"Why? Be specific, Peg. Please." I had not thought much about it since his oath of not killing Marisa or my parents. I'd seen him bullying men in my living room and beating the hell out of the Serova boys, my brothers, outside The Tavern. Maris was concerned Garrett would kill him for stealing the icon but guess who he called when he was in trouble.

"Garrett can be… He won't hurt you." She lowered her voice. "But just you remember he's dangerous." She tapped her finger on the table hard. "He's made a big claim, though. One I don't think he has the right to make. You're his. He's been spreading that shit all over town. I figure he's wanting to protect you best he can, but…"

"He's made me, a Serova, a target. Damn, damn, I warned him…shit!"

"Yep. But that's your family. Folks say trouble is usually thieving Serovas."

We finished, and Peggy was telling me about more photos when my three Serova brothers stalked in like bullies on the hunt for victims. I expected someone from the family, but not like this, not this soon. They headed straight for us.

"June!" Peggy called. Her voice climbed in alarm.

"I can deal with it, Peggy." I stood and stepped to meet them.

I'd not had a chance to study them when Garrett laid them out on the sidewalk in front of Leslie. Morgan and Merritt were two years older than me, Randy a year younger. They had the tribe's height, but taut muscles under jeans and a T-shirt stretched and moved like a dancer's, not the bulky hardness of a body builder.

Such pretty faces for men, all three of them. Coal black hair, falling to disobedient curls, dusky skin made an attention-grabbing contrast to my paler shade and blonde hair. Another realization? I was the ugly duckling of the bunch—or at least the Plain Jane. I could no more reach their level of attractiveness than I could outshine Garrett.

The one in the lead, I couldn't tell if he was Morgan or Merritt, glared at me like a petulant child. Aggression? Jealousy of a new-found sibling? Oh, hell. Why did they smell like that?

I winced, stepped back, and held up my hands, palm out.

"You boys haven't had your bath this month, have you?"

They jerked to a halt. For the briefest of moments, they appeared confused. The one in the lead—Morgan? Merritt?—attempted an expression he probably thought was a sneer. He glared around the room as if daring anyone to interfere with family matters.

"You come with us." He leaned forward to intimidate. He didn't. "Pa wants you."

Too bad. His melodic voice wasn't credible enough to bully with words alone.

Behind him, the other boys kept glancing around like they thought the cavalry—in the form of Garrett Dain—was on the way. Customer phones were out, recording and broadcasting every second.

I didn't want a scene. Too bad. It was here. I tried to defuse. "Hey, guys, I understand. This is all new to me, too. Please. Let me finish my coffee and I'll come outside and talk to you."

The lead brother glared. "Pa said you should—"

"No. Later." I pointed at the door. "Go."

He flinched. What's this? Then, I understood. I was a sevishtå, a leader, top dog. My siblings were not. They had to follow me. *They would follow me.*

His eyes narrowed. He grabbed my left wrist and jerked. Such a juvenile mistake. He hauled me close enough I made a fist and punched him smack in the center of his face. Oh, yes, I know what it looks like on TV or the movies. The fact is, a solid blow to the face would debilitate anyone except a fighter trained to accept the inevitable. A trained fighter would never let me get close enough to hit him. Superwoman I am not, but I'm strong and I practiced. Rado made me train, but I bet he never even dreamed of this scene.

So, Katrine, start your reunion with violence.

My target instantly released me. His eyes crossed. He staggered, then dropped to his knees. Blood spurted from his nose. I didn't hit him that hard, did I? To my surprise, his brothers suddenly caught him under the arms and dragged him out the door.

I stood for a few seconds, my face and body broadcasting my surprise to the world. I went back to the table, flexing my sore hand. Peggy was grinning. Then she laughed out loud.

"Shit and damn, girl." Her voice carried around the room. "Garrett usually has to hit him two or three times to put him down."

That received a laugh and a smattering of applause. I grabbed the pictures Peggy offered me and stuffed them in my bag. "Is everything around here such a drama?"

"Only if you're a Serova." Peggy laughed again.

Other sounds of amusement continued from my audience. Well, hell. I guess tribal heritage was impossible to escape.

When I walked out of the diner, I spotted Peter Serova standing by his black pick-up truck in the parking lot, only steps away. An older, rougher version of his three boys, he projected vast strength, and like Garrett, danger. Like Garrett, he stood apart from the world and the tribesmen around him. A powerful man, my biological father.

His dark hair had no gray. The lines on his face might have come from the sun. The deep brown of his skin agreed. He betrayed no emotion, not even curiosity.

"Good morning." I didn't know what else to say.

He nodded slightly. He kept his eyes on me, studying me. A car pulled in the lot. No way did I want an audience.

"Could we walk?" I turned, not waiting for an answer. He followed. I could feel his presence behind me. He had a towering aura, like the mountains around us. They might both be wolves, but Garrett carried the scent of the forest. My father carried the scent of the deep earth. I wondered what it would feel like to have that kind of strength myself, to project that aura of surety. Yes, I have extraordinary powers denied to what Darrell called regular people, but I'm so inept and afraid of the damage I might do.

There were picnic tables and benches behind the Rize and Shine, not completely out of view, but they offered a bit of privacy. The morning had rapidly burned away, but the leafy shade made a green canopy over us. I sat on a bench, and he sat beside me. He rested his elbows on his knees and stared at the ground. Then I was back to, *I don't know what to say.*

Thankfully, he started. His voice was deep, but smooth, unlike his rough appearance. That voice stirred a memory I couldn't quite grasp.

"I loved her. You look…"

"I look like my mother." I let out a sigh. I'd have to live with that for a while. "But I am not her. Please allow me to be different."

He turned to stare at me again, a hint of a smile on his face. It quickly faded. "It was my fault. Pissed, drunk, not looking. Not watching." Ah, the guilt. "I killed her. I lost you." He squeezed his hands into fists. "You were mine, my little Lissie. I thought you'd be okay. Left in the car. I was hurt, couldn't carry you. Who would take you?"

Not the question I'd expected, but one I would answer. "You were right to leave me. It would have been more dangerous if you tried to carry me. A desperate grieving man who had recently lost a little girl to illness took me. He admitted it was evil. He…they…Mom and Dad deeply loved me though, and I loved them. I've had a good life." I had to ask, if for no other reason than to shock him to discern a lie. "Did you go to California and murder them? My…parents? Because they took me away."

He jerked up straight. His stoic face flashed to astounded. "What? No. Garrett said he found you. Not who took you. Murdered?"

"Yes. And someone in Rize knows the truth, knows the murderer. I'm here to learn. And you must understand. Vengeance is mine alone. Law, tribe, family, nothing will come before that."

His face went through a series of complex

expressions I couldn't read. "Will you need help?"

Now that I truly hadn't expected. Garrett seemed to stand in my way and my father offered to help me. Well, to help his little Lissie.

"Help? They took me away. You aren't angry?"

He shook his head and stared at the ground again. I'd received an offer of help to avenge the murder of those who had grievously wronged *him*. True to my cause, I wasn't above using my new-found father—a stranger—to reach my goal.

"Thank you. Eventually, I will need help."

"Dain." Peter spoke with deliberate precision—and menace. "He says…you're his."

Breath hissed through my teeth. "No. I've made no commitment to Garrett Dain. We are, for a bizarre and mysterious reason, drawn together." I wanted to stamp my feet and shout in rage. "That doesn't mean I'll allow him to drop into my life and stake his claim. We have already had intense discussions. We will have more in the future. Garrett Dain is on the law, tribe, family list of things that will not stand between me and retribution for my mom and dad."

One side of his mouth twitched like he wanted to smile but didn't remember how. "It's dangerous here. Strange things happening. Too many people coming from outside, messing with shit. Dain's standing across the parking lot, now, watching." He didn't glance that way, but I could see his whole body tighten like he wanted to fight. "Bad blood between me and him. But I'm glad he's looking out for you. If you'd stayed with me, I would have protected…" He stopped. He slowly shook his head as if resigned to some inner truth. "No. It's best you went away. Even kidnapped."

"Someone told me that if I had stayed with you, I would not have lived past my sixth birthday without my mother. Is that true?"

He growled a little in his throat and gave his head a fierce shake. "I would never hurt you, Lissie. I'd most likely let you wander off and get eaten by a mountain lion or drown in the river. Neglect you like I did my boys. Let you be ruined running wild."

That reminded me. "Oh, yes. The boys. They're going to be angry with me. They came in the diner a while ago and demanded that I go with them. I chased them out. I hit one. I hope I didn't break his nose."

"Huh. You did that? Thought that was June. Told them to ask politely that you come talk to me. Fucked up mess."

"That's a good description of my life for the last year. Nothing is simple."

"Not if you're a Serova."

"Why did they smell so bad? The boys."

"They were working at the dairy. I called them. Asked them to talk to you. They should have cleaned up first. Will you come out to the farm? I know you can't call it home. But I need to tell you some things. Show you."

"Yes. I'll come. As soon as I can."

We stood and he gave me a phone number and simple directions on how to find him. He offered a hand to me. I accepted it. He held it and slid an arm around my shoulders so briefly I might have imagined that touch. "I'm glad you're here, Lissie. You were such a fiery little thing from the day you were born. My boys act tough, but they're more like Elaine inside. Morgan's smart as a fox, but thinks he has something to prove. Merritt? He follows Morgan. Randy's the only one with any sense. You were fierce." He stared straight at me. "You *are* fierce."

So, it was Morgan I took down and Merritt and Randy who dragged him out. And I'm fierce? Not exactly, but I was certainly moving in that direction.

When I'd come out of the diner, I'd removed my jacket and draped it over my arm. It dropped when he held me. Peter twisted and grabbed my wrist. He'd noticed my forearms. I'd worn a short-sleeved shirt because only Leslie had to cover them. He recognized the scars for what they were.

"Who?" His whole body drew up, prepared for action.

"Marisa Trent challenged me last year in my home. She changed shape mid-battle and chewed on me."

"You killed her?" He drew back, still holding my arm. Only curious, not surprised, or appalled.

"No. I was in Florida when she died. Too bad. I believe she knew who murdered Mom and Dad. I was looking forward to beating it out of her."

My father, the Serova sevishtå, smiled. Pride? Joy? Talk about a wolf grin. I wanted to be objective. I tried to be cool. His smile grew to a ferocious grin, and his eyes widened in obvious delight. Daddy was proud of his girl. I carried an odd warm feeling with me when I left him. Oh, I'd been proud when Dad praised me, but this…something new, something exciting. My world had just made another seismic shift. I'd made an emotional connection with my biological father. The brothers would come next.

Garrett was indeed standing by the parking lot. I glared at him before I went back into the diner to tell

Peggy I was okay. Garrett wouldn't be the only watcher.

I spent the rest of the day in my hotel room working. Phone calls to my lawyer, another to Danny who couldn't talk, but I assured him I was okay in Rize and how pretty and safe it was. Yeah, so people change into wolves occasionally. Big deal. It's not like they do it on Main Street every other day.

I dressed and left the hotel about six. I wore better gray slacks and a more feminine white blouse covered by a gray jacket. Did my hair, too. Ba'ran went in the jacket and the 9mm in my bag. I wandered toward the closed street where the pre-Solstice festivities were well underway. The vendors selling the usual art objects, soaps, candles, abounded. They were from different localities, mostly around the state. Friendly, yes, but I was a customer. Occasionally I'd come across tribe people. They immediately knew who I was. Some, the women, not the men, would speak. *I'm so and so. I knew your mother.* The men usually turned away, never making eye contact. One word drifted on the air as if spoken with profound reluctance.

Serova.

Chapter Twenty-Four

I'd walked to the end of the street and started back to the hotel when it happened. What do you call it? Premonition? No. A murmur felt rather than heard? Then a sound. The impact of flesh on flesh. No one else seemed to hear, truly I shouldn't have been able to with all the background noise. The need to follow the sound rose and urged me on.

How idiotic. Like the movie heroines, too stupid to live. I quickly walked away from the festival street and down an alley into the darkness. The shadows didn't last long. I emerged into a parking area behind a building. There were security lights, not bright, but enough to see the source of the sound that had summoned me.

Garrett and one of my brothers, the more volatile Morgan I presumed, faced each other. Garrett stood straight, Morgan wavered, side stepped, then charged at Garrett. Morgan was slinging his arms but when he reached Garrett, Garrett slammed a savage punch in the gut. Then he hit Morgan in the head and shoved him backward until he collapsed against a chain link fence. The other two boys rushed to his side. Garrett headed for the three like a charging bull. He wanted more, more action, more brutal battle.

No, that was wrong.

"Garrett! Stop!" I put every emotion I had into my voice, as if the sheer weight of my words would stop him. To my immense surprise, it did.

His head jerked up like a dog startled when chewing a bone. Garrett's hair was charmingly mussed, clothes in slight disarray, but no damage like his opponent. His breathtaking face, frozen in anger, was anything but angelic tonight. His eyes narrowed. He might have remembered the meat sack of a man he'd helped Maris hide. He had no proof that I was responsible.

No proof that I was not. He did know my capacity for chaos when agitated.

"You don't know what you're doing, Katrine. You're choosing sides too soon."

I marched up to him. "I wasn't aware there were *sides.*"

His angry eyes, shining like hammered gold, never left me. He nodded his head as if to agree with some unvoiced thought.

"I suppose blood calls to blood. Kith to kin." That was disgust no doubt. He stalked away, leaving me alone to comfort my newfound family of ruffians.

I went and knelt by Morgan. Blood leaked from his nose and mouth. Skinned, swollen knuckles held cuts and some blood, too. I lifted his head. Randy came and knelt beside me. He was a year younger than me, but he hunched over like a boy, utterly distraught, lost in the violence. He also had a large welt on the side of his face and a blooming black eye. Merritt wasn't much better. An eye swollen shut, he held his arm close to his body. Fine spatters of crimson decorated his shirt like drops of a bloody rain shower. Defeated. Three of them together couldn't take Garrett.

"Randy?" He was the least injured. "Will you get me some water?" I laid a hand on his shoulder. He nodded and rose, immediately accepting my command.

Morgan groaned. He jerked and struggled, then collapsed again.

I lifted and pushed until he was sitting up. Merritt propped him on the other side. It was hard to believe the pair was two years older than me. Randy returned with a bottle of water, and bless his heart, a handful of paper towels. I dampened the towels to carefully wash away the blood on Morgan's face. It had run into his dark hair and down his shirt. His dull, drugged looking eyes concerned me. He did sip some water but didn't speak.

"Do you have a car?" I asked Merritt.

"Truck. Over there." He nodded toward an old pickup not far away.

"Okay, let's get him up. He may have a concussion. He could use a few stitches and an x-ray. We can go to the clinic and let them check him." I nodded at Merritt. "You, too."

Morgan suddenly twisted slightly between us. "No. We don't go there." His words came out a little slurred. Concussion. "She'll come."

She? Randy and I lifted and supported Morgan as we walked to the truck. We wrestled him into the cab on the passenger side. He was semi-conscious at times. I didn't think I could force them to go to the clinic, much as I wanted too.

"Why the hell did he do that?" Randy demanded, as if I would know. I presumed he meant Garrett. "We weren't doing anything wrong. Not drunk or high. This time." His eyes focused on me. Accusation filled his voice. "I heard you belong to him, that wolf?" He laid a protective hand on Morgan's shoulder. "Morgan was pissed about that, too."

"I don't belong to anyone, Randy."

Merritt cleared his throat. "Should have expected it. Copeland house got broken into last night. You know how they are."

"Who are they, Merritt?" Now, this was a curious thing.

"Every time something goes missing, they blame us."

"Should they?"

He wouldn't meet my eyes. "Sometimes. Can't get jobs, and…"

"Shut up!" That was a slightly recovering Morgan.

Randy spoke up. "They're gonna talk now. You know they're watching. Her taking our side. Being family. She needs to know."

What's this?

Morgan on the passenger seat of the truck, me standing at the open door beside him, Randy and Merritt close, all inside personal space, yes, family, banding together to face adversity.

"Yeah." Merritt snapped the word. "Fuckers never say Serova without 'thieving' in front of it. Lock it up when there's a Serova around."

"And…are they wrong?" I had to force down the laughter that so wanted to bubble up in me. Oh, the absurd irony.

Merritt quickly glanced at his brothers. Then he shrugged and grinned. "No angels here."

Hell, and be damned. My tribal family, my brothers, were thieves like me—minus the sophistication and success. I would certainly fix that.

It made me feel better. "Okay, I'll admit your sister isn't an angel either. One day I'll tell you a few stories that will make the devil laugh." *And amuse the supernatural and existent goddess, whatever she was. She considered my past as training for my future.*

We were still gathered by the open door and Merritt reached and grabbed my hand.

"You look like…Mama." Oh hell, was he going to cry.

"Yes, I do. I can't change my looks, so you need to get used to it." Well, I could change, but I wouldn't. Morgan slumped. I had to insist. "He has a concussion. He needs a doctor."

The driver's side door flew open. A girl with long curly brown hair jumped in the truck. She fiercely wrapped Morgan in her arms. Merritt raced around, jumped in the driver's seat, and immediately started the engine. Randy hauled me out of the way and closed the door. The vehicle spun wheels on the pavement and raced away.

Three men came out of the darkness and stalked toward us, poised to fight. Randy, who was acting like a little boy only minutes ago, stood straight beside me. Just what I needed. More protection—or a comrade in arms. *My kin didn't go down easy.*

I'd had enough violence for the night, though. If attacked I would defend. I stood firm and projected a challenge. *Bring it on.* Back straight, feet apart, ready for battle. Randy did the same. My hand was on a now vibrating Ba'ran. I thought about a light show. It wanted blood. Such a malicious thing, that blade. With my brother beside me, I would fight.

The men glanced at each other. One drew a breath to speak…then stopped. They turned fast and left.

"Damn." Randy spoke with a bit of awe. "That's

wicked. You…how did you do…damn."

How did I do what? "Who were they?"

"Annalise Patton's dad. And his pals. That was her who got in the truck. Annalise likes Morgan too much. Won't stay away. She's the tribe's only healer, though. Too important to waste on a Serova. Morgan was just talking to her tonight, though. Nothin' else. She told Garrett she was twenty-four, and she could see who she wanted. Didn't make a difference. We did leave. He followed us. Don't know why. Maybe be sure we was gone."

Young girls did have crushes on bad boys. Bad boys wore a certain aura like charm. I'd had one for a biker when I was fifteen. But Garrett had made these bad boys his special project, to keep them from getting killed—he said. But he'd beat the hell out of them himself. Called them dogs. They may have deserved it, but something inside me objected. Maybe the huge hole left by Mom, Dad, and Rado.

"Randy, can you get home? I can drive you."

"No. Cousin lives a block away. He'll take me." Randy grabbed and held me tighter. He spoke in my ear. "Vîsâi, sister."

Vîsâi? Fenrir's habit of drawing and corrupting words from ancient languages into everyday tribal life confounded me as much as their convoluted methods of determining hierarchy. But I knew this one.

Welcome home, Sister. You're in time for the battle. My brothers, and my father, had accepted me. Morgan a little grudgingly. Did he see me as a threat? Too bad. He'd challenged me in the Rize and Shine. He'd lost. Marisa taught me that game.

When I went back to the street the shops and tents

were closing for the night. People stared, but I kept my eyes straight ahead—until Garrett fell into step beside me.

Chapter Twenty-Five

He walked close, his arm brushing mine occasionally. We didn't talk until we reached the front door of the hotel. I stopped outside and faced him. "Did you have to beat him like that?"

"Yes. Morgan anyway. He's smart, but it all goes away when he throws the first punch. He'd die fighting."

"What did Morgan do that he deserved such a beating? He had a concussion. You could have killed him."

"I told him to leave. That's all. Stupid shit. He challenged me. You know about challenges now, don't you? They're important. Have to be answered."

"You have that authority? To arbitrarily order people around? To beat them into submission if they don't obey."

"Yes. I'm part of the Council and I have that authority in the tribe. Serovas are the only ones who make me use force."

"Why did you tell him to leave? They were sober." He didn't answer.

I stopped and held up my arms to my chest, fists clenched, forearms out, scars flashing the world. "Answer me. I've earned admission to your precious tribe."

He caught my wrists and held them. "There's a girl. She's got a crush on Morgan. He keeps hanging around her. Her father…you don't understand family life here yet."

"Family life? Her father? How old is the girl? Is she underage? Was he stalking her? Don't tell me your precious law says women are property, chattel, subject to Daddy's authority?"

"No. It's about potential. She's a powerful healer, beginning to mature. It's like a man watches his genius daughter—a marvelous star—take up with a crackhead."

"And Serovas are—"

"An absolute waste of the best of the blood traits the tribe has had in a generation. And yes, I know it's not their fault. It's not your fault your parents took you and made you a thief."

I jerked my wrists out of his hands. "Your nobility and superiority disgust me. So, we should all be conformists? Lined up like soldiers following orders? God forbid…*Goddess* forbid someone should be a free thinker. Make their own choices. That's your problem, isn't it. The damned Serovas, they—we—won't lay down, roll over, and piss for you, will we?"

He didn't speak, so I went on. "Garrett, I remember you telling me in Senica that arguments here weren't settled in bloody battles. Civilized was the word you used. From what I've seen, and dealt with, your idea of civilization has a pretty thin veneer."

Garrett started to reach for me. He stopped. No, I wasn't to be touched right then.

"Garrett, you once said I was textbook Fenrir tribeswoman. That I took what I wanted. You didn't tell me I was a perfect Serova, too."

"No. Remembering you in that basement…I figured you'd find out eventually."

We stood there, close but not touching. My body ached for him. But he had told this world and everyone in it, that I was his. Claimed me. That I could not tolerate. I turned and hurried inside the hotel. Up the stairs, lock my door, and I was safe from temptation—for a while.

****

The white space surrounded me.

"You watching, goddess?"

"Yes. It's easier now that you're here, in one of my places."

"Pure soap opera, right."

"It would seem so, though I have more to keep up with than television."

"Do you just float around watching things, like a ghost?"

"That's an exciting concept, and would be wonderful, if it were so. Float around, independent, go where I wished. I can't explain the actuality or my limits any more than you can your powers. How do you push objects away from you? Can you explain?"

"No."

"I see that you've accepted your family. Never falter. Once you show your true power, the old wolf will follow you. He's a useful one to have on your side. If he commits, and I sense he will, you may trust him."

"Yeah, about that. He, Peter, tells a different story about me. Everyone, even you, paints him as an evil man who would have harmed me if I stayed with him. He personally admits that my leaving was best, but says he would have been neglectful, not abusive. What goes with that?"

"It is complex. He is correct that he would never deliberately harm you. But he can be violent and

malicious. His actions, not neglect, could have killed you. One action killed your mother. He's the kind of man upon seeing a hundred-dollar bill on a busy four-lane highway, would send his young daughter to retrieve his prize. Or take her to a bar fight and leave her to watch and hope he would win and take her home. I couldn't stop the accident, but I could feel the universe ready to mark you that day, set your appointed time far too soon. I rearranged things. More than ever, I know giving you to strangers was the right thing to do."

And eventually those strangers paid for her action with their lives. But there were the years of joy, of love. I needed to stop living in the goddess' dream world. Regardless of her connection to the tribal consciousness, I did not understand. Was she lying to manipulate us? She'd reminded me several times that she was not human. Which was truly terrifying, considering that she's asked me to form a permanent connection to her.

"Katrine?"

"Yes, goddess." Shit. Did she know what I was thinking?

"You need only walk away from this. It would be difficult, and a mistake, but you are strong."

Yep, mind reading was one of her powers.

"Would I escape, truly?"

"You are Tribe. As long as I exist, each of you who carries a part of me will be drawn together, recognizing and gravitating to your own kind. You could fight that need."

She wasn't finished.

"And the old wolf, your father. You have his heart, now. Guilt drives him, and you may, you must, use it any way you wish."

She was right, though I hated it. "Go away and let me rest."

She did so. I was caught and she knew. Garrett, Peggy, Peter, and the boys, all links in the chain that bound me to the tribe. Peter was an unexpected bonus, the sudden solution to a problem. I needed to put my plan in action.

****

I made another mistake the next morning at breakfast with Peggy. I told her I was going to see Peter. I received an explicit lecture on evil and how I should not go there alone. I gave one in return on how it was my business, my decision. Peggy shut up, but she left me alone for a few minutes and of course, called Garrett who met me at my car. Conspiracy, conspiracy, but he knew by now he couldn't stop me. He did give me warning not to stray from the precise roads. There were other *evil* Serovas living in the valley of my original home. He also asked for and received a kiss. Broad daylight, in the parking lot, I'd let him have that. Oh, what a mouth. How much longer could I hold out against what we both wanted?

Destin Road required a sharp turn off the highway and onto a narrow, paved road with crumbling edges. It immediately jogged to a switchback down a steep hill, a testament to a drunken roadbuilder. The tortured path morphed from broken asphalt to gravel and dirt a mile or so later. The BMW complained but didn't disappoint. The compass in the car moved with each twist, but I was most certainly heading down. My clear directions quickly turned to dubious suggestions. Mature fir trees, fragrant cedars, a cool green canopy surrounded me one moment, and next I drove by a rolling meadow of grass.

Sporadic forest breaks would give me an occasional peek at the mountains. Turn right beyond the single-lane wooden bridge, Peter had said, then take the left when you come to a fork.

Dumb luck, but I found the bridge. I slowed to stare at the world around me. Incomparable nature offered a scene of mystical beauty as sheets of shallow water burst and crashed over rocks that lined the creek. Less mystical and picturesque was the single lane, wooden structure to cross. The loose bridge boards gave hollow thumps as I passed.

Down the left fork and there it was. A house and two barns sitting in a field. Not an expert, but the field showed no sign of farming. The house, timeworn and squat, constructed of massive logs, had small windows and a long front porch. Forget the clean-scraped, uniform-size yellow logs of the pre-built and packaged cabins on today's market. Low to the ground, black with age, it embodied the solidity of fortress as well as a home.

Peter came out the front door when I climbed out of the car. The briefest of smiles touched his mouth. He held the door for me.

"Come in."

I walked up the steps. "Never been in a log house before. That I remember."

"It's one of the first built in Rize. 1890, 1891. Serovas, Dains, and Anexts were the original families here."

I had no expectations, but the inside of the house was clean, orderly, and homey, even if it had little natural light. Windows weren't so grand when you heat with a fireplace. Decidedly feminine objects, pictures, colorful small ceramics, decorated the large living room. Neat, dusted, but it all spoke to another generation. It spoke to my biological mother who seemed, I'm told, as if she did not belong among the wolves of Rize.

"This is nice." I felt I needed to say something.

"Yeah. It's like…it's like your mama left it. This room anyway. I made the boys build a place out in the barn years ago, so it wouldn't get messed up." He gazed around the room like he hadn't seen it in a while. "Not healthy my sister said. Holding on to the past. Sarah Jane, she's the smart sister. Educated anyway."

"For a while, in Senica, I pretended that if I changed nothing in the house, one day Mom and Dad would come home."

Another almost smile. "You want coffee?"

"Yes. Thank you."

He looked much as he had yesterday, dressed in jeans and a western shirt, but his movements, hands, eyes, had relaxed a bit. He was home and not on display.

"Come on in the kitchen." He turned abruptly and left me to follow.

The kitchen wasn't modern, but it was adequate and again, clean. I'd bet the boys' bachelor pad in the barn was atrocious.

"Sit there." He nodded at the table, one aged like the house, and scarred with years of use and abuse. I liked a table in the kitchen. Mom and I would sit at ours and… Stop, Katrine. Focus.

Peter poured two cups of midnight black coffee. "You want sugar? Got no milk." He set the cups on the table.

"No. Black's fine."

He sat and stared at his cup. A frown creased his

forehead, so I decided to start.

"I don't remember anything about my life here. Last year, I lost the only family I've ever known. That and other events have made me feel…vulnerable. Something I'm not used to. Mom and Dad taught me to be adventurous, to take chances. They taught me to figure the odds, not jump in without looking."

"But you did. You helped the boys. Last night. Strangers to you. Claimed them and stood up to Dain for them."

I had to forcibly unclench my teeth. "He had beaten Morgan, and he just kept hitting him."

Peter shook his head. "He has to. Not that I like Morgan getting hurt." He leaned forward. His intensity surprised me. "Morgan keeps challenging him. Stupid ass. He won't submit like he should."

"Why should he? Sorry, I'm a never surrender type myself."

"My mama is educated, too. *Stratified.* That's what she calls the tribe. Said it's a caste and sub-caste system. We're all equal under the law. But some of us are the warriors, the fighters. Some lead. Some follow. Lots of warriors in the Serovas—and the Dains."

His brows pinched together as he frowned. "Morgan leads his brothers, but he's not like you. He can't match you. He knows and won't admit it." He cocked his head, and the smile became more real. "He…they will follow you, Lissie. I knew that when you were small. You lead."

"And that's the role you think I should play?"

"No role. It's what you are."

I had to change the subject. "I know Garrett's put out the word that I belong to him. That he says it does not make it true." I sipped my coffee.

Peter chuckled softly. He allowed more genuine emotion to seep in with each passing minute. "I hate to say it, but it's true. Lissie, you're Fenrir. So is Dain. The Tribes…we…know when we meet our mate. If it wasn't so, you'd have rejected him long ago. Instead, you let him kiss you in front of everyone. Mama said that knowing is part of the…tribal consciousness. Because of the…"

"The goddess? Yes, I know about her. Too much about her."

He stared out the small window behind us, then went on. "Recognition draws us together. It keeps us together."

"Is Mama around? I could probably learn much from her."

He grinned at that. "You bet."

"And my own mother? I know it hurts you, but could I know a little about her?"

When he spoke, he sounded so troubled. "Elaine was…" He picked up his coffee. "Elaine was a good mother, a passionate wife. She'd defend you and the boys with her life. But she didn't have the will to do some things she needed to do. Oh, honey, I loved her. Knew it the minute I saw her. We belonged together. But she shouldn't have married a Serova. She wasn't strong enough." He smiled. "I bet you'd have been a trial for her."

"I would have. I had a few disturbing skills as a child. I'd been born with them. From what I've experienced, I'd have stood out even here, among family. If you consider your boys trouble…"

Morgan walked in the door, stark naked.

"Morgan!" Peter snapped the word at him.

"What?" He glanced up and saw me. A flash of confusion flashed over his face. Then it sank in.

I laughed.

For a few seconds, he appeared not to know how to react. He blinked, drew a breath, then mumbled "sorry" and walked out.

Peter sighed. "We are a household of men."

"Who change shape."

"Clothing is a nuisance at times. We know how to behave in town." He stared at the door. "Some of us anyway."

I had noted one thing. "He seemed hurt pretty bad last night. The girl…?"

Peter shook his head. "Annalise Patton. Her family's pissed. He's a sorry-ass Serova, and she's the first healer the tribe's had since 1901. She saves her healing for major illness, injury, kids. But Morgan? She'll heal him. She has to. He's hurt, and she feels. That hurt calls her. She can't help it. Like you and Garrett."

"The tribal mating dynamic again? The way Garrett can't seem to stop hovering over me."

"And you had to reject him at first, didn't you? Your mama did the same thing to me." The sorrow and longing on his face hurt me. "I had to chase her. Prove I was the man for her."

Use him, the goddess had said. His guilt for your mother. If he commits, you may trust him.

"Peter, Father, I wish this could wait, get better acquainted, but it can't. I'm driven. I cannot resist. I must act now. I must act for the tribe." I drew Ba'ran from its sheath. As usual, the rune lines had a golden glow. They twisted like tiny molten rivers across the blade. The gem on the hilt flashed once, subdued, not brilliant as it had in the past. It sensed it wasn't there to kill. "Do you know what this is?"

He stared, silent. He reached out a trembling uncertain hand, then drew it back. "It's Ba'ran. They taught us. In history. It's...real?"

"It's as real as the goddess." The glow rose, then faded. "I don't want any knife. I don't want this one. But it came to me. It is a fearsome thing I don't always control. That doesn't matter. I've accepted responsibility for its...my actions."

He nodded ever so slightly—his gaze locked on the knife.

"Do you believe in your goddess, Peter?" The red stone on Ba'ran flashed again.

This was a man who could change into a wolf. Whose sons could do the same. I would have thought such a thing would equal belief, but what if it didn't? The shape change he'd lived with all his life. But did he equate that with her? With her power? "I believe. What do you want from me, daughter?"

"I need you to listen to my story. I need you to believe. Believe in me. You offered to help. You may change your mind. I can't carry out part of my plan without you." I sheathed the blade. I told him my life story. As if someone slipped me a truth drug, I told of my childhood, my psychic powers both lost and retained. I spoke of my lifestyle, my ignoble occupation, and the family I had for so many years believed to be my own.

The theft of the icon in Seattle, murder and what came after, he would know all my mad existence—including his goddess and how she haunted my dreams.

"She said I could trust you."

He sat silent, absorbing words. I couldn't read him.

276

His voice deepened as he spoke.

"You…changed? Your face? I saw you. As Leslie."

What? That's what had the most impact on him? I'd misjudged how much the ability to shift shape dominated his life. I wouldn't ever turn wolf, but what I could do surprised him.

"I manipulated and molded my bone structure. Made tiny adjustments. That's all. It's not actually a true change. Changing personas, and character, that's in my training. That's mostly how I played Leslie. I don't feel it's quite the same as your shape shifting. According to the goddess, it's been a while since anyone in the tribe could do what I do."

Then I explained my plan and how and why I needed him to help me. "My scheme is dangerous. There's nothing in it for you. Except deep trouble. You only have my word that she told me to continue to pursue my desperate and selfish need to know who murdered my mom and dad. It's my deep, desperate guilt that I failed to protect them. I don't know if I have anything you might value, anything I can give you for your aid."

He held up his hand and silenced me. There was no hesitation when he asked, "I know how to help you. I will give you what you need. In your mother's name in the family's name, I will obey you in this. I see Ba'ran. It's the goddess' will. When do you want to go?"

No deliberation, no hesitation. Troubling, how easy it came.

"Tomorrow morning. While everyone is focused on the Solstice Celebration or sleeping off the celebration of the night before. Can you send the boys somewhere public, so they'll have an alibi? I doubt they'll question you. Me? I'll be in for suspicion because of my authentication job and the fact that certain people know I stole the icon in Seattle. I can deal with them."

He didn't ask why I came to him and not Garrett. I couldn't trust my own wolf to be a part of a scheme that was not his alone. Against his nature, his need to dominate his world. Soon, Garrett and I would have to settle in our roles, determine how—or if—we would proceed.

I gave him a chance to back out. "Peter, please, take tonight to consider what I've asked you to do. You've known me a day. And this crazy scheme of mine…it's against all your tribal rules. Just be sure."

"The rules were created by the goddess. When she spoke to you, helped you, it was above those words." He gave one sharp nod, then stood. "Come. I'll introduce you to the family."

So, I spent the rest of the day meeting the Serova clan. Mama Serova, my lovely grandmother, pronounced me too skinny. I sat in her kitchen, and we talked while she prepared a feast. She was, as Peter had said, an educated woman. While she remained guarded, I did learn a few things about Fenrir and what it means to be a Serova. They—we—have always caused trouble in Rize.

Peter had sent the boys out to round up my long-lost relatives. That afternoon I met multiple Serovas and associated kin. Didn't see any obvious evil personalities. No shifty eyed scoundrels materialized, though a few appeared a little dubious in nature.

My reception ran the gamut from suffocating hugs to a few sneers. If the scorners came too close, Peter growled, and they backed off. My brothers were ridiculously protective, always touching me, moving close around me. Even Morgan. An observant Mama

Serova quietly explained that it was in their wolf nature to touch a family sevishtå like that. It was a form of submission, and I should adapt. Wolf nature. Did I have that. Touching? I didn't like touching because of the unbidden visions that could shock me.

It was dark when I left. Randy rode with me to be sure I made it back to the hotel. Before we got into town, he had me pull over. He opened his door.

"Are you going to walk back?"

"No. Run. You keep my clothes until later?"

"Yes."

He laid his shirt across the front seat. The pants and boots quickly followed. He closed the door. I didn't watch him—but I felt it. Like a whisper in my mind, it washed over me. Fenrir. The connection of the Tribe? Or family? Blood kin. I was beginning to understand—and experience its pressure.

Chapter Twenty-Six

It was early evening and a fair bit of traffic rolled through town. Garrett waited for me to return from my family excursion. I felt him somewhere close. He stepped out of the shadow of a tree when I climbed out of the car.

"I'm here, safe and sound."

He gazed into the car and frowned.

"They're Randy's clothes. He rode with me to be sure I safely made it back into town."

He gave a long sigh.

"Garrett, I enjoyed a fascinating day, met a few interesting relatives, had food thrust at me every possible minute. I need to go let my system digest things." And I had plans for tomorrow that required rest that night.

He did smile then. He brushed my cheek with his fingers. I so wanted to ask him to come to my room, stay with me as he had in Portland. But it wasn't fair, not to him or me. I wasn't ready for that step in our relationship. He left me at the hotel's front door with a soft kiss.

I rose early. Breakfast with Peggy, then out with a vague explanation that I was going to Limbough. Peter waited for me on the front porch when I arrived at the log cabin. We parked the BMW in one of the barns and climbed in a truck much older than the black one he drove to town.

Peter had sent the boys to town with instructions to remain visible until late afternoon. I hadn't shown them Ba'ran, and Peter had told them nothing. He didn't warn them not to talk about us at all. They asked no questions.

I would have. But I was beginning to learn the sevishtå's role—or roles, since my father and Garrett had declared me a sevishtå too, in a complex and confusing way. None of the deceptive, dangerous, and illegal activities of my life had prepared me for immersion in a culture beyond anything I could have imagined.

Talk about roads where angels fear to tread. The truck, a real trooper, crawled across paths I'd have sworn a bicycle wouldn't go. An hour later I found myself on the side of a rock mountain staring at a black hole the size of a garbage can lid. Claustrophobic? Not me. But my tight places were ducts and pipes and crawl spaces. Straight edges measured to a sixteenth of an inch, none came close to jagged rock.

I'd stripped too, but I had a tear resistant funeral-black catsuit under my clothes. I'd had a *just in case* premonition, so I'd purchased it before I came to Rize. My flexible shoes wouldn't slip on anything—if I believed the advertisements. If I did slide into a rocky chasm, I'd be sure to give them a one star on the review. A small cheap backpack I did not buy locally went over my shoulders.

I glanced down at Peter, who had gone behind bushes to change shape. How utterly amazing. He was easily as massive as Garrett, and his coat was a surprising warm red brown. I wish my hair was that color instead of dishwater blonde that required bleach to create a good pale shade. I swallowed hard and said, "Let's go."

He quickly and easily disappeared into the maw of

the mountain beast. I dropped to my knees and followed him.

I crawled through the oppressive rock portal on my belly. The tiny passageway opened into a space as dark as the end of the universe. The rancid, appalling odor of animal musk filled my nose. Had I entered the earthy lair of an immense ogre, strewn with bones and offal?

Frozen, I lay there in the purest terror of my life. I'd sloshed through storm sewers of stagnant water and human waste. I couldn't move. Peter, sensing my distress, came to my rescue. He lay beside me and rested his head on my shoulder. Air exploded from my lungs.

"I'm okay. Okay. Yes, I am."

No, I wasn't, but I'd committed to this path, and I would go on. I pushed myself to my feet and turned on the flashlight. Peter whimpered. Too much for wolf eyes.

"Sorry." I dimmed the light. "Let's go."

He could obviously lead me in the dark, but I needed to see any obstacles I'd trip over, or low hanging rocks. I pushed on behind him. The rank air soon cleared. My hand trembled, and the soft flashlight beam danced and cast moving shadows that would become nightmare creatures if one gazed too long at a single place. I had entered a subterranean tomb, the mountain's cold heart.

He guided me through tunnels, around black holes and bottomless pits, stumbling over floors littered with fallen rocks. We walked through a chill hollow cavern not touched by the warmth of the outer world's sun in millions of years.

Then I felt her. It was not like the dream, the bright white space where she seemed so human. I laid my hand on a rock wall. It shivered and hummed with her presence, much as Ba'ran hummed with the desire for violence. The sheer magnitude of her existence in the rock here made me want to weep and flee in terror.

Goddess? Is that what she is? Ageless, terrifying, and by her own admission, *never human.* And she wanted me to belong to her, serve her. She'd said I'd have a choice. I'd choose her or some unnamed trauma to myself or someone I loved. Part of the rules she had to obey, she says. *Who made rules for someone with this magnitude of power?*

That thought drove me to my knees again. Peter immediately came back.

"I'm okay," I lied to him again. "You feel her here, don't you?" No wonder he required no proof of her existence. He, of course, said nothing. I forced myself to my feet to push on.

He stopped, and his head bumped the flashlight. I turned it off. Ah, light. Pale precious light. Now I listened. Nothing. He cautiously stepped forward. We went past a wall but remained in shadows. And there it was. The tableau of the Calx Icons. Garrett had returned the one he'd shown me so eight of the holy relics remained.

Light bulbs hanging from wires draped over outcroppings in the rock illuminated the room. I'd seen the electrical wires run through the outside cave opening in one of Aristide's photos. Nothing was secured to be permanent. I'd bet they got on their knees and begged forgiveness if they accidentally chipped a rock. I needed to check for cameras. Peter started forward, and I pulled him back. He stopped. I knelt and opened my backpack. I hadn't had time to give him details.

Rado and I had talked and agreed that technology was getting far ahead of our time-tested methods of avoiding detection. That didn't mean I couldn't learn to use a few gadgets. I followed each wire with the flashlight looking for cameras. Nothing. I'd purchased an expensive security camera detector to check for wireless cameras. Again, nothing. *Did they honestly believe that their goddess had the power to protect this room?* Remembering her presence deeper in the mountain, I'd bet she did. So why didn't she stop the theft of the two icons? That was the thing that troubled me most. She spouts drivel about her powerlessness and inability to communicate, but shit that shouldn't happen, does.

Since this theft could have deadly instead of mere financial and prison consequences, I would take no chances. Standard equipment in my backpack—black gloves, black mask. I draped myself completely in a long, hooded cape made of the thinnest metallic looking fabric. No clue what it might be. It weighed next to nothing. For an astronomical price, a colleague swore it would screw with cameras. Not invisible, but it would reflect in the lowest of light and hide my shape. Since I was tall, I could be a man or a woman. I asked him if he patented it and he said no, he was afraid the government would steal all his inventions. The man was a genuine genius. Unfortunately, I had promised the genius I'd destroy the magic cape when I finished.

I bent low and whispered in Peter's ear. "You stay here. I don't see cameras, but don't show yourself." He sat and stared at me. Message received? What did I know?

I walked to the tableau. I quickly picked up and slid the icons one at a time into a stiff cloth case I also carried. A padded slot for each one made a small bundle. Then I opened a plastic bag I'd carried and dusted the entire area with a strong scent blocker powder.

My former jobs should have been that fast and easy. All I had to do was crawl through a mountain's heart. I finished in a little over two minutes. I returned and quickly packed my backpack.

"I need a place to hide the icons where no one will find them. I'm not taking them out of the cave. That way we can tell the truth if someone asks if we stole them. We only moved them from one place to another."

An inadequate bit of rationalizing, Katrine.

I spread the rest of the scent suppressor around and behind us as we moved back into the darkness. I glanced back. Tiny whirl winds scoured the floor erasing our tracks and admirably spreading the suppressor.

Back inside the mountain we crossed a small stream that we hadn't crossed on the way in. Peter stuck his head in a niche in a rock wall. I carefully slid the cursed relics inside. Yes, I trusted him to know where he'd stashed them.

The trip back through the darkness was nowhere near as bad as the journey in. Still, I hoped I'd never have to go that way again. Peter went out the opening first. I waited for his signal that it was safe for me, that no one had discovered our little journey.

"Come," he called to me. He'd already changed and dressed.

I stripped off the catsuit and dressed. When we returned to the cabin, I tossed everything, including the backpack, into a hot fire Peter built for me. Years of successful thievery produced caution. It's a good thing I stood back. When the fire ate in the pack and hit the metallic cape it whooshed up like a jet airplane.

Dangerously flammable. *Thanks for warning me, genius.*

The entire journey had taken less than three hours.

Peter's phone rang. He listened. "I'll come." He closed the phone. "My boys. They make me proud. Occasionally. They're in jail. Been there since not long after they left here. You want to come? Be a Serova with us." Peter's eyes grew bright. Was it a trick of the light—or unshed tears.

Did I want to truly be family? Be Serova? Stand with Serova? To take sides as Garrett had said. *Nobody's perfect.* Was I a sham Katrine Dolinski or a true Lisa Marie Serova?

"Let's go. It should be interesting." Decision made. And Garrett? I was one step closer to knowing who killed Mom and Dad—I hoped. He could accept or leave, but… *goddess, please don't let him leave me. Let him love me the way I am.*

****

I parked at the hotel, quickly changed into a pale blue silk blouse and gray slacks. Professional, I thought. But the blouse's short sleeves again left my forearms and their vivid wolf bite marks visible. My battle scars.

The pleasant thing about Rize? All necessities from food to law enforcement were within three to four blocks. Better, you could talk to Sheriff Darby, pay your fines—or sit in a cell—all in the same multipurpose building. A simple brick box a block off the main street, it could have been a grocery store in a previous life. Large glass heavily tinted windows covered the front.

We walked into a labyrinth of bland, boring beige. Beige walls bled down to beige carpet and butted up against four-foot beige cubicle dividers. Tiny pops of color provided by the few employee's clothes certainly didn't break the curse of neutrality. Employees only filled half of the cubes.

With a high flat ceiling, any sound echoed back two-fold. There would be no secret whispers in this place. The jail cells were visible in the back through an open double door.

Sheriff Darby had his own office to the right. A sign proclaimed his domain, so he couldn't hide. I had to be careful around Darrell because Katrine had never met him. Not likely he would see Leslie in me, but now was not the time to take chances.

Peter walked up and silently handed the woman at the first desk a credit card. She immediately accepted it. Okay, he'd done this before. She scanned her computer screen, frowned, and handed the card back to Peter.

"No physical damage this time, Mr. Serova."

He blinked and glanced at me. Surprised? Apparently so. There were chairs to wait, but we went and stood quietly by the front windows. I leaned against him, barely touching, but feeling the importance of contact. Everyone in the room stared. My father, the infamous Serova family patriarch, and myself with my highly visible arm scars—yep, we were a picture. I even saw one phone pointed our way.

"What?" I nudged Peter. "You have a running account for damages?" I spoke softly, but given the emptiness of the now silent room, those who were interested would hear.

"Yes. Expensive brats. I keep hoping they'll mature one day." His brow wrinkled in a deep frown, but his voice carried a touch of humor.

Darrell's office door opened, and he and Garrett stepped out. Garrett's eyes focused on me and opened slightly in surprise. I glanced at Peter. He nodded. I could almost hear his voice.

You take the lead here.

Garrett didn't appear damaged, so maybe he hadn't beaten the boys too badly if he'd locked them up. I crossed my arms and stood directly in his path.

"What did they do? This time."

Darrell suddenly spoke up. "Mr. Patten called and complained. He said they were harassing his daughter. Asked me to pick them up. They didn't object." He waved his hands in front of his chest, so flustered and embarrassed I felt sorry for him. The sheep among wolves.

Peter grunted behind me. No clue what it meant.

My three wayward brothers strolled out the double doors leading to the cells. Rascal grins, easy sauntering gait, a stranger wouldn't know the two oldest were pushing thirty. No injuries this time. They stopped, close enough to us to talk, and each made it a point to brush up against me like puppies. Peter gave the tiniest of nods toward me. We were getting skillful at silent communication. *Oh, the evil things you could teach them, Katrine.*

The situation required a serious expression. "You didn't break anything? Or anyone?"

Morgan shook his head. "No. Not harassing. We was just talking. Sheriff came and we went along nice and peaceful."

Now I had a focus. Not outraged, but stern and in control. I locked on the weak link. "Tell me, Sheriff, is that all it takes to get locked up around here? Someone calls and says take them away? Do you have a hierarchy list?"

Darrell had told me—told Leslie—that he didn't deal with tribe, that he wasn't qualified. Obviously, there were exceptions.

"Katrine!" Garrett snapped the word at me, sharp, angry. "Stay out of this."

What? He gave me orders? How dare he. *Calm, Katrine. Be calm. Oh, shit no.*

"Stay out?" My voice rose to a controlled level of disdain. "Well, sir, I remember that a notable member of the Fenrir tribe invited me to come here to meet my family. I accepted the invitation. I've met my family. If I must—as you so graciously informed me—choose sides, I choose them. I choose those who do not feel the need to regulate my life." I turned to my brothers. "You guys hungry?"

"Oh, yeah." Morgan gave me a tooth flashing grin. "Locked us up right after breakfast."

"Perfect. I'm buying." I glanced at Peter. He was family sevishtå. I was merely a sevishtå member. I had to publicly acknowledge his authority. I had his permission to act. He'd offered me trust and family, even if it was via guilt. Peter nodded once, a quick bob of his head. His expression remained neutral as the beige room.

We went out and started laughing as soon as we hit the sidewalk. Me putting Garrett down was the best thing to happen to them in a while. We walked to the Rize Above Tavern where I first saw my father scraping my brothers off the sidewalk. To my surprise, the Tavern had excellent juicy burgers, grilled rare and smoky, and super crisp fries. I could see how it would be a rough place when the serious drinking started at night, but lunch was superb.

Morgan told us that he decided that since he had to

be public, he called Annalise and had her meet him at the Rize and Shine. They went there, making sure they asked June for permission to enter. They swore they were all *please and thank you* polite. She allowed it, probably because of Annalise. Of course, they'd just finished the meal when Darrell had arrived to take them in.

Morgan chuckled. "Boy, Annalise was pissed. She shredded Darrell."

Merritt, a cool actor, mimicked Darrell's humble demeanor. "Annalise got in his face, big time. So did June. Thought he might shit his pants."

But they quietly went with him and spent most of the day in jail.

I had to shake my head. "That's amazing. This place is confusing. Some jerk calls the sheriff—"

"Who is not tribe." Morgan said over a mouth full of burger. "That's a one time in a hundred. Annalise's father must have not been able to get hold of Garrett. And Garrett's gonna be pissed at you."

Randy's face lit up with a boyish grin. "He's going to have a lifetime of getting pissed at her ahead of him."

"You think so? Me and Garrett for a lifetime?" Their certainty amused me.

Randy shook his head. "Not think. I know. It's tribe, Lisa…Katrine…"

"Call me what you wish, Randy."

He nodded vigorously. "Well, you know we recognize each other. Anywhere, I'd know a Fenrir. And we recognize…bindings. Annalise and Morgan. You, Garrett, you're bound. You're fighting fate."

Wow! Remarkable relationship advice from my little brother. I was barely beginning to understand that tribal connection. I had so much to discover.

We talked and laughed, and I heard multiple stories about what a hellion I was as a two-year-old. I also heard their wordless sorrow. I managed to be compassionate, but I didn't remember her at all. I did, however, remember Peter's words for his wife. *"I loved her, but Elaine couldn't be Serova. She didn't have the strength or will."*

We left a little after one o'clock and we agreed to meet and attend the Solstice Festival that evening. They'd pick me up. Randy badgered me until I promised him I'd let him drive the BMW one day. Morgan and Merritt cared nothing about any mechanical vehicle, other than to know it would get them from place to place. I left them and walked back to the hotel, to my room, where I found the last thing I wanted to see. There on my bed, was a large box from Saks Fifth Avenue. The box I'd sent to my sculptor with instructions. Damn, damn. It was supposed to go to my office in Senica, so I could go pick it up. Why did he send it here? Why so soon? How did he know to send it here?

Hide! Fast!

Goddess? Her words flashed through my mind. What had it cost her to communicate like that? I tore the box open and among the designer clothes I'd sent with the box was my prize. A padded box with ten white stone icons, precisely carved to match the ten that belonged to the tribe. I'd sent the artist photos and asked the goddess to subliminally aid him, so they appeared perfect. Ten icons to fool Aristide, who would soon know someone had pilfered the originals from their sanctuary. Had she also subliminally given him this address along with coaching his art?

Chapter Twenty-Seven

Where could I…no, not in the room. I jerked the door open. The hallway was clear. I'd studied my surroundings when I arrived. I always looked for an alternate escape route in any new place. There. A small door by the elevator. *Please, goddess, don't let it be locked.* Again, the urgency hit me. *Hurry, hurry.*

The doorknob turned in my hand. A janitor's closet, one not frequently used. Up on a shelf, behind a box of floor cleaner, thick with dust. that no one had touched in years. Careful, disturb nothing. Best I could do.

I checked the hall and rushed back. I heard the elevator ding as I closed the door. A few minutes of silence then someone banged on the door.

"Police! Open up!" Shouts and more bangs.

I rushed to the door. I reached…it flew open. The edge smacked me in the face. Impact, a heavy thump. Brilliant flash, explosion of light…I flew back. On my ass. Oh, shit. Blind. Stunned, I couldn't see, function, focus. Rough hands flipped me over. On my stomach, massive weight on my spine…can't breathe, can't scream. Bedlam stomped around me with heavy feet.

Shouts…suffocating, push it off. Push and crush it into the floor above. Blind and immobilized…push Katrine.

The pressure eased. The pain stayed. I sucked in air as fast as I could. Not enough, not enough oxygen. Don't hyperventilate…shit. I choked, tasted blood. It drained out of my mouth and down my chin.

"Katrine?"

Who? Oh, Garrett. I heard him. It would be okay. Everything would be okay.

The pain intensified, my shoulders to my waist. My face? Warm liquid ran down my cheeks. I coughed. More blood. Almost blind seeing only a blur I struggled against the hands holding me.

"Be still, Katrine, please. He may have broken your back or ribs. Punctured a lung."

Garrett again. I tried to speak but the pain overtook me. It was too much. I could hear voices. Only far away.

Garrett? Yes. He shouted. First time I'd ever heard him do that. He roared. "I will tear you apart!" Oh, yes. He could do that. "Shut the fuck up, Isabell!"

Garrett spoke more of those words I should know but didn't.

"Get out of my way!" A furious rumbling voice vibrated in my ears. A voice with enough rage to kill with words alone. My pissed off bio-dad.

It all stopped. Time stopped—the world stopped. Then my body warmed as if I'd climbed into a soothing bath in the dead of winter. I could do nothing else. I gave into a welcome silent peace and slept.

I opened my eyes—was able to focus—on the face of a pretty girl. She had tightly curled mahogany brown hair and the oddest green eyes.

"Be quiet a moment." Oh, the sweetest voice. "Let me finish. Oh, goddess."

I wanted to speak, to say…something. No…I fell asleep again. I woke lying on the bed, filled with a deep weariness—but no pain.

Garrett sat beside me. His hand brushed my face, smoothing my hair back. I struggled to sit up, but hands pushed me back down, tried again…damn! Finally, I prevailed…sort of. With my head propped up on pillows. I'd had a drink of water, so I could talk.

Oh, shit. Too many people in the room. A crowd, a throng, a mob. Standing silent, what were they waiting on?

"What happened?" My voice sounded like a rasp across a piece of rough wood.

Garrett answered. "Harat kicked open your door. It hit you, knocked you down. He rolled you over and put his knee on your spine. He weighs 260. I thought he had…"

Garrett thought he'd broken my back. I remembered that.

"Peter sent Morgan for Annalise. She did… whatever healers do." Garrett nodded at one of the large comfortable chairs by the window. The pretty girl with the mahogany brown hair and green eyes sat there. She smiled at me. Her eyes shone bright like I was a special birthday present. The rest of her slumped in weariness, dark circles under her eyes. Morgan sat on the floor at her feet.

"Wait. Harat? Why did…?" Just in time I remembered that only Leslie had met Isabell and her bully. "Who's Harat."

Garrett made a small sound in his throat. "Forget him. Harat and I will meet and discuss things later."

Annalise stirred and whispered in Morgan's ear. He smiled, and I'd never seen a man so in love. Bound? Oh, yes. These two would not be separated in this life. She rose and came to the bed. Garrett relinquished his place, so she could sit.

I touched my face. Insignificant swelling and soreness.

She gently grasped my hand. "Rest, sister. The goddess. I felt her when I touched you. She's in you. She helped me. She showed me where, how, to heal. That never happened before." I saw something in her eyes and in her expression, that I had to stop immediately. What words could I use to tell this woman who helped me I wasn't what she thought I was? I made up something. Banal and clichéd words in a story or B movie dropped from my mouth.

"Annalise. Listen to me. She's in all of us. She doesn't want worship. Respect, that's enough."

"And who are you to say that?" That forbidding scrape of a voice came from the doorway. Isabell Anext still stood there. Her super white tunic that could double for a tent draped over her shoulders and massive breasts, then down to her feet. Leslie had seen her sitting behind a dais at the Council meeting but was paying more attention to Peggy at the time. Isabell was easily as big as June. Only June was solid muscle. *Remember, Katrine. You don't know her. That was Leslie.*

I glanced back at Annalise. "Who's the fat lady in the bathrobe?"

"Don't mind her." Annalise squeezed my hand.

Okay. Friends and foes. I had three unruly brothers, one Big Daddy Serova, and what? A pretty little faith healer who called me sister. And of course, I couldn't forget the manipulating, overprotective, big bad tribal enforcer—Mr. Dain—who always showed up *after* I got hurt. Not bad for my first two days in town. I didn't need to check the odds to know things would get worse.

"Okay, someone want to tell me *why* this happened?" I wasn't going to make it easy on them.

"We have a search warrant." Isabell announced with authority and more than a little pompous posturing.

"Let me see." I held out my hand.

A woman standing by the wall stepped forward and thrust a piece of paper toward me. Plain and timid as a five-foot schoolteacher in a class of six-foot delinquents, she hunched down. Her gaze darted back to the door where Isabell's massive body blocked the only escape route. I grabbed it with shaking hands. At least I could read the sparsely worded paragraphs of pure bullshit. I'd never seen a real search warrant, but I watch TV.

"This isn't legal. It doesn't say what you're looking for. You can't just go on a scavenger hunt. Where's the probable cause? The judge's signature. Where's his name, even."

Isabell huffed. "I am Chair of the Tribal Council and Priestess of the Goddess. I authorized the warrant. We are searching for stolen property you have in your possession."

Was this a battle I wanted to fight? If I didn't let them search it would look bad. I didn't need that. I started to rub my face, then remembered the damage. "Okay, search. But don't mess up my stuff. Then get out."

Isabell remained like a monolith at the doorway. She didn't move, and she hadn't exactly entered the room. How odd. Was she afraid of something?

Annalise helped me stand and sit in one of the chairs. *I appreciated it because Garrett had silently deserted me. How did he get past Isabell?* Peter stayed, as did Morgan and Annalise.

I stared at Isabell's flush face and those teensy coal black eyes stared back. Such bad timing. Someone must have noticed the missing icons soon after we lifted them and hidden them in the goddess' cave. Isabell, on the Council, knew about Garrett and my icon theft in Seattle. Either he or Marisa would have told them. Otherwise, she wouldn't have come to me first. I'd expected it to happen. I hadn't expected my package to arrive here and this soon. I caught Isabell staring at the visible scars on my arms. Did she know about Marisa's attack, too?

Annalise kissed me gently on the cheek, then she and Morgan left. Peter came to kneel beside my chair, ever vigilant, ever silent. I laid a hand on his shoulder and squeezed. My father, now my co-conspirator, how deeply we'd become involved in mere hours together.

The searchers, a man and the mousy woman, were careful. They kept glancing at me as if apologizing. The woman lingered over the Saks' box and the girly things inside. I froze for a second when she lifted one piece. She was wolf! Did she smell something odd? No, only closely observe a gorgeous feminine piece of clothing.

Only one thing in the room might have caused questions. The label on the box. It was not from Saks. If they checked delivery records, they would find it came from a man in New Mexico who had shipped it to the wrong address. Neither of them paid attention. Obviously uncomfortable, they hurried through.

Isabell stood silent, splitting her observation time between glaring at me and her minions. I froze again when they picked up the case that held my gun.

"Be careful. There's a gun in there. License is in my wallet. The blue bag over there on the floor."

Isabell perked up. *No way, bitch.* I'd checked the

laws, Rize, county, and state. I was legal.

The man opened the case, removed the 9mm, and laid it on the bed. I noticed my knife sheath at my side was empty. Ba'ran was gone. Of, course it was. Damned knife. The only thing that might give me credibility here went on vacation.

"Take the gun." Isabell snapped an order.

I stood, and Peter rose with me. I grabbed his arm for support. "No. You are not the police. You have no reason, no justification, to disarm me and confiscate my private property. If you consider it so important, go find a real judge, give probable cause, and get a real search warrant."

She lifted her nose higher in the air. "I am the Council. You are Tribe. I will take what I please."

"That's the way it works here? The Council can steal whatever they please from tribe members?" I glanced at Peter. "I thought we Serovas were the thieves."

Peter broke his silence. "Alleged thieves, daughter."

"Oops. Alleged. Right. Got it." I squeezed his arm again. Fatigue drained me.

Peter stared straight at Isabell. "The Law of the Tribe gives Council members great authority, Isabell Anext. It also warns them to use it with a hand soft as a sparrow's wing."

I'd say she whirled and marched away, but with her size she rotated and lumbered down the hall. The man laid the gun down with the rest of my stuff, then he and the woman hurried out.

Peter guided me to the bed and shoved my belongings out of the way. The gun he laid on the nightstand, obviously admiring it as he did. It was a nice piece. I'd give it to him when I finished here. I stretched out on the bed. Rest sounded fine to me. Then I would check my face. It hurt. Not as bad as when I first learned to rearrange it months ago, but it throbbed bone deep.

An older man with a toolbox arrived to fix the door where an asshole had kicked it open. He kept cautiously eyeing me. *The newcomer, Katrine, a.k.a. Lisa Marie, was the cause of holes in the walls of the hotel—and the community.* Tribe, regular people, all were curious—and suspicious. My family, the notorious Serovas, had accepted me. Everyone else was on guard. They were right to be. For all her talk of weakness, I'd felt the power of their goddess in the mountain. I was now a believer, if not a worshiper. *The flashy knife and I were the harbingers of that monstrous thing called change.*

I heard Peter say, "Rest. You must go with us tonight, even if we carry you."

What? I started to ask but dropped off too soon. I didn't dream. The next moment, as if no time had passed...

"Katrine? Lisa?"

What? Who was that? Someone touched my shoulder. I opened my eyes. Ah, yes. Randy, my youngest brother hovered over me. Of the three, he looked most like the photos of our mother.

"Pa said you should wake up. He wants me to take you to the tavern by 8:00."

"Oh. Okay."

Wow. My befuddled brain had kept me asleep during a changing of the guard inside my hotel room. Wonder what else had happened while I was out?

Randy touched me carefully as he helped me sit up on the edge of the bed. He wasn't as big as Merritt, Morgan, and Peter, but he had tension in his muscles that spoke to veiled strength. Regardless of his mild demeanor, he was a physically grown man.

I did feel better for my sleep. Not good, just better. I wore a shirt, stiff with dried blood. I cautiously fingered my nose. A bit of swelling left. Healer? The warmth I'd felt, that was the most truly magical thing that ever happened to me. All my childhood talents and adult skills couldn't surpass that power.

I made it to my feet on the first try. The more I moved the stronger I became. Randy hovered. "Randy, I know you want to help, but you need to move back."

"I'm afraid you'll fall." Yeah, that might happen.

He stood back, but not far, while I made it to the bathroom. I closed the door and shut him out.

First thing. The mirror. No. Shower first. Blood dried in my hair. Ick! After depleting a week's supply of warm water and applying half a bottle of shampoo, I finally felt clean.

The warning about the search was the first time the goddess had provided immediate personal help. Annalise said the goddess had given strength to heal me. I again suspected she had more power to manipulate things than she admitted. And of course, I didn't understand exactly what she wanted from me other than her, *be my servant* pronouncement. She seemed content to let me go on with my agenda for now, to find out who murdered Mom, Dad, and Rado, as if my goals were her goals.

I stared in the mirror. A leader? Me? Peter seemed quite willing to foist familial duties on me—and I'd as willingly accepted them. I'm not a virgin to the strange. I'd dealt with it all my life. I'd used odd tools in my elected occupation. Changing into a wolf—even if I could or wanted to—was a far less feasible or useful skill. The healing Annalise did? The *ultimate* beneficial use of whatever power the goddess bestowed upon these people. My people. If there were more like her in the past, they lost so much over time.

My bone structure line was flawless. I remembered how hard the edge of the door hit me. Brutal. The only visible sign? Spectacular blue-black racoon-masked eyes and a slight swelling on my cheek bone. I wrapped myself in a towel and cracked the door.

"Randy. Close your eyes or go outside."

"Okay. But I've seen…" He chuckled, and I caught a hint of mischievousness in his voice. "We get undressed all the time. Don't want to ruin clothes."

"Girl wolves undress in front of you, too?"

"Well, they do go behind a bush. But you're my sister."

"Eyes closed or go out. Only options here, brother." He gave me a honey-sweet, little boy smile that made me wonder why he didn't have a girl following him around like Morgan.

I quickly dressed in suitable jeans and a soft blouse embroidered with multi-colored flowers. It hung below my waist to my hips. Short sleeves again so everyone could see the scars. I'd earned them, I would flaunt them. The short, dyed platinum blonde hair curled a bit and could use work, but it would do. Katrine of the past had always preferred a light brown to blend in, but Katrine, new resident of Rize was a bit more prominent.

My strength held. High quality concealer went on the purple under my eyes. Countless times I'd wielded a brush and sponge to make myself someone else. And countless times the question hovered in my mind. *Who am I?*

Randy chuckled as he appraised me. "Oh, boy. You look great. Like you never had your face bashed. Or the shit squeezed out of you."

"Thank you, Randy." I received a compliment—I think.

Ba'ran had returned while I slept. The blouse covered the knife and sheath at my hip. I had a light jacket, too. I slipped on the messenger bag with the 9mm and secured it over my shoulder. I hadn't planned to use it but if violence found me again, I wanted all available resources.

The empty lobby was presided over by a middle-aged woman I'd never seen. Narrow-eyed and hostile, she stood behind the registration desk. Her gaze followed us across the room to the front door. Randy, shadowing me, didn't seem to notice—or he was accustomed to such unconcealed disapproval.

We walked four blocks to the tavern and passed closed shops and smiling people in festive summer clothes, headed toward the lakefront park where excitement rose for the Solstice festivities. The city promised entertainment along with the fireworks set to begin at eight minutes after midnight. I had briefly read about the calculations for the current year's exact moment in an almanac.

Flower filled baskets hung from the lamp posts. Summer had arrived. Temperate days, pleasantly cool evenings, Summer delivered what Spring promised.

A delicate pink light lingered to stain the sky above the peaks, but it was dark enough the lights had flickered to life. The only blemish on the perfect scene were cars parked everywhere they could be wedged in. Two businesses, a tire store and garage, and a dry cleaner, had someone standing guard and selling tickets for the privilege. The Summer Solstice Festival brought significant out-of-town money to fill the coffers of Rize. I made Randy step away for a few minutes and called Aristide. I needed to get my fake icons out of my possession, soon.

"Good evening." Aristide sounded disinterested. We'd agreed to use certain numbers and not speak names.

"You in Portland?"

"No. I'm near a certain mountain resort town."

"Now isn't that a coincidence." *Run, Katrine, run. Rado's voice shouted in my head. Run, run away!*

"I consider it a convenience, Katrine. You know I have business here."

This I hadn't expected. He was up to something. I had to go on, though.

"I have the items you requested."

"So soon?" Skeptical? Oh, yes. I would be, too.

"An unexpected opportunity arose. I'll call you when I'm ready. When I can get away…alone."

"Of course. Anytime. I don't sleep."

I'd expected to make a long trip to Portland, not have him come to me. Randy gave an audible sigh of relief when I returned. I wouldn't hijack his assignment to get me to a certain place at a certain time.

The Tavern reeked of beer, as if someone spilled a few gallons and made only a half-hearted effort to clean up. It hadn't been that way when I'd gone with them to eat lunch earlier. Unlike the Rize and Shine and most retail shops, tacky Solstice ornaments did not compete for attention with the beverage advertisements. Nothing drew the eye from shiny neon. No reminders to disturb the serious drinker, the outlier, who eschewed all communal merriment that didn't come via a beer mug.

Tribe people filled the bar and most of the tables. Yes, I could spot them now. Tension, invisible, but thick as a morning fog, made the air barely breathable. The men and women in the Rize Above Tavern conversed in subdued voices. *Kidnapped girl comes home. Was that it? Or something more sinister.* I'd give respectable odds that, as I had accepted my blood family, the tribe had classified me as another troublesome Serova. Randy laid a hand on my back and guided me toward a table in the corner. Peter, Morgan, and Merritt waited there. The chatter in the room resumed, but it still seemed too intense to be ordinary.

Peter sat with his back to the wall, dark and brooding. He gestured to a chair beside him. I noticed that neither he nor the boys had beer, only soft drinks. Their fingers touched but did not grip the full glasses before them.

Morgan spoke up. "Annalise said Harat had torn muscles in your shoulder joints and displaced discs in your back. If she hadn't been there…"

"I'm aware of what I owe her, Morgan. She's beautiful and kind. I haven't figured out what she's doing with you, though." I hadn't figured out how she managed to be close when I needed her, either. *Just another troubling coincidence.*

Morgan grinned like a man with a secret he was bursting to tell someone. "Oh, yeah. She says you…you're different. She said the goddess is strong in you."

"Is she talking about me? Spreading the *G* word about me?"

"No. Of course not. Why does it matter?" Peter spoke, his lips barely moved, his low deep voice pitched only at us.

"It matters because people might decide a Serova could have what Isabell Anext wants for herself. The ability to speak for the goddess." Peter's mouth twisted into a sneer. "When Harat hurt you, Garrett hit him to get him off you. He knocked him unconscious. When Harat woke, he issued a battle challenge to Garrett. *Â-ŷas morte*."

The words spun through my brain. *Damn these people*. They kept spouting words from different languages I'd struggled to translate and… "He's…no. Wait. *Morte? Death?* That's bullshit. And murder if it happens."

Peter shook his head. "Harat bypassed the law that requires a complaint and trial before the Council. A direct challenge to Garrett takes precedence over complaints. They'll fight until one gives in…or dies. No one's died in my memory, but the risk is there. One of the many brutal flaws in the law. And life in the Fenrir Tribe."

"When Marisa attacked me, Garrett said it wasn't supposed to happen."

Peter slowly shook his head. "No. It happens. He wants to change us. We need to change. He can't do it by himself."

I suppressed laughter. "So, you have a tribal law, written a few thousand years ago with help from a goddess, and official government law that theoretically supersedes that tribal law. And on occasions, both are ignored. Do I have that right?"

Morgan chuckled. "Welcome to Rize." He

mimicked the smug expression of an evil entity who has tricked the buxom blonde into going to the attic/basement to check out a funny noise.

"What's going to happen? They turn into wolves and fight?"

"No." Morgan shook his head. Harat can't shift, so Garrett must fight him as a man."

"Does Garrett have to kill him? When he wins, does he have to kill Harat?"

"He should." Peter's voice hardened. "To leave an enemy alive is dangerous."

Unless you cut his balls off and cripple him. Wait. Did I just think that? We sat in silence for a while. Then Randy chuckled, low and mocking. "So, you have the goddess on speed dial." Brothers were such annoying shits.

"It's not like that. It's complicated. Anyway, what's the plan? For tonight."

"No plan." Randy again. "We go see what happens."

Peter reached over and gripped my hand tight. "You are Fenrir. You were injured. Your mate issued a challenge on your behalf. You carry Ba'ran. The goddess—our goddess—speaks in your dreams. What are you, daughter?"

"I've asked myself that question many times. I'm Fenrir and Serova by birth. By a twist of fate, I'm a successful thief with millions hidden in overseas bank accounts. I have a flashing, teleporting knife that gives me lessons on how to kill. I have telekinetic power that I can't control." *Stop, Katrine, stop talking.* No, I had to go on. "And yes, I have a scheming, ineffectual, and possibly neurotic goddess who babbles in my sleep. So, you tell me. What am I?"

The Serova boys sat there open-mouthed.

A waitress approached. Peter rose and like puppets, we stood with him. Most of the tavern patrons had left while we talked.

Peter led us to his truck. No struggle over the shotgun position ensued. A given? It was mine. We didn't go far. He turned off the highway onto a rutted dirt road. The truck grumbled as he steered it deeper into the forest. We rolled through a funeral-black tunnel of trees and followed headlights that bleached the roadside from summer green to shadowed gray. No idea where we were, except that it couldn't be far from town.

Chapter Twenty-Eight

The forest parted and we entered a flat field where cars congregated, and probably others hidden in the darkness beyond immediate sight. The boys had fallen silent and as in the tavern, tension swelled. Peter purposely maneuvered and parked so the truck faced the exit. We climbed out, fell in line behind him, and walked into the night. The path we followed across the field was wide, and easily passable. We entered the forest again. Ahead, brilliant lights illuminated an empty circle, surrounded by trees. A hundred-fifty feet of flat packed earth, the circle stood as an arena by any standards. I could hear portable generators in the distance. Tribesmen and women gathered in groups around the edge. They spoke to each other in tense, hushed tones nothing more than a murmur of voices.

I spoke softly too. "Are all these people tribe?"

Morgan frowned. "Yes. Most Fenrir, but a few are from other tribes. They come because we have the best Solstice."

Ba'ran vibrated like a deep note on a bass drum. I laid my hand on the hilt under my shirt. Ah, mega balls of shit were going to fall like dirty hailstones. My weapons? A flashy knife prone to disappearing at odd times and the dubious ability to shove stuff away—and four strong men who obviously were not strangers to battle. Overkill, really, so I'd left my bag with the 9mm in the truck.

Where was Garrett? Ah, there he was. Barefoot, he'd stripped down to his jeans. That perfect face, hard sculpted body—it wasn't fair. When people saw us together, they would say, *"What does such a fantastic looking guy want with a plain skinny creature like her?"*

The answer came when his golden eyes found me. Instant connection. It hit me much like the power I called on to push things away. It hit me as it had in that Seattle basement when I first met him, and again in my front yard when he asked me to read him.

He came to us. The four Serovas beside me tensed, but he adopted a no aggressive posture as he came close. Garrett kept his eyes focused on me. Our disagreements stood unchanged, but we were bound together and had been for some time. All we had to do was live and learn how to deal with it. And hope for happiness or at least contentment along the way.

I moved closer to Garrett. I could smell the forest on him. Heady pine, deeper resinous conifers, all tranquil, waiting for the storm. The scent of human reigned over that, masculine, sweet, and salty, the intoxicating odor of desire. I couldn't hold out. I raised my hand and laid it on his bare chest. *Mine.* Before the tribe, before my Serova family, I claimed him.

The murmur of voices around us fell to silence.

I wanted to ask him not to fight. I didn't. I would allow him what he had been so reluctant to allow me. Freedom to act as he thought best, without interference.

He caught my hand and raised it to his lips. Ah, that smile. His eyes turned to Peter who was standing close. "I had intended to ask you to be *via bitîm*. But another has claimed that place."

Peter nodded. "She is worthy."

Via bitîm? Again, with the ancient words. Bitîm? That meant second. *Garrett's back-up was me.* This powerful man had acknowledged that I was a force of my own. Now all I had to do was not falter or fail in the face of what was sure to be pummeling violence. I suppressed a massive spike of fear. Not fear of what would happen to me. Fear of what I might do. I had no desire to kill again.

I had made sure my blouse covered Ba'ran. I wouldn't draw it until necessary. I also silently and facetiously ordered it not to do a light show—not yet. I had disregarded all Rado's caution about conflict. Fenrir appeared to be conflict defined. And I was Serova, not Dolinski. Once I found who killed them, had my revenge, Mom, Dad, and Rado would be beloved memories. I'd mourn them all my life. But I would remain Serova. Remain Fenrir.

Harat, also barefoot and wearing only jeans, stood across the clearing. Obscenely muscled, oozing intimidation, he broadcasted a threat with his actual presence. Beside him stood a tall lean man dressed in jeans and a leather vest. This one stood straight, silent, arms crossed…dangerous? Hard to say. He might have been attractive if he didn't have a face that looked often broken and poorly repaired. Was this Harat's back up? I glanced at Garrett.

He'd seen what I'd seen. "I don't know his name. Or his tribe. He's related to Isabel."

Garrett nodded to the path where Isabell strutted forward, projecting hate with every step. Ted Balcome was with her but appeared restless and apprehensive. Apprehensive hell, he looked like a man walking to the gallows. Terrified.

Isabell ceased her arrogant strut and waddled into the clearing.

"Come, Katrine," Garrett said as he stepped toward them. I followed him. Surly Harat and his unspecified second did the same. I wished I knew the exact role I should play.

"Isabell." Garrett acknowledged her. "This is not necessary. Tell Harat to withdraw. We can settle in other ways."

Harat's head jerked. He spit on the ground. "Coward."

Garrett relaxed. He'd resigned himself to battle. "What do you want, Isabell?"

Isabell's focus went to me. "You brought her here." She hiccupped a breath. "Marisa…"

"Katrine did not kill Marisa, Isabell." Garrett's voice carried sympathy. "Marisa made her own path. Now tell me what you want to end this farce. There is a challenge, but you and Ted have the authority to forbid such actions."

Her massive chest rose, arrogance, superiority encircled Isabell. "What do I want? I want you to respect the goddess. I am her priestess. Acknowledge me as such before the tribe."

"No, Isabell. You want power over the tribe. Over our lives. My respect for the goddess does not involve worship or bowing to a priestess. You're willing to risk lives for what you believe is superior rank. For prominence you haven't earned. Prominence you don't deserve since you're resorting to this travesty."

Isabell's eyes narrowed to black slits in her face.

A wolf howled in the forest. The mournful sound

echoed off the surrounding mountains.

Garrett spoke to Harat with resignation. "Katrine will stand as *via bitîm* for me if you insist on going through with this."

Harat made a grumbling sound in his throat. His head gave a slight jerk toward his shoulder. "Boker is mine." The man standing behind Harat chuckled low under his breath. Damn, I needed to know the scope of duties for a backup.

Garrett turned his attention to Ted Balcome. "Ted? Do you agree with this farce?"

Ted stared at Isabell.

"Ted agrees with me." Isabell snapped the words.

"So, the Tribal Council is worthless."

"The Council will be what it should be. Ruled by the goddess' chosen."

I didn't mean to speak. Didn't want to speak. The sound forced its way unbidden, out of my mouth. *"Ama âmruyê."*

Two words I didn't recognize, spoken not by my will, but clear and explicit.

Isabell jerked back like I'd slapped her face with a dead fish. It was a good show, but I'd have to speak to the bitch goddess about inserting words in my mouth. Especially since I hadn't officially agreed to serve her.

Garrett turned and we walked back to the side where Peter waited. I followed, and with significant effort, resisted the urge to glance back.

"What is my part here?" I had to know.

Garrett sounded grim. "The *via bitîm* stands guard to repel any interference with combatants. It's mostly ceremonial. They may not act unless attacked or they see a dishonorable action."

Peter focused on me. "Will you show the blade? You could end this. No one will stand against Ba'ran. The knives are not the worst, but we all know them."

I turned to Garrett for advice. He laid a hand on my shoulder. "I doubt Marisa spoke to anyone about the blade. She'd know Ba'ran gives you legitimacy. Use it as you see fit." He gave me a calculated raised eyebrow stare. "What does ama âmaruyê mean?"

"Those were not my words. Someone else spit them out of my mouth. Something about depravity or the lust for power, I think. I haven't memorized all the lines, yet."

Garrett winced. "I can take Harat. Without interference, I can take him. Everyone here knows that. Harat knows. I suspect they assume you make me vulnerable. That I will forfeit the battle to save you if they attack you. Which almost guarantees it will happen."

"And they knew I'd be here?"

"Yes. Peter made it clear that you were Serova when Harat hurt you. Since you were the aggrieved party, you should be here by right. And I suspect they planned this farce for that."

Okay. Fine. "I can deal, wolf. Remember that car door and watch your own ass."

Garrett glanced over his shoulder at his opponent, then back at me. "Defend yourself, Katrine. If you're attacked, use anything, Ba'ran or any power granted you by the goddess. Don't hesitate." He walked back into the ring. I stood on the edge to wait.

Harat stepped to the center at a slow deliberate pace. He shifted his weight from foot to foot in an odd, brazen dance. Grinning wide, he flashed his teeth.

Boker, his *via bitîm,* stood back to the edge as I did.

No bell, no words, no signal. The brawl began. Fast, fierce, two men collided in what might end as mortal combat. Brutal impact of flesh and bone, then the sharp intake of multiple breaths in the crowd. I am a non-violent person, or at least I was until I ran into the Fenrir bunch. Other than my defense in the park, I'd never struck anyone with any intent to injure. Only in the lessons Rado insisted I take had my hands or feet contacted a human body with force.

I knew one thing. I'm selfish. If necessary, I would cheat. That's the Dolinski in me. Tribe, goddess, or law, I would not let this man kill or cripple Garrett. I checked Ba'ran. Still there. No way to check on my push-power, but while erratic in force, it wouldn't let me down. Crush and cause a catastrophe, yes, but never disappoint.

Harat had started with a fist punch. Garrett dodged. He slapped—slapped, not slugged—Harat in the face. Harat's foot lashed out. A solid on Garrett's knee. Oh, shit. I remembered Marisa's knee, bent backward when I kicked her. Garrett was stronger. It didn't move him.

My hands squeezed into fists. A solid blow put Garrett down. He rolled away from Harat's feet. Harat jumped on top of him. Tried to jump. Garrett's foot shot up and hit Harat's face hard enough to send him staggering back. Garrett jumped to his feet.

No gloves, no referees, no shouts from watchers, only the thick heavy noise of battle.

Blows—fists on flesh. Ragged breaths, every sound amplified in the silence. The scuffle of feet across the dirt. Garrett always moving, Harat remaining stationary at times. Obviously less nimble, most of Harat's kicks went to Garrett's legs. The punches to the face, eyes, or temples. Mouth, nose, fists. Both men bled. Neither showed pain. Neither appeared tired. How long could this go on?

Horrified and engrossed, only when Ba'ran vibrated did I notice Boker, Harat's *via bitîm* approaching me. I don't know what he intended, but the determined expression on his face gave certain credence to the idea that it wasn't good. Ba'ran vibrated and whispered in my mind. *Free me. I will kill.*

I strained to give Boker a slight push back. I didn't know his intent, but I wanted to keep him away from me. I slapped at him, gently.

He jerked to a stop. Lost his footing and staggered back. He'd collided with an invisible wall. *Oh, sweet relief.* No major damage. Boker shook his head, confused. Then he lowered his head and charged toward me. I slapped again. It slowed him, but he plowed on, slinging his arms like swimming through something thick. I tightened up and he stopped. Then I pushed back. Oh, oh, mistake. And it was going so well. He flew backward fifteen feet toward the edge of the ring. Only he kind of…hung in the air for a few impossible seconds. He landed on his ass, legs spread, arms flailing. One quick glance told me that the men grappling in the center of the circle had paid no attention to us. Blood drenched Harat, but Garrett bled, too.

I went to Boker who sat like a kid who'd fallen off his bicycle. I kept my hand on Ba'ran as I knelt on one knee.

I slapped his face with an open palm. "Look at me!"

He did. His eyes wide and prominent, his lips quivered like a fish gasping for water, not air. "Boker, I don't know what they told you to do, but by the goddess, you know it's wrong." Isabell wasn't the only one who could use religion for control. I'd manipulated my own father to further my goals. I would not stop now.

He kept gaping. Pretty unnerving because I didn't know what he saw in me.

"Now, get up and go back to your place. Act and serve according to the goddess' law, *via bitîm.*"

I stood, turned my back on him and walked back. Peter waited there—his face as shocked as Boker's. When I turned back to Boker, he was, as I instructed, up staggering back to where he'd come from. He glanced over his shoulder at me every other step.

The combat in the center of the ring had slowed. Garrett had Harat pinned down. Harat was jammed down on his stomach with Garrett's knee on his spine. The position the ass had used on me earlier in the day. Garrett had Harat's right arm twisted behind his back. The odd twist of his other arm…acute, probably broken. Garrett had his fist raised to punch it into the back of his neck. Garrett had the strength to crush his spine. There were no cheers from the observers, no urging one strike or another. The only sound came as the pop and thunder of midnight fireworks began at the lake.

Please don't kill him, Garrett. Please, please. As you begged me, I beg you.

Garrett raised his head to stare at me for a long moment. Had he heard me? The light gave his golden eyes a dangerous gleam. Men would kill for countless reasons good, evil, or boredom. By his own tribal law, he could justifiably claim a life.

My bloody faced fighter gave me the briefest of smiles. Amused? What? At something in me. Or that were we so connected that he'd heard my thought, my silent plea. He released Harat and stood. Harat didn't move.

Garrett made four steps toward me and staggered. He straightened. He stopped and fell to one knee. Something was wrong. Confusion filled his face. He swiped his hand at his upper arm as if brushing an insect away. His muscles contracted as he forced his body up— and didn't make it. His eyes widened as they stared at me. "Run!"

Harat struggled to his feet. Garrett had hurt him, but...ah, he stood. He still had one good arm and the potential to kill.

Oh, hell no!

I dashed to Garrett. I drew Ba'ran and pointed it straight at Harat. The blade screamed in my mind. *Free me. Let me kill.* It flashed gold and the runes went molten. They cast glowing rune patterns in the air around us like a gigantic laser show. I stood between Garrett and Harat. Harat, covered with blood came on. An instant before I drew back to throw Ba'ran—to kill Harat— Boker, Harat's *via bitîm,* stepped in front of him. He grabbed and held the combatant he was supposed to protect with ease. And it did protect him. Because an eager Ba'ran, clutched in my hand, solid and trembling on my palm would kill the instant I relaxed. I wouldn't even have to throw.

Garrett, pale and shaky, had slightly recovered. I ran my free hand down his arm and found it. A needle. I plucked it out. So tiny, invisible at a distance, it seemed improbable that it could carry enough drug to kill him, but slow him down? Allow Harat to kill? Oh, yes.

Silence filled the clearing. I raised the needle to scan it. I didn't need to, but I wanted the watchers to know what had happened. Someone had cheated on Harat's behalf. I glanced over at Isabell. She glared, then rotated her massive body and shuffled away.

Peter and the boys surrounded us. Merritt and Randy steadied Garrett. Raised voices sounded behind me. I glanced over at Harat who faced off with his second. Boker stood firm. In the face of potent magic, he'd decided to stand with the law and take the appropriate action.

The sounds of people leaving came, then all lights blinked out.

It left me blind in the dark.

"Peter, I can't…"

He had my arm. "I'll lead you, Lissie."

Randy tried to ask a question. "How did you—"

"Shut up!" Peter again. "Talk later."

No one else spoke. It was a silent journey back to the clearing where Peter had parked the truck. One thing I noticed. The animosity between Garrett and my father and brothers had eased—for now at least.

"My car is over there." Garrett slightly slurred the words. "I'm okay now."

"No, you're not!" Peter and I spoke simultaneously.

"I'll drive." I wanted a few private words with Garrett.

Peter had to help him into his car. I quickly climbed in and started the engine. "Should we go to the clinic? What was in that needle? It might have a delayed action."

"No clinic." Garrett was adamant. I wouldn't change his mind.

"Okay, the hotel. I can dress your wounds."

"I'll heal." I barely heard the words.

I pushed for getting medical care. Again, he said no.

The hotel would have to do. Peter helped me get him upstairs. A silent empty lobby and a sign propped up on the registration desk by a phone said enough. *If you need service, please dial 001.*

We had to take a chance on the elevator I distrusted. Peter then left me with a semi-conscious man sprawled across a far too small bed. I cleaned his wounds, the ones I could reach, and he did come around, but immediately fell back asleep. I watched him for a time, then quietly left the room. I retrieved the imitation icons from their hiding place in the utility closet and went to my car. There would never be a better time.

When I made my living as a thief, I usually left the premises in the pre-dawn hours. Here, light would come, but the sun had to climb the mountains to show its face. It's usually the quietest time in any city, and Rize was no exception. It was cool enough I could wear my jacket and not look odd even though midnight had marked the first day of Summer.

I climbed in my car and called. Aristide answered on the first ring. "In my car, got the things, need directions."

"Leave town. I will guide you."

I glanced up at the window of the room where I'd left Garrett. I wanted this game over. I did not want him involved. It was mine. My mother, my father, my hurt, my guilt, my pain. All logic and reason I possessed told me to go back, stay with him. Love him. Even the goddess had placed little value on the icons. Instead, I followed Aristide's instructions and drove out of town. Not far, less than a mile then onto another single lane road cut into the side of a mountain. This was not one of those rutted dirt tracks that led to other summer homes.

Aristide wouldn't have dirt roads, of course.

The road ended at an imposing but oddly constructed frame house. I could see it all because of the dramatic triumph of electric lighting that fulfilled a paranoid Aristide's security concerns. If one were on the next mountain over, it would shine like an inexplicable, misconstrued lighthouse. Surely astronauts could see it from space.

The structure, a sharp-angled multi-storied box seemed to be attempting to climb a mountain. A respectable feat of engineering allowed it to remain perched there and not collapse in the valley below.

With one push, I could...stop, Katrine. Just stop.

A significant area flattened for parking had been created by digging, blasting, into the mountain itself. I parked the BMW facing out toward the road. I'd made a few dashed getaways before. I knew I wasn't going to get in with Ba'ran or a gun, so I left them in the car. Ba'ran made it through a metal detector in Portland, but it was unlikely that sophisticated hardware would be here. I'd be hand searched. Unreliable Ba'ran might or might not stay in the location I'd chosen. I pretended to stumble and left my keys under a small bush where I could snatch them on the way out. The door opened and I walked into a spacious foyer. Four bruisers in black suits surrounded me, hulking, pushing close. I enfolded the fake icon box in my arms and fought not to push back.

Chapter Twenty-Nine

"Aristide, if I drop these…"

The bruisers stopped pushing but remained in place.

"I told you to search her. Not crush her." Aristide rarely raised his voice. He communicated with the nuance of tone.

"Forgive me, Katrine, I am not comfortable in this place."

The gang moved back. One stepped up. I held onto my pack and raised my arms. He fingered me everywhere and searched my jacket pockets. Each touch was exact and professional. No lingering and no leering. He stepped back and said, "Knife sheath. Empty. The box?"

I carefully opened it and let him inspect the icons.

He stepped away.

Aristide stood behind him. Gun in hand. I raised an eyebrow.

"Aristide, I know security isn't prime here, but this is intense."

"There have been threats from people in this town. And stories. Strange stories. I'm told your newfound family has fully embraced you. *Serova*? Is that it? My adamant contact whispered when he said that name."

Serova? Oh, Aristide, you wouldn't believe what that name signified in this place.

I made one step forward. His guards tensed. "You're

not wrong to be vigilant. The cult of fanatics here is real and more lethal than you can imagine. But I've kept my part of our bargain. Now you keep yours."

He pocketed the gun. "Please. Come in."

I noticed that he'd dressed for the wilderness town of Rize. He wouldn't stoop to jeans, but his dress pants and a button shirt made him appear almost casual. The foyer opened to a large two-story living room with a massive wall of windows that would have a magnificent view when the sun finally rose above the mountains.

And the house? Wood walls, wood floors, and a behemoth stone fireplace that soared the two stories to the roof. That fireplace might be the thing that anchored every splinter of house to the mountain.

He led me upstairs to a balcony that overlooked the massive glass walled living room. The room we entered was, yep, wood paneled. His single white carved icon lay upon a large table—a wood table, of course.

"This place feels like a coffin, Aristide."

He chuckled. "Oh, you noticed, did you? I'm leaving shortly. I thought I could learn a few things if I came here occasionally. That did not happen. You apparently have had more success." He gestured at the table with the single icon. I'd had no firm plan when I came in. As a last resort, I'd get my hands on his icon and blast out the walls to get away. Everything depended on deception—and my skill with my hands. As a juvenile pickpocket, I had the advantage of size. I was eye level to the back pockets of most men, and I could easily peer into open handbags to lift my prizes. I'd grown but retained my skill and speed. I set the pack down on the table. I drew the fake icons out one at a time, carefully taking a few minutes to place them in the correct order.

Bending forward, the loose jacket fell around me.

Aristide watched, but he stood behind me.

I fumbled, almost dropped one of the pieces, caught it with both hands and drew it tight against me. At the same time, I switched his real icon for the matching fake and slid it in my inner pocket. When I finished, nine icons, all imitations carved by a skilled artist, guided by a goddess, lay on the table. I stood straight and flipped my hand toward the masterpieces.

He nodded, his eyes on me. "May I inspect them? Or would that offend you?"

"No. It would not offend me. I'm an authenticator. People pay me to tell them if the things they bought—or plan to buy—are genuine. Or remarkably often, counterfeits."

"Would you mind going downstairs while I examine them?" He held up a case with a CD. "I have what I promised you."

This would put the goddess inspired artist to the test. At least Aristide no longer had a real icon to compare them to. He was not an expert. He seemed relaxed, happy. Then why did unease suddenly fill me like a pool of dark water? Like any second, I'd drown.

No con was ever easy. I kept a neutral face and walked out. He closed the door behind me. On hyper alert, I eased down the stairs to the entrance foyer. So close, so terribly close. I touched my knife sheath. Wrathful Ba'ran had joined me, longing for blood. I had only the blade and the ability to create a directional, invisible explosion of pressure. I readied myself to do that.

The odd house construction made for two branching hallways and stairs down to a lower level by the entry way. Sounds drifted from the lower level. Then came the sound of a fist on flesh and bone. Once you hear that you remember it, always. The cry of pain came next.

Stop, Katrine. Don't interfere. In minutes, you could have what you need, what you've searched for. Why take a chance?

Another moan of pain, long and low, the sound of someone who had given up, and wanted to die. It could be a fight between the brutal men Aristide employed.

I knew better. Something powerful had led or dragged me here to this place, these people, my family. It had grabbed me when I touched the icon in that Seattle museum basement. It had brought me brutal, unbelievable sorrow, joy, love, and a sense of belonging I'd never thought I'd want or need. Either the goddess had more power than she led me to believe, or she'd drawn some emotion from me I'd never known existed.

I slipped down the dim stairwell, step-by-step with full knowledge that I'd have to risk my life to fight my way out. Ba'ran immediately sent me sensations of joy and longing. All I had to do was set it free, let it kill. When I reached the bottom, at least I could observe unnoticed.

Oh, no.

Maris Balcome lay on the floor, trussed, arms behind his back. Shirtless, his face and body were bloody as raw meat. Two men stood not far away, bickering. And Maris, oh, goddess, his blood smeared the floor where they'd dragged him. His face, eyes swelled shut, and thick red drops fell from his lips. How long had they been mauling him like wild animals?

No mercy, Katrine. No mercy. Premeditated murder did not allow leniency. Peggy's image came to me. Her love for her only child even with his atrocious behavior. Unconditional love. I'd had that my whole life. I could save Maris or crawl silently up the stairs. I made the decision. Oddly enough, it wasn't that hard.

A long row of windows stretched across the wall. Certainly not as impressive as upstairs, but windows broke easier than walls when you slammed bodies through them. I drew all my will and gave it the preternatural Push.

The standing men flew out with the window. With the window, not through. The entire wall blasted out, flying in one piece. Flat, it winged out and glided like a frisbee, far down the mountain. At first it made remarkably little noise, as if I'd cut out a piece of paper with scissors. That didn't last.

The massive glass wall of windows upstairs, losing the support of the wall below, shattered like a giant mirror. It sent vicious broken shards down and through the trees. The whole house creaked and then screamed like an amplified saw blade. Snap, pop, timbers broke in rhythm. In minutes it would collapse.

I raced down. Ba'ran cut Maris' bindings like threads, but that was a minor problem.

"Maris, get up!" I pulled at his arm. Damn. I could *create a disaster* with a Push, but I *remained a disaster* when it came to lifting and pulling.

Maris struggled. Peggy's boy had a little fight left in him. It seemed forever, but with my help, he made it to his feet. His blood soaked my clothes. With his arm around my shoulders, we staggered to the stairs. He missed the first step and dragged us both down. Try again. Where was everyone? If they had any sense they'd be running away as fast as they could.

Okay, up the stairs one step at a time. We'd just gotten out of sight when I heard voices shouting below. They'd entered the room behind us a separate way. When they followed the blood trail Maris had left behind him…I readied myself to push again. Another one like the last would bring the two floors overhead down on us. I had no doubt I'd destroyed the entire structure.

More yelling went on behind us. I could only get bits and pieces, but one of the men who went out the window was clinging to something to keep from falling. The others rushed to rescue him. It would keep them busy.

Maris moaned low and deep in my ear with each step. At least he could cling to a stair rail to take the pressure off me. Blood oozed from his wounds, not gushing, but it needed to stop if he was going to live. A few more agonizing steps. The house thumped. It dropped a few inches. We had to get out.

Finally, at the top, I could see the front door. I couldn't bother with lock or key. Pow, I blasted it out into the parking area. Flat and airborne, it made a first-class flight. I hauled Maris over the threshold and grabbed my keys from the bush where I'd stored them.

"Come on, Maris, another hundred feet. Think of Peggy crying over your grave."

He gave a sob, followed by an uh, uh sound low in his throat. He punctuated it with an occasional gasp. He left bloody foot smears on the parking lot asphalt with each step.

Shouting came from the house—and the sound of more splintering wood. At least they were busy. At last. The car. I opened the back door and unceremoniously shoved Maris in. He cried out as I folded his legs at the knee to shut the door. I'd apologize later.

Okay, around the car to the driver's seat.

"Katrine!" Aristide shouted at me from the house. He rushed out the doorway and hurried to an SUV that was already running. He carried a package in his arms. The icons I presumed. I stupidly turned toward him. Then the most remarkable things happened.

This time, it mimicked the movies. Slow motion. One of Aristide's seriously armed thugs stood twenty feet away. His gun? Massive. And pointed straight at me. He pulled the trigger.

A sledgehammer hit me in the chest. It didn't hurt. It forced all the air out of my lungs. I flew back...I don't know how far. I landed and rolled onto my side by the wheel of my car. I saw two things in the seconds before darkness closed in. A big black wolf flashed before me. Airborne, his jaws closed on the gunman's throat. A fantastic red fountain shot everywhere. Then the wolf was suddenly a man running toward me. A car rolled by. I glanced up and saw Aristide's shocked face peering from an open window. He'd seen the wolf and the man.

Surprise, surprise.

Darkness closed in. My last thought? *Oh, hell. Not again.*

I woke to a brilliant light. I immediately knew I wasn't dead because absolute agony shrieked through me. Crushing weight on my chest...air...I needed...

"Take deep breaths." A disembodied voice ordered.

Breaths...I couldn't...one gasp. I could feel the tube on my nose. Oxygen. Oh, to be able to scream. Panic, people holding me...black out again. The next time...enormous waves of pain throbbed in my chest. I could breathe—and choke. I tried to open my eyes. Nope. They were stuck together. A cool damp cloth blotted them. Okay, open this time. No focus. Just blurs.

Garrett stood over me. I could smell him. I could feel others in the room.

"Water." I mouthed the word. No words came out.

Every breath felt like knives sticking in my lungs. I don't know how much time passed. It seemed so long, gasping for breath, and crying. Finally, I could talk, sort of—after they brought me water. I demanded that they raise the head of the bed. Lying flat was panic inducing trauma.

Garrett and Annalise stood close. Peter and the boys leaned against the wall.

Okay, a frog croak was better than nothing but... "Maris. Help Maris?"

Annalise spoke softly. "He's in the hospital in Limbough. I was there when they brought him in. I helped as much as I could. I must be careful when I'm not around tribe. He'll live, but it's bad. It will take time. I did a little work on you, but if you need..."

"No." I lied. My voice had cleared a little. She didn't say it, but healing took a toll on her. "I'll be okay."

Annalise's sweet smile brightened the room. "Maris told me what you did for him. You saved his life."

"Which wouldn't have been in danger if he'd listened to me." Oh, oh, the voice of pissed off Garrett. "And that fucker shot you. I saw...I couldn't reach him in time."

"Garrett. I'm alive. I did what I had to do."

"Katrine." Garrett let loose a thick shuddering breath. "You stopped breathing. Your heart...I did CPR for...I don't know how long. Annalise wasn't there. You..." He turned and stepped to the window to stare outside. Yep, the big bad wolf had to regain control before he broke down in front of everyone. The big bad wolf who loved me.

Then the fun started. An ear-splitting screech raked our ears. And that voice like a food processor grinding rocks. "I told you she's a thief. It was in her coat. Damned Serovas!"

White robed Isabell Anext burst into the room, flapping an icon in one hand and Ba'ran in the other. Stupid woman had wrapped my jacket around the hilt. As if that would stop Ba'ran from killing her. "I told you! You didn't believe me."

Oh, hell. All I wanted was pain pills and to rest. Goddess give me strength. I didn't—couldn't—shout.

Somebody, Peter I think, did it for me.

"Shut up, Isabell!"

Silence. Absolute. Wow!

They could hear me in the ensuing silence. "Isabell, put Ba'ran down before it hurts you." My voice still came out like a frog croak. "It hasn't killed anyone recently and it gets cranky without blood."

She dropped icon, blade, and jacket on my bed and snatched her hands away.

Pain aside, I had to do this. "Okay. Here's what happened."

It took a while. Between sips of water and a little whimpering, I lied. At least to Isabell. The others knew more—and less. "I had a plan. I had to get the stolen icon that Aristide had in his possession." It was all about the icon. I said nothing about my deal for information. "I had fake icons made. I had to steal the real icons from the cave so Aristide would get the news and believe I'd stolen them for him. It had to be credible. When Aristide accepted my fakes, I stole the real one back. Peter will get the other eight originals for you, Isabell. They never left the cave. I still don't know the location of the tenth. But if you spread that story and Aristide realizes he's been duped, more trouble will come."

"You were shot. In the chest." Isabell had recovered and, of course, was suspicious. Yeah, I would be, too. My story was full of holes. My chest should have one too.

They'd removed my blouse and bra and dressed me in one of those gowns that opened in the back. I didn't want to flash everyone, but this was too trite, too coincidental, too B-movie drama. It couldn't be real. I lifted the gown to expose my chest. There it was, the five-inch square of small cuts and massive bruises where the icon in my coat pocket dug into my chest as it deflected a bullet. I dropped the gown. I stared around at the wide-eyed spectators.

"You had broken ribs." Annalise's voice came soft, clear and with a bit of pride. "I fixed them."

I picked up the icon Isabell had dropped on my bed. "What the hell are these damned things made of?" Indestructible. That's what Garrett had said when he handed me one of the original icons. Hard to believe, but the square white tile had indeed survived a powerful bullet. I tossed it away. I never wanted to touch one like that again.

Isabell cleared her throat. She did speak softer. "Bones. The icons are made of the Goddess' bones. When she gave up her body."

I'd screwed myself by helping Maris. For now. I wouldn't give up my hunt, but it would wait. I shoved the sheet covering me down. They hadn't removed my jeans at least, but Maris' blood streaked them, and I'd have to throw them away.

Garrett was staring out the window, not looking at me. Everyone suddenly decided they needed to leave. Isabell took the icon and gave Peter a furious look that should have raked the skin off his body or snatched out all his wolf hair. But this was Peter. He ignored her. To me, Peter said, "You know this isn't over, don't you?"

"No. Wait. Why?"

Garrett answered. "Because your hair remains blonde."

Oh, yes. He'd asked me once before if my hair had turned white. I had no idea what that was about. Everyone left the room and Garrett came to my side. Now I had to pay the true price for my actions.

"You trusted Peter, a stranger, not me, to help you with the icons." Garrett's voice was soft but carried all the hurt in the world. "You left me asleep. If Peter hadn't been watching the hotel…"

Anything I said would be an excuse. "After Portland, when you offered to restrain me, I couldn't be sure of you. And I didn't want you to pay for any of my actions if I failed."

My chest still throbbed like a giant toothache. "Garrett, you've tried to push, shove, and manipulate me ever since I met you. Despite that, I've thought of you, dreamed of you. I claimed you before the tribe as mine— as you claimed me. I want you so much." I fought bitter tears. "You trusted me when you fought Harat, yes, but I still don't know if I can trust you to let me live life, make necessary decisions. I don't know if there's an answer for us. If we can't be partners, we can't be anything."

He left the room without a word.

Cry later, Katrine, cry later.

I had a needle in my arm hooked to a hanging bag of fluid. It came out easily. I didn't feel it over the deep lingering pain in my chest. My jacket still lay on the bed. No blouse but it would cover me. After several painful attempts, I pulled it on. They'd taken my belt and sheath, so I had to shove Ba'ran in a pocket.

The clinic wasn't a hospital, so I had no problem sneaking out. Just trouble walking. Something was wrong. Did I have a head injury? One step forward, two sideways. My chest protested, lancing me with sharp, immediate spears of pain with each breath. Wait? Where was my car? My keys? My bag? I gripped Ba'ran, my murderous true companion. The hotel. I'd go to the hotel and make them let me in my room. Each breath seared my throat and lungs.

What time was it? Early evening. Where had the day gone? The world I could see fogged up like a bathroom mirror. I stopped by a patch of green grass. It looked so comfortable. I could lie down and rest there, couldn't I? Just a few minutes.

"Ms. Serova?" A nervous male voice came from behind me.

I slowly turned around. "Sheriff Darby." Such a soft mushy man. He wobbled a bit, but I could see him. "It's okay. Sure. It's…I'm okay."

"No, ma'am. You're not. You're going to fall or get hit by a car."

Strong arms caught and lifted me. Garrett.

"No!" The word came out like a gasp. I hit him with my hand. It barely brushed his chest.

"You can't walk, Katrine. They gave you heavy pain meds in your IV earlier. I'm taking you home."

"Where is home?"

"Home is wherever you are, my love."

"Home is…" I finally said the words, the right words this time. "I love you, wolf. I'll try to be what you want. I promise. I'll try. I will."

"Then you wouldn't be Katrine. Or Serova."

Blessed be the opiate gods. I fell asleep.

****

I woke once, lying next to a big warm male body. He smelled right, so all the world was okay. The bed felt too big to be the hotel. Pain? Still there, but not so bad. I dropped off again.

Next time I opened my eyes light blasted through the windows. To my surprise—and irritation—the goddess had not interrupted my sleep. I wanted to have a few words with her. Maybe it was the drugs. Or she's a coward. Where was I? Wherever, it had log walls. Clean new straight-cut log walls, not dark ancient trees like Peter's place. King-sized bed. Empty, except for me. I stretched. No super pain. More of a deep ache. Someone had undressed and redressed me. A T-shirt, no underwear. I stood on the first try. It hurt, but I'd survive. I walked to the window. The deep forest surrounded the place as far as I could see.

"Home is wherever you are," he'd said.

And I'd told him I loved him. The deep longing to be with him, to make love to him came stronger with the words. Share our days and nights together. I would die for him because I suddenly couldn't imagine a world without him. Garrett, in his expensive lawyer's suit and silky voice. Garrett at his bare-chested best, pounding the hell out of an opponent. Garrett the great black wolf rubbing his fur against me. Yes, it was him.

"What are you thinking?" I turned at the sound of

his voice. He stood in the doorway, as bare as when I'd first set eyes on him. Oh, such a sight.

"I was wondering if I could make myself think of *you* before I act. Make you complicit in every disaster."

He winced. "You anticipate disaster? If you talk to me, trust me, I swear by the goddess I will never try to stop you. I may scream and rage. I may go with you, follow you, and yes, be complicit."

"Garrett, If I don't tell you something, it might not be a matter of trust. I act before I think. I've lived my whole life making decisions on my own."

"But if you marry me, we will be together more. Have better communication."

He stepped in and gathered me in his arms.

"Where are we?" I leaned against him. Such a lean hard man.

"In a house on the mountainside over town. Mom and Dad built this place for retirement then decided it was too close to Rize. I live here now. They moved to Florida."

"Ah, I've been there." Good memories for me. "The beach is pleasant. No ice. No snow."

"Yes, Katrine, and no bloody battles over ancient law, hierarchy, or who marries whom." He rubbed his face against mine. "You left me at the hotel. Had duplicated icons made, took a dangerous chance, just to retrieve one original? For me? For the tribe?"

I had to laugh. "No. You're giving me too much credit. I'm so far from that altruistic. Aristide said he would tell me who killed Mom and Dad if I got him the eight in the cave. Retrieving one true icon he had was a bonus."

He rubbed his hand down my back. "And did he?

Give you the information?"

"No."

"Because of Maris? You took the time to save
Maris. And destroy a house."

"Yes. I'm a thief, Garrett. By nature and nurture, an
immoral, scheming, lying Dolinski/Serova. Mom and
Dad are dead. Peggy is alive. Maris is alive. I couldn't
leave him to Aristide. I'll have to find another way for
Mom and Dad."

I stripped off the T-shirt. He kissed me and the
connection I'd first felt the night we met and standing on
the sidewalk in Senica exploded through. Oh, we'd fight.
Growl and throw words of rage. He wrapped his arms
around me, and I knew what I had. My mate, my life. His
lips skimmed along my throat. I relaxed and molded my
body to his...oh, that body. He was so flawless he could
have stepped out of a romance magazine, and I
was...Katrine. Too thin, not beautiful, flawed in so many
ways. His hands cupped my breasts. Adequate. Right?
He moaned and locked his lips on and...adequate was
okay.

The bed, we made it to the enormous soft bed.
Breathless, no words, only sensations. His mouth, his
hands on me. My hands had held diamonds and other
priceless shining jewels, I'd clutched incomparable
objects that whispered of ancient times. I had creeped in
and crawled through museums, mansions to pilfer the
most exquisite possessions. Now this most precious of
all things had come to me. I had no trouble letting my
stolen goods go. This was mine. I'd keep it as long as we
lived.

Chapter Thirty

Garrett and I sat in the kitchen waiting for my jeans to dry. The square imprinted on my chest had bloomed magnificently around the edges. It hurt, but not as much.

We were going to go into Rize to get my belongings and car from the hotel. A gourmet lunch at the Rize and Shine was also on the to-do list. My phone rang. Garrett picked it up from the counter and handed it to me. Answer it or not? I didn't recognize the number. What the hell?

"Hello."

"Katrine?"

"Aristide."

Silence, then. "I saw…" he cleared his throat. When he spoke again, the old Aristide came out—sort of. "Our bargain was not complete, my dear. You brought what I wanted, but you—"

"Decided I wanted something else." No accusations yet about the fake icons. I started to say *sorry I broke your house,* but he would never believe that catastrophe was my doing.

"I saw…" He stopped. "I saw a wall blown out of my house without explosives. The front door. I saw…wolves. I saw a wolf tear out a man's throat then turn human."

"Oh my God! How amazing. Did you also see bloody Maris Balcome crying agony? Did you see your man shoot me?" I wanted to swap stories. "I don't know anything about a wall. Wolf tear out a man's throat? Change to a man? You haven't been reading paranormal romance novels, have you? No telling what that might do to a sharp brain like yours." I glanced at Garrett. He smiled. No, there were no bodies. And no concern from Aristide about his men.

"I didn't see anything, Aristide. I was busy trying not to die when a bullet from your minion hit me. A bad angle, something in my pocket deflected…but it stopped my heart." I waited.

"The wolf…" He was stuck on that. I would be too.

"Yeah, yeah, if you have a video put it on YouTube. I'm sure it will get millions of hits." Time to end this. "You got what you wanted from me. What about my fee?"

He didn't speak for a moment. "Unfortunately, the information was lost when the house collapsed."

"How convenient."

"But I listened. I remember details. We'll talk in the future, Katrine. Talk about many things."

He hung up.

"Garrett, how's Maris?"

"Annalise stabilized him in Limbough. He's back at the clinic on drugs. They want to send him to a hospital in Portland. I objected. Peggy agreed. He wouldn't be safe from Aristide there. I…we couldn't protect him."

"Are my pants dry? I'm starving."

I believed Mom and Dad would say I made the right decision to save Maris. Thieves yes, but we were not killers.

****

Danny and Melanie came for a wonderful visit.

They rented a cottage down by the lake. The town had an abundance of planted hardwood trees, so fall color flourished along the streets. Excitement bubbled out of most everyone as the town prepared for Halloween, the last big festival of the year.

June and Peggy agreed to babysit the kids one afternoon, so I took Dan and Mel out to meet my Serova family. Mama Serova cooked another feast. No wolf drama, other than a bit of sniffing. I'd never paid attention, but the wolves of Rize were a bit obvious about their sense of smell in all things on their own turf. Danny and Mel politely ignored them.

On that last day, Danny and I walked in the park. A fitful chill wind blew from the mountains, and rolling gray clouds promised snow at higher elevations. We located a sheltered bench to sit and talk. He pulled out his phone. "There. I sent you the scan of the full evidence report on Rado. Had to pry it out of Barnhouse. I know you wanted it."

"I did. I do. Can we talk about Aristide?"

He stopped walking. "If you'll be honest."

"I will if you will." I wouldn't lie and claim morality.

Danny's mouth twisted, and a frown creased his brow. "Aristide has…withdrawn. That's the only way to say it. He's closing all business here in the states. We may have to hand our work over to Interpol. And he's acting…peculiar. Like he's had a revelation, or God help us, a religious experience. Do you know what happened?"

Well, my friend knew me, didn't he? "Aristide and I had an agreement. He'd tell me who murdered Mom and Dad and I'd give him certain objects he desired. I kept my end of the bargain. But when we met for the exchange, I found he had something more valuable than information. I took that instead. He saw a wolf pack attack his men. And he saw Garrett change. When he contacted me, I insinuated that he'd been delusional. He didn't believe me. He's running away."

"Something you wanted more? You didn't get your murderer."

"Unfortunately, no. Not yet."

He sat silent but not for long. "Honey, I love you. But your new *family* talks. I heard you were shot, but your…their goddess saved you. I heard that you saved the life of someone Aristide was going to kill. Is that what you wanted more than who killed your mom and dad?"

"Yes. But there are other things." My love for Peggy and my diner friends for one thing. Danny and I sat for over an hour, and I told him the whole story. He didn't interrupt. I clasped his hand tight, and we leaned closer together.

"Okay, I know you have a pagan goddess now, but will you come to Portland for Christmas?" He gave me that boyish grin that so pleased me as a child.

"Christmas? Okay. I'll follow the snowplow out. Or find a dogsled. Rent a helicopter." I so wanted things to be right by then.

****

Time moved on and the temperature moved down. Garrett remained on the Council and was busy reorganizing something in the legal and business system of the tribe. I took over the task of controlling my Serova brothers. Peter decided he would relinquish that duty to me. We had a hell of a party when Morgan and Annalise were engaged.

And I got a job. Besides the icons, the tribe had a climate-controlled warehouse of relics ancient enough to make me drool. I would date and catalogue them. Certainly, a labor of love, and I was qualified. I saw brief images of past times beyond my imagination. Tablets, scrolls, items people would have used in their everyday lives thousands of years ago thrilled me. Not so the weapons, swords, knives, axes, but I made it through.

Historians from the other nine tribes contacted me, and it looked like we might build a true history of the weirdness of our communal legacy. A legacy that spread thousands of years, a migration from the area around the Caspian Sea to the west.

But the one entity who could help most hadn't shown up. I slept with no interruptions.

I loved Garrett, loved my life. We were going to Las Vegas in a few months for a special grand meeting of all the tribal leaders. The prospect energized him.

I had put something important off. I sat by a window in the cabin and read the report on Rado's murder. Enough time had passed. I was cool.

I skimmed over the words with unemotional ease. Until a certain photo slapped me in the face. *I knew where the missing icon was.* At least I hoped it was there. I climbed in my car and headed out. I had to make a long drive to Senica.

Garrett was in Portland doing lawyer stuff. We'd talked, he'd promised not to give me mandates, and I tried to keep my promise to involve him if I made extensive grand plans. But this wasn't grand. Just a simple pick-up. I made the turn onto the interstate before I finally got through to him.

"Hey, I'm on my way to Senica. I shouldn't be long. I'm pretty sure I know where the last icon is located."

"Wait! Wait for me. Don't go alone." Hard sharp voice—and a command?

"Garrett, I don't need supervision. I have Ba'ran and my 9mm."

"That's not enough. I haven't found Aristide's spy in Rize yet." His last words came through clenched teeth.

"Garrett, this is a surprise trip. Few people saw me leave, and no one in Rize knows where I'm going. I'm trying to keep my word, love. I'm involving you. Yes, I probably should have waited for you but…"

"And I gave you orders. Sorry." He sounded genuine. "I'm on I-5 now. I'll head your way and I'll meet you in Senica. Where?"

"That's not necessary, but…okay, I'll be at my office. You remember where that is."

"Yes. Wait for me there. Please…please wait."

"Okay. I love you."

"Katrine." Just my name. A single word filled with all things I never believed would come to me. I ended the call.

It was after dark when I rolled into Senica. Since I owned the office buildings, I'd kept sporadic contact with the manager. I'd told him to find a real estate agent. Both buildings remained profitable, but I didn't have any time for them. When I got close to town, I called the manager, and he gave me the code to unlock my office door. I'd told him to obtain better security. The hallways remained open 24/7, but he'd had cameras installed last year, and a security firm checked it regularly.

I pulled into the parking lot and turned off the car. My back was to the building across the street where Rado died. I sat there long enough to get a chill. Finally, I went in and made my way to my office. The code opened the door and I beheld…boxes.

Oh, yes. I closed the door and locked it behind me. I had ordered the manager to save all my mail and he was diligent. Now I had to sort through it. Oh, well, I promised I'd wait for Garrett before I headed back. I had no idea of the amount of junk mail that could accumulate in two years. The boxes weren't labeled but I could tell by dates on the mail. It was in the corner, my prize. The mail from two days after Rado died.

The report on Rado's murder had vital information. He had a gun in his hand, but a photo told me the story. It showed me what I hadn't seen. He had also carried keys with a bright blue tab. The only reason would be that he'd gone to the basement with that key was to mail something. He needed that blue tabbed key to enter the mail room.

Now came my leap of faith, my hope. Near the bottom of the box, was a package. Yes! The right size. My fingers trembled, so awkward in my hurry. I tore it open. And there it was, the treasure that had cost lives. The tenth icon. I made a mistake though, I handled it with my bare hands. The world disappeared, and it caught me in a vision. Clearer this time, probably because it involved her.

The Tribe's goddess stood shrouded in a white robe. I knew her. I'd seen her, spoken to her in my dreams. But her face, rigid and pale as a statue, barely resembled the faded image she'd presented to me. She stared down at two men and a woman, ancient warriors, each gripping a bronze knife in their hands. They knelt at her feet. They didn't move as she stepped up and, one by one, slit their throats with brutal efficiency. I shook, but I held on to the icon. Blood gushed in furious scarlet fountains onto the bronze they held, splashed her robe and to the floor. So much blood. It puddled around their goddess' bare feet as they slowly toppled over.

The next image thrust me through a tunnel where men with hammers labored at a white-hot forge. I didn't need to see more. Created by sacrifice, steeped in unfathomable and unimaginable power—inhuman— power, Bi'ar, Ba'ran, Ben'zir endured. The blood and souls, the self-sacrifice of warriors gave the blades, not life, but an awareness, a power as inexplicable as a man becoming a wolf.

The vision faded. Now imbedded, clear and precise, it would remain in my memory forever. I laid the icon down on my desk and drew Ba'ran. It flickered gold down the runes. But this time it offered me nothing. No desire to kill. I sheathed the blade, slipped the icon in my jacket, picked up my bag, and walked out of the office. The door automatically locked behind me. Home, I needed to go home. I'd call Garrett, find out where he was and meet him on the highway. I turned to the exit. And there down the hall, stood Aristide. The gun in his hand pointed straight at me.

Ba'ran quivered. I need only touch it and it would be in my hand. I didn't have to aim, merely get it in the air in the general direction of my target. Just as I had when I'd saved Peggy. Even with that, I didn't think it was humanly possible to draw and throw faster than he could pull the trigger.

I made a slight turn and managed to free it from its sheath.

"Hello, Aristide."

He smiled. Not pleasant at all.

"You have it, don't you? The last icon. The one from the museum. My agent followed you when you rushed out of the mountains and to Senica. I knew it could only be for one reason."

Oh, goddess. Wonder of wonders, he hadn't discovered the icons I'd given him were fake.

He made one step forward. "Marisa kept me amused with wild tales of her so-called tribe. She didn't say anything about wolves. I understand why, now. I'm not insane, Katrine. Nor am I blind. Can you…?"

"No. Not in my skill set. Or one of my superpowers."

"That's a pity. And Maris Balcome? You gave up Telek and Alina's murderer to save him." He raised the gun. I could see the barrel wobbling. "I do know him. The murderer. I would have told you."

Now, this is the point where there's a convenient miracle. The lights flicker, a noise outside, a moment's distraction. Wasn't going to happen. Yes, I had an icon in my jacket, but the dismal odds of two bullets hitting the same spot weren't even worth consideration. Without thought, I grabbed Ba'ran and threw. I dropped instantly to the floor. The bullet hit the wall behind me with a sound I'll never forget. That's because it skimmed by my arm digging a blistering, burning furrow through my coat, shirt, and a layer of flesh.

Hey, it looks cool on TV. Just a flesh wound. On my arm, even. I can jump up and save the world. Bullshit. It hurt. Hurt so much I rolled into a ball on the floor. I don't know how long I lay there. Long enough for Aristide to kill me if he shot again.

I fought the hurt and struggled to sit up and see.

Aristide wasn't going to kill anyone. Ba'ran stood buried in his chest, the ancient red jewel on the hilt glowing like a fiery star in the crown of a queen of a long-lost world.

Another struggle and I made it to my feet. I approached him with caution. Aristide lay in much the same position as Rado had when he had fallen in the building across the road. On his back, arms thrown up and spread wide. Not as much blood. He'd released the gun when he hit the floor. He wouldn't use it again, but I kicked it away and knelt beside him.

Ba'ran's jewel pulsed with a slow beat. And it had missed his heart. He reached for it with one shaking hand.

"Don't." I stopped him. "I'm calling for help. Leave it in place and you might live."

I brushed my finger silently over the hilt and ordered Ba'ran not to move. To stay there until help arrived for him. Not to kill him. I suspect it was enjoying his suffering, bathing in his blood. Was that the nature of the warrior who offered his life for its creation thousands of years ago? Blood bubbled from Aristide's mouth, not an appalling amount, considering he probably had a punctured lung. I called 911, gave a clear message. Then I called Barnhouse and told him to get his ass over here if he wanted in on the action. I sat beside Aristide, and we waited.

"You killed Rado, didn't you?"

A brief nod of his head.

"Because he chose not to give you the icon? He said it belonged to someone else."

A tiny touch of a smile. No way I could decipher that. I might never know what really happened.

"What about Mom and Dad?"

He gave a tiny shake of his head.

That's when Garrett charged in. The EMT's were right behind him followed by a truly and justifiably pissed Detective Barnhouse. It was going to be a long night.

I called the building manager to come in and give the camera images to Barnhouse. I did show the people searching where the bullet that wounded me hit the wall. Garrett was at his cold, powerful executive lawyer best.

I'd made a mandatory trip to the ER for my wound, my wolf lover hovering over me the entire time. I finally fell asleep with my head on a table in an interview room at the police station, after repeating my story to Barnhouse and other detectives multiple times. My arm injury had subsided to a deep but bearable ache from shoulder to elbow. There was no position that eased the suffering. I needed drugs. None were offered.

Garrett woke me when he came in. "Come on, Sleeping Beauty. Let's go get a hotel room."

"Are we done?" I rubbed my eyes. It didn't help.

"Mostly." He glanced around, a warning not to speak.

"Okay. Aristide?"

"Still alive. In intensive care. I called Danny and told him you were okay. And Peter."

Garrett wrapped a comforting arm around my shoulder, taking care with my wound. I fell asleep in the car, and he practically carried me into the hotel.

I woke to the sound of the last voice I wanted to hear. "No. I want an explanation." Barnhouse. I rolled over. I was missing my shoes and jeans but had my shirt and panties. Good enough. And wonder of wonders, my wound had eased its seemingly endless complaint.

Garrett, the luxury hound, had sprung for an elegant suite in the most expensive hotel in Senica. I made it to my feet and staggered to the bedroom door. "Is there coffee?"

"Yes." That was Garrett. Of course, he'd had a fresh pot sent up from the kitchen. My stomach grumbled like broken gears in a worn-out machine. I'd need food soon.

Barnhouse sat at a table by the window with an open laptop. I plopped down in a chair across from him. Garrett set my coffee in front of me. He had a playful grin on that perfect face. What had he told the cop?

I felt anything but playful. "Now what, Barnhouse? You didn't get enough of me last night?"

"I did until I saw this." He turned the laptop toward me and pushed a key. There, in high resolution, was a movie of Katrine and Aristide. It wouldn't win an Oscar, but I watched it while it replayed from two different angles. With sound. My building manager hadn't gone cheap on those cameras. Now what was I going to do?

"Self-defense, Barnhouse, you saw it was self-defense. He had a gun ready, and he shot me." I laid my hand over the wound on my shoulder. "All I had was a knife. It wasn't a shoot-out."

"Self-defense. No problem. Now, how the fuck did you draw and throw that knife so fast your image distorted, blurred. Everything else stayed sharp. Only you moved." He leaned back and sighed. "What you did is impossible. You know the force it takes to…that blade cut through a fucking rib bone."

"Trick of light, buddy. Angle of the cameras. A genuine miracle?" Pat me on the back for that one.

"Well, let me quote you statistics." He plundered in his jacket and pulled out a ragged notebook that should have been tossed last year. And he did have a few facts. While I sipped blessed coffee, he went over data from knife throwing professionals. He covered the details on the speed and force required for a thrown knife to cut through human ribs. He was right. It was virtually impossible.

"So, I got lucky. Okay, Barnhouse. What do you want? And did the camera's pick-up Aristide's confession?"

"What confession? He nodded his head when you asked."

He slumped in his seat. He'd obviously not slept at all last night. "Katrine, I checked with the surgeon at the hospital. He called it a miracle. He said your knife cauterized veins in Aristide's chest or something. How?"

"Would you believe it's magic?"

He stared straight at me—eyes full of rage. He stared at the laptop and watched the video again. When he looked back, the rage was gone. He closed the laptop. "If I believe you, if I let it go now, will you tell me everything?"

"Yes." I stood and offered him my hand. "Come to Rize. You know, in Oregon. Come in the Spring unless you bring snowshoes. I'll tell you the whole story and prove it to you."

He accepted my hand. "Your knife is evidence. I'll try to get it back for you."

I had to grin. "Don't worry about it, buddy. The damned thing will come back on its own. I don't think it's going to like an evidence box."

He left without saying goodbye. There were people in Rize who were not Fenrir but knew more than they should. Why not add him to the list?

We spent the day busy. We'd slept until noon, made love, and then I went to talk to my Senica lawyer. He'd been a friend of the family for years. I did show Garrett the icon. They hadn't searched me, so it was still in my jacket pocket.

"He mailed it to you?" He turned it over in his fingers, examining it with light from the window.

"I don't know why. There was no note. I'd bet he planned to call me when he got back to his office. Explain. Or give instructions. I'll probably never know."

It was almost dark when we were ready to leave for Rize. I didn't want to tackle the mountains but didn't want to stay another night in town. We climbed in our cars, and Garrett's wouldn't start. He made the arrangements, but he rode with the tow truck driver who'd agreed to drive to Oregon for an obscene sum of cash. I hit the interstate and left them behind. I wanted to go home.

I watched the abysmal outside temperature gauge on the dash drop every mile. One more mountain to climb. According to Peggy, the HOR, the Heroes of Rize, the men and women who ran and maintained the snowplows would soon begin another season of toil. Nothing would delay the postal service or UPS truck delivering consumer commodities.

One more switch-back and I topped the mountain at the rocky cliff overlook where I'd stopped the first time and gazed down into a place that would change my life forever. To my utter surprise, the man who greeted me— or more accurately Leslie—on that day, was standing there. Sheriff Darrel Darby waved his arms frantically to flag me down. I pulled over and stopped. I thought he'd come to my car, but he motioned for me to get out and come to him. Okay. I climbed out and the bitter wind hit me like the slap of a frost giant. It cut through my light jacket, and I jammed my hands deep in my pockets.

I went to him. "What's wrong, Darrell?"

"Look down there." He moved over to the guard rail, and I followed. I peered into the darkness. And I fell for the hackneyed unoriginal B-movie shit. I'd walked right into the situation like the stupid, stereotypical big-busted babe. A flash and a rope went over my head. I couldn't scream. I couldn't breathe. And I had my hands in my pockets!

Blind panic hit. I fought to jerk my hands free. I could push, but if we hit something too hard it might break my neck too. Or I'd throw us both off the cliff. My lungs ached with the violent need for a single breath of the sharp frigid air.

"This is for Marisa, bitch." Marisa. His girlfriend. The love affair the tribe broke up? "I killed them. For her. Not enough. Never enough. Should have been you." He grunted and sobbed as I twisted in desperation.

Them? Mom and Dad? I had one hand free. I reached back and clawed his face. It made no difference. My throat burned. Air, I needed air. Darrell kept talking.

"Old man, old woman, easy. She said…" He moaned. "I killed for her." He jerked me back and screamed in my ear. "She laughed at me."

Then he shoved me over the guard rail and into the darkness around a cliff that ended in rocks two hundred feet below.

Chapter Thirty-One

Oh, I could fly. Such a sweet and brief sensation. Impact. Didn't feel it. The world went black.

Then, of course, she came.

"Where am I?"

"Lying on a small ledge about thirty feet from where you fell."

"Thrown. I was thrown. I'm alive?"

"Yes. If you lie still, they'll find you at dawn. It's not that cold here. The rock face shelters you. Your back is broken. So is your leg. Other injuries are minor."

"And?"

"I don't make the rules, Katrine. It's time. I can heal you, save your life. Then you belong to me."

"You can use me? Like Ba'ran does when it kills."

"It's similar. Ba'ran has never acted except in your defense. But it's a purity of function, not a reasoning entity. I'm more complex. I could swear I'd never force you to do anything odious. It would be a lie. At best, I'll say I'll try. And our relationship will change. You'll know me, understand me, better."

"The icon I picked up in Senica. The one from the museum. I touched it. You killed them. Ba'ran. The other blades. The warriors didn't move when you cut...how could you?"

Silence.

Finally, "I loved them. They made the sacrifice. You

can't understand. I was under siege. But now is your time. Choose."

"Your slave or die."

"No. You won't die. As I said, they'll find you in the morning. But I doubt—I know—you'll never walk again. At least your child is not injured. It's still so tiny."

"Child?"

Garrett and I hadn't been using birth control. He told me that women in the tribe had extreme difficulty conceiving. My biological mother, who had four and carried another that died with her, was an absolute miracle. I didn't care. I had Garrett and I was ready for a child.

Sure, I could raise a child from a wheelchair. Garrett wouldn't desert me. I shivered, more from fear than the cold. I wanted to walk. Unlike Bi'ar, Ba'ran, and Ben'zir's human donors, I wanted to live.

"Okay, bitch. Do it. But you know I won't submit to everything gracefully."

"Of course not. I expect that. I didn't choose you because you were malleable, Katrine. I could choose any tribeswoman and have that. And you are not a coward. I, and my tribes, will not survive without strength and sacrifice. You will lead. Because you carry a part of me, their own inbred instinct will make them follow."

I woke up lying on biting hard stone. I flailed in panic for a few seconds, then realized I couldn't feel my legs. She'd said one was broken. Panic bubbled up in a choking fountain. Darkness gathered all around. So cold. I wasn't so sure about her assertion that I would survive. I could feel the outside edge of my stone bed with my right arm. I knew how far I'd fall if I fell again. The solid mountain cradled my left. Warmth rolled down my spine.

Yesterday I'd have said the pain that came from molding my face bones was the worst of my life. I didn't know shit. Agony, burning, a razor slowly slicing away my skin—adequate words didn't exist. She fused my spine with screws of molten lava. My broken leg bone moved inside my skin tearing at muscles to fuse with its other part. I found voice to shriek, but the wind carried it away. No one heard.

Finally, it eased. I could feel my legs again. I could also feel the smaller wounds and contusions she hadn't touched. I could ignore those. I struggled to sit up.

"Stop." The words came directly into my mind. No dream. She owned me. No way could I shut her out. "You're going to fall."

I ignored her. If she wanted to stop me, she'd have to use force. The resolution, the climax, the final act of my journey was at hand. Careful, though. I'd be careful. I made it to a sitting position. My savior ledge stuck out about four feet. I ignored knowledge of the chasm below. I could see lights above, voices shouting. Someone had come, but too late. Flashlights, strobe lights probed the area to my left. They'd never spot me here.

Rocks protruded from the mountain above me. If I could get to my feet...

"You stupid bitch." My goddess was pissed. She spoke in my mind, again, no dream necessary.

"No." I shrieked like a banshee. "Let me have this. You owe me."

I made it to my feet. Clinging to the mountain, I started up, scrabbling, clawing at any hold I could grasp. What's this? The rope he'd tried to strangle me with still draped around my neck, a sign of his failure. I moved on.

Clutching rocks, digging in the few soft spots for handholds. Forget fingernails. I had a mission. Did she help me, my goddess? Climbing a stone wall by feel alone required a miracle. Occasional gentle pressure on my back kept me jammed against my precarious ladder.

Higher, inches at a time. The rush and chatter of small rocks I'd dislodged accompanied me. Lights flashed above in inordinate number and pronounced intensity. If I shouted, would they hear me? I bit my tongue. No warning allowed. Blue, yellow, red, beacons flaunted their urgent omens in perfect rhythm. My foot slipped, a hand lost its grip…again and again. I clung to the mountain like a bat cleaving to the rock walls of a cave.

I reached the guard rail. I pushed and dragged my raw scraped and cut body under it. No one could spot me out of the immediate range of light.

I used the railing as a hand to stand by force. On my feet. Amazing. Feel the cold? Feel pain? Yeah. But ignoring came easy. Blood-soaked jeans, blouse, black stains stood out in the weird colored radiance. Damn, I was a sight.

I needed a weapon. Ba'ran was MIA, in evidence after careful removal from Aristide's chest. Besides, this was personal. It didn't belong to a sentient knife. Several rocks lay on the ground at my feet. I chose one. A twelve-inch rock with a razor-sharp edge along one side. Shaped like a football, it was rough enough I could hold it tight with my bloody hands. Darrell Darby was going to suffer the wrath of a woman he'd wronged.

Sound ceased. Time slowed. I stepped into the light. Darrell was sitting his ass on a low stretcher. Ha! Like he was injured. His face pantomimed emotion. Fake despair, fake sorrow. I had scratched his face. Wonder how he explained that.

Garrett stood over him, ready to pounce. He wasn't accepting Darrell's bullshit.

I lifted my chosen weapon high over my head and charged. My chest vibrated. I screamed. Not far, only a few feet…Darrell saw me. His mouth popped open. I slammed the sharp edge down.

The monster, the murderer, jerked away. The rock, aimed at the center of his skull, plunged down and skinned the whole side of his head. My stone knife pared away ear, skin, flesh, all to the bone. A single piece, it flopped on his shoulder like a rag tossed aside. I wasn't finished.

I raised the rock again. Hands grabbed my arms. *No, no, let me go*. I wasn't done. I didn't grapple with them. I couldn't win. But they made a brace when I lifted and planted my boot square in a killer's face. It caved in like a melon hit with a bat. I twisted, desperate to get to him again. No, that wouldn't happen. I collapsed.

"Katrine. Katrine." Garrett. I heard him. Wait, was he crying?

Then his face came into view. With the last of my strength, I said, "No drugs. Pregnant."

****

I woke to silence. Empty silence. My life, ravaged and torn by murder and an obscene, devastating goddess with no name, would go on. I forced my eyes open. Long seconds drifted by as I fought for and regained focus. I hurt everywhere, and my hands, securely bandaged, lay across my chest like a mummy in a coffin. Hope my fingernails grew back. I hated glued on fakes.

Garrett sat in a chair beside the bed. My Garrett, my

love. He stared at the floor. I had to be a trial for him. My nature wouldn't allow any other way. But he was there. He would remain faithful, no matter how ruinous my life's path through time. I strained to say his name, but only managed a choked sound.

His head jerked up. "Katrine?" Again, that sob in his voice.

I managed word. "Water."

He held a straw with a nifty little accordion bend. Liquid relief rolled into my mouth. I had to rest from the exertion of swallowing.

"Garrett?"

"I'm here." He hovered over me.

"Where am I?" Ah, that was better.

"Limbough Medical Center."

Then I realized Garrett was shivering like a man lost on a glacier.

"You were…damn it, Katrine. Why can't I keep up with you?" I'd never heard him sound so desperate. He reached for my hand, and prudently stopped at the bandages.

I swallowed. "Did I kill him?"

"No. But you terrified him to the point of insanity. You maimed him. A shrieking demon from hell charged out of the dark." He did smile then. "Those were June's words. She happened to come along and stopped to see what the fuss was about. I had no idea she could be so articulate."

Neither did I. "He moved. I wanted to bash his head open."

"You skinned the whole side of it and his face. I think they're going to try to sew it back on. You split his nose and took out all his front teeth when you kicked him. His story, how you fell…we were questioning him when you appeared. Later he babbled out a confession, even without teeth. He killed your mother and father. And Marisa."

"He told me. Mom and Dad…yes. Marisa? But I thought he loved her."

"And she used him. He stopped and confronted her by the roadside that day. Told her he'd done what she wanted in Senica. And what he wanted, in return. What she promised him. She laughed at him. She misjudged him, though. He struck first."

Once she went down, he had to kill her. If she ever got up, her wolf would slaughter him.

I shifted my butt and it sent pain spikes down my legs. "Marisa? Why did she want Mom and Dad killed?"

"I don't know for sure. She may have believed it would keep you away from Rize. Or maybe it was Darrell's crazy scheme he hoped would please her."

"I was tired and careless. But I knew him. Turned my back. He put a rope over my head…I panicked. Then I went over." Calm, cool super thief Katrine had panicked. And like Marisa, I'd misjudged Darrell.

I cried then. It made my body hurt more, but I couldn't stop. Garrett held me, wiped my face, and said nothing, which was the best thing he could do. Was it over? This scene, this act, yes. More would come. No doubt about that. How many times had I been beaten or drugged unconscious since I met Garrett Dain? Three? Four?

When I settled, he asked, "What are you going to tell everyone about your hair?"

"My hair?"

He handed me a mirror he must have brought for the

occasion. Pure white. Not a substantial change from platinum blonde. People would notice, though. Like they'd notice the purple band from the strangulation rope around my throat first.

"I'll think of something. Garrett, will you take me home?"

"Tomorrow when they release you. Katrine? Are you really…"

"Pregnant? *She* said I was." I reached out and touched his face. "Is that okay with you?"

The kiss he gave me answered my question. I asked him to take me home again. He refused. I was too exhausted to fight.

Peter and my boys came later. Male staff stared and discretely moved away. Females stared and discretely edged closer. My boys were tribe. They were bigger, stronger, and each carried a wolf slumbering inside. Fierce, prone to violent confrontations, I'd never seen them compared to people who didn't live in Rize.

Peter didn't speak of it, but he touched my white hair. I had no idea how she'd changed me otherwise. And my baby? Would it be affected? I hadn't heard from her. She'd get around to me eventually.

Danny called. His concern, after me, was, of course, Aristide.

"You hurt him bad, honey."

"Yeah. Knife in the chest. Bam! That'll teach him."

To protect myself, I'd tossed a knife carrying the spirit of a warrior at Aristide. No skill, only flinging the blade in the right direction. Ba'ran chose where to strike. No way did I believe it missed his heart by accident. Ba'ran *chose* not to kill him. I'm sure the *why* would come later.

Danny said that after the doctors had stabilized Aristide in Senica they air lifted him to a trauma center in San Francisco. Though gravely injured, he would live. His lawyers were already challenging the recording of events in that office hallway, particularly a certain blur when I threw the knife. And once Ba'ran inevitably disappeared from the evidence and came back to me, it would get wilder.

I had, however, succeeded in what I hope is the final con of my long criminal career. I'd pulled off a stellar exchange on a man who'd lived his life and built a fortune on guile and treachery. With his injuries and legal problems, he might never realize the fakes. It would make Rado proud, but it wasn't enough. I'd eventually have to deal with Aristide. And, of course, Garrett would have to deal with Harat. All part of the life I'd accepted. And my goddess? The one I'm supposed to serve? Still hadn't heard from her. I'd forgotten to ask her about the Calx, the icons. Were they made from her bones? How long since she had a body, anyway. No way from Mesopotamia to Hell, do I buy her *I'm so powerless* bullshit. My guess? Somewhere, she had another poor woman on the hook to jerk around. Ba'ran returned while I slept that night. I woke with my hand curled around the hilt.

Garrett drove when we left the next day. He made a sharp turn onto a winding forest road halfway between Limbough and Helle. Over a mountain and there it was. Home.

A word about the author...

Lee Roland is a writer of urban fantasy and paranormal romance. She lives in Florida with her family.

http:/leeroland.com